DOOMED
DURANGO

C & C BEAMER

Library of Congress Registration Number: TXu 2-172-789

ISBN 9798658890333

Acknowledgements

Undertaking writing a book can be quite a feat. Deciding to write with another author is additionally challenging. However, both of us were amazed at how in sync we were in creating this novel. As mother and daughter we are close. It was a pleasant surprise to discover that as authors our like minds were still there. Busy schedules sometimes interfered, and like any relationship, we had to have a few heart to hearts. However, we came away from this experience better for it and excited to start book number two.

We also want to express our appreciation to the people who helped make this endeavor possible, especially our friends and family who supported us in this project and had the faith that we could do it. Also, we want to thank our beta readers: Mary Kean and Lawson Seropian. We'd also like to say a collective thank you to the shrimpers along the coasts of North and South Carolina who so patiently answered our questions in order to make DOOMED DURANGO as accurate as possible. And lastly, thank you to our readers. Until next time, Christine and Caroline

DOOMED DURANGO

No captain can do very wrong if he places his ship alongside that of the enemy. Horatio Nelson

Adrift

Present Day

He was on his back. Floating. The sun low in the sky, the sea so chilly he could no longer feel his hands. Yet, surely they were there. Moving back and forth. Keeping him afloat.

His ears rang from the screeching, unsure if it came from Durango's failing propellers. Or the crash of the Esmerelda. Or from him. The racket had his head throbbing along with the pressure of tears dammed behind his eyes, so many they couldn't escape.

Smack! The coarse burn of a salty wave swept against his face, scorching his nose and eyes. But even the wave's sear couldn't distract him from his anguish. His body convulsed from grief, not the icy waves.

His vision hazy, he could make out chunks of splintered wood bobbing nearby. Parts of her... His beloved Esmerelda. His brother wasn't the only one he had failed. A small piece was near his hand. He grabbed it. Holding tight. He didn't care that it was sharp and splintered. A part of her. He wasn't sure if he needed to feel it to feel her, to know she was truly gone. Or was he hoping still, that after all this, she would keep him afloat?

Something was tugging at him from behind. *God tell me that's not a shark.* But his body made no effort to move. Couldn't move. He was shivering too much. Did he even want to move?

The ocean suddenly became hard and unrelenting. He was turned over, then face up again. He caught a flash of orange and felt two large hands pressed into his back to keep him above water.

"See how it's done, Hutchins? Like cleaning a pool," a man joked. "You scoop 'em out just like you would some leaves."

"Yes, sir," a female responded back. "He's secure to move now."

The voices became muffled. The pain in his ears sharpened with the sensation of wind. Instinctively, he wanted his hands to cover them, but he couldn't. Straps locked him in. Had the screech from Durango's propellers burst his eardrums? Or had he burst them himself from yelling for Trevor? He decided it was a small price to pay to be the brother who survived.

Now someone was pulling at him again, grabbing his clothes and limbs with no regard for his comfort. He felt himself hoisted up, swinging gently in the air before coming down with a thump on the deck of a ship. His wits returning, he knew it was the Coast Guard.

The Coast Guard. The Coast Guard... yes, that's who it was. Bitterly, he realized they were just as much to blame. Had they ever noticed they had saved only one brother?

His anger warmed him, allowing his screaming to return. Erupting in a fury, he wanted them to know his grief, to recognize what they had done. What they had cost him. As he shouted, his head felt like a loaded gun. Were his words coming out? His shouts of "My brother, you idiots! You killed him! You killed my boat!" swirled around him.

A voice interjected, the pool cleaner. "But Mr. Starnes, your brother—"

He didn't want to hear excuses. He drowned the man out by yelling so fiercely he hoped his ears would ring too. Then silence. He began moaning, the pool cleaner getting impatient. "Damn! Tell Lopez to hurry it up! We need to get him knocked out. I can't take this."

Moments later he felt a bee sting. He wanted to slap it, but his arms remained prisoners by his sides. As he wondered where a bee came from, he heard, "No, give him the other one, too. I want him out cold."

Another voice said, "If you say so. This oughtta' give him some sweet dreams." Another bee sting.

So curious there were so many bees so far out to sea, and so quickly this fog is rolling in, so foggy...

Chapter 1

Two Days Ago

Fabulous sea. Fabulous voyage. Can this keep up?
Let's hope not! #CummingsAndGoings

Jason Cummings, renowned restaurant reviewer,
watched the waiter present his meal with a theatrical
bow and swoop of his arm. His expression neutral,
Jason was thinking, oh brother, spare me. By now, he
was aware that the entire staff knew who he was, but
it just couldn't be helped. He was a big deal.

He shooed the man away before placing his linen
napkin in his lap, knowing perfectly well that he was

about to have another five-star presentation served on the High Cotton's maiden voyage, even though Jason was dining midday. Hitting memo record on his phone he began in a sad monotone, "Ah yes, predictably, as I prod the fish, it's falling apart," much like my enthusiasm, he mused. Where is the scandal? My twitter feed will soon be as soft and buttery as this meal. "And now for the puree." He took a few bites, then began again. "The flavors complement one another, bringing out the best in each, much like a good gin and tonic," he chuckled. "The salty shellfish, the sour sorrel and the sweet smoked sauce intersect delectably. And who wouldn't admire the chef arranging the food as a miniature High Cotton?" Rolling his eyes, he could hear the rest of the composition now. The High Cotton has mastered haute cuisine and exemplary service. For discriminating cruise ship travelers it makes for an enjoyable voyage. For this reviewer, there's little to sink his teeth into.

Normally, Jason's articles were literary feasts unto themselves. His clever wording and tasty metaphors describing restaurant mistakes provided excellent information, but more importantly, entertainment, the exact ingredient missing from his High Cotton reviews. He sullenly considered, I feel like I'm a groveling public relations whore, and I'm not even getting any sex out of it! The food, the staff, his cabin's appointments had all been flawless, so no delicious negative commentary. He ran his hand through his hair, light brown with a hint of henna, styled by the ship's salon that afternoon. Even that was perfect. Well, he consoled himself, I do have great hair.

It wasn't that he actually wanted anything terrible to happen. No need for a repeat of the Titanic, just a transgression. Perhaps a staff member losing his temper and slapping a guest. The oysters a little off and somebody puking on the ice sculpture. A tipsy honeymooner tripping over a cheap rug and landing thong up---just SOMETHING to spice things up. His followers expected it. But the constant vanilla-flavored reviews were getting revolting. His fans had actually tweeted to see if he had finally been paid off. "The positivity is sickening, Jason!" one wrote to him.

He had a reputation to maintain as the most popular national reviewer. Jason was proud to report that his tweets for dining recommendations were used more often than Yelp. He wouldn't even be surprised if Google's ratings depended on him. Jason considered his work vital. But it had to be fun to write and, of course, read. No one had an appetite for the same thing over and over. To maintain interest, a commentary shouldn't be bland; it should have some viciousness to add seasoning. And a good photo-op didn't hurt.

He took a sip of complimentary champagne, glancing around and seeing the usual gathering of happy, satisfied passengers. When he looked back, he noticed someone approaching his table, the beautiful Captain Padma Patel.

"Ah, Captain Patel, a pleasure to see you," he said somewhat sarcastically, as he rose slightly then sat back down.

She stood very straight in her starched white uniform; her black hair tucked neatly under her cap. Her dark eyes sparkled as she replied, "Thank you, Mr. Cummings. I hope you are having a pleasant voyage."

"Yes," he sighed. "I was just thinking how incredibly pleasant it has been."

"I must apologize that you and I haven't had an opportunity to do an interview. I hope our First Mate, Brian Chambers, gave you a satisfactory tour and answered your questions."

Jason's memory reunited with the first mate in question, a veritable Adonis who wouldn't respond to a single flirtation.

"Oh, yes, and I quote, 'The High Cotton is a retro upfit of a small but luxurious cruise ship, 50,000 tons, 950 passengers and equipped with aero-derivative gas turbine engines, computer designed and operated for green efficiency.'" He picked up his glass and waved it in a mock toast. "Simply scintillating."

She laughed with perfect white teeth. "Well, when you put it that way it does sound dull. However, I hope he told you about the Morrow family, owners of the cruise line. Very noteworthy people, philanthropists and conservationists."

"Yes, I've seen the website. But I think our readers are ready for something different, such as what goes on off the books?" He used his foot and pushed out a chair next to him. "Please, won't you join me?"

Her brow furrowed before the engaging smile reappeared. "Perhaps for a moment. Thank you." She lowered herself onto the chair then folded her hands on the table. The waiter brought a champagne glass.

and quickly filling it, asked, "Captain, will you be dining?"

"No," she said, her eyes watching Jason. "I'll only be here a short time." When they were alone again, she remarked, "I'm not sure I understood your question, Mr. Cummings."

He leaned in. "Well, to put it bluntly, my tremendous following doesn't come from writing syrupy brochures. The ship has gotten its something nice. Now it's time for the spice."

"I don't understand."

"What socialite was kicked out of the bar for being drunk and disorderly? Whose husband has been seen mixing up room keys? That kind of thing. A word with your staff would be all I need."

The little frown returned. "I think what you need is a complimentary trip to the spa."

He looked away, irritated. Then he caught sight of First Mate Chambers heading their way. He gave him a wink, but the man didn't notice, intent on reaching the Captain.

"Excuse me for interrupting, Captain," he said, removing his hat, freeing his glossy blond locks.

"So formal around here," Jason muttered.

"Yes, what is it?"

He leaned over and whispered in her ear, his face turned away from Jason, but Jason, in addition to being a savvy critic was also gifted with outstanding hearing. He couldn't make out all that was said, but he heard enough.

She rose immediately. "I've enjoyed our chat, Mr. Cummings. I must leave you now and return to the bridge, but I'll give some thought to what you said."

Jason rose with her. "Thank you, Captain. I would appreciate that. By the way, is anything wrong?"

"No, of course not. Merely a small matter needing my attention. Good day."

Jason watched them exit, and through the bank of windows, observed the two moving quickly across the deck rather than stopping to socialize with passengers, their usual form. It was at that moment an idea struck him. This quirk of fate could be the answer to his prayers. He would follow them.

Keeping a distance, he never let them out of his sight. They were talking back and forth, their heads down, speaking confidentially. Up three more decks they rounded the last corner that Jason knew, thanks to the First Mate's tour, led to the bridge. They opened a gate with a plaque on it, 'No Passengers Beyond This Point' and passed through. Jason stopped, sucking himself inside a doorway in case they looked back. Peeking out, he saw them pass a steward carrying a tray and upon reaching Jason's doorway, the man caught sight of him.

"May I help you, sir?" he asked.

"No. I'm fine. Just enjoying the view." He attempted to discreetly put his hand on the doorknob behind him, hoping to make his leave; however, as he took hold of the knob he found it locked. The steward waited.

"Well, if you don't mind, sir, you're going to have to return to the lower deck and enjoy the view from there. Passengers aren't allowed in this area."

He had no choice but to retreat, as the steward followed him to make sure. Going down to the main deck, every step of the way Jason could hear the treading of the steward's shoes closely behind him.

It was unseasonably warm, the passengers wearing swimming attire or shorts, crowding the decks to enjoy the sun. An enthusiastic bunch had gathered around a volleyball game, giving Jason an opportunity to dive behind a group of people. Peeking back between two women, he watched the steward go indoors. Making an abrupt turn, he stepped on one's toes and she responded with a little whelp. Calling out, "Sorry!" he then quarterbacked around her frowning husband, intent on returning to the restricted area. Feeling bolder, he continued beyond the doorway that had been his hiding place minutes ago.

As he opened the gate, he recalled the highly mechanized operational zone of the bridge. It had looked as complicated as the cockpit of a Boeing Airbus, everything seeming to be digitalized. He recognized the sonar as well as the radar system, and noted it was so sophisticated it not only pinpointed surrounding vessels, but also larger ships were identified with their call names to allow radio communication, should it become necessary. Moving closer, Jason crouched down so he wouldn't be seen. The door was open, presumably to allow the breeze inside, so he slipped out his phone and pressed memo record and slid it closer.

The minutes ticked by, his thoughts drifting back to when he was a young, struggling writer waiting tables in New York. While he was on break one night and standing in the alley, he chatted with the dishwasher, Leon, from the exclusive restaurant next door. Puffing smoke out of his nose, Leon told Jason mockingly, "The chef is selling illegal goods, served in the private dining room to rich people willing to pay big bucks for shark fin soup and other black market stuff that tastes like crap."

The startling statement gave Jason an idea. He told Leon he'd give him two hundred dollars if he allowed him to take his next shift, to which Leon readily agreed. The following evening Jason arrived, saying he was a temporary replacement, as Leon had taken sick. While Jason scrubbed pots and pans, he recorded sound and video of the chef preparing the contraband dishes that he confirmed for himself did taste like crap.

The next day Jason wrote an article that appeared in several news outlets. By the end of the week, the restaurant was closed by the Fish and Wildlife Service after Greenpeace protesters gathered on the sidewalk. The New York Times ran Jason's story on the front page. After CNN covered it, it went viral. When NBC asked for a copy of the video, they did a brief on-air interview, which was so spectacular it led to a job offer from *America Today*.

Thinking on his feet had brought about a happy ending for him and the sharks. Now, as he considered he may be on the edge of discovering another news-breaking event, what good fortune would come this time? Perhaps #CummingsandGoings will become a regular spot on morning television.

Chapter 2

Twelve Hours Ago

Long before the sun graced the sky for a new day, the sounds of 93 Jams waded into Nick's consciousness. He grouchily slapped the snooze button for the second time, as always. He'd had the same old-school clock radio since he was thirteen, back when it seemed new school.

Grunting, he rose and fell into his well-worn routine. And yet, no matter how many times he awakened in the dark, it never felt natural. That was why God invented coffee. With cup in hand by the time he reached the docks, he would be ready to face the new day and the hope of a bountiful catch.

After parking his truck, he stopped to admire the view of distant lights twinkling on the Charleston bridge. He followed the path he took every morning across the driftwood planks towards the harbor, the regular beat of the buoy bell setting his pace. He held the Esmerelda's key in his hand, rubbing his fingers over the grooves. With each circle of his thumb he felt the tackiness of the day's humidity growing, the smells of fish and sea clinging to the thickening air.

The air was thick with something else too, something Nick didn't want to think about. He promised himself he wouldn't. He needed this day to be like any other. When those heavy thoughts crept into his mind he sent them back, and rubbed the key a little harder.

Beyond the dock, terns worked their way along the marsh's banks. Behind them, bending succulent grasses, blue in the pale light, met black streaks of sand mottled at the water's edge merging into a creamy froth. It's so beautiful, he thought. Too bad I never bothered to notice.

Approaching the Esmerelda, or Esmereld, as her paint now read, he considered that he really should have fixed that lettering. But how many times could he get excited about re-doing a paint job? And now... He stopped the encroaching thought. It was time to prepare for the day. And maybe, he suggested to himself half-heartedly, it was time to pull out that seaweed hanging in the shrimping gear. It didn't help the old girl's looks to have putrid greens from the previous catch dangling in the netting, or, well, catches if he were being honest.

A gull circled above. "Right on time you little beggar," he chided, but actually he liked seeing his old pal. Somehow it had become routine. This gull, the one with the chip out of his beak, came by every morning when Nick was breaking into his breakfast. He'd felt pity the first time he saw the bird, thinking it wouldn't live long with that damaged beak, so he'd shared. Now, as reliably as he knew his wife Carly would pack him fresh fruit and an egg-white sandwich, the gull would appear. He didn't mind sharing the sandwich. Carly and her fretting over his cholesterol. Who knew cholesterol was so critical to food tasting good?

"I see Bo back again for some egg-white sandwich." Ray's baritone resonated behind him.

"You know it," Nick answered back. Bo was preening himself, pleased with his breakfast. Ray had been the one to name the bird, calling it Hobo, then later shortening it to Bo.

Nick's eyes crinkled into a smile when he saw Ray carrying a cooler. "Oh please tell me you've brought Aunt Jenny's fried chicken." He pulled on a line to steady the boat for Ray to board.

"I did, and potato salad and coconut cake for dessert. She said she baked it with extra love for today." Dressed in a denim jacket and cargo jeans, Ray climbed aboard to place his gear in the wheelhouse. He pulled out his fishing hat, a well-worn Atlanta Braves cap that he fit snugly over his wiry hair, his black skin weathered from sun more than age. He was grinning like a schoolboy rather than a man with a slight stoop from working too hard and too long. Deep creases channeling his cheeks from a lifetime of wind and salty air moved into his ever-present affectionate smile.

Nick was peeking into the cooler. "That is one fine lady, never mind her making a cake just for me."

"Hah! That cake ain't just for you. It's for me and Trevor, too. And speaking of your brother, where is he?"

"I told him to get here later. I thought you and I could load up, since, you know…"

Ray turned and looked hard at Nick. "You sure about this?"

"I'm sure," Nick answered. "I'm tired of the long hours and shrinking dollars. And Ray, you said yourself you need easier work. We've been over it a thousand times."

"I know, but it don't seem right, just to walk away." His hand rubbed the gunwale.

"We're not walking away. We're selling." Nick's expression belied his stern tone of voice.
Shaking his head, Ray argued, "That man will use her for scrap. And you know it."

"If he wants her for scrap, it's his choice. Besides…" Nick countered as his toe nudged a bucket out of the way, "Maybe that's all she's good for."

"That's a mighty cold statement you're making there. She's been good to us a long time."

"Stop being so damned emotional! We're not talking about a person. It's a boat---and this is business. Besides, nobody else is interested. And are you forgetting your cut?"

"Have you told *him*?" Ray didn't look Nick in the eye, just continued pulling his gloves on.

"Not exactly."

"Man, you're going to be on this boat with him for maybe two days. Not telling him will be like a lie. Just saying..."

"It's not that simple. I haven't found the right time, and believe me, it needs to come at the right time. You know how he is." Nick pulled his hat off to rake a hand through his reddish-brown hair, his temples sprinkled with gray. Looking at Ray, whose back was to the newly risen sun, he squinted with green eyes surrounded by crows feet, his freckled skin tanned and rough. "He acts like I'm some kind of God, that I can do anything. Been that way his whole life."

"You *were* some kind of God, Nick! If it hadn't been for you---"

"And you!" he cut in.

"Okay, okay, but you gotta be honest with him. You're not kids anymore."

"Well, that's for sure. He didn't get to be a SEAL actin' like he's still twelve. But, come on, Ray, it's the end of a fuckin' era, ya' know? This poor old shrimp boat is the last thing he has that reminds him of Dad. I gotta ease into it."

Ray nodded thoughtfully. "Whatever you say, but your 'easing into it' better happen sooner than later."

"Loud and clear. Now it's time to get some work done, so let's load up and get ready to go. Then we can shove off as soon as he gets here."

"Uh-huh. You worried one of them other fishermen gonna say something. I know you," Ray chastised.

Nick, wanting to drop the subject, made no reply. They worked silently as they stowed the ice, situated the bait and readied the boat for departure. They had just finished when music blaring from an old fashioned boombox cut into the morning air. Looking up, they saw a tall, well-built man singing along to the twangs of a Grateful Dead song.

"You know, it wouldn't be so horrible if you could carry a tune!" Nick said with a laugh. "I can't believe you're still listening to that shit."

Trevor jumped on the boat and threw his bag into the corner. He pushed his cap further back on his head, the waves in his black hair curling in all directions. His brown eyes were dancing from Nick to Ray. Inheriting his grandfather's Armenian coloring but his mother's fine nose and brows, he was what many women would call handsome. Trevor, however, always seemed oblivious. "Shit! You wouldn't know good music if it walked up and kissed your ass. And the voice of public opinion says it all. They're having a comeback. Another generation is listening."

"Two is enough," Ray chided. "Your father drove me nuts with his Dead-head music."

"My father, I'll have you know, saw a dozen Grateful Dead concerts and even got to go backstage once and meet Jerry Garcia."

"I remember. I had to hear about it every time we went to sea. He'd make me wanna jump overboard!" Ray finished with a raspy laugh.

"Okay. Let's wrap it up," Nick said. "We've got to get fuel." He started the engine, its rumble drowning out Trevor's music. After the diesel warmed up, Ray untied the line.

Chapter 3

The Captain seems alarmed. Is Jack Sparrow about? #CummingsAndGoings

Jason couldn't hear what was being said inside the bridge. He had to remain crouched below the window next to the entrance. His phone, placed strategically with *memo record* on, was hopefully gathering information. His only problem was that just before he had seen Captain Patel at lunch, he had been at the pool, enjoying the sleek fabric and sense of freedom his Speedos gave him.

He still had them on.

Naturally he hadn't walked into the dining room for that splendid meal wearing only his banana shaped trunks. He was not one of those guests who found that the dinner rolls could be served both on the table and the flesh. He had slid on terry cloth shorts and a white polo. For shoes he sported espadrilles, and *Voilà!* Perfect *après* swim attire.

Now squatting outside the bridge's door and doing what he believed any good investigative reporter should do, the Speedo was doubling as a tourniquet around his twig and berries.

Suddenly at the doorway, he heard a voice. "Yes, Captain. I'm on my way."

With lightning reflexes Jason grabbed his phone and slipped it into his shirt pocket. He knew he was about to be busted, but by God he wasn't going to be caught with his balls nearly cut off. He sprang up to face his accuser but forgot about the heavy metal railing above him.

Womp! went his head, and he fell back with a plop only meant for a fluffy mattress, not a steel floor.

"What the hell!" First Mate Chambers said. "Captain! It's that reviewer guy. He's hit his head!"

Captain Patel stepped out and looked at Jason, who was flat on his back with a strange smile on his face. A small patch of blood had pooled above his forehead.

At first glance Padma thought to herself... seriously? He followed us up here?

She told Chambers, "Get him to the infirmary. And let me know what they say." Before kneeling and dabbing the blood from Jason's head, First Mate Chambers got on his radio and called for a stretcher.

With the problems of the day mounting, Padma wanted to prevent one of her headaches, so she stretched her shoulders and did some head rolls before going back to the bridge to check on the Chief

Engineer. He was busy on a computer, watching the gauges as a red light on the console continued to flash.

She sat down in her swivel chair, discouraged that she began feeling the dreaded pain at the base of her skull. At first a tightening, it was now blossoming into a full muscle clench at the top of her spine. If she wasn't careful she would end up sunk with a migraine.

These headaches had been her nemesis since she was in middle school. "You are holding onto your stress," her mother had chided, then suggested, "You must channel that energy into your studies."

Padma knew her mother secretly took pride in her headaches, because it meant her daughter was striving for perfection, a quality her parents insisted upon. However, being perfect had its pitfalls, not the least of which were migraines.

She considered the conversation she had yesterday with Chief Steward Dawkins.

"Captain, a lot of passengers are objecting to another emergency drill. Since we're nearing the end of our voyage could we not skip this one? I think everyone knows what to do since we've already had two."

"Absolutely not. It's protocol to have three drills on every Morrow voyage. We'll proceed at eleven hundred hours as planned."

"Are you sure, Captain? That reviewer is on board, you know. He's bound to hear the grumbling---he seems to be everywhere."

"I'm sure. No bending the rules, he'd certainly notice that."

Dawkins was right about unhappy passengers. She had four couples personally complain and one woman demanded partial repayment "for all the lost time doing school fire drills!" Padma knew her response had been correct.

"Had there been a real fire you would have been prepared. Preparedness is the key to any emergency."

"That's your job," the woman snapped.

She felt sure she would call the cruise line, but so be it. Procedure was procedure. And besides, Padma was the first female captain the Morrows had employed. She wasn't about to jeopardize her fresh start by cutting corners.

She went back outside and walked over to the railing, looking below to see the High Cotton moving easily through the water. Her radio buzzed.

"Patel here."

"Captain, Mr. Cummings is conscious now. He has a slight concussion and is to remain in the infirmary overnight," explained First Mate Chambers.

"All right. Tell him I'm on my way to personally check on him. Has he said what he was doing when he hit his head? I don't want this to end up in a review as a ding for our lack of safety."

"No, he hasn't. I did ask him, but he says he has no memory of it. But Captain, I believe he was following me. I told you how he was on the tour. What if he heard something!"

"Yes, you may be right. I can see I may need to do some damage control. It could be a blessing he's confined to the infirmary."

"I should say so!

Chapter 4

Shrimp or Tuna?

Thirty minutes later, with the Esmerelda refueled, Nick, Ray and Trevor were leaving Mount Pleasant, moving across a gleaming bay, the lone gull following.

Once they were away from the harbor, Nick pulled the throttle back to a medium speed. All three looked across the Esmerelda's bow to the endless ocean ahead, silent and comfortable, feeling the contentment that going to sea gave each of them.

Ray decided to get a conversation going so Trevor wouldn't restart his music. "I remember the time Cam took you out and you was green as a gilfish, Nick," he said, winking at Trevor.

"What's this? I never knew Long John Silver here ever had a spell of seasickness!" Trevor nudged Ray's arm.

"I wasn't seasick, and you know it! I was hungover. But I couldn't tell Dad because I was only seventeen. God, it was awful! Me, Benny Graves and Peter

Westover drank rum the night before. And to make matters worse, mixed it with cherry vodka! I've never touched the stuff since."

"Rum?" Trevor asked.

"No, Cherry Vodka! Never been so sick in my life."

The three laughed and Ray said, "We didn't get much of a catch that day. We ended up coming in early for fear the fool would get dehydrated. That, and he stunk so bad from puking all over his shoes!"

"Hey, we've all had our bad days." Nick commented good naturedly.

Ray sat back in a chair and related, "You know, you never fooled your daddy for a second."

"Yeah, I know. I could never pull one over on him."

"So you drank in high school, 'Mr. Do as Daddy said.' Why didn't I know about this?"

"Because you were seven years old at the time," Nick retorted.

"There's more to this man than you know, Trevor," Ray commented.

"Yeah? Like what?"

"Nothing," Nick said, cutting off the conversation. "You won't get any more confessions out of me. And *you*, Ray, do not need to tell him any more stories."

"Oh, quit being such a wuss," Trevor said, punching his brother on the arm before walking out to feel the warmth of the sun.

His gaze followed the water to its edge where the mysterious line of the horizon always appeared to be the end of the world. He shut his eyes and stood there feeling the heat on his face as his body rose and fell with the swells. It was good to be out with Nick and

Ray, just guys being guys. That's how his father always described their escapades. He only wished there had been more. He felt cheated, grieving for something he never had. Yet he wasn't bitter, accepting the cards dealt to him. Still, so many unexpected changes in his life. Someone told him once that was what had made him so resilient. Perhaps. Then he thought about the recent change he hadn't planned on, returning home a few months ago. He rubbed the top of his shoulder to feel the outline of the fresh scar.

With his back to the wind, it dawned on him that he no longer constantly had his guard up. Having survived so many missions, he felt like he had lived on adrenaline for as long as he could remember in spite of the SEALS having regular down time. This morning with the ocean spray mixed with the sun to create a thousand tiny rainbows, he sighed at the tranquility, feeling relaxed and happy as he sipped his coffee. He was glad he was feeling more normal, going about his daily life like a regular person, though he still found himself tensing at certain sounds or movements. He may never lose all the hypersensitivity that had saved his life so many times, but he hoped to never need it again. Being alert wasn't a bad thing, however, never letting go would kill him.

As South Carolina's coastline faded away, Trevor began lowering the towering outriggers that had been raised and secured to the cabin roof while the boat was docked. The outriggers held the shrimping nets. Now at sea they needed to be lowered to keep the boat stable and to prepare the netting, except when Trevor moved to unfasten them, he heard Nick shouting to him over the wind.

"No! We're not shrimping!"

Puzzled, Trevor ran his fingers across the nets, so worn in places he found holes. It was uncharacteristic of Nick and Ray to let things go like that. He walked into the wheelhouse where Nick stood at the helm to find out what was going on. Ray stepped out on deck.

"What do you mean 'no' and why are your nets in such bad shape? Isn't that why we're here? Or you just wasting my time?"

Nick shook his head. "Fuck no! But we're going after tuna, not shrimp."

Trevor studied Nick's face. Was he joking? "Tuna? We don't do tuna," he said warily.

"Well, we're doing it this time."

Nick didn't crack a smile, and in fact, seemed overly serious. When Trevor and his brother got together it was usually hijinks, wisecracks and stupid stories, all the good stuff. Today, he was attempting to act normal, but he wasn't. Marital problems? No way, Carly was a brick and had put up with Nick for too long to bail out now. So, what was it?

"What the hell, Nick? Tuna? What gives?"

"Because we want a big score and this is the season for it. Not only that, I got a tip where to look for them. Do you know if we pull in a big fish it could bring in eight or nine grand?"

"And we could also spend all of our time wasting money on fuel, ice and chum---that is, I'm assuming you've got chum, because you need some kind of bait."

"We've got it plus some live fish," Nick said with a wave of his hand. "Look, I know I didn't mention it when I asked you to come with me, but fishing is fishing, right?"

"I don't know shit about hooking tuna."

"You don't know shit about most things, but how hard can it be? Ray borrowed a couple of rods and I've got two spearguns. The sonar is adjusted to detect tuna. When we get a bite Ray will take the wheel. You take the rod and let the tuna run with the bait to get the hook good and solid in its mouth. When you reel it in I'll spear it. Simple."

Trevor shook his head, "Simple," he mocked. "Then why isn't every idiot with a string on a pole out here doing it?"

"Dude, we're trying it."

Trevor walked back out on deck and looked at Ray. "You knew about this, too. What the hell, Ray?"

Ray shrugged. "Ain't no harm in tryin'."

"It's just so… different. You've always done shrimp."

He thought of the irony of this conversation and how their roles were reversed, with him being the reasonable one and Nick the risk taker. Nick was the rock, always stable and taking the safe route on everything. Trevor didn't want to make a big deal out of it, but it seemed odd.

He called to his brother, "Okay, Captain. But just for the record I think you're nuts."

"Duly noted," Nick replied. He remained at his post, while Ray and Trevor chatted then fell into a lazy silence.

A few hours later they stopped to savor the fried chicken lunch. Trevor was helping himself to seconds when he remarked, "You know, Ray, you are one hell of a lucky man to be married to Aunt Jenny. Nobody--- and I mean nobody---can cook like she can. If she's gonna pack a lunch like this every day, you may have a third crewman."

Ray smiled and patted his stomach. "How do you think I got this?"

Nick nodded, slicing a piece of cake. "I had to be really careful around Mom when I was still living at home and Jenny would bring us dinner. Oh, my God! It would be so fucking good, and poor Mom, I, love her to death, but she's a horrible cook! I'd be licking my plate clean and finishing off all Jenny had sent, in ecstasy! Then I'd look over at Mom. She'd be givin' me that sad puppy face. I'd say something like, 'but you know this has nothing on yours.' Man, we both knew it wasn't true."

Trevor jumped in, "Oh, but do you remember Mom's meatloaf? One time I found a peanut in it and asked her what a damned peanut was doing in my meatloaf. I knew what had happened. She'd been drinking a little wine and munching on peanuts while she was cooking, and a peanut fell into the mix--- probably straight out of her mouth!"

Nick was laughing. "I remember that! She was red as a beet as soon as you asked her. You never did let her live that one down."

"Well, she didn't cook meatloaf anymore!" Then Trevor started another story, "One time she boiled---"

But Ray cut him off. "Your momma did the best she could and had a lot going on after Cam died---and I'm talking about raising you two hoodlums and working full time while making a decent home for you. Show her some respect, now."

"Awww, don't be like that, Ray. You three raised us right," Nick said, giving Trevor a wink.

Chapter 5

Everybody Loves a Secret Agent

Leaning back in a plush leather chair, Lee Jin Hein was having a shoeshine in the lobby of an exclusive Zurich hotel. Taller than most North Koreans, he was intensely watching the glittering female travelers, beautifully attired and so at ease carrying their Bucherer, Louis Vuitton and Hermes shopping bags. It amazed him to hear these citizens talking idle gossip or discussing where they would like to dine and what delicious treats they desired. Where he was from this lifestyle did not exist, or perhaps only for a few. Fortunately for him, he was one of them, while still working for the cause, of course.

When he was first sent outside North Korea, Jin had to learn how to behave casually around such things. Being offered more food than he could eat, or for that matter, having choices, was utterly foreign to him. His eyes would widen when he saw so many people in fine clothes. But most extraordinary was to hear and read what these citizens said about one another and their governments. Yet, he had seen no one arrested because of it.

Being a patriotic agent, he put in many hours studying Western culture so that he would become an expert in fine food, wine, art, jewelry and dress. This knowledge made him a valuable agent as someone who can comfortably mingle among the rich.

Catching his reflection in a shop window, it was clear he was attractive by Western standards. After taking a sip of his dirty martini, he straightened the tie on his Brioni suit then checked the time on his Patek Philippe watch. An attractive blond walked by and gave him a look, which he agreeably indulged.

His shoeshine now complete, he looked down, satisfied he could nearly see his reflection. He reached into his pocket to find a few bills to tip the young man. He chuckled, believing the boy would feel fortunate to have such a generous reward, while to Jin it was nothing.

That morning he and his underling, Kwon, had gone to the *Banque Suisse International* to remove an entire suitcase full of money, stacks of crisp euros. The funds were the result of black market trading by North Korea. The money will pay for Jin's new mission.

Jin and Kwon were leaving that afternoon to begin their journey overland to the coast of Italy, where Jin had an appointment at a shipyard day after tomorrow. He couldn't fly and risk the money being found by airport security. He and Kwon were traveling by limousine, with Kwon posing as Jin's driver, though in Jin's mind it was an appropriate distinction. Kwon certainly fit the part, peasant looking with his broad face and square body.

They checked out, leaving promptly. Jin kept the suitcase next to him in the backseat. As they changed lanes to negotiate traffic, he barked to Kwon in Korean, "Have you finished the requirements yet?"

"Yes. They're supposed to send my captain's license to our hotel, so I should have it in time. If not, we'll have to wait."

After cursing under his breath Jin said, "Idiot. I can't believe you didn't clear that up before we left."

"I tried. It couldn't be helped. The bribes sped things up, but it still takes time."

"You could have done better."

"And draw unwanted attention? I have no control over these laws."

"I had hoped we could avoid delays. You know how he is---he won't be happy about this, and he'll know whose fault it is." Looking at Kwon's dark eyes in the rearview mirror, Jin pressed the button to close the window separating the backseat. Then he made a call, being one of the few able to directly dial The Great One.

"There could be a delay before we can sail. It's due to the paperwork. I'll keep you informed." The voice on the other end of the line grunted a response and hung up.

Conversations with The Great One were always brief. He only cared to know the details of a mission's success. Nothing less was acceptable; however, any delays he had to know about, and there was no way to hide things from him. The result was that the call left him with a nagging tension in his neck.

He opened iTunes on his phone. Scrolling down, he found what he needed, the album *Saturday Night Fever*. He clicked on the song, *More Than a Woman,* and shut his eyes, resting his head against the seat as he hummed along. Slowly, as his shoulders loosened, the music returned him to his first mission. Ah, yes, he said to himself, the beautiful Soo-Min. The memory lingered...

He was sent to Seoul to penetrate a traitor's cell, an amateur group that had been smuggling intel about North Korea to the west, as well as stirring up unrest among farmers and factory workers. He had received a tip that one of their contacts worked at the docks in Incheon, South Korea.

As planned, he crossed the border overland one night and a few days later had a job at the Incheon dock, driving a forklift and loading freight. Keeping to himself, he gradually began to chat with his co-workers about neutral topics, but would join in when the men made lewd comments about the women who walked past to report for administrative jobs. During their breaks, the men would sit around an old bench outdoors, laughing and speculating about what the women would do for their bosses. Once he became accepted, he began venturing into political discussions, griping to his co-workers how the North was so cruel to its people and how concerned he was about his grandmother, who couldn't leave to be with Jin.

Time passed with no one approaching him in spite of his making subtle hints about wanting to find a way to smuggle his grandmother out. He heard nothing. So astutely, he adjusted. Perhaps he shouldn't be looking for a man. The contact could be a woman, and if that was the case, he needed to get to know the office personnel. Instead of associating with the men on his breaks, he began hanging around the offices. At the water cooler, he made some political opinions known, and soon a woman began chatting with him, a middle-aged accountant, who handled the dock workers' payroll.

He was careful to be polite and deferential, having her believe he felt honored to make her acquaintance. He began to drop by her office once or twice a week to bring her little things: a new pencil, a flower, and then a box of candy. Knowing that she was at least forty and probably had never been with a man, he made sure to make her feel desirable before asking her out. He was strategic, taking her to the movies or going for walks, only being together in public places and always maintaining propriety.

Eventually she introduced him to her mother, with whom she lived. As Jin patted her hand, he flattered the old woman with compliments, then told her what he needed for her to hear: how important family is and how he had been searching for a nice girl for a wife. When she asked about his parents, he wiped a tear from his eye and said all he had left was his grandmother in Bukhan---the north, which meant he could never see her.

"I would give up my life to spend one day with her."

He could see the mother and daughter's eyes meet meaningfully. When he arrived at work the next morning he was told to report to the office. He did so and found his lady friend looking demur.

"I've been thinking about your grandmother," she said to him as she closed her office door. "I might know someone who could help you get her out."

"Really?" he asked tentatively. "I don't think I have to tell you what it would mean to me." He looked away shyly and then added, "It would open the way to our future together."

"Yes, I thought so too."

He waited for her to say more. She searched his eyes then continued, "It would be dangerous if you spoke to anyone about what I'm going to tell you. If it becomes known, you could possibly be killed."

He appeared shocked. "You surprise me. I had no idea you were a woman involved in such things, but I admire you for it."

"Are you able to keep this silent?"

"Yes. I won't say anything."

"And you must be committed entirely."

"I am, but I'm not sure what you're asking me to do. Do you know people in the North?"

"This will mean danger and expense for those who help you."

"Ah, yes, I understand. But I don't have a great deal of money."

"I realize that. But perhaps there could be other ways of making payment."

"What do you mean?"

"You may be able to help someone bring something back into our country."

"I won't smuggle drugs!" he cried indignantly.

"No, not drugs. But perhaps information."

"Information..."

"You would be given complete instructions."

"I'm not sure. What if I can't do it?"

"It won't be anything difficult. The main thing is that you not discuss it with anyone and act normal. Can you do it?"

"I would be putting my life in your hands."

She nodded. "Are you willing to do that?"

"You know I trust you completely."

She put her hand on his arm. "Yes, I see that, but you must remember that I'm trusting you completely too."

He kissed her passionately. She pulled away, her face flushed, and then took a piece of paper from her pocket.

"Go to this address tonight. Eight o'clock sharp."

*   *   *

Once darkness descended he stole a car and drove to the address in Seoul, parking the vehicle around the corner from a working class apartment building. Climbing the steps to the third floor, he knocked at number twenty-eight, waited, then knocked again.

When Soo-Min opened the door, he was taken aback. He had not expected someone so beautiful. She had large, light brown eyes with long lashes and perfectly shaped brows. Her skin was as soft as any woman's he had ever seen. Her mouth was a lovely frame around flawless teeth. She smiled with dimpled cheeks that gave her a young, almost childlike expression. Her body was provocative in a plain dark tunic over tight fitting jeans, her bare feet had toenails painted dark blue.

She invited him in. Then, her phone in her hand, excused herself saying she had to finish a call in the other room. He waited while listening to the muffled sounds of her voice from behind the closed door. A minute later she joined him, gesturing for him to sit down. As he eased into a comfortable chair, she sat on a settee and curled her legs underneath her as agile as a cat.

They chatted about his work at the docks and whether he liked living in a large city. She asked him about his family and in particular his grandmother. He told her how she had raised him but had to return to the North to care for her brother, who later died. Soo-Min seemed to accept his answers or at least didn't let on if she didn't. After a while she offered him Soju.

He discovered she was quite intelligent and he could feel an attraction to her as they both sipped their drinks. She never discussed politics, but judging by the titles of her books, most written by contemporary Western authors, and from the pictures on her walls, she was thoroughly corrupted by Western influences. Luckily, Jin was well versed, having read many of the same books and studying art created by the very same artists, but for entirely different purposes, or course. Her eyes were alive with the discovery that they had so much in common.

He poured more Soju. It was when they both were feeling tipsy that Jin discovered she had an old fashioned turntable and a Bee Gees album.

"Could I play this?" he asked innocently.

"Go ahead," she replied, rising and taking his hand once the music started. The two began dancing and laughing, and he discovered she was quite good. After a couple of songs they collapsed onto the floor in an embrace and began kissing passionately. They had sex while the Bee Gees sang in the background, something Jin had never done with the hired women he frequented back home.

They climaxed together and remained in each other's arms, her finger outlining a tattoo of the number 33 inked along the bottom of his neck.

"Thirty-three. What does that mean?" she asked.

He tensed momentarily, then forced himself to relax again.

"It's the year my grandmother was born."

She giggled, then said simply "Oh."

His anger rose instantly as he considered she was mocking a symbol that represented his service to his country, one that was personally selected by The Great One himself. Disgusted by this young woman and her wanton ways, he was eager to stop the cuddling and just kill her, but reminded himself to be patient and to stick to the plan. He smiled and kissed her hand.

He looked into her eyes and said, "Are you going to be able to help me, Soo-Min?"

There were several seconds of silence before she got up, her naked body like ivory, and retrieved a piece of paper from a drawer. She handed it to him. "Be at that border location on that date, exactly at that time. Without fail. You will be getting your grandmother out if you do exactly as you are told."

He took the paper from her and said, "Thank you. I'll never forget this."

"There will be something you will be bringing back, so don't thank me yet," she replied, then rejoined him on the rug, snuggling against his shoulder.

He needed to continue to cultivate the moment, and her emotions, so he held her and lightly stroked her skin. She told him about her family, and how in 1951 her grandfather had been captured and killed at the Battle of the Imjin River. He listened patiently, but she would not let it go. He tired of it after a few minutes and said, "You can't blame Bukhan for your grandfather's death. It was war."

She sat up. "That was no excuse to torture him. He was only a soldier obeying orders."

He quickly reversed and said, "Yes, you're right. I don't know what I was thinking. The stinking dogs probably killed him for the pleasure of it."

The spell was broken. She got up and put on a silk robe. As she tied the sash she said, "I'm hungry. I'm going to cook something now that you're leaving."

Rising next to her, he reached out. "I'm sorry. I didn't mean to offend you. Please allow me to stay for dinner." His hand delicately pushed her hair aside so he could kiss her neck.

She moaned, closing her eyes for a few seconds before she pushed him away. "Okay. But only because I want you again for dessert." She moved towards her kitchen and said over her shoulder, "Get dressed, you're helping. You can chop."

He cut garlic and peppers as she began cooking on a brazier set atop the table, and judging by the smell, she was an excellent cook. When she passed him the plates she gave him a kiss. With her back turned, she opened another bottle of Soju, which gave Jin the opportunity to swiftly pull a vial from his pocket. Using the eyedropper contained in its lid, he dripped deadly toxin into her empty cup, before she passed the newly opened bottle for him to pour.

As she sat down, the song, *How Deep Is Your Love,* began playing. She smiled, admitting to Jin it was her favorite track. Then she raised her glass to make a toast. "To family reunions."

Their glasses touched and after taking a sip, he watched her taste a mouthful of food. She frowned as the toxin took immediate effect. While she lay on the floor, her mouth frothing and her body jerking, her eyes watched Jin as he wiped his fingerprints from everything he had touched. He had used a condom when they had sex, so was careful to remove it from the trash and place it in a plastic bag he put in his pocket. He washed his glass, then slipped out of her apartment into the darkness.

Doomed Durango

*   *   *

There in the limousine, he was listening to *How Deep Is Your Love.* His tension gone. Jin was so relaxed he felt a little sleepy, and sighed as he murmured... yes, such a great song.

Chapter 6

The Whirlwinds of Change

Nick, Trevor and Ray cleaned up the lunch and raised anchor to resume their trip. The morning was nearly gone, but they continued another two hours until Nick slowed the Esmerelda then cut the engine.

"Okay, boys. Let's get the chum out, then we'll raise the outriggers so we can have complete freedom to reel in our big fish. We're lucky the water is so still."

Trevor scoffed, "Damned lucky! With the outriggers up, this tub would be going sideways like a hobby horse if we didn't have the dead calm."

"What can I say? I'm a lucky guy," Nick replied with a grin, clearly enjoying himself.

Now that's the Nick I know, Trevor thought to himself. Then he considered the other times he had seen Nick since he had been home. He had seemed so down. That was why Trevor agreed to be here today, to feel like it was the old days when it was like they had no cares at all. Maybe he needed it too.

They tossed the chum, the chunks of bait attracting more gulls; then they baited the two rods with the live cod. While they worked, the sun exploded in sheer white light. The blue-glass ocean reflected with barely a ruffle. Ray yawned and after a while nodded off to sleep in the captain's chair. Nick sat down on deck to untangle some rope. Trevor slid down to lean his back against the gunwale, his eyelids getting heavy. The only sound was the water lapping gently against the boat.

Trevor was snoring after a while. His hands would periodically twitch when his fingers loosened their grip on the rod. He'd somehow tighten them again in his sleep. Then, the rod quivered, and the whirring sound of the reel began. His eyes snapped open and he was on his feet in one movement.

Nick called out, "Take it, Trev! Ray, you're at the wheel! Gentlemen, start your engines!"

As soon as Trevor took a sturdy stance, the sound stopped. "I'm hardly feeling any pull." He reeled the hook in, and rather than finding a big tuna, it was a small skate, a flattish creature, with a white belly and a brown speckled head. Keeping its barbed tail at a safe distance, he unhooked it and tossed it back in, the skate melting into the water. "Now what do you want to use for bait since he ate your cod?" However, before his words were finished, the other reel began spinning.

"Forget that one and take this!" Nick said excitedly.

With the new rod in Trevor's hands it arced from the pull of the fish, a totally different feel from before.

Doing as he had been told, Trevor allowed the tuna to run with the bait. Nick was talking excitedly as he watched the line, telling Ray to back up or go forward depending on which direction the fish took. Trevor held a fierce grip, bracing his foot against the boat.

"He's going straight out, Nick. Let's bring him in." Where the line submerged in the water, a tornado of bubbles gave clues to the strength of the animal below.

"Do it!" Nick agreed.

Trevor turned the crank on the reel, the great fish darting in different directions to free itself. As the battle ensued, Trevor wondered how the hook didn't just rip through the animal's flesh. "It feels like fuckin' Moby Dick!" he said, his veins visible across his taut muscles.

Nick shouted to Ray, "Back her up!" And then, "Stop!" And again, "Move her starboard!"

"We've got to cross over!" Trevor said, gritting his teeth.

Nick helped him grip the rod as they followed the tuna to port side. Trevor cranked the reel again, sweat stinging his eyes.

"I can see it!" Nick shouted as he reached for the spear. The fish neared, thrashing sideways, exhausted but still fighting.

"I can't get him any closer. This is it!" Trevor stated. Nick took aim with the speargun and pulled the trigger, but missed. Trevor, frustrated and tired, yelled at him, "What the hell? Come on, Nick!"

Nick cranked the spear back and readied it for another shot. The fish rose to the surface as Trevor gave a final turn on the reel.

The spear erupted from the gun. "I got it! I fucking got it!"

Ray cut the engine and ran to help raise the beast into the boat. It gleamed translucent blues and greens, the sun highlighting every detail of the silver scales cascading across its stomach like perfectly sewn sequins. With all three grabbing hold, they lifted the creature over the side and dropped it into the boat.

"Holy shit! Look at the size of that bastard!" Nick happily shouted.

"It's a hell of a fish, Nick," Trevor agreed, wiping his face with his shirt tail. "A real beauty."

"We need to cool it down," Ray told them, and taking his knife, cut its throat then ran the blade down its belly.

Trevor got a hose and cleaned the gape of the fish, blood and innards splashing onto him and the deck. Nick pushed the gunk into a bucket and tossed it overboard, the gulls diving excitedly, scooping up dangling entrails and gulping them down on the wing. By the time the fish was cleaned, their clothes were streaked all colors from guts. Trevor ran his fingers across his shirt to scrape off bits of blood then smeared some on Nick's cheek.

"Dude!"

"You're blooded. It's your first kill."

Ray laughed and said, "That's right, Nick."

They put their catch on ice and closed the cooler, standing back up, the three of them looking at each other, suddenly laughing and giving one another high fives.

"This calls for beer," Nick said. He went to the cooler and pulled out three bottles.

"To success!" Ray announced, clinking the brothers' drinks.

"Hell yeah, success!" Trevor added, then took a long swig. "How much will you make on this?"

"As big as that monster is, I think we nailed a ten-grand fish." Then Nick cocked his head back and yelled, "Woo-hoo! I cannot believe we just did that!"

Gesturing with his chin towards the birds, Trevor said, "Are we going to try for another? Because it looks like the gulls have gotten your chum."

"Let them have it. We're done!" Nick answered.

"Good. Then I'm going to change." Trevor belched a ferocious burp.

"Wait a minute! Change? Why? I like your fish-gut outfit. Surely a Navy SEAL has had to sit around in worse? Then again, you do smell like shit!" And with that he catapulted Trevor over the side and into the water with a splash.

Nick was laughing and took a swig from his beer, though his eyes never left the spot where Trevor went under. Having looked after his little brother for so long, it was instinct to do it, even though Trevor was one of the strongest swimmers he knew. Ray remained silent next to him. When the last of the bubbles rose to the surface, Nick kept waiting. "I know he's staying down to just to scare me," he said to Ray, then whispered, "Come on, you idiot." After more than a minute passed, he set the beer down and was about to kick off his shoes.

Trevor came rising out of the water like Poseidon and shouted, "Come on in, Nick! It's like a bathtub down here!" He splashed some water towards the boat then swam closer.

Nick stared at him relieved but pissed off, though he wouldn't give Trevor the satisfaction of letting him know it; he was also wary of the invitation. "No way, that water's got to be fifty degrees." He leaned over to put his hand in. "Plus there are probably sharks from the chum. You'd better----" Trevor grabbed Nick's wrist and yanked him in.

He hit the water so hard the gulls scattered, Nick came up screaming, "Mother of God! This is cold!"

Trevor swam up behind him and dunked him, then climbed into the boat with a hand from Ray and turned around to reach out to a coughing Nick, who didn't hesitate to take it. Nick climbed onboard, laughing and cussing, stripping off the wet clothes. They grabbed some towels and were drying off feeling like they were boys again and still grinning about the fish and the dip in the water.

"I'm going to miss this," Nick said casually, his expression holding a sad smile. They had gotten fresh clothes from their kits and stood naked in the sun changing.

"Miss it?" Trevor said, throwing his towel at him.

Nick picked it up and tossed it into the wheelhouse. "Yeah, I'm selling the Esmerelda. Well, Ray and I are selling." Nick pulled a fresh shirt over his head then yanked on some pants.

Trevor looked at his brother, searching his face to see if he was joking, but it became clear he wasn't. His grin disappeared. He pulled up his pants and raked the zipper up so hard Nick wondered how he didn't break it. Then Trevor said, "Are you kidding me?"

"It's time." Nick replied, focusing on his dry socks.

"Let me get you boys another beer," Ray suggested, moving towards the cabin.

"No! No beer for me, thanks Ray," Trevor responded, then looking back at Nick, he called out, "Turn around so I can see your face while you tell me this! Selling? Why? The Esmerelda supports your family and Ray's."

Nick sat down on the edge of the boat and looked hard at Trevor as he laced up his shoes. "You've been gone, Trevor, for a long time. You haven't been around to see the changes in the industry, in the fishing, the money to be made," he paused, "in me... I can't do it anymore."

"That's bullshit! Dad was fifty and still shrimping."

Nick stood up and moved closer. "And Dad died! I'm not going to leave Carly struggling with our kids the way Dad left Mom. I'm just not doing it, so get used to the idea."

The words renewed the raw pain of Cam Starnes' death, making Trevor feel like that lost little boy again. "We did alright," he responded.

"All right? You did all right! Me? Not so much, at least not now. I've had it," Nick shot back.

They stood there, Trevor staring at him, shirtless and barefooted, feeling like he was seeing his brother

48

for the first time. "Why didn't you tell me? Why didn't you talk to me?"

Nick shook his head. "Because you had your own shit to deal with, why do you think? What was I gonna do? Call you on the cell phone you weren't allowed to take with you while you were God knows where? And besides, this is something Ray and I had to decide, and we've been talking about it a long time. Tell him, Ray. We had this idea ages ago, didn't we?"

Ray answered, "Now, don't go dragging me in. It ain't like all that, Trevor."

"But you support this? Just giving up shrimping?" His voice felt strangled in his throat.

Ray was heartbroken to see it going like this, Trevor so hurt, and Nick in pain for causing it. Ray knew he had to support Nick, but it didn't make it any easier. "Honest? It ain't givin' up. We don't have no choice. I'm sixty-five now. I got arthritis in my knees. Your brother is forty-two, and no offense, Nick, sometimes after the end of hard day you look fifty. It's hard, a hell of a lot harder than it used to be. Not the same game when Cam and I was out here."

"So, what are you going to do?" Trevor asked, looking at Nick.

"I don't know. I'll figure it out."

"Have you sold her already?"

"We've shaken hands." Nick crossed his arms against his chest.

"Who's buying her?"

"Dick Sims."

"Dick Sims? That asshole? He'll scrap her the day he gets her once he scavenges anything he can make a buck on."

"If he buys her, he can do what he wants."

"Have you signed anything?"

"No! I just told you. We shook hands."

"Okay then, tell him the deal's off. I'll help you. Let Ray retire. He deserves it. I'll help with shrimping."

"You don't get it, Trevor. I'm done! It's over!"

"It can't be over! You're acting like a bitch. Just giving up and sending Dad's legacy to the junkyard!"

"I'm not acting like anything! This is a decision I've been forced to make. Forced to make while you were gone, by the way. I'm physically and mentally not able to do it anymore."

"You're crazy. You can do anything."

"No, Trevor. I can't! We can't all be out there doing what we want all of the time."

"What the fuck does that mean?"

"You know what it means."

"No, I don't, Nick. I've been risking my life for the last four years, and before that I endured two years of the most brutal training any man can go through. It hasn't been a walk through the park."

"But *you* got to choose!"

"No! I didn't get to choose! I didn't choose that my father died when I was a kid. I didn't choose to be raised by a mother who was never there, and an older brother always out shrimpin'!"

"That's right! You just said it---always out shrimpin'! You think that's what I wanted? I had no choice! My father died too! I had a mother and a little brother to support. I couldn't go to college and have an illustrious military career!"

"Oh, that's hilarious. Act like you didn't jump into Dad's shoes to take all the glory. And now you're resentful because I went to college?"

"I'm not resentful of anything! I'm just trying to live my life the way I want. I've never been given that chance, like you have."

"I didn't just decide to join the SEALS because I needed a day job. It was because of the sacrifice *you* made. I wanted to give something back, make a difference, you know, get some glory myself!"

"And what did it get you? You're not the same person, so resentful that they made you leave!"

The statement hung like static in the air. Nick seemed shocked that he had said it. He heard the words as though they had come out of someone else's mouth. Trevor started to speak, but couldn't. Finally Nick said, "Trev, nobody forced you to take it so far. You didn't have to become a SEAL to make a difference. You could have become an average citizen for all I cared. Don't put all that on me."

Both held tight fists and looked like two junkyard dogs posturing to fight to the death. While each was deciding whether to take it to the next level, a place that could be the point of no return, time seemed to have stopped. The lower sun penetrated their eyes. The air quit moving and the gulls departed. It felt like they were the only two people left in the world, standing at the edge of an abyss, where their decision was to take a step back or go over.

Ray's feet scraped; Nick turned to look at him. With his head down, Ray sniffled, hiding his face as he rubbed his eyes with his sleeve.

Nick said in a whisper, "Now look what you've done."

"Me? You're the one acting like a prick."

Nick called out, "Come on, Ray. It's not like that. You know we were angry. We had to clear the air, so we were saying shit we didn't mean."

"It's true, Ray," Trevor added. "This isn't about you. Nothing will ever change how we feel about you."

Ray stood up. "This isn't what your daddy wanted. Ya'll are his legacy. Don't you get that? It ain't the boat. It ain't shrimping. It's you two. And I done him wrong to let you get to this place today. Saying those things..."

"I'm sorry, Ray," Trevor said.

"Yeah, me too, Ray," Nick added, both responding like obedient children.

"Don't be sorry for me! You need to say it to each other! All you have is one another when it comes down to it. Who else in the world can you really depend on, aside from me, and I ain't gonna be around forever."

Trevor's eyes were tracing the grain in the deck. Nick stared at Ray, who moved towards them.

"You two shake hands, let all of this other stuff go. If not for yourselves, do it for Cam." Neither moved. Ray stepped closer. "*Nick*."

His hands still in fists, he looked at Trevor and saw his younger brother's were the same. His shook his head in disgust, in himself, in his brother, in the unfairness of a world that threw these hardships in their way. Then slowly his fingers relaxed, his hand extended.

Trevor looked intensely into his older brother's eyes. Their palms met and gripped one another hard.

After releasing a long sigh, Ray said, "Good. Now let's get home before you get into another one, probably about something like who's the smartest or better looking, or whether or not that sky up there is blue."

They laughed, short and tense, but it was a laugh that rose from their hearts. Yet the air around them was singed, charged from the earlier tension. Nick broke it, suddenly slapping his brother on his back. Trevor grinned at Ray, who nodded understanding as Nick headed to the wheelhouse and cranked the engine. Relaxed again, he thought to himself that a lot of things have changed over the years, but thank God not Ray. No, not Ray.

Chapter 7

How's Your Russian?

Tree studded hills dotted with red-roofed houses rose above the Salerno harbor. On this sparkling day, the sea glimmered like a green jewel in the tiny bay. Moored along the piers were elegant yachts, a small cruise ship as shiny as a button, and fishing boats, some for hire.

Anchored further out was a lone cargo ship, a scab on the seascape, red and rusty, like an old boot kicked to the back of the closet.

It made Jin nervous as he examined the vessel from the dock. With such a contrast, people were too aware of the old wreck. Would they be curious who was inspecting it for purchase? Perhaps the locals will be so glad to see it go they won't care who buys it, just as long as it leaves. Jin's main concern was that no one ask questions.

He walked up and down the wooden pier, his fingers tapping impatiently against his sides. His appointment was fifteen minutes late. The sun was unduly warm making him hot in his suit, and the smell of fish, particularly old fish, wafted his way cutting through his Fendi cologne. Two gray-headed men down the way argued over their catch, which if Jin's Italian was any good, was primarily squid. He pushed his Gucci aviators snug on his nose and checked his watch again. Then a voice called out behind him.

"Do not worry, my friend," the man said in accented English. "I have not stood you up. A matter of some small urgency kept me detained and I apologize. I'm Uri Naminski." He extended his hand, his fingernails black with grease and dirt.

Jin reluctantly took hold of the Russian's palm then immediately dropped it. "I'm Jin. You're lucky I waited." He whipped out his silk pocket square and wiped his hand, then chucked the exquisite cloth into the trash bin.

"Again, my apologies," the large man acquiesced. He looked Jin up and down. "Nice suit. Looks expensive." Then with a raspy laugh he added, "You look like James Bond." Jin nodded, making Uri laugh again, realizing that Jin thought he really did look that good.

Jin waved him off. "Let's get on with it."

With stubbly cheeks and a crumpled brown linen suit, Uri's dark hair looked as though he had just tumbled out of bed. He stopped to light a cigarette, his gray eyes taking measure of Jin. After waving the match and dropping it to the ground, he said with his head slightly cocked, "Jin, is it? Isn't that Korean?"

"My mother was born in Seoul, my father was Chinese," Jin lied. "Now please, I'm short of time."

In an overly magnanimous tone, Uri said with his hand making a sweeping gesture, "By all means. I have a skiff we can use."

He led the way to a small motorboat tied to the dock. It appeared to be the kind of vessel a lone fisherman might use on a lake. It had two seats and was equipped with oars as well as an ancient looking oil-soaked motor. One at a time, the two men stepped gingerly into the tiny swaying boat, carefully seating themselves. With his cigarette dangling from his lips and the ashes tumbling onto his suit, Uri pulled the motor's cord, then motioned to Jin to untie the line. After another yank the engine responded in a puff of exhaust and a loud patter.

They traveled in silence, the old cargo ship at Jin's back. His stiff posture and gaze away from Uri made it clear he was not interested in small talk. He kept his attention on the shoreline that curled its way around the water in the shape of a seahorse. The sharp light highlighted patches of green between houses, revealing small gardens and then closer to the harbor, planters overflowing with flowers cascaded down to the pier. Taking all of this in, Jin's hands, perched on his thighs, did their best to avoid contact with the filthy boat.

Within minutes, they were pulling alongside the ship where Jin saw a trap door and a welded ring to tie off the motorboat. Once done, Uri turned the crank handle on the hatch, having to make several attempts to wrench it open. The little boat waggled precariously back and forth. Finally, he got it to heave-to with a screech of metal and a crumbling of rust. He climbed inside and then offered a hand to Jin.

Entering the dark, dank interior, Uri pulled from his pocket a small flashlight to navigate his way toward some steps, climbing two flights to reach the top with Jin following. He shoved a heavy door open to be greeted by sunlight. They both stepped out and sucked in fresh air after being in the musty cargo hold.

Walking across the deck, Uri began, "As I mentioned, it's a gearless SID general cargo ship, built in 1991. The beam is ten meters, depth 4.7 meters, overall length 56.40 meters." He paused, looking about and saying wistfully, "She's been a fine ship. Never let us down."

Jin took a moment to scan the deck, seeing rusting cables and cracked glass in the window of what must have been the navigation room. Red paint was peeling everywhere in curls of crimson. Even the deck seemed to be decaying, their footsteps gritty from bits of crumbling metal. Finally, he said skeptically, "Is it seaworthy?"

"Of course she's seaworthy!" the man replied, rubbing his hand along a railing. "She's crossed every sea in the ocean."

"Will it pass inspection, though? It looks like shit."

"Sure. She needs some work, but basically she's seaworthy." He leaned closer. "You said you needed something that we could reflag, and everything has to be done under the table. If you want that, you will have to take this vessel. She's been here so long her certificates are scrapped. She's no longer registered, so she's----what do they say in English? 'A blank slate.'" He smiled a board grin revealing yellow, jumbled teeth.

"Your price includes the upfitting, getting her ready for inspection?"

"My price was for the ship only and arranging for certificates under a new name and ship number. If you want repairs and upfitting, it's extra."

"You can't provide certificates without it."

"I can provide you with anything I want. She'll be sailing under a Ukrainian flag."

Jin studied him. His frumpy clothes and careless appearance belied the crafty look in the man's eyes.

He answered, "Sounds like you have it all worked out, then."

Uri grinned and said happily, "Now you understand! Good! We will be friends, you and I." He slapped Jin on the back, and added, "Come. Let me show you the pilot's room."

Though Jin knew nothing about navigation equipment, he could see that everything looked old. An opened drawer had torn and stained maps spilling out. Trash and dusty soft drink cans littered the floor. Sea air had clouded the glass covers on the instruments. Uri kicked garbage out of the way.

"Naturally this will all be cleaned up," he allowed. "And through there," he indicated a doorway, "Is the salon with a bath and shower. Four people can sleep comfortably, and there's a captain's berth that can be closed off."

"It reeks," Jin responded nudging what might have once been an apple.

"Yes, well, these old ships take on an odor over time."

"I've seen enough."

*   *   *

On the ride back both men were contemplative. Uri considered that Jin will be an easy mark for raising the ship's price with the upfitting to be done. He surmised Jin was secretly representing someone else, which will mean that a bigger price will be no problem. Big fish never do their own shopping.

However, he wasn't an expert in black market sales without being good at reading people. He could tell that he should tread carefully with Jin. He was clearly someone who thought of himself as terribly important, and those types could be unpredictable. He decided that he will need his men to keep an eye on him until the transaction is complete.

Jin kept his expression neutral. It didn't concern him that Uri was setting it up to overcharge. He had plenty of money to pay, should it become necessary, which it wouldn't. Jin knew just how to handle Uri's type.

When they reached the shore and climbed onto the dock, Uri suggested, "I'd like to invite you to dine with me tonight. It is a local place, very nice. And just your style. We can get to know one another."

Jin answered, "All right. We can go over more details of the purchase."

"Yes, of course. Meet me at eight o'clock at *La Bella Vita*."

Jin nodded and began walking away as he heard Uri call out, "Ciao!"

*   *   *

That evening, Jin made his way to the restaurant, having no difficulty, even though it was fairly dark on the moonless night. A few street lamps dotted the city interior. It was a slow time of year for tourists, so things were quiet and the sidewalks mostly deserted. The air was cool as he walked briskly along. Reaching the old district, the road became bumpy with cobblestones and the buildings were tucked tightly together separated by narrow alleys. He could hear music drifting towards him, a concertina and a mandolin. Delicious odors of excellent cooking met his nostrils as he neared the entrance of the restaurant. Jin suddenly recognizing his hunger, inhaled the delectable smells again, hoping the place was Michelin Star quality. He wasn't in the habit of taking business meetings anywhere substandard.

Uri was already seated in a booth, a bottle of red wine on the table and his glass filled. Jin looked at him, his brow furrowed. How presumptuous that he would choose a wine with no input from his guest.

He waved Jin over and said, "I've taken the liberty of ordering some calamari to start off." Jin nodded as Uri poured him a glass, then said, *"Buona salute."* After both men took a sip, he told Jin, "They don't have menus. I would suggest you allow me to order what they've cooked fresh today. It's always delicious."

The proprietor took their orders by asking in Italian, "The pasta and fish for you both?" and Uri responding, *"Sì, grazie."*

Jin looked around the small eatery, consisting of about six tables and a few booths, all occupied and everyone seeming to know one another. Wooden chairs scraped against the flagged floors and dark beams crossed the stuccoed ceiling. At the end of the room there was a small bar, tended by a mustachioed bartender. The clamor of conversation and tableware made for a pleasant background.

"Where are you from?" Uri asked once they were served the pasta.

He gave him a neutral smile as he dabbed his napkin on the corner of his mouth. "I was born in Seoul but raised in China."

"Oh? What part of China?" Uri pursued, a forkful of noodles poised in front of him.

"You are familiar with China?" Jin asked, knowing that whatever part Uri knew of, Jin would say he lived elsewhere.

"Only Hong Kong," was the answer.

Jin nodded. "I lived in the interior for a few years, then along the coast."

Before Uri continued the query, the main course arrived and he attacked it with gusto, a whitefish cooked in a garlic and herb sauce on a bed of risotto. Jin was relieved the conversation had paused. It was the part of the job he hated, having to make friendly discourse with people he cared nothing about. He had no interest in Uri, hearing about where he grew up or his family. He preferred to stick to business. Why was it people felt it necessary to discuss their life story, as though anyone cared? Furthermore, Uri knew nothing of how to dress for a business dinner. He hunched over his plate in his crumpled blue shirt and jeans, his table manners crass as he held his fork like a trowel. Tonight he had an earring in his left ear, a gold hoop that gave him the look of a washed-up boy-band member.

After dessert Uri drained his wine glass, then wiped his mouth on his sleeve. Jin could see that now he would dispense with light conversation. "How soon do you need the ship?" he asked, his voice lowered.

"Immediately," Jin answered.

"It will take at least thirty days," was Uri's response, right after a breathy belch.

"Impossible. I need it right away."

Jin could predict Uri's reply, that it will cost more to have the repairs done quickly. He didn't like to negotiate from a point of weakness, so he needed to switch things up. He folded his napkin and stood.

"Thank you for dinner. I will be doing business elsewhere. I have found a ship that can be ready to sail in a week. Good evening." He had turned on his heels when he heard Uri call to him.

"Don't rush off, there's still more wine. Let's be reasonable. I'm sure this can be worked out."

Jin sat back down and said in a low voice, "I am not interested in your games of cat and mouse. We decided on a price over the phone that included having the boat ready for inspection and sailing under a new flag. I want it in a week. Can you do this or not? It is not negotiable."

Uri met Jin's eyes, the two men sitting there silently until the proprietor appeared with the check. He stood there waiting for instruction as to who to hand it to. Uri finally grabbed the ticket. He then cut his eyes back to Jin and snorted, "All right. A week it is."

"Now, that *is* reasonable."

Uri picked up the wine bottle to pour more. Jin covered his glass with his palm and said, "I must be leaving. Call me when the ship is certified."

"Just a moment," Uri said, his hand on Jin's arm. "Before you go, we must arrange another meeting, unless you have half the cash on you now."

"We never agreed to that."

"Maybe not, but I have to pay people up front. I need money to get repairs done and to bribe the right officials. And of course, you want the workers to keep their mouths shut."

"That's what I'm paying for. My privacy is not optional."

"Yes, yes. Calm yourself. Everyone is reliable, for the right price."

"Fine. Meet me tomorrow at the dock. I can give you twenty-five thousand euros."

"Twenty-five thousand! That's not even shit in the bucket for what I'll be spending."

"That's your problem, your cost of doing business. Twenty-five thousand or no deal."

Uri licked his lips, mentally adding up the expenses. "Okay. The dock. Tomorrow at ten."

"My man will be there with the money."

"I prefer it be you," Uri cried indignantly.

"I'm not an errand boy. You'll get your money."

"When I do business 'under the table' I like assurances."

Jin laughed. "Don't we all." And he walked out.

Stepping into the fresh air, Jin felt relieved to be away from the man. He brushed off the front of his suit as though he were brushing away Uri himself. Then he began walking back to his hotel, his eyes alert and his ears quickly noticing the sounds of two sets of footsteps behind him.

Earlier, he had counted the blocks between the restaurant and the hotel: six. He was halfway when he saw an opening between two buildings. He slipped in and hid behind some boxes. Two men trotted in, as he was sure they would.

As the first one approached, Jin sprang from hiding. Grabbing the man's hair, he pulled back his head and cut his throat in one swift, precise movement. The body fell to the ground as Jin turned to face the other, who had stumbled backwards in confusion. Moving in quickly, Jin kicked his feet out from under him and put the knife through the man's ribs killing him instantly. He wiped the blood off the blade onto the man's clothes then put it back in its sheath.

At the street entrance he checked to see if anyone else was lurking. No one. Stepping out, he resumed his walk, pleased that his terrific skill had once again saved him from getting blood on his clothes. It would have been a terrible waste to ruin such a fine suit while taking out the trash.

He had gone less than a block when he saw a car up ahead, idling on the side of the road. As he neared the glowing red lights he realized it was Kwon, waiting for him. He hadn't arranged this with Kwon, but without speaking, Jin climbed into the backseat and they left, driving the short distance that remained to reach the hotel. Neither spoke.

Later, Jin got into bed, pleased with his day's work. Then, not typically a problem, he tossed and turned for an hour or so, assuming it was the rich, Italian food that was keeping him awake. Finally, he drifted off and eventually climbed through the mists of sleep to have a recurring dream that hadn't visited him in a long time. It was always the same thing, a childhood memory stored in a deep, dark recess...

A woman and small child walked towards him on a dusty street. As they neared, and with her clutching the little boy's hand, she looked up, revealing the face of Jin's mother. He knew that the child was himself. His mother led him into a building, where they climbed narrow steps surrounded by dingy walls. They were going to the shabby apartment where they had lived all those years ago.

Once inside, there came a pounding at the door. A large man entered, speaking gruffly and flinging some money. After scrambling to pick it up, his mother played a scratchy record on the old turntable, the Bee Gees, her favorite, and began to dance. The man had a long snake wrapped around his waist that shifted into a leather belt. Removing it, he licked his lips with his serpent's tongue. Jin saw the frown on his mother's face. She kept dancing while he snapped the belt like a whip. Welts rose on her arms and legs while screams and pops crackled through the air. Grabbing her and pushing her down he mounted her, his thick, grizzled fingers around her throat, squeezing so hard her eyes bulged. He grunted satisfaction, his hips moving backward and forward.

Crouched behind the kitchen counter, Jin peeked out to see her face change to a bluish-purple. A gurgle rose from her throat. He felt himself opening the drawer above him, his hand finding what it was looking for. Gripping it like a javelin, he ran with his mother's kitchen knife aimed for the man's back, the blade diving into the flesh as easily as an overripe melon. Crimson splattered then oozed like molten lava. Jin's face spritzed, he could smell blood as the body tumbled over like a landslide. He ran to his mother, staring at her black marble eyes about to roll down her face.

"Umma! It's alright, you can stop pretending." He waited for her to come out of her trance, but the eyes failed to return to their normal places and the lids never blinked. He then knew. He had seen death before.

He got up, calmly washing his hands and face. After he dried off, he used the towel to pull the knife from the man's back, his foot pressing for leverage. He washed it, then carefully returned it to the drawer. "There. That's better. Thaaat's better…"

*   *   *

By the next morning, the dream returned to its hidden place. Jin awoke early and had coffee in his room, hearing the sounds of police sirens in the distance.

"I wonder what that's about?" he chuckled to himself. He called room service for breakfast and then showered and dressed for the meeting with Uri.

Making it a point to arrive late, he found Uri standing where he kept the skiff. His mouth was clenched and his gray eyes were like storm clouds.

Jin stepped lightly down the steps and said, "Good morning. Beautiful day, isn't it?"

"What did you do?" Uri demanded.

"I'm sure I don't know what you mean," Jin replied, withdrawing the envelope from his pocket that held the twenty-five thousand euros.

"You didn't have to kill my men!"

Jin kept his smile. "As I said, I like my privacy." He held out the envelope. "But I don't think they'll be saying anything. Do you?"

Hesitating at first, Uri took the envelope. "One week. Be here in one week with the rest of the cash. Then we're through."

"Exactly," was Jin's response. He turned to go back up the steps, then said over his shoulder, "*Ciao*."

Once he reached street level, Jin began humming, enjoying the sun and pleasant morning, glad he had chosen to walk instead of having Kwon drive him.

Chapter 8

Polish the Purple Heart. I've been injured in the line of duty! #CummingsAndGoings

Jason woke up to the sensation of bright light penetrating his eyes. When he blinked, the light withdrew and a man dressed in medical scrubs spoke to him.

"You're in the infirmary, Mr. Cummings. My name is Doc Charlie. I'm checking you over because you've got a nasty bump on your head."

As he was getting Charlie into focus, Jason raised a hand to touch his forehead, only to have Charlie gently move it back to his side.

"I've put a bandage over a small cut. That area will have a pretty good goose egg before long."

"Have I been in a coma?" Jason asked with a scratchy voice until he cleared his throat.

"A coma? No, of course not. But you have been unconscious for a few minutes. And you've got a concussion."

Jason thought back to his childhood when his sister knocked him cold by swinging a bat and not knowing her little brother was behind her. His mother stayed with him overnight in the hospital, and he smiled inside with the memory. Spending time with his mother was one of the reasons Jason took up cooking when he was so young. He wasn't especially close to his father. Thinking his son would be like his two older brothers and enjoy Scouting, Reverend Cummings finally gave up when he realized that the only part of Boy Scouts Jason enjoyed was sewing the patches on the other children's uniforms.

"Will I have to be here overnight?" Jason asked Charlie.

"Yes, you will. But not to worry. I'll be here then nurse Mazy will take over. You won't be left alone."

"Oh, good," Jason said with a sad smile, thinking that with somebody constantly watching him he won't be able to listen to the recording on his phone. His hand went up to his shirt pocket. His phone wasn't there, then again, neither was his shirt. He had been undressed and was in a hospital gown.

"Where's my phone?" he asked frantically.

Doc Charlie soothed, "It's perfectly safe, stored in that locker over there along with your clothes."

"I'd like to have it," Jason said meekly, wishing he felt a little sharper so he could speak more forcefully.

"No phone for now. I want you to stay quiet and rest."

First Mate Chambers knocked on the door and stuck his head in, his cap pushed back on his head. "How's the patient, Charlie?"

"Just woke up."

At once Jason knew from the glint of the golden locks that it was Chambers. His mind began to wander, wondering if the First Mate was blond all over...

Jason asked with a bat of his eyes, "Did you two undress me?"

The men looked at one another and Charlie said, "Don't be embarrassed, Mr. Cummings. I undressed you. I'm a trained medical professional."

"Are you feeling better, Mr. Cummings?" Chambers asked, ignoring the previous question.

"Please, call me Jason." Jason attempted to sit up, then felt a little dizzy.

"Here, let us help," Chambers said, getting on one side and Charlie on the other. Jason liked the pale hair and freckles on Chambers's arms. The two men lifted Jason higher on his pillows.

"Oh, my. Thank you," he said, realizing he couldn't get the smile off his face.

"Better?" Charlie asked.

"Definitely," Jason replied. "By the way, what happened?" he asked sheepishly, remembering exactly what had occurred, but wanting to avoid blame for it.

Chambers answered, "I was hoping you could tell me. I found you outside the bridge. You hit your head on the railing. Were you looking for something?"

"I can't seem to remember a thing," he answered, looking from one to the other.

"That's quite common with a head injury, so don't concern yourself," Charlie explained.

"Is there anything you need? The Captain wanted to personally ensure your utmost comfort." Chambers asked.

Charlie informed Chambers, "He wanted his phone, but I told him no phone for now, he needs to rest."

The First Mate nodded. "Sounds like good advice. Rest sounds like just the thing." He said the words with a half smile, one of his dimples crinkling.

"I hope it wasn't too hard for you to carry me down here, Chambers." Jason said in a small voice.

"Charlie and I carried you on a stretcher."

Jason began smiling again and decided that yes, Chambers was blond all over.

Then Charlie said, "We're glad you're okay."

"I'll let the Captain know you're comfortable, though I'm sure she'll want to see you just as soon as she can step away," Chambers commented as he walked out the door.

"If she must," was Jason's response, trailing behind him.

"You get some rest. I'll be right in there doing paperwork." Charlie indicated a desk in the admitting area, which Jason could clearly see since his room had only a half wall.

"My goodness. I hope I don't sleep with my mouth open," Jason remarked as he pulled the sheet up to his eyes.

"Won't bother me a bit," Charlie assured him. Jason watched him get on a computer before the intercom buzzed.

After a few minutes, he realized he did feel drowsy. Yawning, he turned on his good side, staring at the blue locker and its shiny, chrome handle. He decided he would sneak over to retrieve his phone the first chance he got. However, that would have to wait, because his eyelids were feeling ever so heavy.

There was a knock at the door. Turning back over groggily, he saw Captain Patel. She removed her cap as she walked in.

"How are you, Mr. Cummings?" she said, walking over and hiking one hip up on the bed. The overhead light bounced off her glossy, black hair.

"I'm okay, Captain," he managed.

"Were you outside the bridge to see me?"

He looked closely at her, her black eyeliner so subtle, and yet, he could imagine her ancestors living in India with kohl painted around their dark eyes. "It's like I told Mr. Chambers, I can't seem to remember," he answered, still fixated on her face.

She nodded, Jason noticing how nicely she smelled of the ocean. "Charlie said you are to remain in the infirmary tonight. I hope you'll take his advice."

"Do I have a choice?" he said resignedly.

She laughed, "Well, it's not prison, but we certainly don't want to take any chances with your health."

She said it so seriously, yet her eyes seemed playful. He decided he couldn't help but like her, but knew he must be mindful of what was at stake and not be taken in by her charms.

He sighed. "It's a pity since this is the night of the formal dinner. I was really looking forward to it. I interviewed your chef, you know. The man is from Naples. Everything will be authentic Italian."

"There will be other dinners you can enjoy," she said appreciatively.

"Well hardly, Captain. We'll be back in port in two days."

She swallowed, then took in a deep breath and perceptively relaxed.

"Won't we, Captain Patel?" he asked, feeling his brow crease.

Smiling, but more stiffly now, she rose. "Of course. I'll tell you what, if Charlie gives his approval, why don't you join me for dinner tonight. A few other guests will be at the table, as well. It might be fun to get out for a bit."

His eyes lit up. "Yes, all right." He considered that this could present an opportunity to glean more information. With that, she left, stopping at Charlie's desk to speak to him in quiet tones.

With their backs to him, Jason wasted no time and slipped out of bed, his bare toes shocked by the cold floor. It was chilly in general in the infirmary, and with the hospital gown open in the back, he felt breezy all over. He moved to the locker, pleased that the dizziness was gone. His hand took hold of the metal latch, slowly lifting the lock. It made a little squeak when it opened, but it was worth the risk.

There, sitting on top of his folded polo shirt was his phone. He grabbed it and didn't even bother latching the locker door, just pushed it to, then turned back to his bed. As he snuggled into the neatly pressed sheets and blanket, Charlie glanced at him. Jason gave him a little wave, then turned back on his side and put the phone down where it couldn't be seen. He hit the play button to listen.

There was a great deal of background noise that Jason determined must be the hum of the ship's engines vibrating through the decking. With the voices muffled, he could just make it out. Two words on the recording made him shiver as Captain Patel's distressed voice echoed in his ear,

"How long?"

He replayed it over and over. How long before what, he wondered?

He thought about calling to her before she left, but when he looked up, she was gone.

He slid down further under the covers so Dr. Charlie wouldn't see his grin. His imagination running wild, he thought to himself… this is going to be my big moment. When my story breaks, every news outlet in the world will want to interview me. I can't wait for my press junket. Then a thought suddenly panicked him. What will I wear on the Jimmy Kimmel Show?

Chapter 9

A Rose By Any Other Name

His phone rang. A damned inconvenience. Jin was at his tailor's in Milan, getting fitted for a suede jacket. When he saw it was Uri he was extra irritated, but he knew he must answer in case there was a problem. The ship was due to be ready tomorrow.

"What is it?"

"What name?" Uri asked, his voice slightly menacing.

"I told you. Register the ship in the name of Flouris Enterprises out of the Ukraine.'" Jin had to switch the phone to his other hand so the tailor could measure his right sleeve.

"I know that. I'm talking about the name you want on the ship. I need it for the registration. Also, we will need to paint it on the hull."

"Oh," said Jin, noticing that the tailor was making his sleeve too short. He gestured impatiently he wanted it to fall exactly on his wrist bone. He said to Uri, "I don't know. Why don't you pick something?"

"If I pick it, I'll name it after you: Mother Fucking Killer."

Jin laughed. "Well, that won't do. All right, let me think for a second." He paused, and then thought of a name that would have some irony, one that harkened back to the Old West in lawless America. "Call it Durango."

"How do you spell that?"

"You fucking moron. D-U-R-A-N-G-O."

"I got it. Meet me tomorrow evening to finish payment and I'll turn everything over. The dock. Six o'clock." He hung up.

Later, leaving the tailor's, Jin returned to Salerno in good humor. Things were going smoothly, in fact, decidedly easy. However, he wouldn't discount the challenges ahead. The first of which was meeting with The Great One for final instructions. That would happen once he got Durango to the Yellow Sea. Until then he would keep his happy mood.

*   *   *

It had been raining off and on all day, so by six o'clock darkness had descended. When Jin and Kwon pulled up, Uri was waiting on the dock, his form nearly obscured by heavy fog drifting in from the sea.

The tip of his cigarette was a tiny red light as if he were in an assassin's scope.

"Get in," Jin called down from the car.

Hesitating at first, Uri dropped the cigarette and stamped it out. As he climbed the steps, he watched Jin open the back door and slide over to make room. He looked at the driver, unable to see his face. His hand slid into his raincoat pocket where he felt the security of a nine millimeter pistol. He then got into the car.

"Where are we going?" he asked, as the rain returned in big drops dappling the windshield.

"I want to show you something," Jin said lightly, as their vehicle pulled away. Then he added, "Where's my paperwork?"

"I have it. And the money?"

Jin flicked his chin towards a briefcase sitting at his feet.

"I want to see it."

Impatiently, Jin snatched the case and put it on the seat between them. Uri turned it around and unfastened the latches. Inside were stacks of euros. "It's all there," Jin remarked peevishly.

Removing his hand from his pocket and leaving the gun behind, Uri dug his fingers under the top layers of money to assure himself. He then closed the case.

"And my papers?"

"On the ship, in the drawer in the navigation room. All except this title, which you must sign." He removed the document from his jacket and set it on the case, pointing out where the signature needed to be.

Jin picked it up and looked at it. "It seems to be in order." He said something in Korean to the driver, who turned around and handed Jin a pen. The name he signed wasn't his own; it was that of a fictitious Ukrainian national, the supposed president of Flouris Enterprises. After signing, he folded the paper and put it in his pocket.

"How far are we going?" Uri asked. "My car is back at the harbor."

"There is a fish market I want you to see."

"Now? At night in the rain?"

"Yes, they're keeping it open for us."

"I've seen the local fish market."

"Not this one. It's exclusive."

As they drove on, the rain intensified, the racket making conversation difficult, though no one seemed eager to speak. Pebbles of hail briefly pinged off the car as streams of water and ice gathered on either side of the windshield. The wipers slashed back and forth. The rumble of the storm and the last vestiges of the hail made for little comfort as Uri grew increasingly tense.

He searched out the window, wanting to determine where they were. He knew the driver hadn't made a detour to return to the dock where any fish market would be. A flash of lightning exposed the guardrail that he knew ran alongside the coastal road out of town. His hand moved back to his raincoat pocket.

"No fish market is out here. Do you take me for a fool?" He removed the gun and pointed it at Jin.

Jin glanced over and seemed unfazed. "Put that away. It's just ahead. I told you, you've never been there before."

Back and forth went the wipers, the water streaming like liquid mercury. He glimpsed a turnoff ahead, the right angle of the road given shape by the headlights of a passing car. He lowered the pistol, setting it on his lap so he could pull a handkerchief from his pocket. He mopped his brow, then heard the muffle of Jin chuckling.

Their vehicle slowed then turned. He let out his breath and looked pointedly at Jin, who sat motionless staring ahead. He put the gun back into his pocket. The driver pulled in front of a house only slightly larger than a garden shed. The only light was a dim illumination behind a battered window shade.

"Come on," Jin said, as he and Kwon got out. "The rain has eased up. This man is a marvelous fisherman and you can get anything you want," he added with a wink.

Uri reluctantly opened his door and stepped out, seeing that Jin was knocking at the entrance of the little house. Kwon waited nearby, his face shadowed. Moving slightly forward, Uri's hand slid back into his pocket in an attempt to caress the gun, but his fingers were trembling. He looked sideways, wondering if Kwon had left the car's key in the ignition. He hadn't.

The front door cracked open. Jin spoke to a small man inside, then turning to Uri, said, "Come on, what are you waiting for?" When Uri didn't move, Jin strode towards him, extending his arm. "You're acting ridiculous."

"With good reason. I'm not going in."

Jin slapped his hand on his thigh and said, "You've got your gun, but if you insist, we'll head back to the dock." Turning again to the house, Jin said something in Korean and the man shut the door. Looking disdainfully back to Uri, Jin griped, "Are you happy now? You've insulted him." He moved closer. "Here, let me put you in the car like the child you are."

The blade of the knife moved so quickly Uri never saw it, only the reflection of the pale light on the metal as it flashed near his eyes. His body crumpled, a pool of blood spreading quickly on the already wet earth.

Jin wiped the blade on Uri's clothes then sheathed it. While Kwon got back into the car, Jin returned to the house and again tapped on the door. As before, it opened only a few inches. He passed over a thick envelope and it slammed shut again.

When Jin climbed back into the car, he said to Kwon, "Let's go. I'm no longer in the mood to shop their delicacies. Besides, now they've got another fish to gut tonight."

With the skies clearing and a few pinpricks of stars beginning to appear, they drove back to the dock. Jin opened the briefcase and handed Kwon a thick stack of bills. "Uri's tip for the discrete driver," he joked. "And here you thought he was cheap. You can use it to enjoy your travel home. You know, you'll be getting home later than I will," Jin said cryptically.

Kwon knew better than to ask what he meant, knowing that Jin wouldn't tell him. He looked at Jin in the mirror, his face neutral, but his eyes held a simmering darkness as he replied, "So generous."

Jin sat back and considered how pleased The Great One will be with his results, thinking... I'm sure he'll treat me with a bottle of my favorite champagne and a lovely lady to share it with.

Upon reaching the dock, they used Uri's skiff to reach Durango, Kwon having to make a second trip to get their luggage. True to his word, Jin found the ship's papers Uri had left in the drawer. He put the new title away, and they prepared to launch as Jin popped a chilled bottle of Dom Perignon and poured two glasses.

"To life," he toasted, tapping Kwon's flute. They drank with the clatter of the diesel engine warming up before Kwon pulled the lever to raise the anchor.

Chapter 10

Arriving on schedule or not at all?
#CummingsAndGoings

It was a deep sleep, the kind where it takes several minutes to wake. He had been having an X-rated dream involving First Mate Chambers. That smile he had on his face earlier had reappeared, in fact, Jason was happy all over. Then he had a very blunt interruption, the sound of a woman's voice, low and raspy.

"Finally awake, Sleepy Head?"

He turned to see what he had fantasized would be the First Mate, only to discover inches away a middle aged woman wearing scrubs in a Betty Boop print. She stared at him through large red glasses perched on a similarly large nose. Her mouth was stuck in a grin as if she had caught him doing something. Well, she kind of had.

"I'm nurse Jenkins. You can call me Mazy." She cocked her head. "You've had quite a nap."

Did she just wink? Jason sat up. "How long was I sleeping?"

"Three hours."

He began struggling with the bed sheets so he could get up.

"Need some help?"

"No. But I need to ask you where the powder room is?"

"Right over there," she pointed. "I'm happy to assist."

Jason replied sarcastically, "I've been taking care of that by myself since I was three years old, thank you."

The bathroom was complete with a shower. He felt grubby and thought about getting in, but he wanted his own salon-quality ablutions and clean clothes. When he stepped out he had a plan that started with giving Mazy a winning smile.

"Listen, Mazy. I'd like to return to my cabin to shower and change. I am very particular about my grooming, and need my own products." He could see her demeanor stiffen. He put a hand up. "Now, hear me out. You could go along to make sure I don't slip in the tub or something. Then when I'm freshened up, why don't the two of us go and get something to eat? The Captain has invited me to dine with her tonight and you could be my guest." He figured the old girl would get a kick out of being seen with a famous reviewer.

"How about we order room service, and you shower and eat here?"

He shook his head. "No. Emphatically, no. This is a formal night and the chef is doing authentic Italian. I want to be dressed properly and dine in style." Then adding for emphasis, "It will show my respect to the Captain to be presentable. And I am sure my attendance will be valued."

She hesitated, then said, "Well, let me call Doc Charlie and ask him. Don't you go anywhere."

While she called Doc Charlie, he dressed in the terry shorts and shirt, *sans* the Speedo, which he slipped into his pocket. She came back and announced the plan was approved.

An hour later they entered the dining room with Mazy on his arm. Lucky for Jason, Mazy only took five minutes to ready herself, giving him the remainder of the time to properly prepare.

She looked a little out of place next to him wearing his custom-tailored black silk suit and royal blue tie. Nevertheless, Jason was determined that they make an entrance. It was nearing eight o'clock.

The only restaurant on board with a dress code, they stepped into the room as a quartet played selections from The Barber of Seville. The decor was done up like an Italian villa, complete with statuary. Everyone was in fashionable evening attire. The Captain, wearing her dress uniform, sat at the head of a large table filled with guests. When she caught sight of Jason, she waved him over. Sadly, Chambers was nowhere to be seen.

"Mr. Cummings! I'm so glad to see you up and about. How's the head? We were not sure you would make it," she said ironically.

Mazy spoke up. "He's had a long nap, a shower and change of clothes. I'd say the patient is doing well, Captain."

"I see. And will nurse Mazy be joining us too?"

Seeing only one available seat, Mazy answered the question by stopping a passing waiter. "We'll need another chair."

Much to Jason's dismay, they had to take their places at the opposite end to the Captain. Jason held Mazy's chair, then sat in his own while everyone chattered about the arriving Carbonara and shuffled to make room. A wine steward began filling everyone's glasses. Looking forward to smelling the wine's bouquet, which he got a whiff of as it was being poured, Jason put his fingers around the goblet then got his wrist slapped.

"Not after a concussion!" Mazy huffed, then turned to the wine steward and said, "He'll have water with lemon."

The steward gave Jason an inquiring look. He sighed in defeat and said, "San Pellegrino." Then he turned to Mazy. "This means you'll have to drink extra so my glass doesn't go to waste," and considered to himself that should work out well.

As the meal progressed to the next course---anchovy salad followed by scallops and linguine, to be finished with an entree of Braciole---Jason watched the Captain to see if she showed any signs of distress, but she did not. She smiled easily and looked striking with her hair down, long and glossy, held on one side with what had to be a real diamond barrette. She was deft at felling the advances of a passenger to her right and spoke fluent French to the one on her left.

A woman next to Jason said to him, "I've so enjoyed your tweets, Mr. Cummings. I'm a regular follower, you know. But I didn't understand that one about Jack Sparrow."

The man next to her jumped in. "I thought you didn't give Le Jardin in Chicago a fair shake. That's an excellent establishment."

Jason sniffed, "Certainly. If you enjoy microwavable freezer meals."

Another woman said, "Tell me, when you dine is it complimentary?"

A British man next to Mazy answered. "I'm sure it is. And this cruise, as well, I daresay."

"How can you be impartial when everything's paid for?" another asked.

Jason hated this part of his job. Every fool in the world thought himself a critic. He wasn't in the mood for it, as he actually did have a headache. To his surprise, Mazy rose to his defense.

"Listen, everybody. Mr. Cummings took a fall today and knocked his head so hard he sustained a concussion. So it's doctor's orders he have a quiet evening, then bed."

Jason gave her a look that said *thank you* as he re-filled her wine glass.

"Oh, I'm so sorry, I had no idea," a woman said.

"Well, I'm sure the Captain has earned only the best reviews," the adoring man next to Padma volunteered.

Padma was spared comment as the braciole arrived, and everyone went silent as their wine glasses were filled, and they started the main course.

What Jason wanted was an opening to speak with Padma privately, and it finally came when the waiter brought dessert: Lemon Ricotta Granita and Florentines. Out of the corner of his eye, he caught sight of a young officer entering the restaurant, then stopping a few paces from their table. She gave a subtle signal to Padma, who immediately stood, and without explanation said, "Goodnight, everyone. It's been a pleasure." Much to Jason's good fortune, Mazy was powdering her nose, which he knew would take a while.

"Captain!" Jason said, springing around the table.

Padma turned. "Yes, Mr. Cummings?"

Jason quickly improvised a reason to speak with her, though all he could think of was, "Do you know something about the dessert we don't? Was the cream curdled or the chef flummoxed with the Florentines?" They began moving towards the exit.

"Not at all. Any *dolce* our chef prepares is always to perfection. No, it's merely that I need to call it an evening."

They reached the door, opened graciously by the maitre'd. The two of them stepped out onto the windy deck, the young officer following.

Jason continued, "You know, I would really like to do that interview before our cruise ends. I mean, it can't be easy being the first female captain the Morrows have hired."

She looked at him thoughtfully. What he said was true; nothing had been exactly 'easy'. She graduated from high school as Valedictorian and went on to Wellesley and finished Summa Cum Laude, but instead of marrying the Indian husband her parents had selected, she joined the Navy and spent six years at sea. That decision had cost her dearly. She hadn't seen her mother, father or younger brother since her college graduation. She had been disowned. She finally received a letter from her father a few months ago, not to make amends, only to say that her grandmother in India had died, and she had missed the funeral.

"I don't know why my life would be of any interest to your readers. Really, it's quite boring. This ship is the real star of this tale."

"Oh, I doubt that. You're a beautiful woman. The sea is a romantic place. Are you involved with anyone on board, perhaps?"

She laughed. "I don't have time for shipboard romance." Then with a mischievous smile, she added, "What about you? Anyone catch your eye?"

She gave him a knowing look and he actually blushed! He tended to get that way around unusually attractive people. He recalled his first love, David, whom he met at college. He couldn't even get his own name out of his mouth when David introduced himself. David was good natured about it. He was used to people getting tongue-tied when they met him, especially girls. He had an exquisite face and body, so lovely that when he entered a room people often just stopped and stared. Jason became instantly infatuated, and the two had an intense, though brief, affair until David decided to switch to the straight and narrow for a while. Last Jason heard, David dropped out to travel the world with a wealthy, and not to Jason's surprise, much older man.

"Captain, this isn't about me. It's about the High Cotton and the people who keep it running so smoothly."

Her expression became more serious. She was about to say something when the junior officer interrupted.

"Captain, Engineer Dobbs said we need to return to the bridge *immediately---*"

Padma's eyes flashed anger as she put her hand on the young woman's arm in an attempt to prevent her from saying more. "Yes, of course, Pullen. Excuse me, Jason. I must leave."

Jason made a split decision. He ran after them, trotting behind until he caught up and said, "Captain, I know about the ship's problem."

She stopped and turned around.

"What do you mean?" she asked, trying to sound casual and looking from Jason to the young woman, who shook her head as if to say, 'I didn't tell him a thing.'"

"I mean, I'm aware that the High Cotton is having issues. What I'd like to know is how they're going to affect us for the remainder of the cruise?"

Her response was quick and abrupt.

"Please don't go around spreading rumors. If ships ran without problems they wouldn't need captains and crew. There's nothing for you to concern yourself with and no cause for alarm. Do you understand?"

Jason stood his ground, quoting coyly, "How long?"

Her shocked expression gave it away. She attempted to recover by saying, "Excuse me?"

"How long will it be?"

"What?"

"Until you admit the truth."

She didn't answer, just did an about face and left with the young officer struggling to keep up. Padma's hand was raised signaling to the girl not to speak.

Jason returned to the table triumphantly; he had rattled the seemingly unflappable Captain. He sat down and looked at his dinner companions, all tipsy from the wine, and relished his sobriety. He would take full advantage. After all, loose lips sink ships.

Gloating, he looked over at Mazy's empty chair and saw that she was speaking with a passenger across the room, having left her wallet behind. Her tacky purple lanyard and ID badge were haphazardly stuffed into an outside slot. He slipped it out and examined it under the table. It was a security key card and easily unclipped. It went neatly into his jacket pocket. Then he poured Mazy more wine.

Chapter 11

Who sits at the right hand?

Jin decided to have Durango detour to the port of Piraeus, so he could get a flight out of Athens. Sharing sleeping quarters with Kwon, or anyone else for that matter, was not his style, and neither was menial labor. That kind of thing he quit doing years ago. Instead, he took a much deserved vacation, spending a few days in the Greek islands. His tan looked spectacular, and he found a couple of Dutch girls for entertainment.

Once he was back in North Korea, he contacted The Great One's office and was told by an assistant to be at headquarters in an hour. Quickly showering, he dressed in a black Armani suit. He left his building to find a car waiting. On the way he gazed out the window and considered how he was looking forward to the meeting since he had done such an outstanding job.

Government offices were in central Pyongyang located in a sprawling, modern structure. Spanning across the building's exterior, the top floor had carved reliefs representing the common man's struggle, the symbolic toil in the fields and the factory worker with hammer in hand. The artwork brought pride and beauty to the city, which was spotlessly clean and inhabited only by those especially selected. Passing a sweeping fountain that misted passersby as if anointing all who entered, Jin made his way inside and across the spartan foyer to the elevator.

The Great One's office was on the ninth floor and heavily secured. Jin breezed past the guards, who all knew him, of course. Without having to acknowledge the soldier blocking the entrance to The Great One's quadrant, he knocked. He heard no answer. A different officer walked over and gestured to a closed door across the hall. Jin had been in the conference area before, a few years ago when he received a commendation for his dedicated work. He smiled and straightened his tie before putting his hand on the knob and entering after a quick wrap of his knuckles.

Taking a step inside he stopped. Faces turned to look at him. The Great One was seated at the head of an expansive table, examining papers neatly stacked before him. The others present were all older men wearing matching gray uniforms that were not military, and Jin speculated that they must be technicians and scientists. Judging by their surprise at his entrance, it was clear he had interrupted an ongoing discussion, which was odd since he had not arrived yet.

"Close the door," The Great One said, without looking up.

Jin saw an empty chair nearby and another on the other side of the table next to The Great One, which he obviously was to take. He pushed the door closed and waited for his cue to sit down.

The leader was still thumbing through his paperwork. He had a pout on his full lips as he held a pair of glasses in his left hand. Stout with a broad face, Jin thought he looked puffier than normal. His simple dark suit fit snugly around the rotund body, the material tailored to fit his particular shape. In his right hand he held a pen with the top glittering from a large ruby, which looked too feminine held in the chubby fingers. His dark hair was coiffed off his face, product keeping it firmly in place. The wisps of gray Jin knew he had around his temples were camouflaged by black dye.

"Now, let us look at the timeline and go over it carefully." Glancing up, the Great One said impatiently, "Well? Sit down, Jin, so we can continue."

As Jin began to pass the closest chair, a paper was handed to him, indicating *that* was the chair where he was to sit. Recoiling, he took the document and sat down, trying to recover from the fumble. Quickly reading, he saw the date of the first port of call for Durango and then its ultimate destination. Sixteen days.

SIXTEEN DAYS! Confused, he wondered how that would be possible.

"Everyone please note the updated installation date." The Great One looked at one of the men, who then nodded along with the others, all except Jin. "Good," was The Great One's response. "Then the most important detail is taken care of." Turning to another man, The Great One asked, "And the digital navigation system?"

The man nodded. "It can only be controlled remotely once it has been programmed, as you requested."

"And what is the maximum distance the digital remote can function?"

"Three kilometers."

"I see." The Great One looked at Jin. "So you had better get your coordinates correct. You wouldn't want the Durango to become a sitting duck. You know how 'seals' love duck." He laughed and the others quickly joined him.

"Excuse me for interrupting," Jin began, doing his best to sound respectful and calm. "I do not understand the timeline."

"Why?" The Great One asked impatiently.

Just then the door opened without announcement. Everyone briefly froze and watched the man entering the room, first making a slight bow to The Great One, then confidently taking the vacant chair next to him. It was Kwon.

As it was Jin who had previously asked a question, the meeting continued with all eyes shooting back to him. He couldn't recall what he had asked, as his mind was racing with the question of why Kwon was there. Kwon was Jin's 'fetch-it' man, not someone to be on The Great One's radar. Kwon didn't exist to The Great

One, let alone sit next to him. At least, not to Jin's knowledge.

"Well?" The Great One asked Jin, again sounding impatient.

"Yes," he said, trying not to sputter. "As I mentioned, I was concerned about getting the ship from the Yellow Sea to the final destination within the time allowed."

"The Durango will not be leaving from the Yellow Sea." The Great One looked at Kwon, who had a half smile on his round face.

"There has been a change?"

With a flick of his eyes, The Great One gave Kwon permission to answer.

"The ship is in Odessa, port of Azovstal," Kwon said, looking only at The Great One, who gave him a slight nod.

The Great One then looked at Jin sternly and added, "It only makes sense, does it not, that a ship with a Ukrainian flag would be upfitted with additional equipment in its home port and then depart from there?"

Jin swallowed and said, "Yes, of course," feeling diminished.

"I'm glad we cleared that up. We don't want any more hiccups like the one a few months ago. And as usual, you will have your 'underling,' Kwon, to assist you."

Everyone was uncomfortably silent, as if they knew something Jin didn't. He nodded in agreement, seething inside at The Great One's knowledge and use of his term for Kwon.

As the meeting progressed, Jin stared at the itinerary, hardly hearing what else was said as his mind jumped to a memory of the night in Salerno when Jin killed the two Russians. After stepping out of the alley to resume walking to his hotel, Jin found Kwon waiting with the limo. The engine was idling as Kwon sat with his foot on the brake, the red lights a beacon in the dark as Jin approached. It was not something the two had planned. What at the time seemed unimportant, now became significant.

Feeling an icy wave of paranoia, Jin realized that Kwon had been sent as a spy, and he had played right into his hands leaving Kwon alone to bring Durango home, or rather to Odessa. Perhaps the change in orders had come while Jin was relaxing on a Greek beach. Kwon's stock had risen, whereas Jin's had possibly shifted. Determined to fix this, Jin would find a way to ensure his top slot in the pecking order.

Then he remembered the money----the money that was to have been used to pay for Durango. After killing Uri, Jin kept the balance once he paid Kwon a handsome bonus. But was it enough? Had Kwon told The Great One and labeled it as treachery? Jin always kept money that hadn't been spent, after all, was it not most important that the job was completed? Doing so under budget was Jin's bonus to himself. It was how he maintained his lifestyle. He assumed The Great One knew this.

Realizing that everyone was rising and The Great One was out of his chair, Jin stood.

The Great One said, "I will expect us all to return to this room when the mission is over, so we can celebrate a plan properly executed."

They bowed in unison with smiles on their faces, all except The Great One, whose eyes remained on Jin before he turned and left.

After The Great One made his exit, Jin skimmed around several men to promptly leave, not wanting to see Kwon's look of self satisfaction or the scornful stares of others. Leaving a meeting with The Great One and feeling so insecure was not something Jin was used to.

Even six months ago when they conferenced to dissect the close call that had happened on an earlier mission, Jin didn't feel sidelined or chastised. Kwon's presence today was a message for Jin. What, exactly, he didn't know, and he doubted that Kwon knew either. The Great One enjoyed his games, so he told himself not to be overly concerned. He was the best man for this mission; for this most daring operation that he or anyone else will have undertaken. Still, he felt wary.

Making his way out of the building, popping in his earbuds, he clicked 'play' on The Bee Gees, then selected 'loop.' Ah... he thought to himself, that's better.

Chapter 12

Reinspired

Midnight was approaching. The air was so sharp the stars glittered like jewelry. A curling moon hung low with a faint shimmer on the water. Alone, leaning against the railing and hearing the High Cotton move through the ocean, it reminded Jason of listening to the surf when he walked the beach at night.

Mazy had to retire early due to her abundance of wine, so he was on his own now. Having allowed himself a glass of brandy, he was enjoying the solitude as he thought about his next move. He had tweeted a review of the superb Italian meal they had enjoyed earlier, and sent another glowing tweet about the High Cotton in general, but his heart wasn't in it. His followers expected more from him. He was so ready to write about hard news. What really mattered. Something like the intrigue and cover-up by Captain Patel and her attractive staff. The ship may be on course, fully powered, with functional plumbing and without passengers sick with an onboard illness, yet Captain Patel was increasingly on edge.

As he mulled the facts, he felt his phone vibrate. Removing it from his jacket pocket, he saw that it was his editor, who texted, "What's with the weird tweets teasing that something's wrong with the ship? The only thing your readers want to know is how the onboard massages are, not your cryptic ramblings. Stop pretending to be a news reporter!"

Jason rolled his eyes before writing back, "Even if I'm sure there's real drama here?"

The reply was, "Yes! My wife and I will be taking that cruise next month, thanks to your favorable reviews. Don't screw it up! In the meantime, get a facial or something."

Disappointed with his editor, he put his phone back. Walking along the deck with the breeze against his skin, it felt like a cruel awakening was suddenly filling him with self doubt, something he rarely experienced. Perhaps his editor was right. He should admit defeat and just end the cruise in blissful ignorance. Tomorrow was the last night on the High Cotton. When everyone awakened the following morning the ship would be in the Charleston harbor. If it had problems it would have become apparent by now. He took the last gulp of brandy and gave the glass to a passing steward and ordered another.

A few passengers strolled on the deck near him, two couples in their forties. The women, both attractive, wore long, satiny dresses with impressive displays of diamonds around their necks and hands. The men wore black tie.

"It's glorious, isn't it?" the blond said.

"Breathtaking," said the other, who was the color of ebony and wore a stunning emerald gown.

The man nearest Jason commented, "You know, I wasn't sure if Morrow could pull this off. I mean, a cruise ship strictly for middle agers and above."

"No, not just middle agers," the woman in emerald chimed in. "The wealthy, or people willing to pay to have fine food and wine rather than kiddie entertainment."

"Sort of like those European river cruises, you mean?" the blond asked.

"Exactly. I think it's a clever idea. Let the larger cruise ships entertain the young families. This one is for the discriminating traveler."

"Certainly the reviews have been good," the other man said.

"Yes, but what's with those odd tweets? Jason is so reliable with his tell-all information, he's kinda got me spooked. Have you seen them?" the blond asked.

Jason turned slightly so they could only see his back.

"Yes, I've seen them. Very puzzling. I thought he was trying to say something between the lines, you know what I mean?"

"Yes, like he was hinting that the ship has problems."

"Exactly! But what? All I've seen is flawless."

"Now, that is a clever marketing tool," the woman's husband responded.

"Marketing tool?"

"Keeping everyone wanting to know more, so they follow his tweets devotedly."

"Oh, yes! I see!" the lady chirped. Then, "Darling, could he be that devious?"

"Honey, if the price is right, he'd probably stab his own grandmother. Wouldn't you?" They laughed, and with that, the two couples walked away.

Jason pondered the conversation. He was offended they questioned his integrity, at the same time, they were loyal followers. His tweets had only alluded to the problems, and he had planned to have them fully revealed by now. It made him almost wish the ship would break down to prove them all--especially his editor---wrong. Happily, he recognized that his anger was bringing back his old self.

As he finished the second brandy, he realized it had taken the edge off his headache. He hoped this would enable him to get a good night's rest. Walking slowly along the deck, he came to the stairwell door, his hand pushing it open. After stepping inside he paused, moving just enough to allow the door to quietly close. One floor below was where his cabin was located. He looked up, the lighting dull but adequate to see the steps. His hand moved to the railing when he heard voices.

They were above him and getting fainter. Not sure why, he began following the sounds, quietly climbing. Nearing close enough to hear, he could tell the voices belonged to two men.

One said, "I knew we had made the switch, but are you telling me there could be another malfunction?"

"That's what she said, and it's all computer related. Can you believe that? What operating system are they using, Windows 97?"

"Man, I feel bad for the Captain, this being her first voyage and all."

"What about us? We'll probably be late getting back to port. The passengers will riot if this gets out. People don't take problems with ships very lightly."

"Oh, shit. Does Dawkins know? As Head Steward, he'll be the one who needs to pray this doesn't get out."

"I told him just a few minutes ago. But it was a heads up, really, since everything seems okay for now."

"How did he take it?"

"How do you think?" was the reply, then the sound of a door opening and they were gone.

Jason stopped his ascent and leaned against the wall, taking in gulps of air. He had been so careful not to be detected that he had held his breath.

He retreated back down to his floor. Returning to his room, he took his suit off, strategizing. No, his editor won't see a tweet tonight, telling the world that something is definitely wrong with the High Cotton. Jason decided he would get some sleep, so that when the shit hits the fan tomorrow, as he predicts it will, he will be on the right side of the wind, and with his twitter feed ready.

Chapter 13

It Begins

Jin arrived at the Odessa harbor on a drab afternoon. Drizzling rain left the dock slippery and few people were about. He didn't want to have to find someone to ask where the Durango was moored; it could create unwanted attention, but the shipyard was a large place. Pulling his collar up and shifting his duffle bag to his other shoulder, he walked up and down piers, having difficulty seeing around the larger ships. Finally, after searching the last row of vessels he looked out into the water and saw it.

Just as it was in Salerno, Durango was conspicuously shabby. The rusty anchor chains had already left stains in spite of the new paint. The thin coat of white designating Durango's name was becoming ghost-like as the old red was beginning to show through. Did no one take pride in their work anymore?

Jin had been given no instructions as to how to reach the ship, so he located a small boat for hire with its owner willing to ferry him. Pretending he couldn't speak English or Russian so he wouldn't have to answer questions, Jin and a young Ukrainian man set off on choppy waters. The damp air gave Jin a seeping chill as he perched miserably in the bow of the boat.

Once inside Durango's hatch door, he was met with a lighted chamber, rather than the previous darkness when Uri had given him the tour. Overheads had been installed as two North Korean technicians were finishing the placement of new wiring in conduits.

He climbed the steps and entered the navigation room to find Kwon receiving instructions from In-Su, one of the men who spoke at the meeting two days ago. An older gentleman, In-Su was instructing Kwon on how to turn the transponder off when they no longer wanted to be tracked by other vessels. Jin watched and listened.

In-Su stopped speaking and said to Jin, "I was told to instruct only Kwon on these matters."

"Told by whom?" Jin said.

The man looked at Kwon and replied, "Him."

Jin laughed. "Well, Kwon can't do it all," then more pointedly, "even if he wants to. Besides, there could be something unexpected. People get hurt or worse. I need to know how to complete the mission should that happen." He looked at Kwon, who held his gaze.

In-Su considered the comment, then said, "Yes, I suppose you are correct. The Great One expects this to go exactly as planned." He stepped sideways to a computer screen and continued. "This laptop will be the device that controls the ship remotely when you are ready." He looked at Kwon then Jin. "You will have to follow in another vessel and remain within three kilometers, as I said in our meeting."

"Yes, we heard," Kwon said.

"When you start the system, you will be prompted with instructions." He smiled. "I designed the program, so it is user-friendly."

"We know how to use computers," Kwon said angrily.

"Of course," In-Su nodded. "However, I saw no need in having unnecessary complications when you are at sea."

Jin chided, "Don't be upset with such a dedicated worker, Kwon. He doesn't know how competent or *incompetent* you are."

"And you as well," In-Su said.

"I presume once the final coordinates have been set we no longer must be within three kilometers?" Jin asked.

"Yes. The required distance won't be necessary if you no longer need to make changes in direction or speed. Program it for ten knots. You don't want her going so fast another vessel cannot get out of her way."

"So theoretically we could begin our journey home once we've programmed the settings, and Durango will continue to its destination?"

"No," Kwon said. "We should stay close to make sure no one interferes."

Jin looked at the older man. "What about it? Could someone board her and take over?"

"Someone could board, however navigation of the ship will no longer be possible, except by this," he said, pointing to the laptop. "I designed it that way, so you can make your escape and no one else can interfere."

"So there's no manual override?" Jin asked.

"None. This was designed intentionally, so that you can leave ship at the predetermined coordinates and ensure both your safety and the success of the operation."

As the three men sat silently thinking. Jin was wondering about their escape plan. They were leaving port tomorrow. Was Kwon in charge of this detail?

"It would seem you've thought of everything," Jin said.

"I have. Keep the laptop charged until you're ready to depart ship."

"We will," Kwon said.

The man packed up his gear and left the navigation room.

"That was clumsy of you," Jin said to Kwon.

Kwon looked up. "What do you mean?"

"Telling him you were the only one to handle the navigation system."

"I'm Captain of the ship." A frayed toothpick he'd had in his mouth all morning glittered across his lips.

"Indeed, you are," Jin said mockingly. "But you're going to have to get some rest once in a while. Then I'll need to take over."

Kwon shrugged. "It makes no difference to me."

"The itinerary at the meeting said we have one stop: Agadir. Are we picking up anything there aside from our... cargo?"

Kwon smiled. "Are you worried about our escape boat?"

"Well, I'm not yet ready to be a martyr to our cause, Kwon. Are you?" He stepped closer, inches away from Kwon's face.

"It's all set up."

"I hope you've arranged for something suitable, and will have it stocked with my Dom."

"I did. It's a touring yacht. Probably just Americans onboard. We'll be the Chen brothers," Kwon said, putting a hairy arm around Jin, who immediately shrugged it off. Kwon laughed, his toothpick dropping to the floor.

*   *   *

Darkness arrived with the technicians leaving ship and boarding a small cruiser. After their departure Jin went back up the steps to return to the salon, wondering where Kwon was. He saw that Kwon had put no personal belongings in the room. Had he found Kwon's suitcase, he would have searched it. An hour passed with no sign of Kwon, so Jin went to sleep in the captain's berth that could be closed off with a bi-fold door.

He had dropped off when a noise awakened him. Quickly reaching for his knife, he sat up and listened to someone bumping into things in the dark and finally falling with a heavy thud. Opening the folding door and then turning on the light, Jin found Kwon on all fours, reaching out for the edge of a table.

"You're drunk." Jin said to him, clearly amused.

"What of it?" Kwon rose by bracing his hands on the table.

"The Great One won't be pleased to know his new dog can't handle his drink. Pathetic."

"I needed something to drown out that shit you listen to."

"Shut up, Kwon."

"If you insist on the retro stuff, try something decent like the Grateful Dead."

"I'm warning you, Kwon! Do not speak again about the Bee Gees!"

Kwon took a few unsteady steps before plopping down on his cot. He removed his shoes, muttering, "Asshole…" Then he fell back and was fast asleep.

The next morning the Odessa harbormaster boarded Durango at dawn to check the ship's certificates.

A short, stocky man, he spoke brusquely to Kwon, who had introduced himself as the Captain. "You are leaving port today?" he asked in English.

"Yes," Kwon replied.

"And your next port of call?"

"We are to pick up our cargo in Agadir," answered Kwon.

The man's eyebrows raised. "And what will you be loading there? I see nothing on the manifest?"

"I believe I have that information over here," Kwon said, moving to a drawer and removing a manila envelope. "This has everything you need." The man took the envelope as Jin remained silent in the background.

After looking inside and seeing it thick with money, he replied, "Yes, it appears that everything is in order."

Jin chuckled to himself, watching Kwon enjoy his moment of power. Kwon dismissed the harbormaster by turning his back on him and starting Durango's engine.

"Normally I insist on a tug to escort you. However, since you are out in the harbor you can leave without assistance." The man had to say this to Kwon's back. He then turned and left the navigation room.

Jin went below to see the official off the ship. As they walked through the cargo hold, he stopped and looked curiously at the newly welded supports centered in the expanse of empty floor.

"What did you say you're picking up in Agadir?"

With an easy movement, Jin's hand was on his knife's holster, hidden under his jacket. "I don't know what it is."

His eyebrows raised, the harbormaster said. "Whatever it is you must be making quite a profit. These welded walls cut your cargo space in half."

Jin said nothing. The man met his eyes and made a quick assessment. "I should be going now."

He exited through the hatch to a waiting vessel, whereupon Jin sealed the door for the voyage. As if

Kwon had been able to see this, the Durango began
moving out to sea.

Chapter 14

Does anyone have some Propel? I think we may need it... #CummingsAndGoings

Jason cracked his eyes open and saw light seeping in around the curtains. He opened them to discover that the ship appeared to be traveling effortlessly through the water. But why? Wasn't something supposed to be wrong with the High Cotton? Did it still have electricity? He turned on a light and it brightened the room. Puzzled, he showered and dressed.

In the dining room he breakfasted and took note of the general attitude of the staff. Nothing seemed untoward there. He got an idea, asking the waiter for a cup of coffee to go.

Out on deck, he pulled his jacket tighter around him as it was a cool morning. Recalling that on his floor there was a detailed map of the ship framed in the hallway, he backtracked and studied it carefully, making note of how to get to the engine room, which he knew would be off limits to passengers. He then patted his pocket where he had Mazy's security keycard.

He rode the elevator down as far as it would take him, then found a stairwell that required the keycard to gain entrance. Once inside, the door closed, echoing with a loud clang. Listening, he heard no one, so he began his descent. At the bottom was a locked door with a sign that read: No Entrance. Again, he used the keycard, thrilled that as a nurse, Mazy had clearance to go just about everywhere.

His heart pounded with excitement as he entered the large chamber, drumming with the sounds of the power station, its engines separated from personnel by an actual chain-linked fence with a lock on it. The area had the faint odor of diesel fuel. No one seemed to be about, so he began to look around. Giant turbines filled most of the area that was sectioned with doors on either side leading to other working parts of the ship. He had read that the huge engines were compartmentalized for fire safety, and if the outer wall was compromised, water would fill only that chamber. His mind went to watching the movie, Titanic, with a vision of him and Chambers in the baggage area, alone in the backseat of a Rolls... He sighed, and told himself to focus, as the cup of coffee was hot in his hand.

Exploring various rooms, he found one door labeled, Authorized Entry Only. Then below that, written in red lettering, 'Danger! Do Not Enter!' Putting his hand to the knob, he found the door locked. He thought about knocking, but suddenly the door opened and out came a man in a jumpsuit with the High Cotton logo on it. His nametag read 'Carl.'

"Hey! What are you doing here?" Carl asked, clearly alarmed.

Having prepared for this, Jason calmly responded, "The steward asked me to bring this to you, Carl. He was suddenly called away, some emergency about a toilet, I believe."

The man's eyes lit up when he saw the coffee. "Oh! Right. It's about time. I've been waiting for over an hour for this. Thanks." He took the cup and immediately enjoyed a sip. "Mmmm, black, just the way I like it. Half the time they get it wrong." He turned to go back through the door, pulling keys from his pocket.

"What's in there?" Jason asked, moving slightly so he partially blocked the door.

The man laughed. "Nothing that interesting, I can assure you. It only leads to where the ship's propellers are operated."

"Oh, how fascinating!" Jason said, extending his hand. "I'm Jason Cummings, the travel reviewer. I'm sure you've heard of my Twitter."

The man frowned. "No, don't think so."

"Oh, come now. No need to be bashful. I'm sure you've checked to see what my opinion is on a restaurant?"

He laughed. "Not me. Give me Applebee's any day of the week, and the wife and I always go to the same one."

"Oh dear," Jason responded. "Well, Carl, since I'm down here, how about giving me a tour?"

The man hesitated. "I can't do that sir, not without the Captain's permission."

"Then we're in luck! She was the one who suggested it, and mentioned you, specifically."

"Really? There's not much to see in there…" he hesitated with a slight smile, then muttered, "Why would she want to do that?" The man cocked his head at the door. "Problem is, my orders are to continuously monitor the situation."

"Oh naturally, 'the situation.' I won't take up your time. I'm happy to explore by myself."

"Oh, no sir! I can't let you down here alone. It would be my head rolling when you lose an arm or worse."

"I'm quite hardy you know. But if you insist, we'll just make it a quick tour."

Carl took his cap off and scratched his head. "Now I didn't say that. I've gotta get back to my post. I really don't know what the Captain was thinking, suggesting this with everything going on now."

Jason gave him a coy smile. "Well, Carl, she was thinking of you. She thought that highlighting your...," he paused, searching for just the right words, "Excellent problem-solving skills would be a great addition to my coverage of the ship. You know, with all that's going on."

The hat went back on. "Oh my, well if that's what the Captain thought, who am I to argue with her. Then I guess we should start the tour in my control room down here."

His attitude changed perceptively, pride taking over. He began at the engine area. "Aero-derivative gas turbine engines generate heat. Then the heat is converted from mechanical energy into electrical power, as you can see," he pointed to a mammoth cylinder with pipes leading to another room. "What happens is that compressed air is ignited in this combustion chamber. Then, you see, the hot exhaust is forced over a turbine that spins to a mechanical drive shaft, and here we have the example of that. The result is that the power can then be used to spin our electrical generators. Now, the output shafts connect to electrical generators, and they produce the electrical power."

Jason waded through Carl's overly enthusiastic explanation of his controls and duties. Carl clearly wasn't used to having anyone to talk to, let alone someone who had an interest in his ramblings. Undoubtedly, it was up to Jason to redirect the conversation.

"Yes, Carl, this is truly fascinating, but the readers will need this next quote in simple terms. How could you describe the problem that has you and the Captain on alert?"

He turned around and said, "Oh, well, I don't know how I could say it any simpler, Mr. Cummings. That one propeller just isn't working."

Jason had to hide his astonishment. How many propellers did the ship have? "Oh, yes. That is simple. I meant more the implications for the trip. Potential impact for the journey and passengers?"

Carl rubbed his hand over his face. "Well, you know, I'm sure Captain Patel already explained. If the computers don't get sorted we could lose the other propeller. But we just don't know. That fella that's supposed to be the computer whiz, well you know about him…"

"Oh, I believe we've hit a detail the Captain left out. Who is this person? She was mainly telling me about you."

At first hesitant, Carl replied, looking at the floor, "Now, I don't want to get him in trouble. She probably doesn't want people reading about it."

"Naturally. But this could be off the record, you know, *entre nous*."

"Right. Well, they got him up in that crazy nurse's office drying him out, and she keeps insisting he's not up to leaving her care. Doc Charlie is supposed to weigh in soon. Problem is, the computer man is the only person who can fix what's going on. And he got himself into quite a state celebrating what he supposed was his perfect work. He's the one who designed the system, ya' know. A little too soon though. But them boys at the bar should've cut him off. You wouldn't see me actin' like that. I don't know what that says about him, but it's not too good in my book, and Captain's fit to be tied with her, that nurse, I mean."

"Oh yes, I've met Mazy. She's certainly diligent in her care."

"Yeah, for a fella like you and that computer guy, I'm sure she is." Jason was a bit taken aback by that statement, but he remained on track and listened.

"And because we're down to one, we're moving slower, delaying our arrival time back to Charleston."

"I see. And the one propeller can do the job?" Then he made what he thought was a clever little joke. "Seems like since it's on one side of the ship, we'd just keep going in circles!" He tittered a laugh.

Carl sighed. "I've got to quit jawin' and get back on duty. Excuse me, sir, I mean, Mr. Cummings."

Jason reached out and put his hand lightly on Carl's wrist. "Just tell me this, Carl. The only problem is the computer glitch, isn't it? That's what I was told last night."

He appeared relieved and said, "Oh, they told you, then. Yes, but that's bad enough. Don't need any more problems to worry us. Damned computers!"

"You've got to monitor things, because that one propeller could, I don't know, overheat?"

"It's under control, don't you worry," Carl assured, and tapped the side of his nose. Then looking at the door, he said, "I really do have to get back now." He squeezed around Jason, unlocked the door and slipped inside, the door closing with a thunk.

Jason smiled and thought to himself, "I should be with the CIA."

Chapter 15

A Different Kind Of Storm

Durango sailed out of the Black Sea through the gray waters of the Bosphorus Strait. They passed both commercial and private vessels, including colorful houseboats with families doing their laundry on deck. Next they saw a massive oil tanker, that for all of its size appeared bereft of human habitation. Eventually they proceeded through the Sea of Marmara, with Kwon continuing to man the ship through the busy waterways.

Once they reached the Mediterranean they stopped at the Port of Piraeus so he could sleep. Jin wanted to enjoy some fine dining in the city, but his orders were to remain onboard. Had he not been left feeling insecure about his status with The Great One, he may have defied that command. However, he considered he had to possibly deal with the port authorities while

Kwon was out of commission, so he did as he had been told.

The following morning they left before sunrise, negotiating between Greek freighters and container ships. The next evening they glided through the Strait of Gibraltar.

"We're making good timing," Jin commented.

Kwon downed another Red Bull, then said after belching, "I think that's about to end." He tossed the can into the corner, where it landed on a pile of snack wrappers.

Jin looked up. "What do you mean? And quit throwing your trash on the floor, those damned dried anchovy snacks are stinking up the entire ship! I can't escape the smell."

Shorter than Jin but heavier set, Kwon pointed a thick finger towards the radar, ignoring Jin's comment. "A squall. We're headed right into it."

"Then let's reroute this tub. I don't know if she's up to it."

Kwon shook his head. "Our orders are to move south, around the northwest coast of Africa to Agadir. The storm system is up and down the coastline. We'd have to travel at least two hundred miles out of our way to miss it."

"Then do it, Kwon! The storm may throw us off course anyway."

"No. They'll be waiting for us."

"Don't be a fool. We're risking the entire mission if we lose Durango."

"Go into the salon and hide if you're afraid."

"You're an idiot! It's not my fear that should concern you. Are you trained in handling a squall? We probably need to adjust the ballast since we're carrying no load."

"I'm the Captain, Jin. Don't you forget it." He put the boat on autopilot and said, "Watch her for a while. The sea is calm right now, so you should be able to handle it."

Jin cursed under his breath and remained in the navigation room. From the salon, lilting sounds of New Age music drifted his way. He turned around to see Kwon doing Tai Chi. After a while Jin walked out on deck.

The sky was thickening as whitecaps began rising in lengthening swells. Nearly dark, in the distance he could make out another ship, its lights blinking through rain. A few minutes later a patter of raindrops began falling as a cooler wind grew stronger and rattled the cargo equipment. On the horizon a finger of lightning ignited the sky. He walked back into the navigation room to find Kwon at the helm wearing a heavy wool sweater.

"It's started," Jin said glumly.

Kwon gave him a grunt. "We're in for a long night."

A half hour later they were peering out of the navigation room window through drenching rain accompanied by whistling wind. The cargo ship moved through the churning ocean lumberously, cutting its way through the swells like an old sea turtle. In the lightning's strobing light, they could make out the tops of waves splashing over the bow, leaving rivulets winding around the hatch covers before returning to the sea. With the tapping of a loose chain, the cargo crane twisted back and forth like a writhing dinosaur. Keeping a steady tempo for minutes at a time, the rain would stop momentarily before resuming in renewed intensity. As low clouds blew across deck then disappeared, the ship's lights captured raindrops in triangular tableaus. A punishing wave hit Durango broadside, the ship listing. Jin was knocked off balance and had to spring from his chair, his feet landing in water.

"Look at this! Fucking Uri didn't fix that window. And we just *had* to go through this storm. Now there's water everywhere and my Gucci loafers will never be the same!"

The ship straightened with a moan and chugged onward. Then Kwon said, "What did you expect from a Russian? Besides, we got the work done for free."

Jin glared hard into Kwon's eyes. "And does *he* know that?"

Kwon didn't answer, a satisfied smile crinkling his taunting eyes, the usual toothpick protruding from his teeth.

Another towering wave hit Durango, the ship shuddering. They dipped into a valley before the bow slowly rose again. Jin began to consider that they were at the mercy of Uri's definition of 'seaworthy.' How ruthless had he been? Did he bother to ensure the hull could withstand this kind of punishment after sitting for years decaying in the Salerno harbor? His eyes caught the flicker of Kwon's lamp that he kept over the console.

"Are we losing power?" Jin knew that without the engine pushing them through the storm they were vulnerable to capsizing.

Kwon looked over and said in English, mocking Uri's accent, "Well, my friend, that lamp needs a new battery. Getting jittery?"

Jin didn't bother to respond. He crossed his arms and set his chin, looking out the window to see the cargo derrick outlined against a violent sky erupting in successive lightning strikes.

Then, like a bomb, the cockpit exploded. Glass and seawater burst in. Jin yanked his arms up to cover his face as fragments of glass flew past him like a shotgun blast. He could hear Kwon screaming, then the sound of more glass tinkling as it bounced off the console and into the water puddled at their feet. The racket stopped, the only sounds the beating rain and howling wind. Jin looked around, finding Kwon on his feet, one side of his face dripping blood as a dagger of glass protruded from his cheek. Another flash of lightning illuminated the deck in time to see something large and bright green---either plastic or fiberglass and as big as a tree limb---slide back into the sea. He looked back to Kwon, who was pale and trembling.

"Get it out!" he yelled at Jin.

"Where's the first aid kit?"

"How the fuck should I know! Just pull it out!"

Jin looked around then decided to seek supplies in the salon. Sliding in his soggy, slippery shoes, he managed to grasp hold and begin opening the drawers, only to find nothing. Clearly Durango had no first aid provisions. Seeing a tee shirt on Kwon's bed,

123

he clambered over and grabbed it. In the tiny bathroom he found Kwon's aftershave. Taking that too, he then reluctantly pulled a clean shirt from his own bag, and using his knife, cut it into three strips before returning to the navigation room.

Kwon had to remain behind, perilously steering Durango in an attempt to keep her steady. He couldn't stop, not even for a second.

Jin stood before him and waited, no longer in a rush.

Kwon yelled impatiently, "What are you waiting for?"

He didn't move. Finally, he said, "Did you tell him?"

"What the fuck are you talking about!! Get the glass out, motherfucker!"

"Did you tell him?" Jin asked again, patiently. "Tell me or you can pull the glass out yourself." He pressed his thumb against the glass, moving it around in the wound. Kwon screamed and Jin relented.

Then Kwon said. "I should have, only because you are such a shithead, Jin! But no, I didn't tell him about the money."

Smiling, Jin wrapped the cloth around his hand to use it as a glove.

"How bad is it?" Kwon asked.

He pulled Kwon's collar back to get it out of the way, noticing the tip of a tattoo that began below Kwon's neck. It didn't surprise him to see this, but he was glad of the opportunity to know for sure.

Kwon had been 'tattooed,' an honor bestowed upon agents who had shown exceptional bravery or done exemplary work. Receiving his special number and having it permanently inked, was a symbol that the agent was in The Great One's inner circle. This is why Kwon has been so puffed up with self importance, he thought to himself.

"Well?" Kwon fumed.

With a tug, Jin removed the glass from Kwon's flesh and pushed one of the strips of cloth onto the wound.

"Press on this," he ordered Kwon.

As Kwon did as he was told, Jin soaked another strip with aftershave, knowing it would have alcohol in it. He moved Kwon's hand aside, the first strip falling to the floor. Then he placed a bandage on the wound, Kwon wincing from the alcohol's sting. Jin smiled. Using the last piece of material, he wrapped it around Kwon's head to hold the bandage in place.

"That's the best I can do for now," he stated over the din of the storm, rain and spray soaking the controls. "You'll need stitches when we get to Agadir."

"Yes," Kwon stated through clenched teeth. Even in the dim light, Jin could see the pallor to Kwon's skin. He hadn't lost an inordinate amount of blood, but the glass had penetrated nearly completely through the cheek and into the mouth. A membrane of skin was all that had protected his tongue from being sliced.

Jin suggested he take over, but Kwon insisted on remaining at the helm. Nevertheless, he seemed diminished, his shoulders bent, his eyes squinting as he endured the pain. He returned to his seat, not trusting Kwon to pay attention with the distraction of the wound, so he watched him to make sure he remained conscious.

Not letting up, the storm seemed to follow the ship, making for a miserable night as the sea and rain drenched the navigation room. Then, as dawn neared, it was as if the foul weather needed darkness to do its work. The sky cleared with steely gray streaks until the sun fully rose and moved those out of the way too

When Durango reached Agadir, the sea was as calm and blameless as a baby's bath. Kwon maneuvered Durango into port; then once they were moored, went into the salon and crashed onto his cot, one arm slung over his eyes. Jin also took to his bed, with restless sleep quickly overtaking him.

Chapter 16

A Call For Help

They had started their journey back home, moving towards an afternoon sun captured in a sky so blue it was almost purple. The gulls followed, and the sea spread before them, a deep green blanket with the gentlest of wrinkles.

"Too bad we don't have water skis," Trevor commented.

"Or a wakeboard," Nick added. "You get to do any surfing over there?"

"Not really. I surfed in Australia once. The waves were awesome, but there were sharks all over."

"You're shitting me! Seriously?"

"Seriously. It was some of the best surfing I've ever done."

"Man, I don't know if I'd risk it."

"Well, you definitely don't want to fall."

They laughed, reminding Trevor of being with his SEAL team. He missed it, the joking, the stories, the trust. As the day progressed with catching the tuna, the fight with his brother, and now the Esmerelda's engine humming as they made their way home, his thoughts returned to leaving the SEALS, his other family.

When he was told he would have to retire, he was still in the hospital. It wasn't his C.O. who broke the news, it was a Washington bureaucrat, a woman who arrived with a briefcase full of papers. Though he had known others who were forced to retire due to injuries, he had hoped it wouldn't apply to him. He would heal from the head injury and knife wound. Yet when he asked why things had to be this way after six years of service---four on active duty--- the only answer he got was, "It's protocol, and we find that it's best for everyone." Trevor kept pressing the issue, knowing she was trained in how to answer these questions.

Finally she said resignedly, "With battle injuries so often soldiers experience mental traumas that could put themselves or others at risk. For an elite division, such as the SEALs, this is a chance we cannot take." He attempted to respond to her argument, but she put a hand up to stop him. "Even if you don't think you have PTSD, it can show up later at a bad time. Because of this, we encourage you to seek mental health counseling once you return home."

So that was it. He was out. Like an old plow horse, he was cast aside because he was no longer useful. His teammates told him he was lucky; he'll have a good military retirement with his honorable discharge and he can start a new life. He smiled and shook their hands the day he left, but it reminded him of when he was a kid and Nick made him taste an unripe persimmon. The bitterness wouldn't leave his mouth.

His train of thought was broken when Nick turned to him and said, "You mind taking the wheel for a while?"

"No problem," Trevor answered, rising from his chair. He looked over at a frowning Ray, who had his eyes closed but was breathing heavily.

"Look at that old fool. Sleeping like a baby. I'm gonna miss this," Nick said.

"I know. You said that earlier," Trevor commented. Nick jerked his head around to see if Trevor was picking another fight. Trevor assured him, "I understand why you reached the decision you did, and how hard it was." Nick gave him a short nod. "But it's Ray, isn't it? You're going to miss working with Ray."

"I am. I've known Ray my entire life and worked with him for nearly half of it."

"Yeah, thinking back, I honestly don't know what I would have done without him."

"Like dude, at my wedding I was so scared. I don't know if it showed, but man, I was close to bolting. Then Ray sat me down and told me what Dad would have, how she was the right woman and exactly what I needed, how she'd bring about the most important changes in life---love, children, family, a sense of belonging. And it was just the kind of speech I needed from my best man."

"And he was right to tell you that. I've always said you were damned lucky Carly settled for you. I can't believe you even hesitated. Dude, she's always been great."

"She has, and the kids too."

"Ray sure kept me from going off the deep end. If he hadn't been there to go to the games or fishing or some of the other stuff Dad used to do, I would have become one fucked up kid."

"You were," Nick joked.

"Please, I might have landed in juvie, gotten on drugs---God knows what. I felt so lost back then. Luckily, Ray kept me under close watch, so I didn't end up doing the shit some of our friends did."

"I'm sorry I wasn't around. When I wasn't shrimping I was dating and partying. I'd come in from the boat, no sleep for two days then turn right around and go out that night. I don't know how I did it. Mom would bitch at me, but I wouldn't listen. More than once Ray saved me from screwing everything up."

"You know, he and Jenny pretty much raised us after Dad died. I always wondered why they never had kids of their own."

"They couldn't. Ray told me once that they tried from the time they were first married. They never had any luck."

"They didn't look into it?"

"No. They felt like if it was meant to be then it would happen, and besides, we kept them pretty busy."

With that, Nick walked out on deck. Trevor glanced at Ray again and saw that his eyes were still closed, but he was frowning and rubbing his chest. As he sat down in the captain's chair, Ray stirred uncomfortably, his brow sweaty.

"Ray?" Trevor said. "Hey, Ray!" Ray opened his eyes and looked at him. "Are you okay?"

He sat up. "I feel a little funny, but I'm all right."

Nick walked in and said, "You're feeling funny? How?"

Ray patted his gut. "I'm sure this is the cause of it."

Trevor and Nick cut their eyes at one another and Nick said, "He had a scare a while back. It wasn't a heart attack, but they put him on blood pressure medicine and told him to watch his diet, get some exercise and all that. And we all know how well that has been going..."

Trevor said in a low tone, "He doesn't look so good."

Nick went over and squatted down next to Ray.

Ray squinted his eyes open and said, "Ya'll quit fussin' over me!" He appeared short of breath after the outburst then leaned back against the chair. "Just let me rest."

Nick stood up and said to Trevor, "Maybe we should pick up our speed."

Trevor was already pulling the throttle back. Nick went over and sat next to him. Ray said, "My arms is all tingly. That must be what's making me feel dizzy."

Trevor said, "It could be an anxiety attack. I've seen a lot of men get them. Nick, you got anything strong, like bourbon or whiskey?"

Nick got up and looked in a cabinet. Reaching in the back he pulled out a half empty bottle of Jack Daniels.

"This is why we keep an emergency stash." He handed the bottle to Ray and said, "Take a hit off this, a long one."

"I don't want it. You know I've cut back on drinking the hard stuff. Doc told me to."

"This is different. It's medicinal."

He took a swig from the bottle and wiped his mouth on his sleeve. "That tastes like dog shit!" He sat back, his hand rubbing his chest.

"He's making me nervous," Nick whispered to Trevor.

"I've got her wide open, well, going as fast as I feel like she can take it. I don't want to blow the engine."

"The weather's changing," Nick said, looking at a weather report.

"Rain?"

"I don't think so. It's just a twenty percent chance. But the water's getting rougher."

A few minutes later when Trevor looked at the flag on the bow, he saw that the air had shifted. Small whitecaps were chopping the water, the Esmerelda bobbing over them.

"The wind is coming from the west, we're fighting it," he commented.

"Yes, I see that, but there's nothing we can do about it. Maybe I can get a weather report from Charleston."

He turned on the radio to change frequency. "Hey, look at this. Somebody has got their emergency beacon on. I wonder what the problem is, not that it would matter to us. The Coast Guard will have to deal with it.

Chapter 17

The Dye Is Cast

After napping, Jin showered and changed while Kwon remained in the salon, saying he wanted to rest.

"You really need to go to a hospital, Kwon," Jin chided, as he buttoned his shirt.

"Yeah, later."

"If you wait too long, they will not be able to stitch it up."

Kwon didn't respond, just gave Jin the finger before he turned his back to him on the cot. Someone tapped on the door. Jin went to see who it was and stepped outside to meet In-Su.

"My team is here to do the install. When we move it onto Durango, we'll be covering the main component with tarpaulins, so it won't be recognizable. Once it's in place I want you to erect a cargo hold screen. We'll leave the supplies for you to do that later."

"Good," Jin said, walking with In-Su.

"Our boat is moored at the hatch. If our pulley system works, we'll be able to load right from there."

"Sounds like you've worked out the details."

"We have. Everything is going according to plan. He will be pleased."

Jin nodded agreement, and went below with In-Su to watch the process. The cargo was to be maneuvered using heavy ropes and a pulley that had been installed in Odessa. The eight-hundred-pound bundle was covered so it wouldn't be recognizable. It was carefully raised, and moved sideways with all the men keeping hold to prevent it from swaying. The bomb was then placed into the belly of Durango. Once inside and over its cradle, they lowered it slowly into its newly welded fittings.

The men moved purposefully, taking their time, and when it was clamped in, everyone gave a collective sigh of relief. In-Su took his handkerchief and wiped his brow. It had taken all morning to make the meticulous transfer. With everyone stopping to rest, Jin decided to go see if Kwon had left for the hospital.

He found him still in the salon, sleeping fitfully, an empty bottle of Soju on the floor next to his cot. His appearance was startling. The wound was covered in a juicy puddle of blood and serum. The skin was curling back and inflamed. His face was so swollen it looked like an overripe tomato about to burst its skin. He appeared feverish, sweat beading above his lip. In his current state, Jin realized that Kwon would not be able to complete the mission. He paused to consider this.

He wanted him out of the way, preferably Kwon having to leave due to some fault of his own. Though Jin didn't care if Kwon died, he did not want him martyred. Jin wondered if he could explain Kwon's injury in such a way to suggest that it was due to Kwon's incompetence he was hurt. That would be difficult, though, since two men were currently in the process of repairing the broken window in the navigation room, and Jin had told them how it had happened. Yet, he did so want Kwon to be taken down a peg, or even a few. His death would certainly accomplish that. Problem was, the mission couldn't be completed without him, at least not at this time. Furthermore, Durango may not be able to leave port without its captain able to answer a harbormaster's questions. And Jin didn't think he could make the transatlantic trip alone. He needed Kwon, whether he wanted him or not. His thoughts were interrupted when someone entered the salon

"What's wrong with Kwon?" In-Su said, walking closer to the bed.

"He was hurt in the storm last night," Jin answered.

"He clearly needs medical attention. The entire mission is in jeopardy if he isn't fit to captain the ship."

"Yes, I was just considering our options," Jin replied. "He was too selfish to go to a hospital this morning when he was up to it. Perhaps now you should go ashore and find someone to tend to him."

"Me?" In-Su responded. "I cannot leave now. I'm installing the timer. You'll have to do it, and soon."

Jin sighed in agreement. "I'll leave shortly."

"Yes. Go now. And tell them this man cannot be moved. He must be tended to here."

"I will take no more of your time with this matter, In-Su. You need to get back to your work," Jin said pointedly.

Later he left the ship when he was ready, musing to himself as he walked down the gangplank. He was the one calling the shots and setting the timeline. In-Su had no right to speak to him as though *he* made decisions.

Walking towards the city center from the port, Jin called for a taxi, then wondered where exactly he could find the medical help he needed. The situation was delicate. Kwon's condition could draw attention to Durango and raise questions about its safety standards. What he needed was a doctor who would come to Kwon and be paid for his silence. He consulted his phone and located medical facilities and called several. None were willing to send someone to the ship. His taxi arrived. Hoping that perhaps the driver could help, he asked if he knew of a doctor who would make 'a house call.'

In the rearview mirror, the man's eyes looked at him questioningly. "I could take you to a clinic or hospital. Perhaps you'll find what you need there," he answered in English.

"Yes, I thought of that. However, after calling most of them, I found no one who would help. My friend needs to have stitches, but he can't get out of bed. You see, he foolishly drank too much. Now he's passed out, and I cannot carry him."

"I do not go to the doctor, so I cannot help you. Do you still want a ride?"

Jin nodded. The driver merged into traffic accelerating.

Keeping his eyes on him, Jin finally said, "What about somebody who's not a doctor? Perhaps an attendant or an ambulance driver?" He sat forward and handed the man five hundred euros. The driver took hold of them silently then pulled the car over to the side of the road. His hand stroked his beard as he contemplated the problem. A minute passed. Jin had the thought that perhaps he himself would have to tend to Kwon's wound. The idea sickened him.

Then the driver put his elbow over the seat and looked at Jin thoughtfully. "This is something you do not want people to know about, yes?"

After a few seconds of hesitation, Jin said, "Obviously."

"Okay. I have an idea. I know where the Red Cross nurses stay when they're in town. They're usually nice people."

Jin nodded understanding.

The car moved on silently for ten minutes until the taxi pulled up to a pink stucco building with a sign out front that said, The Takad.

"This is it," the driver announced.

Already with his hand on the doorknob, Jin said, "Wait here." The driver nodded.

Trotting up the steps, he walked inside a small lobby that had a television on with a daytime soap opera, the actors speaking French. He rang a bell on the counter and a woman came out from behind a beaded curtain. She eyed Jin suspiciously and said, "*Oui?*"

Jin said in French, "Excuse me. I wanted to speak with one of the nurses staying here…"

At that moment a young woman wearing black glasses came down the steps from the floor above. In her hand was what looked like a beach bag.

"Ah," Jin said. "Here she is." He walked over and said in English to her, seeing blue eyes behind the Clark Kent style rims, "You're with the Red Cross?"

She glanced at the woman behind the counter, who was waiting and listening. "Yes," she answered tentatively.

"I wonder if you and I could have a brief chat," Jin said, gesturing that they step outside.

She allowed him to usher her to the door, but said, "What's this about?"

He noticed her English was American. Her thick, wavy black hair was pulled into a ponytail over one shoulder. Once out of earshot of the proprietor, he said in an urgent tone, "I have a friend onboard our ship, who needs medical attention due to an accident. He needs stitches and I believe it could be infected. I was hoping you would help. You are a nurse, are you not?"

As she listened, a little frown in her brow deepened. "I'm a nurse, but I'm not going to some ship to care for your friend. You need to take him to the hospital."

"Yes, but I cannot move him. And, well, he is a very private man. He would never agree to leave. I would be willing to pay you handsomely." He opened his jacket and removed his wallet, from which he withdrew several large bills, and said, "I will pay much more when the job is done."

She took a half step back to look him over from head to toe, then replied, "Look, I'm not going *alone* with you onboard some ship. If he needs medical care, then he needs a hospital."

He nodded appreciatively. "I understand. Is there anything I could do or say to make you feel assured that no harm will come to you?"

She laughed and said, "Well, I guess I could carry a big gun with me, but I don't have one."

"Yes, I see," he said, keeping his expression serious. "If I give you a gun when you board, will you do it then?"

She cocked her head and said, "So you have guns? Great. That is not helping your case, you know." Then her eyes narrowed as she continued, "But... if you are desperate... Our village needs a new well. It will cost fourteen thousand dollars. Do you have that much?"

He paused briefly, then replied with a nod, "Yes."

Her eyebrows raised in surprise. "Cash?"

"Of course."

"Then I will need it now. I won't leave with you until I've given the money to Eva," she gestured to the woman behind the counter.

Jin reached for his billfold and said, "This is all I have on me. You'll get the rest when we get to the boat." He handed it to the girl, who turned and went back inside.

Just when Jin was about to re-enter the building to look for her, she came out wearing green scrubs with an identification badge hanging from her neck. Jin walked with her to the car and opened the back door. Climbing in, she said to the driver, "Souss-Massa-Draa." To Jin, she said, "That's the hospital. I need to go get supplies"

During the drive, Jin said, "You have been nursing for some time?"

She gave him an ironic smile and replied, "A few years, mostly in areas of conflict."

The driver dropped her off at the hospital emergency entrance, then turned around to Jin and said, "Found a pretty one, didn't you?"

Jin smiled, but said nothing. The girl returned a few minutes later with a plastic bag in one hand. "Okay, let's go," she said.

He made it a point not to look at her again, wanting her to be reassured that this was professional. Back at the dock, he thanked the driver and said to the girl as they got out, "I will get the rest of your money right away once we board."

"Okay. My name is Beth, by the way," she said, extending her hand.

"Jin," he replied, holding it briefly. They began mounting the gangplank, Jin's eyes searching to see if anyone was about. He saw no one.

He escorted her into the salon, her gaze quickly finding Kwon. She moved across the room and knelt down beside him. From her bag she removed a stethoscope and listened to his heart, then checked his blood pressure.

While she worked, Jin got the rest of her money together and placed it in an envelope, one of the many he carried to pay bribes discreetly. However, when he brought it to her, she paid no attention, as she was giving Kwon an injection. After putting gloves on her hands she began threading a surgical needle.

"I'm going to need your help, Jin," she said, her eyes raising to his.

He saw then how extraordinarily attractive she was, her glasses hiding the fact at first. He moved closer and said, "How can I help?"

"I want you to put on a pair of these gloves. There are some in the bag. And then I want you to hold this wound closed while I put the sutures in. Do you faint at the sight of blood?"

He nearly burst out laughing, but instead said quietly, "No."

The two worked together, their bodies occasionally touching. Telling himself to concentrate only on assisting, he breathed in her scent, a hint of shampoo or soap that smelled of gardenias. On her cheeks he noticed freckles almost obscured by her tanned skin.

"You've tended the wounded before. Military perhaps?" he asked.

"Yes," she answered, not looking up from her work. Once finished, she bandaged the wound and gave Kwon another shot.

"I've just given him some pretty heavy antibiotics, and the first shot I gave him should have him resting for a few hours. When he wakes I'll give him another injection for pain, and I'll leave more antibiotics in pill form."

"Thank you, Beth," Jin said, taking the gloves off. Then he laughed and added, "I just realized, I failed to get your gun for you. Shall I get it now?"

She smiled. "Well, *he's* definitely not going to be doing anything, and you…" She looked at Jin under her brows, "Maybe I'm not so worried about you, anymore."

He looked around the salon and said, "I don't have anything to offer you, but if Kwon is going to be sleeping for a while, I could take you ashore and buy you dinner."

"Thanks, but I need to stay with the patient in case he comes to."

In spite of wanting to sound businesslike, Jin realized that he was doing his best to be charming. Well, he told himself, it's understandable. The girl was impressive. She had a no-nonsense attitude about her, as professional as he was in his job. Women in North Korea could be competent, but frequently were silly around men, if they were allowed to talk. Beth was capable, assured, yet feminine in ways he liked.

"I could go and get us something to eat and bring it back here. Would you like that?"

She smiled, her nose getting a little crinkle in it. "Yes, that would be nice. I never had lunch today."

"What would you like?"

"Anything will do, but if you're walking, all you're going to find this close to the docks will be Arab food, but that will be okay."

Pleased with her response, he turned to go, then suddenly looked back at her and said, "Please remain in the salon for your own safety. There are men working on the ship that I don't know."

"All right," she said.

Before he left Durango, Jin went below to look for In-Su. He found him working on a digital display mounted to the cargo.

"Well, Jin. Did you find medical help for Kwon?" he said as soon as he saw Jin approach.

"Yes, a nurse is with him now. I'm going out to get some food. She will remain with him until he regains consciousness."

"Very good. And will he be able to perform his duties?"

"He will be able to captain the ship out of port. If necessary, I can pilot Durango for the majority of the trip, that way we'll keep to our schedule and Durango will... He made air quotes. "'Arrive' during Charleston's Spoleto when there will be many people about." Jin then gestured to In-Su to walk with him so he could speak privately.

"Yes? What is it?" In-Su asked.

"This injury of Kwon's, it got me to thinking. We need a fail-safe, in case something else unexpected happens."

"What do you mean?"

"It will be on a timer?" Jin said, gesturing to the cargo.

"Yes, you know that, as we discussed with The Great One."

"Right, but if something happens, a delay of some kind, the timer could end and Durango may not have reached the target."

"What are you proposing?" In-Su asked, his eyes narrowing.

"Only that you install a switch. A switch I can use that will cut the timer off, should it become necessary."

"That will stop the detonator," In-Su reminded him.

"Yes, then I could restart the timer at the appropriate time."

"If you don't restart it, it's always possible that Durango will ram into the harbor and the bomb will still go off."

"Correct. Our fail-safe ensures the bomb explodes at the opportune time, and the mission will be a success."

"I can do this, Jin, but I'm not sure it should be done without The Great One's approval. And we will not have time to reach him. I am nearly finished here, then we are scheduled to leave immediately."

"Yes, it's a delicate situation." Jin rubbed his chin in thought. "Perhaps rather than attempting to reach The Great One, it would be best to keep this to ourselves. Once the mission is a success, I can hardly see a need for discussing such a minor detail."

In-Su was silent as he considered Jin's proposal, then said, "It does involve risk on my part should the mission fail."

"True," Jin said, nodding understanding. "But we are not planning on the mission failing, are we? Nevertheless, how could your risk be calculated? Perhaps in Euros or do you prefer US dollars?"

In-Su looked over his shoulder to see if anyone was watching. He said, "I'm sure we could arrive at a suitable figure in Euros."

Jin took an envelope from his pocket and gave it to In-Su, then patted his shoulder and left.

*   *   *

It took an hour for Jin to locate a restaurant, order, receive the food and return to Durango. As he climbed the gangplank he saw lights coming from the salon, but elsewhere the ship was dark. He made his way to the navigation room then tapped on the door. Beth saw him through the window and got up to open it.

"Our patient is doing much better," she announced as he entered the room. Kwon was sitting up, the swelling in his face reduced. His hair was standing on end from tossing and turning in bed, but his fever appeared to be gone.

"Well, Kwon. It seems our nurse has worked wonders for you."

Kwon said nothing, only watched Jin as he crossed the room and smiled at Beth.

The two of them removed the items from the bag and Jin opened a bottle of wine. He found two glasses and poured, then said to Kwon, "Only water for you Kwon, since you've had painkillers." He and Beth touched their glasses together.

Beth fixed a plate of food for Kwon and a glass of water, then set them on the table near Kwon's cot. She and Jin sat at the small dining table.

Delightfully, she removed her glasses. "When will you be leaving port?" she asked Jin.

Jin hesitated to consider his answer and replied, "Not sure. It may have to be tomorrow, though we had hoped to go tonight." Looking at Kwon, he said, "What about it, Kwon? Are you up to leaving port tonight?"

"I stay on schedule," he grunted, not yet taking a bite of food.

Jin sipped his wine and said to Beth, "How long will you be in Agadir?"

"I'm on leave until the end of the weekend." Her eyes met his.

"Are you married?" Jin asked, the words coming out before he realized the implication.

"No. Are you?" He shook his head and cut his eyes to Kwon, who still sat motionless on the cot. "Ever been close?" she pressed.

He laughed, "Not even close." Then he speared an olive and said, "Is Africa where a girl goes to meet a good husband?" He saw the color rise in her face.

"Not really, but it's a good place to escape a bad breakup." She looked over at Kwon and commented, "You're not eating. Do you need help?"

Kwon stirred, moving to the edge of the cot and reaching for the glass of water. He took a sip, most of it drizzling down his chin.

"Disgusting," Jin muttered.

"No, it's alright," Beth said, rising from her chair and going to Kwon. She knelt down and told him, "The swelling is keeping your mouth closed. Gently pry it open and it will loosen. Then you can eat."

Jin said to her, "Don't baby him. He'll be fine."

She rose and returned to the table. "You men are always so hard on one another."

Jin smirked, "Kwon's tough. I know him better than you do."

They finished, with Kwon taking only a few bites. After Beth cleaned up she said to Jin, "I should be getting back. It's getting late."

His eyes moved from her to Kwon; then he said quietly, "All right. I'll accompany you in the cab back to your hotel."

She smiled. "That would be nice."

As Jin rose, In-Su walked into the salon. He looked at Kwon then to Jin and said, "Jin, I need to have a quick word."

Jin nodded to In-Su and turned to Beth. "Do you mind waiting a few minutes before you go? Then I will gladly escort you."

"That will be fine," she said.

He left with In-Su, the two going down to the cargo hold to find In-Su's men packing up and about to leave. "I have completed all the necessary work," he said to Jin.

Jin nodded, watching the last man leave through the hatch. He then whispered, "And the switch?"

"It's below the timer, a wire. All you need to do is cut it. The yellow one. Do you see it?" In-Su handed Jin a small flashlight.

He bent over and had a look, seeing the tiny wire exactly where In-Su said it would be. "Yes, very good."

"To reset it and reactivate the timer, all you have to do is reconnect that wire. You can do that?"

"Of course," Jin replied.

After standing back up, Jin held out the flashlight to return it to In-Su. He shook his head and whispered, "Best you keep it, in case… Oh, and one other thing." He removed a small tool from his pocket. "Wire cutters. I would hide them somewhere close by. These can cut the wire." The two men shook hands. "Good luck, Jin. You should keep your eye on Kwon." In-Su left, and Jin secured the hatch for sailing. He then hid the cutters behind a pipe.

He climbed the steps and walked out on deck for a minute to check the weather. He found a romantic night covered in a starry sky. His thoughts wandered to Beth. Yes, he would like to take her back to her hotel and have sex, yet it wasn't just the idea of having her that was attracting him. He felt a stirring he had never experienced. A woman had always been something for his temporary use, nothing more, but with Beth he was feeling a different kind of desire. He wanted to know everything about her. Then he realized he was behaving like a romantic, as if he were in one of those ridiculous American movies. He chuckled at his own absurdity.

As he turned to go inside, he decided he would ask her how he could get in touch. Once the mission is over he could see himself arranging to spend time with her. It was a strange sensation, to want to be with a woman for a purpose other than satisfying his lust. It was because he had never met anyone like Beth. She had all of the attributes he never knew he valued in a woman. She was making him damn near giddy. What an unexpected turn.

He was surprised with himself as he went through the navigation room door. Closing it, he heard a scuffling sound. He jerked around to see through the window of the salon Kwon squatting on top of Beth, who was prone on the floor. His knees were holding her arms down. His hands around her neck and his squeeze so violent, he was shaking her. His cot was turned over, the bed sheets bright red. The wine bottle was toppled and dripping, and beyond, the dining table was broken into large, jagged pieces.

Jin ran in as Kwon pulled his hands away from Beth's throat, her eyes bulging and staring at the same nothingness Jin remembered his mother looking at. Her face was bloodied, a wound on her head covering her dark hair in blood.

"What have you done?" Jin said, his voice hoarse.

Kwon, still sitting on Beth, turned around and looked at Jin, his breathing heavy, his cheek bleeding again. Jin gripped his hair and pulled him off. Kwon lunged for Jin's legs to yank him down. Jin jumped sideways then stood over Kwon, his knife pulled from its sheath. Kwon froze.

"Why, Kwon?" Jin said. "Why did you kill her?" Kwon looked up at Jin with cold hatred, then pushed himself up to get on his feet. "Tell me, you mother fucker! Because to me this looks like you took an unnecessary risk, you stupid fool!" Jin moved the knife closer. "How about I widen that cut on your face to go around your neck?"

Kwon backed up and leaned down to turn the cot upright. "She was too risky. You should concentrate on the mission."

"She's an American with the Red Cross. The *risk* is your killing her!"

"No, *you* were the risk. You need to be focused." He began removing his clothes, taking a step towards the shower. Then standing there naked, he turned around. "After I shower we're leaving. We'll get rid of her at sea."

"He will learn about this."

Kwon waved Jin away, muttering, "You and I both know you don't want that."

He stepped into the bathroom, closing the door behind him, the nozzles for the water squeaking. Jin went over to Beth and leaned down, closing her eyes, his knife still in his hand. He looked over his shoulder at the bathroom door then rose to take a step in that direction. He could hear the water running. His fingers touched the knob, the knife in his right hand, his thumb pricking the handle in agitation. Then he decisively turned away, the knife put away.

Chapter 18

Change Course! Full Steam Ahead!

Curious and concerned by the SOS, Nick moved through the radio's channels. Quickly, he stopped when a voice came on, faint, almost obscured by static. He fine-tuned to get clearer sound. "... do you read me, over?"

"Sounds like a woman," Nick said.

The voice broke in again. "... the High Cotton, calling the vessel heading North 033 degrees by West 047. Do you read me, over?"

"That's us!" Nick said, grabbing the microphone. "This is Captain Starnes of the Esmerelda. Over, High Cotton."

The radio spat static, then, "...assistance. No other vessel in the area, over."

Nick replied back, "Repeat, High Cotton. Please repeat."

"We are requiring emergency assistance. Can you provide, Esmerelda?"

Ray sat up. "What's goin' on?"

Nick ignored him and said into the microphone, "How can we assist, High Cotton?"

The three men listened intently, but the radio was silent. Nick said again, "High Cotton, how can we assist? This is the Esmerelda. Do you copy?"

Trevor looked at the radar. "Where is it? I don't see any ships or boats?"

Nick put the microphone down. "That's because I had it looking for tuna." He changed the frequency. "There! That's it!"

Ray, looked over Nick's shoulder with Trevor next to him, and said, "What's the High Cotton? A high-falutin' name like that must be a yacht."

"I don't know, but I'd have to guess something like that," Nick answered.

"Cut the throttle, Trev," Ray said. "We've got to recalibrate and not get any further away."

No one said anything. Ray, not giving up, insisted, "Slide over. Let me get to a map." Taking the coordinates from the radar, Ray pulled a map from the drawer.

Nick picked up the mic again, telling Ray, "This doesn't mean we're turning around." He then said, "High Cotton. This is the Esmerelda. Do you copy?"

Silence.

Ray said, "Okay, I've got it! Nick, we need to change our heading. Let me make the adjustment now."

Trevor said, "Ray, they're not even answering the radio anymore. They probably don't need us."

"Yeah, Ray. Trev's right."

"They ain't responding because they're in trouble!"

"No, Ray. *You're* in trouble. We need to get back," Trevor replied.

"What's the matter with you two? We're at sea and somebody has sent us a distress call. This ain't the time for arguing!"

Nick looked at Trevor. "Maybe he's right. She needs our help."

"*Nick*," Trevor argued, "They *might* need our help, but we know for sure that Ray does. He's the priority. We need to go back."

"I ain't goin' to have no heart attack! Now, listen, you two, don't delay because you worried about me! Is that what the Frogmen taught you? Just pretend shit ain't going wrong?"

The brothers looked at Ray, then one another, hesitation keeping them at a standstill.

"Move out of the way!" Ray said, and he turned the wheel to the new heading and gunned the engine.

Chapter 19

Had a massage to relax before my meeting with the Captain. Hope I'm not in trouble! #CummingsAndGoings

Padma was outside the navigation room, watching the ocean change from soothing calm to choppier waters. She knew this development wouldn't greatly affect the ship, but it could cause some passengers to become seasick if they spent much time on deck.

Personally she liked the sea that way, churning and foaming, showing its power and majesty to the smallness of man. It was one of the reasons she joined the Navy, her deep belief that humans needed reminding of their insignificance by being humbled by the forces of nature. Being on the water can do that; however, she didn't want her passengers to reckon with it today.

"Captain!" First Mate Chambers said, coming up the steps. "I've got some news. Our IT man says he's figured out the computer malfunction."

Padma's face showed visible relief. "Oh, that's terrific. How soon before it's repaired?"

Chambers hesitated, then replied. "Well, it's one of those good news-bad-news situations. He says he can fix the program error related to the propeller, but to do it we have to... well... shut both down."

Her shoulders slumped. "You're not serious!" She was afraid this would happen. Blame for any ship's problem was always placed squarely on the captain. Since the Morrows had invested heavily in the ship's new green technology, the result was that she and the High Cotton were under close scrutiny on this maiden voyage.

She was used to the pressures of having to be perfect. Wasn't every woman in a leadership role? She first experienced it in the Navy, handling it by giving the appearance of brushing off unwarranted criticism and microscopic scrutiny. It was interpreted as confidence, yet inside she felt every sting. Hiding it well, she flourished and was promoted, her final assignment commanding a small ship in the Persian Gulf. Career wise it was satisfying. Nevertheless she felt an acute loneliness, and believed that leaving the service would end it.

Now with her new role in civilian life, she was in strange waters again with regards to feminine leadership. It seemed as if it wasn't enough that a powerful woman was an expert in her field. She also had to cleverly navigate the human psyche. It went without saying that the female executive had to be above and beyond in her job. If not, feminine labels were applied: too bitchy, too timid, too bossy, too weak. If she was all business with no soft side she wasn't liked. But the soft side had to be carefully meted out. Too much and she appeared to be 'a pushover' and lost respect from both men and women. She longed for a time when she could just do her job using her intelligence and instincts and not have to devote so much study to calibrating behavior. She had hoped she would experience that with this job. She had a good crew and a good ship, minus the current computer snafu. She set these thoughts aside as she heard Chambers speak again.

"Sorry to have to tell you about it, Captain, but you and I both know I wouldn't joke about something like that."

She looked at him warmly. "You're only the messenger, Chambers." Raising herself back up, she continued, "Did he say for how long? If the choppy water gets worse, the High Cotton may get a sway if we're not moving."

"Yes, I've considered that myself. But Ben said it has to be done. He needs to recode then reboot. At least the only grid we'll have to shut down is the one controlling the propellers, so electricity will be no problem."

She turned back to the ocean. "I suppose that's some consolation, but having power isn't enough to keep the passengers from noticing we're stalled. We need to expect trouble."

"I'll alert the crew to keep a watchful eye."

"Did you get any idea of how long we'll be down?"

"I don't think he knows. When I pressed him for an answer he guessed between three and eight hours."

"What!" Swiftly regaining her composure, she continued, "That's quite a variance. Did you ask him about continuing on course with one propeller?"

"I did. He said we can't do it. Carl agreed. He's concerned now we're going to lose that one too due to overheating."

"It's ironic, isn't it? The Morrows paid a fortune to computerize the link between the engines and propellers. It's more efficient, saves fuel, less trouble, and yet it would seem we'll be zero for three."

"I'm sure once the bugs are worked out it will be worth it."

"Perhaps. For now it's out of our control and in the hands of our IT man and his flask. Is somebody keeping an eye on him?"

"Yes, Mazy, the nurse."

Padma gave Chambers a conspiratorial smile. *"Perfect.* So, we need to get about the business of shutting down. How long before the ship completely stops, do you think? Half an hour?"

"That would be my guess," Chambers replied. "Captain, why don't we inform the passengers when the ship has nearly stopped. After all, they won't notice it at first."

"Yes, delay as long as possible."

"And Captain? There's one more piece of news."

"Yes?"

"It's that reviewer, Cummings. He paid a visit to Carl in the engine room. Somehow he ended up with Mazy's security badge."

She rolled her eyes. "That's all we need." She began walking back to the navigation room. "Find him, and bring him to me with that security badge. Meanwhile, I'm going to inform the rest of the crew what's about to happen."

*   *   *

Jason wasn't difficult to locate. He was in his cabin and answered right away when Chambers knocked.

"First Mate Chambers!" he said. "It's always a pleasure to see you. *Entre,* please."

"Hello, Mr. Cummings," he replied, entering the room. "I've been sent by the Captain. She has asked that you report to the bridge. I'm here to escort you, and you will need to bring that badge with you, sir."

"Escort me!" Jason said wryly. "You know I can't refuse that. But a badge? I have no idea what you mean."

Chambers moved closer, then leaned in. Jason, slightly overwhelmed by the subtlety of Chambers' cologne, prepared himself for the outcome. About to pucker up, he was disappointed to realize that the handsome First Mate only picked up the security badge behind him off of the dresser and placed it in his pocket.

"Are you ready, sir?"

Jason shrugged and reached for his hat and said sarcastically, "I'm all yours."

As they moved through the crowds on deck, Jason felt light pressure on his elbow. Chambers' hand was maintaining contact that Jason knew was only to ensure his arrival at the navigation room, but it would have been nice if it had meant something else.

A few passengers noticed and gave the two an odd look, but no one was brazen enough to make inquiries, much to Jason's chagrin. He would have loved to respond that the ship was having difficulties, and he was evidently being punished because he had knowledge of it. They continued their trek silently. As they reached the last set of steps leading to the bridge, Jason got a good look at the sea, the wrinkled water so different from yesterday.

They stepped inside with the Captain swinging around when she heard the door open, her lovely face in a frown. She said sternly, "Sit down, Mr. Cummings."

Jason removed his cap, noticing it was an order, not a request. "Yes, Captain," he replied, lowering himself into a swivel chair. She remained standing with Chambers behind her, his arms crossed.

"Let's not mince words here, as I realize you are all too aware that I don't have time to waste. Have you communicated with anyone onshore or onboard about the ship's status?"

"You mean my review of the ship's spa? After that fabulous massage from Pablo, I assure you I will be confirming it as five star."

"Don't insult my intelligence, Mr. Cummings. I know about your visit to Carl."

"Carl? Oh, Carl! Yes, that nice gentleman a steward had me deliver some coffee to this morning."

"And I'm also aware of the information you gleaned by deceiving him."

"I don't know what you're trying to imply! That Carl is a chatterbox. Very proud of all he's doing to help get the ship back in order, you know---with that one propeller, and all," he said, mocking Carl's manner of speaking.

"Mr. Cummings, that is not information that you have a right to disseminate. You are on board this ship as a passenger and meant to review the experience of the ship's luxuries, accommodations and dining---not to snoop around in *my* business. And as such, I expect that information not to leave this room."

Jason sat back and cleared his throat. "Well, Captain, I hardly see how you are in a position to stop me. It's my job, after all, to keep people informed---"

She shot back quickly. "Stealing a security badge is a serious offense. I can justifiably put you in the brig if you don't cooperate."

"The brig?" he said, taken aback. "What next? A court martial? I'm sure my doing a stay in and review of 'the brig' is unnecessary. I'm not the enemy here, Captain."

"You have been up to this point, but I think it's time for a truce. I'm going to extend an olive branch and trust you. And to show my good faith, I'm going to tell you exactly what's going on."

Jason sat up straighter. "Well, thank you, Captain. I would appreciate that---finally!"

"Good," Padma stated, no amusement in her tone. Then gesturing to the Chief Engineer and other staff in the navigation room, she said, "All of us are working very hard to keep this ship safe, comfortable and arrive back at port in a timely manner; however, due to a computer issue, we've lost the use of one propeller. Luckily, the man who designed the system is on the High Cotton. He is able to repair the problem; however, we're going to have to stop the ship to do it."

"Seriously? We'll be adrift!"

Padma looked at Chambers who shook his head in dismay at the remark. Then she said, "No, we will not 'be adrift.' The ship will be fully powered. This development will only cause a short delay in our returning to Charleston. When I make the announcement in about thirty minutes, I want your assurance that you will assist me in keeping everyone calm. I'll need all of the help I can get to prevent the passengers from panicking."

"How can I do that?"

"With your tweets and if you hear anyone getting upset, perhaps you could strike up a conversation to settle things down."

"I know I'm good at a lot of things, Captain, but we're going to need more than pep talks to keep these people calm."

"What do you have in mind?"

"Free alcohol, of course. Call it an early happy hour or some other cutesy name if you like, but it's bound to get results."

Padma glanced at Chambers and said, "What do you think?"

"He has a point," was his response.

Jason looked pleased. "Now, for God's sake use top shelf, and don't bring the band up on deck---we don't need anyone thinking we're about to hit an iceberg." Padma continued listening. Jason then said, "And if I'm complicit in keeping this a secret awhile longer and willing to spin the bad news any way I can, I want *carte blanche* to write up the story and," he paused for effect, "I want complete access to the ship. Nothing and no one off limits."

Padma replied, "Some areas are restricted for safety reasons; however, to meet you halfway, let me know what and where you want to 'investigate' and I'll have someone accompany you to keep you out of danger. Fair enough?"

Jason nodded. "Fair enough. And Chambers, feel free to volunteer."

An awkward silence hung in the air before Padma said, "Yes, well…"

Then Jason cut in, "Oh! I just had a brilliant idea! I brought my drone with me. I haven't been able to use it since I didn't take into account how windy it is on a cruise with the ocean breeze and the boat moving along. But if we're stalled, I could fly it over the crowds, maybe get some good videos, possibly some funny ones, too. Naturally, I'll be tactful," he said with a wicked smile.

Padma cut in, "All right, Jason. Use your drone, and tell everyone that we'll show some of the video later

163

on the big screen in the movie room. Make it sound like home movies."

Jason rose. "I'm sure I'll get some terrific footage, just wait and see."

Chapter 20

Leaving Her Behind

He wanted fresh air to clear his head and to get away from Kwon. He turned to leave, his back to the murder scene and its victim, the sounds of Kwon showering in the background.

Kwon was getting out of hand. That conclusion had become obvious ever since the meeting with The Great One. How to deal with him needed cool, calculated thinking, not impulsive reaction, such as he almost had minutes before. Kwon had been poised for a fight. He wasn't a killer with the finesse Jin had, but he was a brute to be reckoned with. And Kwon was no fool. He knew Jin hated him and that the only thing that kept Jin from killing him was the mission and Kwon's vital role as captain of the ship. But that wouldn't last forever. Soon being at sea on Durango would end--- and doesn't the expression go that the captain goes down with the ship? However, Jin also had to consider that Kwon has had the same realization about Jin: that he could eliminate him once their success with Durango is realized.

This gave Jin an epiphany, the idea crystallizing from what was an earlier hunch. The Great One was probably engineering the contest between them. Was it that Kwon's assignment was to be Jin's irritant, the thorn always pricking his side? Is doing this The Great One's method for checking Jin's absolute fealty, to make sure that under any circumstances Jin would be true to the mission and his country? He could not let himself forget that The Great One so enjoys playing his pawns.

Perhaps The Great One and Kwon discussed this plan of goading Jin when Kwon returned from delivering Durango. Yes, that would make sense. They probably had a talk prior to the meeting that very day, maybe only minutes before. Perhaps Kwon's dramatic entrance and taking the seat next to The Great One had been carefully orchestrated for Jin's sake.

Kwon was certainly too dull to have thought of this on his own. It had to be The Great One's scheme, and Jin had played right into his game. His reaction was just as The Great One had desired, although it was an untypical one for Jin. He should have had a face of stone at that meeting. Instead, Jin let it be known he was genuinely shocked by Kwon's juxtaposition to The Great One at the table---not to mention the feeling of importance Kwon displayed at answering Jin's question on behalf of The Great One. Disgusted with himself, Jin could see now how he had been putty in The Great One's hands. Next time it will be different, and it appears that the 'next time' is now. Jin will be the victor in the duel with Kwon. Of that, he was sure. No longer would he allow himself to play the fool. That job will be left to Kwon.

He relaxed, taking a long breath and blowing it out slowly. He understood his position now, and the result was that he felt much better. He would be prepared and have no trouble dealing with his intellectual inferior, Kwon, or for that matter, The Great One. Jin would not be baited by Kwon's clumsy tactics and would remain utterly focused on the mission. Upon its completion it would be clear to Kwon as well as The Great One, that he, Jin, remains the superior agent, not the upstart. Kwon had been used by The Great One, probably by being told that he could be the next superagent. But Jin was sure it was merely to lure Kwon into The Great One's plan.

For Kwon to believe he was even close to Jin's caliber was ludicrous. Kwon only spoke English, Cantonese and Korean. Jin spoke six languages, three with no accent. Kwon had no formal education, while Jin had been sent to Cambridge. And Kwon was too oafish to assimilate into high culture. He lacked the ability to interact in high society. The only role Kwon could play was one of a lowly worker. Whereas Jin could be a chameleon no matter what the assignment. And lastly, Kwon lacked imagination. He wasn't the thinker that Jin was. Jin sneered as he considered that Kwon only needs basic food, a place to occasionally clean himself and the merest pallet for sleep. Anything beyond that was above his station and nothing would ever change it. Kwon's only goal was to be petted by The Great One. A lap dog, that's all Kwon was.

It got Jin to wondering, though, that if Kwon had been meeting with The Great One without Jin's knowledge, what might he have been told about Jin? The idea that Kwon knew any intimate details about him was utterly repugnant. Jin didn't want Kwon to even think about him. The Great One knew everything, but that was acceptable. Was he not The Great One's creation? However, he hoped he could still count on The Great One's discretion with regards to some of the more unsavory events in Jin's past. He felt sure Kwon had no knowledge of these things, for if he had, Kwon would have thrown them in his face by now. Kwon didn't know the meaning of the word 'strategy.' Then Jin considered there is the remote possibility he's developed enough self-control to hang on to this in hopes of finding the perfect moment of impact. Jin should be prepared for those facts to be used as weapons in Kwon's arsenal. Kwon would not shock Jin again.

He smiled to himself, wishing he could be present when The Great One learns that Jin hadn't fallen for Kwon's ridiculous traps. Jin will have passed his test with flying colors by not losing his temper. The Great One surely predicted the outcome, why else design such a ruse? What happens to Kwon afterwards will hardly matter to Jin or The Great One. Jin figured that once they reach Pyongyang it will be ordered for Kwon to have an unfortunate accident, and if not, he would be returned to being just another minion in the ranks, watching a door.

No, Jin had nothing to worry about. This was child's play to him. True, he was momentarily caught off guard, but even The Great One was underestimating him.

Yes, he considered, I'm blessed with a superior mind to Kwon as well as The Great One. My good looks are an added bonus.

*   *   *

With everything settled in his mind now, Jin's thoughts returned to the mission and what his next step should be. Making a quick assessment of his surroundings, he realized the immediate problem. The salon was helter-skelter with broken furniture, glass, bloody sheets and a corpse.

The body was first priority. Since they were going to sea that night, it would be dumped overboard. In the meantime, it should be covered and hidden in case a harbor official should come aboard. A glance told him there was no closet or cupboard to conceal it. He decided on a different plan.

Working quickly, he spread out the soiled sheets and Kwon's blanket, and then rolled the corpse up in the bedclothes. Finding rope in the navigation room, he tugged it tightly around the shroud to keep it in place. He then lifted the body onto Kwon's cot and covered it with his own blanket then stacked belongings and other items around it to have it blend in with the clutter. He decided he would leave the general cleanup to Kwon; it was his mess. When he heard the water stop running, he left and walked out on deck.

It seemed to him the stars that had appeared so romantic earlier now were mocking him. The mild evening was sharpening. He walked around a ventilator, then peered over the railing to see oily water reflecting in the shimmering light. He heard the trickling sound of discharge from Durango's bilge. Far away, a ship's horn rang out like the wail of an animal. Somewhere on the dock men were talking, their voices low.

Hearing noise from the navigation room, Jin looked through the window and saw Kwon on the radio, evidently making arrangements to leave port. A moment later he heard the diesel engines start. Kwon emerged and began releasing the ties to the dock, with Jin coming to assist, as it was a two-man job. A short while later, Durango slipped away from Agadir without any officials inspecting.

They began their cross-Atlantic trip with Jin remaining on deck and watching the lights from the city diminish, the only sounds coming from the ship moving through the water and the hum of the tapping engine. Reaching into his jacket, he removed a cigarette case and then thought of how many times he had shared his cigarettes with Kwon. He chuckled to himself, recalling Kwon marveling at the excellent composition and how smooth they were to smoke, never knowing it was the mark of the forbidden West that made them so satisfying. He took a deep drag and walked around the deck, eventually resting against the old cargo winch.

It seemed that as soon as they reached deep water the temperature dropped and Jin had to zip up his jacket. He saw strange streaks of light occasionally flashing below and presumed they came from fish. When he turned to look back at the African coastline it had disappeared in a shadowy horizon of dark sea melting into midnight sky. He returned to the navigation room.

"Let's dump her now," he said to Kwon, who nodded and put the ship on autopilot. Jin walked into the salon to see that Kwon had attached a cast iron frying pan and a large wrench to the ropes around the corpse to act as weights. The two of them picked up the heavy bundle, struggling as the shroud wanted to unwind from the rope. Once on deck they tossed the woman Jin had found so attractive earlier overboard and heard her body hit the water with a splash, the ocean quickly swallowing it up.

Chapter 21

Reporting For Duty!

Nick and Ray sat in the swivel chairs with Nick at the helm, the boat moving swiftly through the rougher water, spray shooting over the bow and the engine a steady roar.

"How long before we get to that boat, Nick?" Ray asked.

"Not sure. Thirty minutes, maybe."

The three fishermen chatted about where they would sell the big tuna. Then Trevor retrieved his duffle bag and slung it on the bench next to Ray. His impatience was obvious as he considered that they were embarking on a fool's errand.

He didn't care about what was probably a big game fisherman stalled on the water---someone who didn't have Ray on board about to have a heart attack. Yet it was Ray who was insisting they help, and he knew Ray wouldn't hear of turning back. Furthermore, Ray was still a man to be reckoned with, not a doting geriatric or a child, and he deserved Trevor's respect. Still, the unknowns about this errand left Trevor uneasy.

Unzipping the duffle, he pulled out his Glock 23 pistol, and with the efficiency of doing something many times, he dropped the magazine, checked it then replaced it and put another in his pocket. He found his inside-the-waistband holster, strapped it on and snugged the Glock into place. His Benchmade fixed blade knife went into another holster that slid on his belt, the leather supple to the fit and curve of his body. He put a flashlight into a pocket, a folding multi-tool with blades, screwdriver and other necessities joining it. He had a smoke grenade in the duffel and clipped that to his belt, then put a light jacket on to cover it.

Ray was watching him, but Trevor never noticed. Finally, he turned around and said to Nick in a low tone, "What's wrong with Trevor? He's like a Tasmanian Devil zippin' round this boat."

Nick shrugged and replied, "Seems okay to me."

"He hasn't stopped moving since I opened this beer," Ray argued. Then to Trevor he called out, "Trevor! Are you a shark, afraid you'll quit breathing if you stop?"

Trevor snapped, "This is what I do."

"You're not a SEAL anymore. We're just going to see what these people need."

"What they need? This isn't a potluck we've been invited to."

"Oh, come on. It's not like we're going to battle. It's just people on a fancy yacht. Captain probably had too much bubbly, and they need help setting the boat to head home, or maybe it's engine trouble."

"Move!" Trevor said irritably, reaching between Nick and Ray to retrieve his fishing knife from the console. "Where's the revolver you two keep onboard?"

"Umm," Ray muttered as he considered the question. "Where's the key to that cabinet, Nick?" Nick shook his head in reply.

"Why in the hell do you have the gun locked up? You think the hijackers are gonna' wait while you two look for the fucking key?"

"Come on, Trev," Nick started.

"Come on, nothing! You think I enjoy having to think of every shitty scenario we could be facing? You think this is a game? Life isn't a movie where good intentions protect you from the bad guys." He stopped and looked from one to the other, then said, "You're right. I'm not a SEAL anymore. But I'm for damned sure not going to have survived all the fucked up shit I survived to come out here and approach a strange boat---where anything could be going down---with my head up my ass."

Ray said, "Trevor, I didn't mean for you to be feeling all this. I just wanted to help."

"If you want to help, get the flare gun and flares." Ray nodded and gave a little salute as he got out of the chair. Then Trevor said in an easier tone, "I hope you're right, it's just some socialites on a yacht needing a hand. But we're not taking chances."

Opening a drawer, Ray found the flare gun and flares in a waterproof box. He set them on the counter then announced, "I just remembered where that key is!" He reached behind Nick and pulled a keyring out of a cup holder. A single key dangled from a floater. Inserting it into a locked upper cabinet, he opened the door and looked inside. "Here we go, Trevor, one Colt that used to be your daddy's and my old thirty-eight."

Trevor examined the Colt, his fingers running along the stag handle. "I remember this old thing." He opened the chamber and said, exasperated, "Where are the bullets?"

Nick said, "I cleaned it not long ago. There should be a box in there."

"I found it," Ray said, putting the ammunition on the counter.

Trevor set the Colt down and picked up the thirty eight. He emptied two bullets out of the chamber then examined it further. "This one's in terrible shape, Ray." He said, "Do you have more than two bullets?"

Ray shook his head. "No. I haven't fired that thing in, well, I can't remember when."

"This gun is to be used only as a last resort." Then Trevor considered to himself that Ray too should be used only as a last resort. He placed the Colt next to the bullets in the drawer, then closed it. "And for God's sake, leave it unlocked!"

"You carrying your Glock?"

"Yes, and that." Trevor's chin pointed to the M1A.

Ray whistled at the sight of it. "That looks like a lot of gun."

"Holy shit! Put that away," Nick ordered. "You'll scare these people to death."

"I'll move it under the bench and put towels over it. I want it hidden but within easy reach." Nick rolled his eyes. "I mean it, Nick. If we're doing this, we need to be prepared."

"Don't be a dick. We can't go pulling up to a pleasure boat brandishing weapons. It's probably some amateurs having engine trouble."

"That's what I said," Ray agreed.

"But we don't know, do we Nick? We couldn't raise them on the radio, *remember*?"

"All right," Nick said tossing his hands in the air, "So, what's the plan, Marshal Dillon?"

"We approach cautiously, circling their boat. *I'll* do the talking. No one leaves the Esmerelda until we find out exactly what the problem is. We also need to know how many are onboard and what their status is. Most importantly, we ask them if they have any weapons, and remember, they'll probably lie." Nick and Ray nodded. "And no one, I repeat---*no one* boards the Esmerelda. We need to be alert to the possibility that their ship has been taken over and they may not be able to speak truthfully. Watch body language."

"Okay, okay," they said obligingly.

Then after looking at the radar, Nick said, "This must be a bigger boat than we thought. And it should be coming into view. Ray, get the glasses."

Ray pulled some dilapidated binoculars out of a case dangling behind him and attempted to clean the clouded lenses. He handed them to Nick, avoiding eye contact with Trevor.

"Take the wheel for a second, will you, Ray?"

"Aye Aye, Captain." He slowly rose from the bench to take over.

Walking on deck with Trevor, Nick began searching the horizon, slowly pivoting his body as he concentrated. The sky was changing, the brilliant blue dissipating as a gusty wind brought hazy light flirting with clouds. Finding his target, he paused, then pulled the glasses away before looking again. "This is weird. I can't see the High Cotton. There's a cruise ship in the way."

He handed the binoculars to Trevor who stared for several seconds. Then slowly lowering the glasses, he said, "There was only *one* boat on the radar, Nick." The two eyed one another. "Get it? That's the High Cotton!"

Nick jerked the glasses from his brother's hands and looked again. Confused, he glanced back at Trevor and said, "Are we being punked? They can't be serious."

Trevor put his head back and began laughing, his hand slapping the gunwale.

"Shut up, asshole!" Nick said, starting to laugh himself.

Ray called out, "What's so funny?"

Trevor answered, "Nick's gotten another big fish!" Nick went back into the cabin, Ray taking the glasses from him.

"What's going on? Trevor, take this wheel so I can look." He went on deck, returning less than a minute later. "What's that cruise ship doing there? Where's the High Cotton?" The brothers looked at him, their faces twitching, about to erupt in laughter. Ray's chin dropped. "Oh, no she didn't! You tellin' me that cruise ship captain is the one who called us? That's for the Coast Guard!"

Nick grinned. "Well, here we are, reporting for duty! But don't worry, she probably just wants a tow!"

The three of them burst out laughing then almost simultaneously stopped as the chilly breeze found its way inside the cabin. Trevor rubbed his jaw. Nick looked in the direction of the ship. Ray cast his eyes down, their expressions serious in that moment of understanding, all of them knowing perfectly well the big ship wasn't looking for a tow. With such a vessel the possibilities were limitless. So what did they want with the Esmerelda?

Chapter 22

Anyone got a spare jigger?
#CummingsAndGoings

Jason walked out of the navigation room contemplating his next move. Before the Captain makes her announcement about the ship coming to a stop, he needed to prepare his role as host of a cocktail hour that would get everyone so blitzed they wouldn't notice or care that the ship was at a dead stop in the middle of the ocean.

First things first, he headed to meet with the High Cotton bartenders to instruct them on how to prepare his signature drink, The Cummings and Goings. Additionally, he wanted the kitchen staff to prepare some festive hors d'oeuvres with a south of the border theme, the salty snacks encouraging alcohol lubrication to keep everyone happy and distracted. The upshot was that tipsy passengers would provide entertaining footage for the drone. Once it all gets underway he'll need to work the crowds and turn on some of his famous Jason charm to get the ship's party on. With a music selection already at the click of a button---he had a Spotify playlist ready to go at all times---he'll get the passengers moving to the music and later assemble a group to start the cliched, but ever popular, Conga line. For Jason, big parties are no different from small ones. It's all about the vibe, and no one creates a buzz like he does. However, first priority was to strategize how his new liaison with the Captain can best serve *him*---not just alcohol.

As he walked along he considered his career end game, his own television show. He clearly has all of the qualifications necessary. His face is a camera's dream, so he's been told, first when he was interviewed by MSNBC for the illegal fishing catch story, and again when he was invited to assist in a Thanksgiving food-prep gig for the Today Show. That time he was on-air for a full ten minutes, Jason brilliantly judging the best dressing for turkey day, making a particularly notable comment when the hostess spilled dressing on her blouse. Jason quipped, "Savannah, I think you're taking the term 'dressing' a little too literally!" The viewers loved it. His wit and repartee have always been his trademark.

He began fantasizing what the presentation would be like. Filmed live with celebrity guests as well as a regular segment on what's hot in fashion, travel and restaurants, he could also have interviews with popular chefs known for their gossip as well as their cooking. He didn't want it too gimmicky, though, the way so many were. His personality and humorous responses should keep things fun and quirky, providing excellent entertainment and lastly, information. It will be much in the vein of his idol, Ellen, who undoubtedly will be following him on Twitter by the end of this trip.

He was practically salivating at the thought of it all. If the High Cotton situation got a little more dire, he could have exclusive footage and need to be interviewed again by all the major news players, who would ask about his harrowing coverage during such tribulation. He could hear the praise now. Then he thought of something. Note to self. I need a high-profile agent. I wonder who Ellen uses?

Thinking of the matter at hand, he wanted to capture some good drone footage that will be popular with the passengers and the Captain. Trouble was, it would be uninteresting to everybody else, so he'll need to keep the juicy footage for his own coverage later.

The ship being stalled is newsworthy, but playing up a computer debacle is not exactly stimulating, especially since no one is about to die because of it. However, getting the inside perspective of the Captain's point of view could possibly make for an attention-getting video. Maybe he could play up the drama, the intensity of the Captain's decision-making, her concern for the passengers, the anxiety of the unknowns, and what if the IT guy can't fix the propellers? It could make for a good 'woman in the workplace overcoming great odds' angle, which is all the rage.

He would capture Padma's lovely face creased with worry, the handsome Chambers soothing her, her other staff eager to solve what could be an unsolvable problem. And perhaps an interview with Carl down in the ship's belly, the common-sensed engine man bravely attempting to keep the High Cotton in working order. Against this backdrop, the drunken scandal from the passengers could provide comedic relief. Jason's ideas were really beginning to flow. Was this what it was like for Spielberg?

Now that he got all that decided, he would need to speak with the Captain once the party got underway and he has worked with the drone for a while, proving that he's upholding his end of the bargain. As a result, he can remind her that he is to have access to any part of the ship he wants, navigation room included. His steps became lighter as his thoughts continued to gel with ideas.

After locating the head steward, he explained he needed a meeting with the bartenders. While that was being handled, Jason got behind the bar and began looking for the necessary ingredients.

"It's called The Cummings and Goings after my hashtag, but you probably guessed that," he explained once they had gathered. He continued as he loaded Rumchata into the blender. "It's delicious and decorative for special parties, such as the one we're about to start. It's a variation on a Pina Colada, but better, obviously." He picked up a bottle. "Ice cubes in the blender, add Rumchata, vanilla vodka, coconut milk, a splash of lime juice, and use chunks of mango and lemon to give it more punch than sweetness.

182

Whipped cream on top with a cherry on the side, and please, no little umbrellas. If we had miniature sombreros that would be a different story." He turned the blender on then poured the mixture in several glasses and handed out the samples. Everyone clearly loved it.

"Start making batches right away. As soon as the Captain says it's free drink time, have these babies ready to go. They might ask for bourbon, scotch or something else more traditional, but if they try this, they'll change their minds, or better yet, have both!"

Then the intercom crackled and Chambers' voice could be heard, telling everyone to listen, as the Captain had an important announcement. He repeated what he said, the second time around silencing the chattering in the bar.

"Hello, everyone, this is Captain Patel," her voice smoothly rang out, though her tone was more serious than friendly, Jason noted. "I've got two things to tell you, the first being that the ship will be stopping for a short while. You may have already noticed that it has slowed. This means you'll get to enjoy your voyage a few hours longer than expected, while we make a quick adjustment. Just know we'll resume our way back to Charleston shortly. To take advantage of this bonus time we're starting happy hour early with free drinks for those who are of age. Travel reviewer Jason Cummings will introduce you to his signature beverage. Jason will also be taking video footage with his drone, and we'll show some of it later in the movie theater. Anyone who needs to communicate with someone onshore about the adjusted arrival time, or who needs assistance with changing connections in Charleston, please see our head steward, Mr. Dawkins. He wears the same uniform as the other stewards, but his coat is red. Enjoy your extra time on the High Cotton."

The bartenders quickly dispersed to return to their posts as passengers began lining up at the bars.

"If it means free drinks they can have us sitting here another day," a thirtyish man said. His girlfriend pronounced, "I don't know... I'm worried about my babysitter's schedule."

Jason turned to her and gave her a drink. "Try this, and send your sitter a text. Make sure you pick her up a little something from the ship's gift shop." The woman took a sip, whipped cream giving her a mustache.

Her brows raised as she said, "Delicious!"

Jason then looked around for the head steward and when he got his attention, waved him over. He said to him in a confidential tone, "Get the music pumping louder, and I want those hors d'oeuvres out right away." The man nodded and spoke into a radio. Seconds later a lusty Katy Perry song rose over the crowd and feet began tapping.

As Jason returned to his room to get his drone and laptop, he perked his ears for negative comments from passengers, but heard none. When he got back up to the deck, he heard laughter and saw more people than usual looking over the railing to gaze at the sea. He heard a man say, "Let's take a wager on how many minutes before she stops altogether." Another answered, "Okay. Twenty bucks says in ten minutes we'll be at a standstill." A woman murmured behind him, "I think we're stopped now."

Time passed with the sun high in the sky. The sea with the choppy swells had smoothed to calm water again as the wind settled to a light breeze. Jason got out his laptop and the box containing his drone from where he had stashed them behind the bar. Squatting down, he began unpacking the equipment and considered that most of the passengers had now sampled a Cummings and Goings and the food. All seemed pleased.

He was no stranger to operating a drone. He purchased his first two years ago, a beginner's model that he crashed and ruined right away. But the experience had gotten him hooked. Practicing in fields, parking lots or anywhere he could find that was open, he became adept at the controls and eventually graduated to a sophisticated model he could control with ease. Yet he considered that even though he was skilled enough to fly in circles, do figure eights and maneuver in light winds, he didn't want this expensive piece of equipment to end up in the ocean. He would keep it over the decks at all times with the exception of when he wanted to move to a different level. The drone would then have to move over the water to go up or down, unless Jason carried it himself.

Still low behind the counter, he could hear the cacophony above, as the free alcohol had put any fear about the ship being adrift out of passengers' minds. People were chatting and laughing as the music shifted to the next song. There was an unexpected and stark contrast between the Bruno Mars track ending and the beginning of a Bee Gees hit, *Staying' Alive.*

"The hell!" popped out of Jason's mouth. That was certainly not on *his* playlist. He might occasionally do a throwback as he'd planned for Gloria Estefan and the Conga, but lord knows, not the Bee Gees! This would have to be addressed with the DJ.

Then Jason heard a familiar voice, that smooth baritone that he did so like to hear. He was about to stand up and begin some shameless flirting when he heard the ring of a radio phone.

"Chambers," he heard him say. Silence ensued as the other party spoke. "When?" Chambers asked; more silence. "What does the Chief say?" he asked, then a brief pause. "I can't believe---Yes, Captain. I'm on my way---and Captain? I agree, put the call out."

Jason stood up slowly, finding Chambers hurriedly going out the door. "Now what?" he wondered. He considered the tone Chambers had used. He had never heard the man speak with that much urgency. Normally, he, like Captain Patel, was well studied in the poker face and voice. Could there be more problems? Jason decided that his pact with the Captain entitled him to be in the know of any new developments. He left the drone where it was and headed for the navigation room. The DJ would have to be dealt with later.

Chapter 23

Secrets and Lies

Rain. Endless driving rain, day after day, the static sound pinging off the ship's metal surfaces like an old television without a signal. All they saw from the ship's cockpit was gray sky meeting gray sea enveloped in gray fog, a colorless view matching Durango's gray interior right down to the steps entering the cargo hold. Everything dank, dark, graying and old.

With no visual release and no entertainment such as games, conversation, or a computer, it was the most isolated mission Jin had ever experienced. The monotony of the sea and weather had him feeling as constricted as if he wore a strait jacket. He knew action was on the horizon, but couldn't see it coming. All his eyes ever met was the rain, unable to see sea or sky, just more of the damned rain. To make matters worse, their crossing was extended due to having to slow the Durango to nine knots. They worried they might smash into another boat cloaked on the radar by low clouds and more of that damned rain. Should that happen it would not only ruin the mission, they could be instantly vaporized.

Their cargo was both feared and revered. Jin could sense the tremendous power that lay below him, its energy practically pulsing through the ship, its potential resonating into his very core. The enormity of it was invigorating, yet the finality of its detonation left his mind lingering.

He was aware of how nuclear weapons held the fascination and respect of the world. Even Kwon beamed with pride. "Our people are so clever to achieve this---and using second-hand parts from black market sources---right down to the uranium!" He would laugh, "No one will ever trace it to us! They'll say, 'How could it be done?' Ha!" He shook his head, smiling. "And here the West is so concerned about our 'official' nukes! They don't even suspect we could come through their back door!"

Jin listened to these outbursts daily, and usually allowed Kwon the luxury of his boasting, after all, Kwon had so little to be proud of. Today though, maybe it was his dark mood due to the weather and sea, Jin was sick of it. He challenged Kwon with, "What about the hundreds of thousands of people in Charleston, Kwon? Are you sure you can damn them to the consequences of nuclear holocaust? The death and destruction will reach more than just those who have insulted our great country. Do not diminish that by sounding like a simple schoolboy." And then to himself, whispered, "Or a simpleton."

"They deserve it! Their dotard leaders insult The Great One every time they speak! And they are the cause of our people's hunger and pain. Why, I am no 'schoolboy' for recognizing they are the reasons why we have so little. Maybe this will finally teach them a lesson!"

"You speak of the actions of a few. And a leader not even of divine order. By a fluke of their inept political system he became the head of their state."

"You talk like a fucking traitor, Jin! We don't question the wisdom of The Great One! If he believes this is good for our country then we follow through, obey like good citizens!" Spitting the words out, he added, "I've always known about you. You do your work solely for your *dividends* that come at the end of each assignment---to buy your clothes, your fancy cars and your women. Oh yes, Jin! I know all about it, and so does The Great One!" His eyes gleamed with triumph.

Jin, keeping to his plan not to fall prey to Kwon's goading, merely smiled. "Oh, Kwon. You are such a child. Don't speak of things that are beyond your understanding." As Kwon began more ranting, Jin turned and walked into the salon, each step tamping down his anger that The Great One watched him so closely, and here, he, Jin, was a hero to his country!

Not only that, Jin had always been so careful to take precautions to keep his well-deserved privacy from prying eyes. But now he has learned he has failed. The Great One really does see and hear all. What the consequences would be, he wasn't sure. Or perhaps, The Great One knew and approved of his actions, and this was what fueled Kwon's immense jealousy. Should things go well with this mission, he will maintain the good graces of The Great One. Once he confirms his status, he will set about finding new ways to secretly achieve what he wants.

Looking around the salon, he was sickened by the state of it, just as he was the night he walked in and found the carnage of Kwon's rampage. This assignment meant actually sharing a living space with Kwon. He had been disgusted to learn what a true pig he was. His clothes remained piled wherever they were removed. Often so stiff with sweat and grime, they held their wearer's shape days after being shed to the floor.

Dirty dishes and trash littered the room, while Kwon's cot smelled so strongly of body odor and piss that Jin wondered if he had wet the bed. The state of the bathroom was so bad that Jin had quit showering and only used the toilet under duress. The sink was stopped up with a brownish gray water that had hair and yellow foam floating in it. The toilet functioned only because Jin told Kwon he'd kill him in his sleep if he stopped it up. The result was that Kwon's soiled tissue was dumped in a corner on the floor, causing an unimaginable stench.

Jin's sleeping area was his only point of refuge. He kept the bifold doors closed at all times and went inside to lie down and escape Kwon's filth.

He looked at the rain, visible through the porthole above him. Falling in a steady beat, the window was blurred with rainwater, a faint light penetrating the onslaught. His bed was damp from the cold and humidity. He hadn't taken his jacket off since the first night on the ship. Picking up the stub of a pencil he made a mark on the wall where there were nine others. It was the tenth day on Durango.

With their progress slowed, their destination was delayed by twenty-two hours. Luckily Jin knew how to change the timer on the bomb, but what if something was wrong technically and the timer didn't budge from its original setting? That would mean a day before Durango was to reach Charleston harbor all would be lost, including their lives.

He thought about the fail-safe, the little yellow wire that he could cut and therefore change the plan. At times he ventured down to the hold to look at the bomb, a shark-like shape resting in a lumber cocoon to keep it stable. Sometimes he would stand next to the weapon and squat slightly to run his fingers along the bottom until he felt the minute opening where the wire protruded like a hernia in the weapon's gut.

Having the fail-safe was Jin's signature that he was his own man. His tiny mischief-making was his way of telling himself that no one, not even The Great One, could completely control him. It was how Jin remained Jin. His power came from completing his missions as requested by choice, not force.

This tendency had begun when he was a boy, raised after age eight in an orphanage. Every day the children practiced chants and rhymes about death to the United States. Even then, when the boys were programmed to trust only the state, Jin was able to maintain a kernel of his independent thinking, silently questioning what he was told. This confidence came from a book he found one day, a magnificent discovery that occurred completely by accident, but was probably the most formative event of his life.

The day he acquired the book, he had been permitted to leave the school's campus to help staff dump the trash. This honor was due to his exemplary behavior and excellent grades. Jin enjoyed every aspect of it, especially the drive, which was half an hour each way. It gave him an opportunity to see the outside world. They passed farms with people walking along the roadside or working in fields. Everything looked bright and cheerful outside of the drab school. Fields were green as roadside wildflowers grew like speckles of rainbows. Even the sky was bluer away from the inner-city orphanage, located where everything, including the clouds above, was covered in coal dust belched from a nearby factory. Turning into the driveway that led to the garbage dump, Jin admired the towering trees ending before an open pit with a mountainous rubbish heap, half of it a simmering fire. The smoke made his clothes smell of what he imagined to be the odor of a campfire, though of course now he knew better.

That particular day, when he began dumping the refuse, he saw something he had never seen before. A paperback book. It looked so odd, so out of place, resting on the ground near the filth. The edges of its pages were a saffron color, the book's spine creased in little furrows from heavy use. He could see that the title was in English, the cover so worn it was as soft as a wad of cotton. In one stroke, he dumped his trash and picked up the book, managing to jam it into his pocket without notice.

It was several days before he had the opportunity to thoroughly examine it, keeping it hidden behind a loose piece of linoleum where his bed met the wall. Secrecy was necessary because he had observed many times how all of the boys' clothes, sheets and blankets were regularly searched for contraband.

One night as everyone slept, he slipped out of his pallet and without a sound, retrieved the book. Climbing back into bed, he used a shaft of light that stabbed through a high window to read the title and the author's name: Casino Royale by Ian Fleming. Though the setting of the book was decades ago, it gave Jin a glimpse of what living in the West was like. He, like the other children, had received a few lessons in English. He studied the book thoroughly to decipher each word. It wasn't long before he memorized every chapter, and as a result became fluent. Now, Jin possessed the key he needed not only to understand the language but to speak like a proper gentleman.

This enabled him to qualify for higher education, a rare occurrence for a child raised in his meager surroundings. He entered the military as a teenager, as all North Korean boys do, but his abilities made him stand out. He learned other languages quickly and was eventually selected for a top honor after scoring high enough on his national testing to attend college in England. Naturally, once there he read many Western books, but it was that first discovery of James Bond that inspired Jin to become an agent, as well as giving him a model of who he wanted to be, how he wanted to dress, act, and live. Most importantly, Ian Fleming's character taught Jin how to keep his inner self secret from everyone else, especially The Great One. James Bond never lost his cool, and neither would Jin, even with all the damned rain.

Chapter 24

...Should You Choose To Accept It

With Nick at the helm, the Esmerelda made its approach to the High Cotton as stealthily as an aged shrimp boat can. The three men silently examined the cruise ship in the distance, gleaming white and black, her name printed on the hull in an elegant red script. Immobile, she could have posed for a postcard as the sun reflected off her decks. Sparkling clean and fresh, it was difficult to believe she was in distress, but surely she must be.

Nick idled the boat. "Well, now what?" He looked at Ray then Trevor. "Trev? And don't even say, 'I told you so.'"

Trevor squinted as he peered again over the Esmerelda's bow. "Let's radio them."

"Ray?" Nick asked.

Ray scratched his chin and said, "Yeah, I reckon. Let's see if we can get them to answer this time."

Nick returned his glance to the High Cotton, seeing an American flag wafting in the breeze at the tip of the stern. He picked up the binoculars and noticed people crowded on deck. "It's an unusual version of a cruise ship, old timey looking with all the open decks. But---hang on---the passengers are going back in. Must've gotten a good look at this rusty bucket and given up on being saved."

Ray took the binoculars and looked. "It's the staff moving 'em. They're wearing uniforms. I don't believe they've noticed us." He gave the binoculars to Trevor.

Trevor could see the crowds diminishing, moving to central doors like sand in an hourglass. "They're orderly, clearly not panicked." He turned to Nick. "That's a good sign, but we need to talk to that Captain. They're stationary, and I would've said engine trouble, but that wouldn't explain why they would move everyone inside. Something else is going on."

"Definitely strange. I'll try 'em now." Nick turned to the radio, but before he had his hand on the mic, a noise erupted, static, then the feminine voice came through. "Esmerelda, this is Captain Patel of the High Cotton. Do you read me? Over."

Nick said quickly into the mic, "This is Captain Starnes, High Cotton. Over."

"Captain Starnes, we have a situation quickly unfolding and need your immediate assistance. Could you please meet me at our hatch door, starboard side?"

"What the hell does that mean?" Ray interjected.

"Nick, move over and let me talk," Trevor said. Nick reluctantly handed Trevor the radio mic. "Captain

Patel, this is Trevor Starnes, retired First Lieutenant, Navy SEAL, Team Four. Could you outline the nature of the emergency?"

They waited and listened. All they heard was dripping from the Esmerelda's bilge. Then the radio squawked again. "We're stalled, Lieutenant. The nature of the emergency involves our position in the water. I can't say anymore due to this channel being open. However, please know, I'm also retired Navy, former Captain of the USS Chaffee stationed in the Persian Gulf."

Nick and Ray looked at one another skeptically then at Trevor, who stated, "Well I don't like it, but if she's ex-Navy I feel a little better about it. But that's not to say we won't pull up to a shit show."

"That's it?" Nick interjects. "You hear she's retired Navy and you're ready to go just like that?"

"Did you forget who insisted we come out here in the first place? And now you're questioning me? For fuck's sake!" Trevor countered.

"Did you boys realize that was a woman talkin'? And she said she was Captain! I sure ain't ever heard of that. Something's all weird about it." Ray commented.

"Seriously?" Nick replied. "'C'mon Ray. With all the possible shit we're about to pull up on, you're worried she's a woman? Please. Let's just hope she's hot," he chortled.

"Listen you two middle-schoolers," Trevor scolded. "You signed us up for this, so we're going---regardless. Besides, if she's hot she'll go for me anyway." He smirked a smile then responded to the radio, "Agreed,

Captain. We'll proceed to your starboard hatch."
Putting the mic down, he said, "Let's go."

The Esmerelda traveled towards the ship at a moderate speed as the three of them surveyed the decks. No one saw anything that appeared untoward. The ship was sitting perfectly still, and by the time they were a hundred feet away, not a single passenger or crew member was in sight. Trevor maneuvered the shrimp boat towards the hatch and saw it open. Two people outlined the doorway, a tall man in uniform and a woman in crisp white with bars on the shoulders that were not necessary to indicate that she was the Captain. Her face was stern, her dark eyes focused on the Esmerelda and its crew.

They were close enough now for Ray to throw a line. As Trevor watched him take the rope in his worn hand he considered the potential impact of what they were embarking upon. Normally that rope was a lifeline, a tie for their safety, to attach the Esmerelda so she and her crew would be secure. Was that the case this time?

His eyes wandered to Captain Patel, her expression stoic. The man next to her told him more; he didn't have the seasoned poker face of the captain. His brow was furrowed and splotched with sweat. He stood waiting for orders before he squatted down to reach for Ray's line and tie it off, the action of a man who respects his captain explicitly. The stern jaw, the clench of his fists, and the turn of the man's shoulders was the body language of someone ready to act.

Nick peered inside the trapdoor to see what was behind its entrance, but the angled light shadowed the interior. Then Captain Patel said to him, "Permission to board?"

Trevor and Ray were on deck next to Nick, who took their silence as approval to allow the High Cotton's Captain to board the Esmerelda. "Permission granted," Nick said to her.

He held his hand out and she took it and said as she stepped down, "Standing at the hatch is First Mate Brian Chambers. I'm Captain Padma Patel."

Nick nodded. "I'm Nick Starnes, this is my brother, Trevor, and that's my crew member, Ray Carter."

She gave them a curt nod and began in a steady tone. "Gentlemen, I'll lay it out for you. Our propellers are down and I don't know when they'll be operative. Meanwhile, there's a cargo ship moving in a direct line with the High Cotton. She doesn't respond to our radio calls---urgent ones. If Durango remains on the trajectory she's on now, she's going to T-bone my ship, and that's going to happen in approximately…" she looked at Chambers who peered at his watch then responded, "Twenty-one minutes, Captain."

"Why in the hell would that ship not answer the radio?" Nick exclaimed, looking at Trevor.

"I don't know, We had trouble getting Captain Patel. Maybe they're having the same radio problem."

Padma challenged, "Yes, I've considered that, but if that's the case, why haven't they gotten out of our way? By now we're undoubtedly visible on their radar."

"That's true," Nick said. "For their own safety they should make a directional change. If it's a big tanker, they don't exactly turn on a dime. But for all you know, they are planning to adjust."

"The situation is so dire we can't make any assumptions about their intentions."

"Wait---are you suggesting this could be intentional?" Trevor asked.

Padma shook her head. "No. How could it be? Our being stalled wasn't planned. It's a computer problem," she answered.

"Computers can be hacked," Trevor reminded her.

"Not this time. The programmer is sailing with us since it's our maiden voyage, and he sees where the correction needs to be made. What I'm wondering is if something's happened to its crew. That means it will never change course." She paused, then added, "We've got to act now---too many lives are at stake. I've got 950 passengers."

"How do you like that,'" Ray said. "She's adrift right where a damn cargo ship is comin' straight at her! Ocean's as calm as a bathtub, too. Wonder where they headin'---Charleston?"

"That's what we're assuming," Padma answered. Then more urgently she said to Nick, "What's the horsepower of your engine?"

"Three hundred and eighteen," he responded confidently.

"Then you've got enough thrust to push us off Durango's course. I've been over it in detail with our Chief Engineer."

Nick scoffed, "Wait. Push? You're not serious."

"Listen---it is completely possible. Just give us a push on the tip of our bow. The math checks out. And

Trevor, you were a SEAL. I'm sure you tackled missions that seemed more hopeless than this."

Trevor said nothing. Nick shook his head in disbelief. His voice faltering, he said "To push the High Cotton at its bow and actually move her, it would take all we've got. Everything."

Padma's eyes flicked to her feet then back up as she explained, "All the Esmerelda needs to do is change my ship's angle fifteen degrees. If Durango stays on the trajectory it's been on for the last hour, despite our pleas, it will pass us with twelve to fourteen inches to spare at its closest point."

Nick's voice, coming back to him, cut in, "But if we can't get out of the way in time we'll be crushed. This is the ocean, how can you give these precise measurements? You can't be that sure. Your boat is adrift." His voice fading, "Come on."

Padma gently agreed. "Your ship will be at risk---if we're not mindful of time. As far as our calculations, my Chief Engineer is the best in the business. With a calm ocean like today, his predictions will stand, Captain Starnes. We are certainly not enlisting your help because we want a little excitement. We're talking about many lives at stake."

"What's the Coast Guard sayin'?" Ray questioned.

"Their ETA is thirty-five minutes."

Rolling his eyes, Ray huffs, "Just in time to scrape us off the side of your ship like a flapjack."

Nick and Ray exchanged a knowing glance. "It'll take every ounce she's got," Nick said. "I don't know if she has it in her. The ropes aren't the only thing that's tired..."

"Tired! She's plum wore out! We're talking about a suicide mission for the old gal. And us!"

"Please," Padma said, her expression about to break. "We're running out of time."

"I'll do it," Trevor said. "Nick, you and Ray wait with the Captain on the High Cotton. I'm a strong swimmer. If it comes to it I'll jump ship before she's hit."

Nick made a tense sigh, "She's *my* boat. If she goes down *I'm* going with her---I want to know there was nothing I could have done, so I'll be the one doing it."

Ray added, "Well, you'll need every bit of my help."

Trevor and Nick expostulated, "No!" Then Nick continued, "Ray, I'm not having something happen to you, so you're staying back. And that's not an option."

Padma interrupted, "I'm sorry, gentlemen, there's no more time for debate. We must get moving,"

Nick hesitated. Ray put his hand on his arm. "I know I'm the one who got us into this, but I'm countin' on you boys to get us out." His glance moved to the Esmerelda. "All of us."

Nick nodded, looking back at the outriggers loaded with sagging shrimp nets and feeling the Esmerelda gently bob against the big ship.

Then suddenly Ray jerked sideways, and called out, irritated, "What's that? Sounds like a damned wasp---and here I'm allergic without my EpiPen!"

Padma glanced up. "You have got to be kidding!"

Chambers' voice rang out, "It must be Cummings! He's always there! How is it he's always there?"

Jason's drone was hovering directly above them then quickly flew out of Chambers' reach, rising up and ducking into an upper deck.

"Ignore it," Padma said with an exasperated wave of her hand. Nick looked at Trevor, who shrugged.

Just as Padma and Ray prepared to climb up to the trap door, Padma hesitated. Ray followed her gaze and shouted, "There it is! The tanker's on the horizon. Lord don't fail us now!"

Chapter 25

Twenty Minutes Earlier

Jason marched up to the navigation room, full of game, and not surprised that he hadn't been informed about a possible new problem with the ship. He lamented how foolish he had been to trust the Captain. Not bothering to knock, he barged inside poised to make an outburst.

It was quiet, the only sound the tapping of a young man's fingertips on a keyboard. One other staff member was present, a girl in her early twenties wearing headphones. She had her back to him, a red braid hanging between her shoulders. Jason perused the rest of the room. All the controls and computers were lit up but unmanned.

Moving to the girl's side, Jason cleared his throat and said, "Excuse me."

"You'll need to leave sir. No passengers allowed in this area," she said in a clipped Irish accent.

"Where's Captain Patel, or Chambers?"

"I'm not sure, sir. They are very busy. Now please," she glanced over her shoulder, "You'll need to return to the passenger area."

"Listen," Jason approached and leaned over to read her name tag, "Third Officer Pullen, I can tell how busy you are making sure this cruise runs smoothly. I don't want to take any more of your time. I'll just borrow this radio and leave you to it." His eyes moved to the radio sitting on the desk's edge.

He had clearly gotten her attention now, and she turned to face him. Her brown eyes were large and doe like, her uniform perfectly pressed. She squinted in an attempt to appear intimidating, and said, in what Jason could only imagine was her *I'm serious voice*, "Sir, unless it is an emergency, the Captain cannot be bothered by radio. She has," she hesitated, "a lot to take care of at the moment."

"Officer Pullen, I can see why the Captain speaks so highly of you," Jason lied. "And I am sure she has mentioned to you how valuable my experience and reviews on this cruise are to her." He picked up the radio, "I know that the Captain would be happy to speak with me, and I'll be sure to mention what a help you've been."

She held up her index finger and said into the headset. "Yes, I'm here." Her forehead was beginning to glisten, her eyes as big as saucers. "It's room 414. Report back immediately." She looked back to Jason and saw his toned figure approaching the door. "Wait, err, sir," she called out, the hesitation in her voice plain as she weighed how firm she could be with him. "I can't allow you to take that." Hopping up, her slender ivory hand grabbed his bronzed forearm.

He could easily keep walking. Her tiny grasp wouldn't slow him down. The poor girl had forgotten her headset was still plugged in, and another step further and Jason could see that the cord would reach its limit. But perhaps commandeering the radio would not be a good faith measure for his deal with the Captain. And clearly young Officer Pullen would not be letting this go.

She held up her index finger again and said into the headset. "Yes, please proceed." She started to take another step forward when she reached the cord's end and was snapped backwards. Flustered, she moved the earpieces back into place and said into the headset, "All right. Just check back later and give a report." With a scarlet face she took the radio and returned to her seat.

Jason, choking back a laugh, looked at the other officer, who had been oblivious until now. The young man was doing his best to keep a serious expression, then lurched up as he suddenly remembered.

"Oh! Mr. Cummings! I just realized it was you." He cut his eyes over to Officer Pullen who was typing something on her keyboard, head down and attempting to regain composure. "I was supposed to come and find you. Our Steward Specialist, Estevão Gencio, wanted to see you. He's waiting at the bar." Then with a quizzical expression, he added, "Perhaps he can tell you what you need to know."

"I see," Jason mused, then nodded and left, backtracking down the steps and wondering what a 'Steward Specialist' was. He didn't have time to waste with some useless steward the Captain had dreamed up as a way to keep him busy. He would swing by and tell this person he would have to meet later. Although perhaps he has a radio, Jason considered, as he routed around the Conga line and made his way to the bar. There a uniformed man stood, one foot propped on the footrest, his fingers tapping on the counter to the beat of the music.

Jason almost stopped in his tracks to admire this vision. The Steward Specialist was about thirty with a gorgeous tan, thick wavy hair, an inviting smile and athletic figure. "Well, perhaps I do have time for a quick chat," Jason reconsidered.

As he approached, the man turned, his eyes lighting up. "Mr. Cummings?"

Jason grinned reflexively. "Please, call me Jason. And you're Estevão?" The man extended his hand and Jason took it, feeling delightfully smooth skin.

"You can call me 'Steve' if it's easier for you."

Jason considered the name and how it rolled off the man's tongue in that delightful way Latin speakers had, making every word sound like dessert. He replied, "Estevão will do just fine. Is it Spanish?"

"Portuguese. I'm from Brazil. Let's sit down." He gestured to the two empty bar stools next to him.

"By all means," Jason agreed as he hiked a hip up on the seat.

Estevão slid closer, Jason getting a whiff of his aftershave. "It's so loud with the crowds and the music, I hope you don't mind." After a shake of his head Jason ran his hand through his moussed locks, letting them fall gently back into their careful coif. In the process he was admiring the lovely green flecks in Estevão's brown eyes.

"The Captain asked me to assist you with your work. She thought it might be a good time to begin showing the passengers some of your film." Jason looked at him, confused. "From your drone?" he clarified.

Jason chirped back, "Yes, of course. Ah, I haven't gotten any of the footage yet. I had to wait for the party to liven up a bit, you know? But," he explained as he ran his eyes over the crowd, "I would say things are more suitable now." He gave Estevão a toothy smile. Jason had always prided himself on his big, white smile and its ability to win people over. It gave him that delectable combination of Calvin Klein model and Ward Cleaver, desirable yet trustworthy.

Estevão responded with a wink, before adding, "I'd be happy to offer you my services." Clearly the smile had done its work, yet again.

"So tell me," Jason began, leaning back and letting the breeze catch the open collar of his peach button up, his hairless chest flashing in and out of sight. "Is drone-flying part of the Steward Specialist job description?"

Estevão said with a slightly crooked grin, "I was originally hired as a tech specialist for the cruise line to assist passengers with using our WIFI or correcting problems with our digital services. However, during training the Morrows promoted me to Steward

Specialist once they could see how good I was with the customers." He gave a subtle flex.

"I can already tell," Jason agreed. "Well, let's get started." He rubbed his hands together, offering Estevão a quick glimpse of his own flex, then popped off the bar stool. "Why don't you carry the laptop and I'll get the drone. And by the way, I'm counting on you to get us a location where we can get a good view of everyone, without being interrupted." Then he explained, "You know what I mean, don't you? So people can't break the fourth wall?"

Estevão took hold of the laptop with a knowing nod. "I think I know just the spot."

As the two carried the equipment up some steps, Jason thought back to the incident with the radio, and was reminded that he still needed to speak with the Captain, so he asked, doing his best to sound casual, "Tell me, Estevão, do you know where the Captain is?"

"No. I spoke with her by radio about thirty minutes ago. Why?"

Taking a moment to craft his answer, he responded, "I want to get a few shots of her and the First Mate. The footage just wouldn't be complete without it."

His eyes twinkling, Estevão nodded. "Ah, yes. We definitely don't want to miss an opportunity to get some good shots of Chambers."

Jason, throwing him an approving glance, said, "You know, Estevão, we're going to get along just fine."

They found a location suitable for launch with Estevão using his security card to get them into a restricted area clear of passengers. Jason took in a deep breath and said, "Conditions are ideal: a calm wind, a bright sun, and the drone buzzing right along with the passengers!"

Sitting next to Estevão so he could see the laptop screen, Jason first had the drone do a general swoop of the partiers as he oriented himself to the controls and began hovering over particular groups. They could hear conversations and laughter as an old John Mayer favorite played in the background.

"It's going to take some work to find 'bodies that are wonderlands' on this ship," Estevão joked.

"True, besides the obvious," Jason suggested with a sparkle in his eyes.

"Wait, are you seeing this?" Estevão motioned with a nod toward the screen just as Jason zoomed in on a group beside the bar. The pair erupted in laughter at the sight.

"Are they twerking?" Jason giggled.

"Mmmmm," Estevão hesitated, "I would guess that's what they think they're doing, but I don't believe they'll be starring in a rap video anytime soon." Laughing, the two locked eyes, then Estevão said excitedly, "That's what we should do! Turn this film into a rap video! I'm sure the Captain would love it!" he said, tongue in cheek. "We might change the demographic for future cruises, that's for sure. It could start a whole revolution."

Jason, his imagination running wild, could see it now, his legendary footage cleverly edited and circulating the internet. The 'High' in The High Cotton's name taking on a whole new meaning. Yes, he could start such a thing. And his twitter base would eat it up. But would *he* benefit from it as much as the gripping footage of a ship stalled at sea, passengers panicked, sacrifices made---oh, the potential for drama was there. And with that, he realized the drone definitely needded to capture that story, not one of silliness and twerking from a population that thought hip shaking to the Bee Gees was scandalous. No, that had been done by America's Funniest Home Videos hundreds of times. It should be video that told a harrowing story of a ship stalled at sea, tensions mounting, a female captain struggling to be a decisive but comforting leader while innocents feared for their lives. That's the essence. It's the scenario that journalists dream about, and he had exclusive access! This could be his Pulitzer unfolding before his very eyes. He needed to focus!

Jason smirked and turned the drone to face them. A few seconds later he suggested, "Let's see what's happening below." He moved the drone to another deck. He did his best to seem nonchalant, but could feel the edge to his voice. The pressure and excitement were getting to him, but he couldn't let Estevão in on the plan. He needed to keep Estevão's guard down. He could be helpful if he wasn't asking questions.

"Oh look there!" Estevão cackled, "That old guy's out at the pool deck with his robe on! Who does he think he is, Heff?"

Jason reluctantly headed the drone in that direction, his eyes scanning the crowded deck for a sign of the Captain. He needed to know what she was doing, and he needed footage of her, preferably with Chambers glowing by her side, perhaps with his brow furrowed in that sexy but concerned manner of his. Then his attention snapped back to the deck where there was a flash of white. Could it be? Yes, the Captain moving through the crowd! Jason reversed the drone's course to follow her. She was walking up to a member of the crew, Dawkins.

"Wait you're missing it!" Estevão looked at him incredulously. "I think he even has on a chain! We can get footage of the crew later." Just then the Captain began speaking with Dawkins and it was clear from their demeanors that it wasn't about pleasantries.

"Hang on!" Jason shushed, feeling a vein on his forehead begin to throb. "I want to capture this. I need to get where I can pick up the audio too. Quickly!" he emphasized, "Maybe they'll say something funny about the passengers partying" he pretended.

He could tell by Estevão's face this explanation satisfied him, but barely, which was good, because any more tension and Jason's pulsing vein might obstruct his vision. He began to wonder if Botox would help, when Estevão volunteered, "That's the Head Steward, I wonder if she's giving him new orders."

"Why do you think that?"

"Just that look on his face. It's the same one he gives us when we've got a crap job coming our way."

"Well, let's hope it's something dramatic." Jason zoomed in as close as he could without risking the pair hearing the hum of the propellers. He suddenly wished he'd spent the $400 extra to get the model that was nearly silent, but at the time he only intended to use the drone for some interesting aerial footage of his trips, not for sleuthing.

He heard the Captain say, "Begin moving them in fifteen minutes."

Dawkins replied back, "Captain, I've never dealt with anything like this. I don't know what to tell them." She put her hand on his arm. "This is only a precaution. Don't tell them anything but to come in. We absolutely don't want any panic."

Jason watched with mesmerized fascination. The fact that the Captain even suggested that the passengers could be panicked was a new development. Panic wouldn't set in from a mere reboot of the propellers. Something else was going on. And certainly no computer issue would require people to come inside. You make people come inside because of terrible weather to prevent injury or being tossed overboard. That wasn't the case here. There wasn't a cloud in the sky and the ocean was eerily calm. So without there being danger from the weather, why did people need to come in?

He heard Estevão stir slightly as his radio buzzed. He answered, "Estevão here," then paused and said, "I'm with Mr. Cummings right now, Captain's orders." A frown furrowed his brow. "Oh, I see. All right, I'm on my way."

"Estevão? You're looking like Dawkins down there. What's happening? You know you can tell me. Captain has me in her inner circle."

He rose, gently placing the laptop on the ground. "The Captain is ordering another drill. I need to report now." He walked briskly to the stairwell door, glanced back with a regretful smile then was gone, the door closing with a sturdy click.

Jason's mind was racing, trying to determine how he could learn more about what was happening and why the ship was having a spur of the moment drill. He looked at the drone, then launched it again, moving it from deck to deck, surveying the crowds and particularly focusing on staff. More and more stewards, bartenders, kitchen crew and others began lining the perimeters of the decks. Then the Captain's voice came over the intercom.

"Attention, everyone! This is your Captain speaking. For the next phase of our stop, we will need everyone to come inside the ship to the common areas. We are preparing some entertainment for your viewing pleasure. Happy Hour will continue at the bars *inside the ship*, and there will be door prizes for those who get in first! I repeat, everyone must come inside the ship to common areas immediately."

From his perch high above the passenger decks, Jason's drone continued watching crowds. It wasn't long before everyone was gone, not a passenger in sight. It became so quiet he could hear the hum of the drone as he brought it closer, then landed it. He stood up, looking around, then turning so his eyes could scan the sea. "What is she up to?" he muttered.

The lowering sun was keen on his blue eyes. He began searching for his sunglasses, finally finding them in the laptop case. After putting them on he looked again. The glare removed, he said, "Ahah!" For the first time in two days he saw another vessel. Still a good distance from the ship, he guessed it was some type of fishing boat.

"Well, isn't this interesting," he said out loud as he tapped the drone controls with his fingers.

*   *   *

Padma had just returned and was standing outside the navigation room, radio in hand, giving orders to staff and watching the passengers below. Chambers was still in the midst, making sure the 'drill' was properly executed. He radioed Padma. "We're ready, Captain. Everyone is in position."

"All right, Chambers. I'll make the announcement now. Remain on deck in case there are problems." She looked again to see the happy revelers, dancing and playing games. It looked like the most fun they'd had since the cruise began. It was so frustrating! First the propeller problems and now this. The maiden voyage seemed doomed. Then she corrected herself. Bad luck to use that word. If any vessel was doomed it was Durango. The High Cotton would come out of this safe and sound. It had to. She thought about the stricken face of the IT man when she told him about the possibility of impending disaster. His hands began shaking as he rushed to do his work. He hadn't answered her question of whether or not at least one propeller could be put into action to move the ship out of Durango's path. He only looked at her and shook his head. She and the Chief Engineer had met with Carl to see if the propellers could be made to operate on a manual switch. He said he could do it, but it would take time since the switch would have to be rewired. Resignedly, she got on the intercom and ordered the passengers inside.

Finished with the announcement, she sighed. Then she raised her chin and decided *she* would not allow Durango to strike them! At ten knots it would kill hundreds and possibly cause the High Cotton to capsize. After she put the SOS call out she began planning, beginning with assessing the readiness of the lifeboats. All medical personnel had been briefed, and staff had determined which passengers worked in the medical field, then gathered them together in a secluded area ready to be utilized, though none were told why for fear word would leak out. And thank God Cummings didn't know! That's all they needed, one of his tweets causing mayhem.

Her mind continued to go down her checklist. The Chief Engineer adjusted the ship's ballast, as well put into place twenty or so other technical adjustments to mitigate possible damage from Durango as much as possible. All first aid equipment was moved to a central location for easy dispatch, while staff accumulated spare linens and other items that could be used for medical triage. Passengers were to be placed in common areas towards the bow, as the stern would be facing Durango *if* the shrimpers were able to turn the High Cotton. She had spoken to the Morrows, the High Cotton's owners, by phone to keep them abreast. They, in turn, were in contact with the Chief Engineer after rushing together a team of experts to make recommendations for the best possible outcome. Lastly, she was in contact with the Coast Guard, but a lot of help they would be, arriving nearly thirty minutes after the potential impact. Beyond that, it was in God's hands and her seamanship.

God... she pondered. They needed His help, or their help. She was raised in a strict Indian family as a Hindu. Did she still believe? She thought about the phone call she had before the High Cotton left Charleston. It was her younger brother, Raj. She was elated to hear his voice. He was fourteen the last time she spoke to him. How she had missed their time together! Being estranged from her family, especially her brother, had been agony.

When she refused to marry the man her parents had selected for her when she was just a child, they had shunned her and her decision to enlist in the Navy. It hadn't been a difficult choice to defy them. She would have died inside had she been forced to become a traditional Indian wife. Once she was in the Navy it seemed that time flew by so quickly she never had a chance to appreciate the consequences of her telling them that the wedding was off. No wedding meant that she could no longer to talk to her mother, joke with her little brother or confide in her father. She hoped her parents would forgive her after a suitable amount of time and her mother had been able to convince her father that Padma should be admitted back into the family fold. But she had underestimated her father's obstinance, and if she were being honest, her mother was probably being as hard on her as her father was.

Her grandmother's death was her last hope of unification. Then, she was shunned from the funeral, as well. Not being able to return to India with the family for her grandmother's memorial had been agonizing, but she was powerless to do anything to change it, and she didn't dare shame her parents by showing up unannounced.

When she earned the rank of Captain it was the proudest day of her life, but without her family to share her joy, the victory was hollow. Once she resigned her commission the pain burrowed deeper. She had reached out to her mother, but was rebuffed with the tearful explanation of, "You must beg your father for his forgiveness!" Padma had written to him, then tried to call, to no avail. He refused contact with her. All the sadder was that her parents were the ones who had shunned her, not her brother, and they had so cruelly kept him from contacting her. Then out of the blue, the phone call came. It was the happiest day she'd had she since she left home all those years ago. She remembered every word of the conversation.

"It's me! Raj!" she heard a young man's voice say.

"Raj! I can't believe it! How are you?"

"I'm well. I'm so proud that my older sister is the Captain of such a luxurious cruise ship."

"Oh, yes. Well, wish me luck on our first voyage. We depart in two days." Her heart was skipping beats to hear his voice, the voice of a man now.

"I'm going to book a suite on the High Cotton for my honeymoon," he told her.

"You're getting married? Oh, Raj, that's so wonderful! I'm sure Pari will be a good wife. I know our parents spent a great deal of time selecting her. I remember it well even though I was a little girl."

"No, Padma. I'm not marrying Pari. I'm marrying someone else, a girl I met when I was in medical school. Sally. Her name is Sally MacGyver. I've told her all about you and she can't wait to meet you."

She heard the shock in her voice. "Sally. I would very much like to meet her. But dear Raj, I suppose your decision has meant that now both of us no longer have our family."

"I have not been shunned, Padma! I think that since you laid the groundwork it was much easier for me. Our parents have accepted Sally. I believe they even like her."

"Really?" She was astounded, and for some reason, hurt. Her parents had given in so easily to Raj's defiance, whereas she has suffered for so many years. Then she shook it off. She was too happy to have this contact with her brother to think of such a petty thing. "This is great news, Raj. Will they attend the wedding?"

"Of course. It's in September. Sally's parents are from Charleston. They live in one of those beautiful homes on the Battery. Her family has a very illustrious Southern history, and believe me, Padma, getting them to accept ME, a brown man, was more difficult than convincing our parents. In the end, however, love prevailed, I'm happy to say. Though being a doctor didn't hurt," he laughed.

"And, will our Mother and Father allow me to be there? It would make me so happy, but I don't want to embarrass you or Sally by being a spectacle."

"I insist that you be there, and I'm working on Mother and Father, Padma. I know I can get mother onboard. Father is taking a little work, but I feel confident that it will work out."

She began crying. "I'm sorry, Raj. I don't mean to ruin your good news."

"Padma," he said gently, "I know you've been through so much." Then more cheerfully, he added, "Listen, I want us to get together when you return to Charleston. Call me, okay? I'll make plans to come down and we'll go out to dinner and have a good talk."

"I'd like that. I would like that so, so much." The call ended with her heart feeling like the big empty place inside her had become a little fuller.

Now with the High Cotton facing disaster, she was angry that something so absurd was standing in the way of her seeing Raj again. Some idiot cargo ship captain without proper training had gone on a bender and passed out at the wheel, or some ridiculous accident had caused Durango's crew to become incapacitated, surely because of stupidity and incompetence. Her anger and bitterness at her father, suppressed all these years, had found a target at last.

She had done her best to empathize with her father. He was raised in a strict Indian household. It was just the way things were done; rules were to be followed or risk bringing shame to the entire family. Cultural tradition was prided in a world quickly changing in every other way.

She wasn't the first Indian American girl to be treated this way. And yet it was expected that she would always do her parents' bidding. Her father believed he was preserving tradition, the way things have been done for as far back as all generations of Hindu Indians could remember. In his eyes, who was she to question marrying the man her family had so carefully picked for her, following in the line of generations of successful unions before hers? It's highly possible Padma's decision had cost her family a great deal of money to put things right. After all, the young man had planned all of his life to marry Padma, to provide for her and her family, should it become necessary. But Padma had always longed for someone who would consider her dreams, her desires to be successful in a career, and respected for who she was, not who she was with.

As she considered these things her eyes traveled across the sea, and much to her anxious anticipation, spotted something in the distance. She raised the binoculars. A minute later she was filled with relief to see a shrimp boat making its way across the water. It didn't look like much, she thought to herself, but it's here.

Chapter 26

Lest We Be Seen

Jin woke up to a sun glowing like a comet through the porthole window. He felt a surge of relief and clambered out of bed, thrilled that the damned rain was finally gone.

For the first time since being on the ship, he took care while dressing, buttoning up a crisp white shirt and skillfully inserting his cufflinks. Whistling while he made coffee, he ate the last rice cake with a few dried dates. It wasn't just the end of the dreary weather; it was his designer attire that lifted his heart. Today he would leave Durango and return to civilization.

With coffee cup in hand, he stepped into the navigation room to see Kwon staring at the radar. Walking over, he asked, "What do you see?" Kwon turned to him. The wound on his face had healed to a syrupy scab that was so repugnant Jin had to look back at the screen.

"A ship. It's ahead of us, on the same course."

The blip on the radar pinged next to the ship's name. "The High Cotton," he muttered. "You have the radio turned off?"

"Yes, I did that last night."

"So, with that much distance between us it's nothing to be concerned about, right?"

Kwon shrugged. "It's something to watch. I don't want them to get a visual of Durango."

"And what about the AIS?"

"AIS? Oh, right, the Automatic Identification System. Ah, yes," he stammered, "It's off."

"You didn't fucking have it off?" Jin seethed as he watched Kwon's hand reach for the AIS switch, adjusting it to the off position. "If we can see who their ship is, they can see ours! You idiot!" He swatted Kwon's hand away. "Don't turn it off now, it's too late. Not only that, we have to keep it on now so our escape boat can find us." He shook his head. "We have no choice but to keep our distance and hope they move on."

Jin walked back into the salon to get more coffee. Kwon's incompetence once again had caused him problems. He considered how he would have been so much better off doing this mission alone. His anger simmered.

Kwon called out just before Jin was out of earshot, "I haven't slept in two days, Jin. I made one small mistake."

Jin looked back and hissed, "If you needed rest you should have said so. Thanks to this fuck-up, somebody aside from the escape boat knows the ship's name, and they're tracking us." He strode back into the navigation room, running his hand impatiently through his gelled hair.

"Tracking us?" Kwon parroted.

"My God, did they teach you nothing at that so called Captain's School? Of course they're tracking us! Whoever is manning that vessel is watching to see if we get too close." Jin's body shook with rage as he searched for something to wipe the sticky gel off, attempting to rub it on Kwon's sleeve before Kwon jerked his arm away.

"There's no need to worry. They'll move out of our way."

"You had better hope so, Kwon, because we're about to leave Durango."

"Hah! You forget we can control her with the laptop."

"Only up to three kilometers, dumbass!"

"It will be enough to move Durango if we see she's too close."

"And how will we know that?"

"We can check the radar."

"On somebody else's yacht? It's a cabin cruiser with other people onboard. We can't go up to the Captain and say, 'By the way, I need to check your radar.' Not only that, we'll be moving quickly out of range."

"Nevertheless, this is a flaw in the mission. The technicians should have installed a radar in the laptop. Not my fault."

"Not your fault? It wouldn't have been necessary if you weren't such an idiot!"

"How was I to expect this? Besides, it's like I said. They will move."

"Expect this? It's the open ocean! That's why we sent you for training, to make sure we avoided other ships in the water! This *is* a shipping lane, right? We needed a captain to make sure we went unnoticed! Not so that we would barrel up behind a bunch of yuppie vacationers. It's astounding, like you took a stupid pill!"

"I'm tired, and I told you it will be fine. Maybe *you* need to take a 'chill' pill."

"So go the hell to bed! We will see who needs the chill pill when you explain yourself to The Great One."

"Back off, Jin! I've been carrying the workload while you get your beauty rest."

"Those are the roles we signed up for, Kwon. I've got the looks and you actually look like shit."

"If I wasn't so exhausted I'd teach you and your disrespectful mouth a lesson, Jin, one you'd never forget," he said, inches from Jin's face, his breath wafting over Jin like mustard gas.

Grimacing, Jin retorted, "When's the last time you brushed your teeth?" Kwon cursed then went into the salon, flopping onto his cot so hard Jin wondered how it managed to remain standing. Not thirty seconds later he heard the roar of Kwon's snoring.

Sunglasses on, Jin walked outside, his heart still pounding with frustration at Kwon's flippancy. Of all the impossible hurdles that had been crossed to get to this point, how could he let something so small risk it all? It was just not that hard to keep your distance from another boat in open water. It was comically easy, and yet Kwon had managed to mess it up. Kwon would never have Jin's meticulous dedication, let alone his brains. With that thought, he began to walk around the deck to stretch his legs and calm down.

As he regained his composure, he let his mind wander to admire a sky so blue it almost hurt to look at it. The calm sea reminded him of a lake in Switzerland he visited last year. The corners of his mouth turned up, thinking how he wanted to return to the Alps as soon as he could. Switzerland was one of his favorite places, along with the Riviera and Kuwait. There he could mingle among the jet setters and feel perfectly at home. *My people*, he considered to himself. Unhooking a deck chair secured to the wall, he sat down and sipped his coffee. He unbuttoned a few buttons of his shirt, thinking that he could work on his tan for a while.

Hearing only the sound of the wake as Durango lumbered through the water, Jin thought about their escape boat, a large yacht that can accommodate a crew of four, including a trained chef, and up to ten passengers. By the time Durango reached Charleston harbor and arrived with a bang, the yacht should be as far as the Bahamas and on its way to Turks and Caicos.

According to his research---to verify what he was told back home, radioactive fallout wouldn't reach that far unless there were high winds, which were not forecast. By the look of the water today, there was seemingly an absence of wind altogether.

Then a thought struck him. He wondered if he should ask the yacht's captain to drop him off in Nassau and let Kwon go on to Turks and Caicos. From Nassau, Jin could get a flight to Europe, be away from

Kwon, and enjoy a few well deserved luxuries. Both men had been instructed not to make contact with The Great One for thirty days. Jin planned on taking full advantage of his free time.

He dozed contentedly then returned to the navigation room to check on Durango, which was continuing on course to the coordinates where they would meet the escape boat. Then he glanced at the radar. He flinched slightly. Were they closer to that ship? Before he had a chance to investigate, he saw another boat and recognized its name. He switched the radio on and immediately heard a man's voice.

"Come in Durango. This is Sea Frolic, over."

Jin grabbed the microphone. "This is Durango, Sea Frolic."

"Durango!" the man said. "We've been trying to reach you for over an hour! We're scheduled to take aboard two of your crewmen this afternoon, the brothers John and Harry Chen."

"Yes, we are aware of that arrangement and are on our way to your pick-up location."

"Excellent. I wanted to confirm this since it's, well, a little out of the ordinary. Are you the ship's captain?"

"Yes, I am. I'm... "Jin looked up to read the name Kwon had on his Captain's license posted above. "Captain Gorchev."

"Captain Gorchev, do you want Sea Frolic to pull alongside your hatch door?"

"Yes. That's right. It's located on our starboard side."

"And Durango will be anchored? We can't possibly have someone attempt to board from a moving ship."

"Durango will be stationary, yes. And we're so fortunate to have a calm sea today, are we not?"

Durango would not be anchored, but it would be stopped. They would not anchor because it would prevent their resuming Durango's journey by using the laptop once aboard Sea Frolic.

"Most fortunate indeed. Please tell the Chen brothers to be ready to board at approximately fourteen hundred hours. We are running on schedule."

"I'll certainly do that, Sea Frolic. Over." Setting the microphone down, Jin heard a sound behind him and turned to see a bleary-eyed Kwon scratching himself.

"Enjoy your nap?" Jin asked mockingly.

"Who were you talking to?"

"The yacht that's picking us up. They plan on pulling alongside at the hatch door. Did you rig up that screen? We can't risk them seeing anything."

"Yes, I did it," Kwon answered irritably. "But Jin, you should have let me talk to them since I'm Durango's Captain."

"If they had talked to you they would have realized they were speaking to an imbecile, and probably wouldn't come as a result."

"I'm sick of your insults, Jin. It has to stop. We cannot board this yacht with you speaking to me so disrespectfully."

"We're posing as Chinese brothers. Brothers like to bicker. I see no problem."

"Well, brothers fight too. But I don't think you want that."

Jin sneered, "Get yourself cleaned up. You're an embarrassment."

"And another thing---just so there's no misunderstanding, I'll be operating the laptop."

Jin snorted, "Clearly, you're kidding. I'm leading this mission, so I'm taking responsibility for the laptop. In fact, I've already packed it. The plan is this: you talk to our fellow passengers and the Sea Frolic's staff to keep them occupied while I go to our cabin and get Durango moving again towards Charleston."

"As Captain of Durango, the laptop is my responsibility."

"No, Kwon, you need to follow orders, and go take a shower. You smell."

"Fuck you, Jin! I'll find the laptop! I know you've got it in your briefcase along with your usual stash of money. I'm taking all of it this time!"

He began storming around the navigation room to make a frantic search, yanking cabinet doors open and pulling on drawers. He ran his hands along the tops of the soffits then on the floor to see if there was a hiding place. Jin smirked as he watched his futile efforts.

"Where is it?" Kwon demanded. Jin's response was to lean against the doorframe and cross his arms. Kwon pushed him out of his way and entered the salon.

Jin followed and said, "Quit wasting time, Kwon. You're acting like a little girl not getting her way."

Kwon's eyes surveyed the salon, not seeing anything that belonged to Jin. He moved to Jin's bedroom and jerked the vinyl curtain back. All he found was the bed tidily made up. He turned around and faced Jin with a savage look, his unkempt hair sticking out over his right ear like a bull's horn.

Jin chortled, "I'm going back on deck for a cigarette. By all means, continue your searching."

Kwon hesitated, momentarily weighing his options before following Jin on deck. It would be just like him to hide it in plain sight. Kwon lurched through the doorway nearly knocking Jin over.

Jin laughed and said, "You're pathetic, Kwon. Not even worthy of your own number." Kwon stopped and turned around, and looked at him questioningly. Jin, seeing that Kwon had responded exactly the way he wanted, shook his head with mirth and said, "That's right. Your tattoo. I saw it when I gave you first aid. Just thought you'd like to know that thirty-three is my number." Jin's expression changed to contempt. "The Great One didn't even bother to give you your own! You're not even worth the effort to think up a new one. You're thirty-three, because you're an extension of me, always under my guidance." He inhaled deeply on the Marlboro, then blew the smoke towards Kwon. "In other words, you're nothing."

Kwon narrowed his eyes and stood there, fists clenched. His body quivering in anticipation of attack. He said in a low, raspy voice. "After I find the briefcase, Jin. I'll be killing you. There will be only one person who's thirty-three then. That was the plan all along." Now it was Kwon's turn to smile.

Jin flicked his ashes. "We'll see."

He hardly recognized his own voice, as his heart was pounding in his ears. Once Kwon resumed his search for the briefcase, now walking rather than running from place to place like a pinball machine, Jin's expression shifted to uncontrolled hatred. It was time to be rid of Kwon. His hand moved to the leather sheath, feeling the reassurance of the knife.

It went on for several more minutes, his pointless, absurd search. Disgusted by the waste of time, Jin considered how Kwon was not clever enough to find the briefcase and he should know it and stop his blundering attempt. Kwon was such a fool he would never know that Jin employed his fail-safe. He had cut the little yellow wire on the bomb's belly. The timer was off.

Suddenly the ridiculousness of it all overwhelmed Jin like a delayed jolt of anger from Kwon's comment that killing him---Jin---*was* 'the plan all along.' Everything Kwon did was a joke. Surely The Great One could see that. And to top it off, this pathetic search would likely last through the time Kwon needed to make himself presentable, forcing Jin to once again be embarrassed and ashamed to be associated with such incompetence and filth. And yet, without allowing himself to dwell on the impossible idea now, in the back of his mind he believed there could be a kernel of truth in what Kwon said, that he was Jin's successor, the next thirty-three. His anger continued to build, outraged with Kwon, indignant over The Great One's disrespect that he was placed in such an untenable position after years of dedicated work.

The sun was hot, burning his skin. He could feel his blood pressure rising, his veins pulsing and pressing against his flesh. Sweat was tracing the lines of his muscles, and with each heartbeat his pores secreted more. Drip, drip, drip. Perspiration trickled into the creases in his face from his brow to his temples and reaching the corners of his eyes, each salty blink painful.

His hands wouldn't wipe the dampness away. They remained clenched by his sides while the frantic tempo of his anger rose. His vision blurred. He did his best to concentrate what focus he had on Kwon, though he could only discern what was immediately in front of him, the fuzzy shapes of the cargo gear and masts. Then something came closer and stopped to raise what must be a hatch cover, the metal screeching. Jin moved around the cargo crane, Kwon's large back facing him.

The knife was cool in his steaming, sweaty hand. He felt it click open and the jerk of the blade ejecting. Blinking over and over to clear his eyes, his legs moved him silently around a bulkhead. Closer now, his vision sharpened briefly, long enough to discover that it wasn't Kwon he was seeing.

It was his uncle, the uncle who lived next door to young Jin and his mother. It was uncle's apartment where Jin had to go whenever his mother had male company. Jin did just as he was trained. When a man arrived his mother would play her music and dance, but when the music stopped it was his cue to leave. Always dutiful, Jin obeyed, though he hated his uncle, a pock-faced man who smelled of rotten kimchee and foul body odor.

Jin's nose pricked as he inhaled the putrid stench. He made Jin stay inside a cramped, pitch-black closet. Jin had nowhere to sit but on his uncle's dirty clothes. The fumes were so sickening that the first time his uncle locked him in, Jin beat his fists on the door and cried to be let out. All he got for his troubles were a bruised lip and sore ribs. So during his stays after that, to distract himself from the misery, he dreamed of his mother's favorite music, the Bee Gees, and her laugh while she sang along and moved her body to the disco's rhythm.

Those rhythms flowed through his body now, and with the music, he drifted along, floating with the tunes until he realized he didn't know where he was anymore. Anxious, he looked from left to right to reorient himself. Stepping sideways he bumped into a cargo derrick. His hands, still damp and sticky from sweat, gripped the railing, sliding along the metal to make his way forward. He heard a sound, a scraping. He quickly turned to search for Kwon.

Then he was at the end of the deck, glare from the sun reflecting off the water, blinding Jin again. His left hand in pain, he rolled his fist over and raised it close to his face to discover his knuckles scraped and gleaming crimson. He still held the knife in his other hand, warm with the sensation of liquid all around it.

He heard something. A voice. Kwon's? No, it was a soft, sweet sound. His mother calling him. "Come to me, Jin," she said, and in her lilting soprano, she began humming a song he remembered from so long ago. He followed the singing, his feet moving confidently, yet his eyes saw nothing.

"Umma?" he called. "Where are you?"

"I'm here, Jin. Waiting for you."

"Umma. Oh, how I've missed you all of these years." He found her, his arms extended to welcome her embrace. The knife released from his hand, and he heard it clink below him before he collapsed, his fingers touching not the soft skin of his mother, but the cold steel of the deck. Before the blackness completely overtook him, his hot face felt the chill of the floor before being greeted by a thick, warm puddle.

Chapter 27

One More Time

Feeling an unsettlingly gentle wind brushing his cheeks, Nick stood at Esmerelda's helm, steering her towards essentially what he felt was a suicide mission. His eyes met the sea; his fingers gripped the wheel, and he breathed in the familiar shrimp boat smells. Yet, somehow everything at that moment felt unreal, like an out of body experience. His actions were accomplishing what needed to be done, but without his thoughts actually guiding them. He was somewhere else, reflecting on how out of his comfort zone he was at that moment. In fact, the entire boat ride today had been out of his comfort zone.

Nick was someone who prided himself in having a life that stayed on an even keel. Liking consistency, he wasn't like Trevor, an adrenaline junky. He was happy to live inside the lines. However, lately everything was taking him away from his usual patterns, patterns he had been following for so long they had become predictable grooves. He liked his grooves. He didn't have to think too hard about things, at least not until now.

He was an open book to anyone he met. Honest to a fault, Nick couldn't lie about anything. He didn't need to. And because he kept his life as simple as possible, he didn't have to delve deeply to know exactly who he was. He was right there on the surface, what you see is what you get.

Then there's Trevor... Trevor had always been one for change. It flows behind him like the wake behind a boat. He can't help it. He finds a way to save everyone around him. His first year of summer camp, Trevor pulled a kid out of the lake before he drowned. Going hiking with a friend a year later, he found an elderly man lost in the woods. He has that right-place-right time fortitude that Nick never had. Trevor was destined to be a hero if anyone ever was.

Nick was tall and lean, but Trevor was built like a Greek god, with muscle clinging to his body effortlessly. He was every older brother's nightmare, because he could outmuscle Nick since he was fourteen. Surprisingly, that was okay with Nick; he had never needed to be the one with the glory, and Trevor reveled in it.

Nick began trying to remember when the unsettling changes began, when everything was jolted out of the easy patterns.

He recalled his little girl's fifth birthday party six months ago, how it was interrupted with that phone call every military family dreads. When he heard the official voice on the line, the happy sounds of the party and all of the rest of his world stopped.

The military official said he needed confirmation of who Nick was. Nick answered while nearly falling into a chair. He swallowed, his heartbeat pounding in his ears, and managed to ask, "Is he dead?"

He doesn't know what he heard after that, except that Nick made the man say twice that Trevor was alive. Then all he recalls is telling Ray, Jenny, his mother and his wife that he needed to go, packing his rucksack and hurrying to the airport.

When Trevor signed up he knew what *he* was agreeing to. He accepted the terms. But Nick was never asked. He never agreed to have his brother enlist and to have his brother constantly in danger and as a result, leaving Nick with constant worry in the back of his mind.

With Nick being ten years older than his little brother and their father dying when Trevor was only twelve, Nick sometimes had to take on the role of parent. With it came the anxieties every parent has. As a result, once Trevor signed up to be a SEAL, Nick feared that inevitable phone call.

He was anxious about it as soon as Trevor began training. He'd heard how recruits could be injured or killed because SEAL training was so brutal, and that was why so few made it to the end. Knowing it could happen, Nick tried to prepare himself, convince himself and everyone around him that he was cool about it. But in his heart it seemed impossible that his brother could survive the things he had to do. Trevor was good, but he wasn't a cat with nine lives.

Someone didn't get to be a Navy SEAL, go where no one else can go, risk his life every minute while on duty, and not end up one day earning your family THE call. And so, there it was.

The Walter Reid staff had been so positive. They constantly used words like *great* and *progress* and *lucky to be alive*. What they didn't say and perhaps because they didn't know----was that the man lying in that hospital bed wasn't Trevor. Not his Trevor. His Trevor didn't get night sweats, didn't scan the room with his eyes every few seconds, and didn't jump at unfamiliar sounds.

His Trevor would have told him what happened, would have leaned on him for support, would have let him in. Nick still doesn't know what occurred that night, not really, and of course, he would never learn the official version, national security and all that crap. He didn't care about that. He wanted to hear about it from his brother. Nick needed to know what was taken from inside Trevor, taken from his soul, peeled away from him like his own skin.

Everyone told Nick, give him time. He'll come around. It hasn't happened. All these months later all Nick has learned from Trevor was that the mission went sour and a team member died. That, and Nick coming to the realization that Trevor really didn't want to tell his story.

Nick wished his brother wasn't so complicated. Why couldn't he be more like Ray? Ray and Nick were geared up alike. The two were hand and glove. Nick's thoughts then shifted to Ray's expression minutes ago, after he climbed aboard the High Cotton and turned around to give the Esmerelda one last look. Nick knew that Ray's heart was as heavy as his. Ray understood his pain at probably losing the boat and everything else with this hair-brained scheme.

Ray always knew what Nick was thinking. That was the beauty of working with someone for so long. You begin to have your own sort of relationship shorthand, where so much can be communicated without having to say a word. The two could spend hours together every day, saying little but getting so much done. Whenever Nick needed a hand with the nets or prepping something on deck, before he could utter a syllable, Ray would be there, and often he would be there before Nick realized he needed his help. Why was it that it was so easy with Ray but so hard with Trevor? When something was on his mind, he and Ray could talk about it, problem solved. With Trevor it was altogether different.

He and Trevor always communicated in high school, before Dad died. Before everything changed. Once they were on their own, Nick had taken on so much to keep the family afloat. Ray became the person who knew him and his struggles best, who appreciated the sacrifices Nick made. Ray knew the grind of shrimping. He knew that sandbag feeling climbing into your truck in the dock parking lot every evening, where it takes all you've got just to get home. Ray valued a life like Nick had built, a life like his dad and Ray had built together, lives they created on the Esmerelda: shrimping, struggling, sweating, and laughing.

Nick had planned for today to be his final voyage on the old girl, with Ray and Trevor by his side. Today was to be the trip that would end their career together, and have the Esmerelda finish with a profitable catch of tuna. It was supposed to feel good. Now here he was steering her to the bow of a cruise ship, ready to add one last job to her to-do list, about to ask the Esmerelda to give all she's got one last time.

The Esmeralda had saved him many times throughout his life. She was always there to sail off and guide him through wind and wake back to balance and restoration of his soul. Now he was asking her to save the lives of over a thousand people. But he knew what it meant. He knew this time he was asking too much. And he knew that she'd do it anyway.

Chapter 28

Escape

Slowly consciousness rolled over his body. From the darkness his mind gradually became brighter, as if it were on a dimmer switch. His eyes remained closed, his body motionless. It was a feeling of being between sleep and the edge of wakefulness.

He wanted to awaken, and yet he couldn't quite get there. He wondered if this peculiar state was due to the extent of his injuries. His body gradually began to register stiffness and pain along with the sensation of being bound, but he felt no ties on his wrists or ankles.

In the silence, he concentrated on raising his eyelids. Seemingly, they were stuck together. It was a strange sensation to have to tell himself to blink as hard as he could to pry the skin apart. Until it gave way, the world was a pale sheath lined in tiny blood vessels, reminding him of the fibers in paper. Slowly, and feeling crusty, his lids raised and vision was restored.

His immediate view was of crumbling red paint on a ruptured piece of metal that comprised one side of a bollard. Looking up as high as he could, which wasn't far, about knee-high, he was met with bright sun. To his left and right all he saw was more metal floor and red paint on rusty equipment. Finding that he could wriggle his fingers, he rubbed his nails across the floor, then tapped. The faint tone on the metal brought it all back to him, and he knew where he was. Durango.

His face hurt, his cheek resting on the floor burning, whereas the rest of his body was chilled as he remained prone on the cold metal. Mentally, he reviewed the events leading up to his blackout. A thin smile crossed his lips. Now unencumbered by the dead weight of his 'partner,' he was ready to complete the last phase of the mission according to plan. He laughed a little, thinking about the pun *dead weight*.

At last able to sit up, he got hold of a cargo chain and pulled himself to his feet, dizzy at first but intact. A deep breath gave him his balance and bearings, and he began to trudge to the navigation room.

Moving each arm, then his hands feeling around his torso and legs, he made an inventory of his body to determine where he might be hurt. Bruised all over, he discovered no broken bones and no open wounds even though he was covered in dried blood. Clearly, it wasn't his. His pace quickened after a glance at his watch told him he had only minutes before Sea Frolic's arrival. He had to clean up, and somehow stop the ship.

To do that, he maneuvered the throttle so that the gears went into neutral; then he put Durango into reverse to stop the forward momentum. The switch caused the engine to grind and shudder. It took nearly a full minute, feeling panicked that he had stripped the gears. Then it became quiet again as he felt the ship slowly backing up. At that point he moved her back into neutral.

He literally ripped his clothes off and stepped into the shower with the nozzle labeled 'hot' turned all the way and getting only a lukewarm spray. Begrudgingly, he began the process of cleansing himself and grumbled, "Why does blood have to be so damned sticky." His hair was so matted he squeezed what was left of a bottle of shampoo onto his gelatinous locks. The bloodied water dripped from his head, down his body and onto his feet before circling in a miniature pink cyclone around the drain. The skin on his wrists and hands required his fingernails to scrape off coagulated globules, chunks of it joining the swirls below. When the water ran clear he got out, rushing to dress.

Frantically searching for something to wear, he settled on a knit shirt and khaki pants. On impulse, he put on Beth's black glasses that he had days ago tossed on a shelf. "She won't be needing these anymore," he cynically mumbled. He wore no watch or jewelry. As he zipped up the luggage, he heard the blast of the Sea Frolic's horn. He ran with everything he had to reach the hold.

He could hear the hatch opening. Still running, he had nearly reached the door when his shoe sent something scattering across the floor: a small wire cutter. He stopped to look at it, then turned sideways, his fingers reaching over to touch the curtain surrounding the bomb. He cracked them open enough to squat down and see a lone yellow wire with a blunt end dangling from its belly. Ignoring it, he stood back up, quickly making the last few strides to the doorway. He found a middle aged, blondish man about to board. Beside the hatch on the floor, lay a soft briefcase with one corner of a laptop slightly revealed.

"I here!" he shouted in English to stop the man's progress, seeing him about to enter. He was faking a heavy Chinese accent. He grabbed the laptop bag, threw it over his shoulder in relief.

With a voice low-toned and smooth, and wearing a white uniform with gold and black epaulets indicating his rank, the man said, "Hope you don't mind. I hollered, and when you didn't answer it looked like I was going to have to come looking for you. I'm Captain Stewart." With his cap pushed back on his head, the Captain struck a pose with one foot on the cabin cruiser's railing.

"No problem," he answered, handing his suitcase to the Captain so he could immediately board.

The man assisted him with the crossover and said, "Where's your brother?"

He sputtered an uncomfortable laugh. "My brother no coming. Don't worry, no need refund. I am John, Captain." He gave the Captain a little bow.

"Very nice to meet you, John. I'm sorry to hear about your brother. Is everything alright?"

"Oh, yes. He change mind. He fine."

There was an awkward pause before the Captain said, "Do we need to close this hatch? Or is someone coming to assist?" He leaned over to peer inside.

"Yes, Captain, you close. I thank you."

The Captain pulled the hatch closed, then said, "Well, John, I'm going to get us underway while one of my staff introduces you to the others."

The Captain's departure left a gap in a group of people that had gathered around the new arrival, regrettably preventing John Chen's escape to his quarters. He looked over the rim of the glasses to see faces that were all white and American.

A short, wispy woman spoke first. "I'm Taffy and this is my mother, Loretta." Taffy's black crow eyes seemed to engulf him. Her nose was small but beakish. Her incongruously thick lips were covered in blood-red lipstick. Her most striking attributes were her ample breasts, bulging out of a red striped bathing suit. The contrast of her thinness with her large chest was striking. She looked like she had tried the full menu at the cosmetic surgeon's office. Taking hold of his hand, she gave him a firm grip then a teasing squeeze.

Moving aside, her mother closed in, John Chen having to raise his eyes to take her all in. She too grasped his hand, but this time his left. Sausage like fingers caressed then stroked over his bare ring finger before vigorously squeezing his palm. If there was a genetic predisposition to Taffy being her daughter, he couldn't see it. The two couldn't have been more different. She said, "You married, Mr. Chen?"

"No, no marry." As soon as he said the words he winced, realizing his strategic error.

"Just ignore Loretta. She only wants to get her daughter married off. I'm Jim Gaines," a man offered, standing shirtless with white sunscreen on his nose and a Heineken in his hand. He raised the bottle in the general direction of his right side and said, "And this is my wife, Kaitlin. We're from Tennessee."

The group parted to give view to another woman, sitting in a lounge chair. She looked up and almost smiled with pale lips lacquered in something with a yellowish tinge that made her mouth look like a pencil. "I'm Glenda, from Atlanta. My husband, Ernie, is inside." She held an electronic cigarette, and sported a floppy hat and sunglasses that hid most of her face. She took a long drag and then resumed reading her novel.

"I'm Terry, from Omaha," another man said.

"And I'm Connie, Terry's wife," a woman in a bikini added, giving Terry a look of annoyance.

A staff member approached, a college-aged blonde looking tanned in a button-down shirt and matching white shorts. "Hello, Mr. Chen. My name is Josie and I'm a member of the Sea Frolic staff. Heard your brother isn't joining us after all. Such a shame."

"John," he said gesturing to himself, his head giving her a slight bow. "Brother, he change mind. You show me room?" he asked, pushing his glasses up on his nose.

"That's what I'm here for," she replied perkily. He gave the group a little nod goodbye then followed Josie across the deck and through a door that led to a salon paneled with polished wood and furnished with plush chairs and an upholstered sofa. A large television was tuned into a sports channel. A man with his back to them was watching.

"Hello, Ernie. This is John," Josie called out. Ernie's response was a wave, not taking his focus off the screen. She gave John Chen a roll of her eyes before they went up a half dozen steps that led to a hallway lined in more gleaming paneling. Josie stopped at the last of six doors and opened it with a key that she handed to him.

He entered a small room with a double bed lined with two rows of blue madras pillows sitting atop a plump spread. A brass sconce hung over an end table; the other wall held a low dresser. One window gave a view of the deck and the sea beyond. It was spartan, but attractive and in comparison to Durango it was the Ritz.

"Very nice," he stated.

"I'll let you freshen up. Dinner will be at seven. Cocktails and champagne are served all day long," she said with a giggle.

He looked up. "Nice champagne?"

"Sure, the best. Can I get you a glass?"

"Dom." was all he replied.

She gave him a quick up down with her eyes, then said, "Right away, Mr. Chen." Leaving, she closed the door behind her.

The irony of the Dom was not lost on him as he smirked to himself in the dresser mirror. He then went over and listened for sounds in the hallway and heard a man whistling as he passed by. Quietly, he turned the lock before going over to the window and pulling the little curtain across.

On the bed, where he had placed his bag, he got out the laptop. Within moments Durango resumed her journey. That done, he allowed himself a long sigh and put the laptop back in the bag and slid it under the bed just as he heard a knock.

"I have your Dom, Mr. Chen."

"Excellent," he said, opening the door and accepting the drink.

Chapter 29

In For A Penny...

Trevor watched as Ray, without hesitating, threw out the line to secure the Esmerelda. Never one to overthink a situation, Ray usually jumped in headfirst then considered what he had found. Like he did when Trevor's dad died. In the blink of an eye, he and Jenny took on two teenage boys rowdy with grief. He didn't overthink it; he just did right by them, as any father would have, and gave them hell for all the things he should have and let the other stuff go. He had the right touch, at least for Nick and Trevor, and he had held their respect from day one.

Today was the first day Trevor noticed that Ray's knit hair was only sprinkled with the black that once filled it, the gray now predominant. And as Ray climbed back from throwing the line, Trevor could see stiff knees and shoulders mindfully maneuvering back to level deck.

The calm water that had replaced the brief spell of whitecaps barely nudged the boat, something that most would take reassurance in, that the weather wasn't about to turn. To Trevor, however, the gentle bob and soft breeze were unnerving. He had always been suspicious of anything that seemed too good to be true, because in his experience, it always was. When a mission was going according to plan was when Trevor went on high alert. It never failed that something would go wrong.

Nothing in life goes according to plan, not easily anyway. His last mission was a sharp reminder of that. Everything began too smoothly. All was as they had expected. The first two guards were taken out without return fire. Every sequence executed as they had designed. When they were in the final phase of the plan, it was then Trevor felt that telltale pulse he got in his neck telling him that the unforeseen was about to strike, just like Murphy's law says. There was no calm before the storm, merely a storm hiding somewhere.

He pulled his attention back to the tall woman who had boarded Esmerelda. She had to be the Captain. Trevor considered what talent she must possess to have been given such a post. She was visibly of Indian descent, and Trevor had detected only the slightest of accents when she spoke. Her deliberate cadence and firm but not overbearing tone, Trevor assumed, had been crafted by years of practice.

As she explained the situation, he recognized her intelligence. She knew how to divulge alarming information in a way that kept the situation from escalating. As she described the approach of Durango, she was matter of fact. There was no drama in her delivery.

Trevor was all too familiar with this tactic. When you have to get civilians to do something urgently, particularly in a life threatening situation, you must devoid all drama from your direction. You impress importance and urgency without signs of duress and deemphasize the threat. When people are panicked they are dangerous and irrational. Her cleverness made him consider her background. This was someone with tactical training. Although it was unlikely she had experience anywhere near what he had, Trevor felt better knowing that the Captain had her wits about her, at least with handling this bizarre turn of events. He questioned how a new luxury cruise ship ends up adrift in the first place. The odds were... then again, perhaps up until now, things had been going a little too well.

As she continued clarifying information about the Esmerelda, it became clear to him what she had in mind. He considered what such a feat would mean for the shrimp boat and for Nick. At first, he couldn't believe how well Nick was taking it, but then he realized that Nick wasn't understanding what was being asked.

He watched the lines in the leathery skin of Nick's face shift as he began to recognize the true meaning of the request.

It was ironic that just hours earlier Trevor had learned how Nick and Ray had reached the end as far as shrimping goes. In the bright light of day he had seen a lot of things for the first time, such as the gray hair now sprouting from Nick's temples, deeper wrinkles in his weather worn face, and the droop in his clothes where muscle once bulged. For the first time he could see that his big brother wasn't exactly old but definitely getting older. But that wasn't the unsettling part. Even Trevor had gained the odd gray hair and the beginnings of crow's feet. What had aged Nick was different, more than just the slow turn of time.

He could see how Nick was worn down. Trevor, before today, had never appreciated the consequences of regulation-induced quotas and netting restrictions. He hadn't thought of the impact, and Nick never burdened him. Requirements for BRD's so that fish can escape and the TEDs for sea turtles to be freed before they drowned were good things, but they altered what used to be a decent living. Today he recognized that profits were squeezed tighter than Trevor could have guessed. There were too many shrimpers looking for fewer shrimp. More work, more stress, less money. But Nick never confided any of this. Not to him. Nick could never shed his role of strong, older brother.

Trevor's attention shifted to Ray, seeing Ray being Ray. Here's this Captain trying to get them to potentially save the lives of all the passengers on her ship, and he's calling crap on the Coast Guard. He watched as Ray responded with an eye roll to the Coast Guard's conveniently too late to be of any help arrival time. Then, adds *just in time to scrape us off the side of your ship like a flapjack*. Trevor's stomach tightened as he held in a chuckle.

That was Ray. Never one to mince words. He might have made us come over here to save these people, but that didn't mean he wouldn't give them a little hell about it first. Ray had a heart of gold. Then, at the thought of Ray's heart Trevor returned to worrying about his health. There was no doubt Ray had some form of a heart attack today. Maybe that was the moment when Trevor started to recognize what was really going on. He had been gone so long that he couldn't see that while his life had remained relatively the same, Nick and Ray's kept getting harder. The toll of the sea was apparent in them both.

The idea that Ray could have a bad heart was unbearable, and he could only imagine what it was doing to Nick. There would be no question that Ray would go aboard the cruise ship while they tackled this request. He hoped Ray would have the good sense to tell the Captain he had a heart scare and ask to get checked out by the ship's medical personnel, but then again, it's Ray---a mule would envy the man's stubbornness, and he wouldn't make himself the priority anyway. It just wasn't his nature. Trevor only hoped that he and Nick could resolve this desperate scheme quickly so they could look after Ray and make sure he gets the help he needed. He couldn't stomach the thought of losing a second father---or the idea of losing Nick either. And he didn't need help to maneuver the Esmerelda. He could easily swim to safety if anything went wrong, and could then scale back up the High Cotton to where he could board. This was no task Nick would be up to. He was sure of that. So the decision was made.

253

"I'll do it," Trevor stated. "Nick, you and Ray wait with the Captain on the High Cotton. I'm a strong swimmer. If it comes to it I'll jump ship before she's hit."

Trevor heard Nick release a tense sigh and he knew a protest was coming. "She's my boat. If she goes down I'm going with her---I want to know there was nothin' I could have done. I'm the one who's doing this."

Ray predictably added, "Well, you'll need every bit of my help."

Nick jinxed Trevor as they both shouted, "No!" Trevor's jaw muscles tensed. Why couldn't his brother just let him do this for him? Why does he have to pull *Captain of the ship* now? After all the time Trevor spent painstakingly becoming a SEAL and devoting his life to saving the world, and then having it all stripped away over someone else's mistake. Couldn't Nick let him do this? Do what he was trained to do? But it was clearly a hopeless argument, and the Captain of the High Cotton was not interested in refereeing disputes of brotherly sacrifice.

She said, "I'm sorry, gentlemen, there's no more time for debate. We must get moving,"

Just like that, the Captain had made the decision for them. The brothers would do this fool's errand together. The family considerations had to be put aside. It was time for business, to get to the task at hand.

Trevor could feel his body transforming. It was a feeling of every cell in his body receiving news from his brain that a new mission had started, that sudden jolt of exhilaration and intense focus that snaps awake every synapse in his body. Every nerve had been honed and perfected over years of SEAL training to maintain a state of readiness. It was more than adrenaline shooting through his veins; it was like a second sense where his peripheral vision sharpened with all of his other senses. It was a feeling that until that moment Trevor hadn't realized how much he had missed.

He was ready. Was Nick? He had made his way to the wheelhouse and was fumbling around. Nick had prepared himself to take a farewell voyage today then sell the ol' gal off, but there was no way he could have prepared for this. Knowing Nick, it had taken him a long time to work up to what must have been a clear conclusion to get out of shrimping. This was much more than that. He was not only losing precious money from her sale, but possibly sending her to Davy Jones' Locker and taking with her a family legacy and a hell of a lot of sentimental value.

Trevor's gaze was returned by Nick, the brothers making eye contact for the first time since the High Cotton closed its hatch. Nick gave him a nod of understanding.

He began steering the Esmerelda alongside the High Cotton. As they approached the big ship's bow, Nick said, "I'd like to protect the helm. I don't want her splitting apart from the pressure. Let's use those old fenders, that'd be the quickest thing."

"That should work if I can tie them together."

"It'll take two of us. Hang on and I'll help." Now at the bow, he put the engine in neutral. On deck, he made his way over to one of the old tires and began chuckling.

"What the hell's so funny?" Trevor asked, cocking his head.

"Maybe it's all for the best, ya' know? Here at her end, instead of being picked apart by vultures, she'll go down in a blaze---fighting until the very end."

"Hell, yeah," Trevor added, smiling. "How many shrimp boats get to go out rescuing cruise ships?" What he didn't say was "why are we fixing fenders if we know it's her end?" He knew. They weren't going to see her destroyed without a fight.

Trevor began attempting to pull at the clove hitch around the tire. Without success, he said with a shake of his head, "It won't budge. It's soaking wet and this knot's been here forever. I'll have to cut it to save time. Have you got more rope?"

"Yes, but I'll have to find it. Let me have a go first." Working in vain to loosen the knot, Nick said, "Yeah, this one's hopeless. I'll try one more." He went over and squatted next to another fender renewing the struggle.

"Nick," Trevor started, but Nick didn't raise his head. So Trevor urgently yelled out, "Nick! There's no time. We'll have to fucking cut them."

Visible over the stern in a short distance was the face of the cargo ship, pushing through the water like an aged shark bearing down on a baby seal. With Nick jogging to the cabin, Trevor pulled out his Benchmade Infidel, an automatic knife that is a favorite amongst his military brethren, and swiftly cut loose the needed tires. Just as he got them into position, Nick returned with rope.

"I hope this dry-rotting junk will hold," Trevor remarked as he hastily tied the tires in place.

As he stood up, he looked back to see the wake coming off Durango's bow, cutting waves with a hiss into the placid water.

 Back in the wheelhouse Nick grabbed the wheel with one hand and took hold of the throttle with the other. "Damn, that tanker really isn't budging one bit. What assholes. Here goes turning this bad boy!"

With a thunk, the shrimp boat butted the cruise ship's bow, Esmerelda's engine rose in pitch as Nick continued pulling back on the throttle. He looked at Trevor and felt the sweat rise on his face as he cranked her all the way, the roar of the old diesel sounding like it came straight from the lion's belly. As gray, filmy exhaust filled the cabin, Nick called out over the clamor, "Get out there and tell me if we're moving her!"

Trevor clambered on deck to the Esmerelda's edge where the shrimp boat was pressed against the big ship. Lying on his stomach, he zeroed in on the sea and the outline of the High Cotton as she rose from its depths. Using one hand to hold a line attached to the gunwale, he pushed himself as far over as he could without plunging overboard. He couldn't get a reference point to determine if the ship was moving. He looked sideways to Durango, its bulk closing in like Jonah's whale. Guessing they had about ninety seconds before the Esmerelda and the High Cotton were hit, he looked back at the High Cotton's bow and then down to the water to discover bubbles from Esmerelda's churning propellers floating towards him. He had his guide now---the bubbles, and he fixed his eyes on a particular one traveling in the water. He guessed it was ten inches away, then it was twenty, then two feet. "It's working!" he screamed at the top of his lungs.

"I can't hold her much more!" his brother called back. The Durango was so close now it cast its huge shadow across the Esmerelda's deck, the creeping grayness a final warning.

Trevor saw the High Cotton float further away. He jerked his head back to Nick, knowing they'd have to change the thrust of the Esmerelda to move out of harm's way or else jump ship and hope they could swim quickly enough to clear Durango and its slicing propeller.

He heard Nick scream, "Hold on!" Esmerelda lurched sideways, Trevor spinning then sliding overboard into the sea, nearly going fully under, but managing to keep his hold on the gunwale's line. The cold water shot into his legs like daggers. As the boat turned sharply again, he was dropped deeper into the Esmerelda's wake, now submerged up to his neck, his grip weakening as the numbing chill crept over his body. Waves seemed to be coming from all directions until one crashed onto his face sending the sea straight into his lungs. Coughing, he could hear the thump and rattle of Durango's engine and feel its vibration in the water.

He needed to twist around to get his other hand within reach of the gunwale, but he knew the jolt might dislodge his hold. Then the drumming sound of Durango seemed to be on top of him. His instincts were to let go and swim to safety, but with water churning around him it would be difficult to swim in a straight course. The cargo ship's wake put him underwater again before he felt the Esmerelda again lurch.

His hand ached to let go, but he held tight. He hadn't accomplished all he had by giving up now. His body would do what it had to, regardless of fear or pain, despite the fact that it was his left hand holding that line, and the deep wound in his left shoulder still hadn't altogether healed.

His mind fighting the cries of his body, he worked to get his feet up and over the side, but was only able to get the tips of his toes to make contact with the slant of the hull. It was enough. He made one last supreme effort to spring up to get his full grip back, right as another wave submerged him.

His head came out of the water, choking on the sea. After he sucked sweet air back into his lungs, he stilled himself and listened. Silence was slowly emerging like a new dawn. Esmerelda's screaming engine was back to her regular rattling hum, and the churn of the Durango was nearly gone.

Spitting out more saltwater and shaking his head to get the sting from his eyes, he flipped himself around and got his other hand on the gunwale. Next, he had to get his leg up and over the bow so he could climb back onto the boat. He swung, but his water-logged clothes had his kick falling short and his leg dropped like an anvil. He allowed himself to note that his shoulder was in screaming pain, but he forced himself to redirect his attention to climbing back up. Then he felt a strong pull at his shirt and hands around his arms as Nick grabbed hold to get him back to safety.

"Come on, Trevor! Help me out here!" Nick was saying. Trevor got his foot, then his ankle and then his leg on deck, Nick struggling to pull him all the way over. "If you weren't such a tall bastard!" Nick said, as the two gave one final heave and then he was onboard.

Before Trevor rolled onto his back to breathe deeply and stop his panting, he saw the back end of Durango getting smaller as it moved away. "Is High Cotton clear?" he asked between gulps of air.

Nick stood back with his hands on his hips and yelled to the sky, "Hell yes! The Esmerelda is one fucking fine shrimp boat!"

A pandemonium of noise caught their attention, shouting coming from the High Cotton. Their eyes traveled upwards to its top deck, where a dozen officers yelled and cheered, all of them with their attention on Nick and Trevor, hats off, waving back and forth over their heads. It was like a scene from an old movie, completed when one threw his cap in the air where the wind captured it and sent it traveling in an arc before it descended slowly into the sea. The shouting continued in a raucous chorus. All except one.

Standing apart was a woman, tall, composed, her uniform white against the crew's black. Her hand rose, fingers together in formation, elbow bent, fingertips at her temple as she gave them a crisp salute.

Chapter 30

Food Critic, check. Travel Reviewer, check.
Famous Reporter, in progress... Stay tuned for
#DoomedDurango #CummingsAndGoings

Jason couldn't allow himself to be bothered by unknown dangers. His work was too important. He felt like Edward R. Murrow covering the London blitz. It was up to him to record the unfolding events--- whatever they were to be---and to share them with the world. It was his destiny.

He soothed any distraction of fear with rational reasoning. True, all of the passengers had been herded indoors in haste, at least from his crow's-nest perspective, but what could it be about? Certainly there was no surprise party in there, so why did they need everyone inside? If the boat was about to *sink* wouldn't they would want people on deck to man the lifeboats? Taking them inside suggested that it was some type of threat out in the open. It seemed unlikely that terrorists were about to attack. He looked back to the oncoming vessel then shook his head. No way terrorists were executing a threat in that old fishing boat. He knew pirates existed, commandeering vessels, kidnapping people and sometimes killing them, but that was unlikely.

Anyway, the Coast Guard tended to frown on that kind of thing in U.S. territorial waters. And besides, pirates don't radio in advance as a heads-up to protect the women and children. That meant the only fact he knew was that whatever was happening had something to do with the fishermen heading this way, and he hardly thought the chef was looking for fresh seafood.

He leaned over the railing as the boat made its final approach, its engine changing from a full-throttle banshee scream to a low growl.

"What salvage yard did that come from?" he sniggered, remarking at the stark contrast the fishing boat made next to the ultra-luxurious High Cotton.

A sucking sound of metal came from below. Peering over, he could just make out that a small door had opened. Someone caught a line tossed from one of the fishermen. He knew from the glint of the golden locks that it was Chambers. And next to him the top of the white cap and uniform with shoulders lined in black and gold stripes, could only be the Captain.

Jason's curiosity and excitement gave him a jolt that practically sent him pitching headfirst over the side. Reassuring himself to remain calm and keep a clear head, he remembered the drone. This is what a drone was created for---spying. Quickly retrieving it, he got it back into flight, having it travel down the ship in the opposite direction.

Keeping its distance, he descended it over the side of the ship. He didn't watch the craft from the rail, where he risked being spotted. Instead he viewed the live footage from the drone streaming to his laptop---less conspicuous. Once he got his little bird at just the right height, he made his approach with caution.

Stealth was key. The breeze could hide the hum of the rotors only a small degree. No juicy details would be uttered if they knew there was an audience. That in mind, he used the rigging of the fishing boat as cover and flew in as close as he could.

He considered the participants, his eyes making darting glances as he concentrated on his work. The fishing boat had a visible crew of three, all on deck, though Jason's view was somewhat obscured by the outriggers. One appeared quite tall and well built with a ball cap pushed back off his face rather jauntily. It was difficult to see a lot of details, but in general he seemed more like the guy who would model clothes on a boat rather than someone working on one. Next to him was an older man with reddish brown locks falling messily around his tense leathered face. He looked more like what Jason would have expected a fisherman to look: in his tee shirt with threadbare spots allowing his deeply tanned skin to show through. The third one was distinctly older. His shoulders were stooped and he held the ship's railing in a way that was reminiscent of someone gripping a cane. His wiry hair was closely cropped and heavily grayed.

Jason could feel the intrigue growing. This was fascinating! Why on Earth has the captain of a luxury cruise line called this rugged trio? Was she hoping to meet the stars of Deadliest Catch? Or did she want to produce a shipboard version of Gilligan's Island?

Then on a more serious note, he considered, was that why she called in the passengers, so there would be no witnesses to this bizarre rendezvous? Yet again the Captain had underestimated him. Whatever shenanigans were going on here would be well documented. Every twist and turn of the drama... his imagination leapt to the bidding war for his coverage.

A chilly, penetrating wind suddenly shot his way. The sun was lower and the water changed to a black forest green as gentle swells ruffled the formerly placid surface.

He heard Chambers call to the Captain, who was now standing on the shrimp boat, "Twenty-one minutes!" A gust caught the drone and nearly slammed it into the cruise ship. Jason sent it further out to sea for safer distance. He was primed to be caught in his eavesdropping, preparing for everyone to thrust their angry eyes upward. Miraculously, the group concentrated only on the Captain.

Slowly he moved it closer, hearing the fishermen and the Captain discussing horsepower. What an odd time to be comparing engine capabilities. As he listened further it became clear what they were discussing. He could make out the men saying, 'no way we can push....' Then audio was interrupted with sea air gushing into the microphone. How irritating. It had been calmer than a bathtub out here all day and during this critical moment the wind decides to pick up! It was as if they'd planned it. But Jason didn't need to catch every word to understand the intention of the conversation. Why did the High Cotton need to be moved? And furthermore, why hadn't they called in a proper tugboat?

Then he heard the Captain make a reference to one of the fishermen being a former SEAL. Now that is interesting. Something is about to happen that requires the skills of a Navy SEAL. It didn't take much of a deduction to determine which of the three he was.

The wind subsided just as he heard the men saying they were concerned they might not be able to get out of the way and could be crushed. *Crushed?* Jason's palms were sweating now. His focus lasered in on every detail his hearing could detect. Presently the Captain was reassuring them that if they followed her directions all would be well. But the men were talking as if it were a suicide mission. The emotion, the tension, the sacrifice… It was ideal footage, capturing the raw selflessness, the humility of these men. He could see the edited version now.

Then another voice broke in, referencing the Coast Guard. His heart racing and his head dizzy with excitement, Jason heard someone shouting about a wasp. Realization set in, and he jerked the drone up just as Chambers took a swat. He couldn't catch the audio, but judging by Chambers' lips, he was shouting, "Cummings!" Jason chuckled, pleased with his getaway.

He made one final sweep back to catch the final exchange, and captured, "That's it! The tanker's on the horizon. Lord, don't fail us now!"

Jason---and his drone---looked in the direction the man was pointing and saw another ship in the distance.

By the time the drone was back in his hands he heard the hatch door close. Immediately following the sound, the shrimp boat's engine revved. He looked below to see it back away from the High Cotton and then move along next to it. His eyes traveled back to the other ship. It was much closer and hadn't shifted out of the High Cotton's line. In a horrifying moment of understanding, he grasped what was happening.

The big boat was heading straight for them!

It would slam into the cruise ship like a highway head-on collision, and the High Cotton was powerless to do anything about it. That's why people were ushered indoors. If they were on deck they could be bounced into the water or worse---like he will be! That was what the men had meant about *getting crushed*. The cargo ship wasn't altering course, and that dilapidated fishing boat was their only hope of getting out of the way!

Evidently the Captain, in her desperation, had asked these unfortunate people to push this huge cruise ship and risk their lives in the process. Clearly there was doubt on all sides as to whether the old boat was up to the task. Jason couldn't imagine it working. "My God! I'm going to be filming my own death! I'll be like the orchestra on the Titanic, working to keep the people entertained until the end."

A door slammed, bringing Jason back, and judging from the sound, it came from the nearest stairwell. He looked up to see someone in uniform approaching. Estevão.

"They sent me up here to get you inside," he said, his face full of concern.

Relieved it was Estevão, someone he could handle, and not Chambers, Jason said, "Are you kidding? I'm making the film of a lifetime. You've heard about that ship out there, right?"

Estevão gazed at the sea and saw the cargo ship's menacing presence. The red monster was bearing down on them.

Their eyes met in understanding. "Well," he hesitated, "With all that is going on they won't notice if you are gone a little longer. But at least let me help you," Estevão said, his hand lightly resting on the muscle in Jason's forearm.

Jason nodded. "All right. Watch the laptop screen and tell me if I'm getting the best shot. Just call out if I need to adjust the angle or hold steady on something. Okay?"

"Yes, but Jason, only while it is still far out. We have to be inside before it hits."

"Agreed." He stood up, controls in his hands. It was always easier to ask forgiveness than permission, he assured himself, as he took hold of the controls then lifted the drone from the deck. He wouldn't be missing a moment of coverage.

At the railing he could see the shrimp boat stop at the High Cotton's bow. The drone hovered above the outriggers as the buff crew member emerged from the

267

wheelhouse and began fumbling with what looked like an old tire. What an odd thing to have tied to the side of a boat, and even a more peculiar time to try to remove it. The second fisherman came out to help.

Jason turned the drone to the oncoming ship. As it came into focus he could see where the anchor chains had scraped red paint from the hull to reveal years of rust.

"It's an old rusty hulk, isn't it?" Estevão commented. Then he said excitedly, "Hold steady. I can almost make out her name. . . Durango!"

Durango, it was a name that reminded Jason of something but he couldn't quite put his finger on it. He continued mulling it over in his mind and turned the drone back to the fishermen, discovering that the two men were no longer on deck. Then the fishing boat's engine rose to a feverous pitch. The hunky fisherman appeared again, hurrying to the front edge of the boat and squatting down. He stretched out on his belly, his head practically touching the High Cotton.

"What's he doing?" Estevão asked.

The noise from the engine thundered on. Exhaust began fogging the picture, Jason moved the drone higher to face the cargo ship as it closed in. He couldn't imagine why the oncoming ship was intent on hitting the High Cotton.

"Why is it doing this? It makes no sense. They risk sinking themselves too if they hit us. And that fishing boat doesn't seem to be helping much. Looks like they could get stuck in the middle."

Estevão suggested, "Perhaps they are demanding a ransom. When the millions appear electronically in a Swiss bank account, Durango will change course."

Jason said as he looked at the cargo ship, "But even if it shifted now, it would likely still strike us, maybe not in the middle of the ship, but it would hit somewhere just the same. Can't turn a boat like that on a dime."

"Do you think the crew is on a suicide mission? Did they agree to this plan knowing that the ship was doomed?"

Jason's face lit up as he glanced at Estevão.

"What is it? You look like a light bulb should be over your head."

"I'll tell you later," Jason said, keeping the epiphany to himself, that his next tweet would be about High Cotton's smash up with another ship, and now he had the perfect hashtag, *Doomed Durango!* It was as if it was meant to be. He grinned ear to ear in anticipation, amazing himself that here he was facing death, but his thoughts were only on his masterpiece and it's new title.

"Do you see that?" Estevão screamed. "They're actually moving the High Cotton! The shrimpers are doing it! Jason, we are literally less than a minute from certain death and they are pushing us out of the way."

Jason raised the drone higher to capture the drama, as well as getting a shot of himself and Estevão heroically at work. "If we're killed, I just hope someone finds the laptop and publishes my fantastic footage," Jason commented with deathly seriousness.

"Now the cargo ship is heading for the stern, Jason! Move the drone!"

Durango was so close they could hear the clicking engine and the sound of its bulky form cutting through the water. It was right at the High Cotton, so deceptively quick. It was fifty feet away, thirty, ten...

"It's so close, Jason," Estevão said, his voice dropping off. He opened his mouth to tell Jason they needed to run to safety, but he was too hypnotized by Durango to move.

From the drone's vantage point, Jason could see the High Cotton shift in the water again. Durango was at the cruise ship's stern, Jason deftly shifting the video from the shrimp boat, to the High Cotton, to Durango then panned out to all three. So much to shoot so quickly.

He moved the controls to get an overview of Durango's deck. He needed to get a shot of its crew, the men who were attempting to take out the High Cotton and these shrimpers in one fell swoop. Their faces would be infamous---and so would Jason's, to have captured their mugs on film.

As the drone made the pass over, it followed Durango along, moving next to Jason and Estevão so closely they could hear its buzzing. But oddly no one was visible on deck. The cargo ship creaked and rattled, and in a quick but horrifying glance, Jason realized that it was missing collision with the High Cotton by inches. He raised the drone higher so it could show the nearness of the two behemoths. Then he heard Estevão make a strangling noise. "What is it?" Jason asked, not taking his eyes from the drone.

"I saw…"

"What? How close it is? I know it! But don't worry, the film is turning out great!"

Now Jason had the drone capturing the final seconds of Durango's near miss then moving along on its oblivious voyage. Then other action caught his eye, and he moved the drone back to shrimp boat, realizing that one of the men was dangling off its bow, a single hand clinging to a line around the gunwale.

"Send it back over Durango, Jason! Hurry!"

"No way! Are you seeing this? That guy's holding on by his fingernails."

"Do it, Jason! Before it's too late!"

"Listen, Estevão, there can be only one director. I'm staying with the action, not getting another overview of that floating barnacle. There weren't any crew members on deck anyway."

Durango chugged past, its backend now facing them in the frothy water burped out by its propeller.

Meanwhile, the shrimper who was nearly lost at sea was being rescued by his shipmate. "It just keeps getting better," Jason muttered, his hands operating the controls as delicately as a surgeon's.

"You must send it back, Jason, so I'll know for sure what I saw!"

His attention elsewhere, Jason ignored Estevão's pleas and had the drone capturing the two men struggling, and finally, the man rescued and back on the boat, prone on deck and panting for breath. Next, Jason sent the drone to film the High Cotton's top deck, where outside the navigation room crewmen gathered to pay homage to the shrimp boat, shouting with joy and admiration. The two fishermen watched them solemnly before returning to the deckhouse. They didn't seem to be enjoying their moment. Slowly, the shrimp boat turned and began to travel back to the ship's hatch door, everyone above still waving.

When the action ended, Jason brought the drone back, delicately landing it near the two of them. He ran over and picked it up, clutching it as tenderly as a baby. Happily, he looked over at Estevão, who was staring at the laptop intensely.

"What are you doing?" Jason asked. "Now isn't the time for editing. I'll take care of that later. That is the job of the director, so I'll handle it."

Estevão looked up, his face in agony. "Since it's too late to have the drone fly back over Durango, I need to see the film. I must know---what I saw...."

"What did you see?" Jason surveyed Estevão, and for the first time noticed the whites showing around his hazelnut eyes and the beads of sweat above his full olive lips. Why was he so upset over the video? They were alive and well. Everything turned out fantastic.

Estevão's eyes lowered. "I tried to tell you. That ship---there was a crew member...sort of..."

Chapter 31

Those Damn Glasses!

After enjoying a few glasses of Dom, John Chen, as the Sea Frolic passengers knew him, had to have a lie-down before dinner. It had been a hectic day, to put it mildly. As soon as he stretched out, he let out a long sigh of contentment and was immediately asleep.

What awoke him was a tapping at his door and the sound of Josie's voice. "Mr. Chen? I hate to disturb you, but if you don't report for dinner soon, you'll miss the meal."

Rolling over, he rubbed his eyes and said groggily, "Okay, I come."

Seeing that the sunlight no longer brightened the back of the curtains, he got to his feet, yawning and feeling refreshed. He put on a clean shirt for dinner and brushed off his pants while whistling light-heartedly. Then, as he raked a comb through his hair, the rested feeling began to dissipate at the thought of his dinner companions: the mother and daughter with the mother angling for a match-up, the boorish couple from the South, the peculiar woman under the hat whose husband never left the television.

It would be a chore to dine with this bunch, but the idea of a hot meal was too enticing to pass up after nearly two weeks of living off rice cakes and cereal. Resignedly, he buffed off the lenses of Beth's glasses and placed them upon the bridge of his nose, then headed out.

Everyone was at the table, including the Captain, who gave him a friendly smile. "There's our sleepy head," the Captain grinned.

"Dear me, Mr. Chen, you've got creases on your face from sleeping so hard," Taffy said with a laugh. Then she cried, "Ouch!" and looked pointedly at her mother.

Loretta smoothed, "You look very nice, Mr. Chen. So glad you joined us."

He took the only empty chair, which was conveniently next to Taffy, and gave her a weak smile. Immediately, he looked expectantly between the bottle of Pinot Grigio that sat near him and the Captain, awaiting a glass.

The Captain, noticing his expectant gaze explained, "We keep things informal on the Sea Frolic, Mr. Chen, so please help yourself to a glass of wine."

A wave of indignance passed through his body, but steadying himself he poured, filling his glass a little too full. After all, we keep things informal here, he mused to himself.

Dinner plates were arriving with a Cajun styled meal of sausage, rice and seafood. "Mmmm, looks even better than Applebee's!" Jim Gaines said, adding excitedly, "And honey, you know how much I love me some Applebee's." He stabbed his fork into a sausage before the others had been served, then asked while chewing, "How did you get those wounds, Mr. Chen? Looks painful. If you were a teenager I'd say you punched a wall."

John picked up his wine glass and delicately took a sip, pleased to note that it was a decent vintage. With the group silent and awaiting his response, he set the glass back down and inspected his knuckles.

"Accident on ship. It no hurt." He laughed a short laugh. Indeed, his hands were swollen with the recent cuts, but it was something he was used to and had learned over the years to ignore the discomfort. Abruptly, he turned to his other side and said to Glenda, Ernie's wife, "You want wine?"

With her yellow lipstick now replaced with a pinker version, the woman was almost pretty, middle aged with her red hair in a cut that tapered along her neck. She was wearing a hot pink blouse that appeared to be silk, however, not a silk that would have met his mother's standards; although neither would mixing pink with that hair. She gave him a smile.

"Thank you, Mr. Chen. No one else has offered." He poured her a glass then the two toasted one another.

Ernie, seeming piqued by John's attention to his wife, picked up his knife in one hand and a roll in the other. He cut a chunk of butter and stated with it dangling precariously, "Those cuts remind me of how my hands looked in high school when I couldn't control my temper. My buddies and I were just looking for an excuse---some kid mouthing off, getting in my way, or makin' eyes at my girl---I'd change their minds in a hurry. You know what I mean, Mr. Chen?"

Swirling the wine in his glass, he answered, "High school long time ago, yes?" Then took a long whiff of the wine's exceptional floral notes.

The table was silent. Glenda stopped the crickets with, "Ernie, please. No one wants to hear about your school days. John's right, that was ages ago."

"I got into a brawl more than once when I was in the service," Jim shared. "I was a Marine, stationed in South Korea in the early nineties."

John was feeling a throbbing in his temples and behind his eyes. It had escalated quickly from a dull ache he had noticed a few minutes ago. At this rate he wouldn't make it through the meal with anything less than a migraine. Looking to meet Jim's eyes, he realized there were too many. In fact, Jim had more like five eyes blurred across his face. Removing the glasses and rubbing the bridge of his nose, it hit him. It was the damned glasses! Why the fuck did I wear them? he lamented to himself, putting the hated glasses back on. Her face flashing between two of Jim's eyes, Beth's revenge became clear.

Focusing back on Jim's comment, John replied neutrally "After a few of those?" gesturing to the Corona in Jim's hand. Laughter erupted around the table with the spontaneous clinking of glasses.

Ernie spoke again. "Thinking about you taking that nap, Mr. Chen, I did a study once when I was in college. It was about people's natural body rhythms, you know, your internal clock that tells you when to eat or wake up, very interesting stuff."

Glenda sighed. "Oh no, Ernie, not that again. Nobody wants to hear about that Circadian stuff."

"What?" Taffy asked.

Glenda's hand waved dismissively. "Please, don't encourage him. He's talking about Circadians. So boring."

"Why do you think Canadians are boring?" Taffy asked.

"I don't think they're boring," Glenda retorted.

"But you just said---"

Loretta looked up from her dinner plate and cut in. "Are you talking about Canadians? I had a Canadian girl staying in my cabin when I was at Camp Takawanda. She was nice enough, but talked funny."

"Oh, I used to love summer camp," Kaitlin interjected.

Glenda lobbed into the conversation, "For the record, I do not think Canadians are boring."

Taffy stood her ground. "Well, that's what you said. I mean, you can't just generalize like that, saying millions of people are boring."

"You don't understand," Glenda attempted to explain.

"It's that kind of intolerance that causes so many of our world's problems," Jim Gaines chastised.

"So true, Jim," Loretta agreed. "I myself always try my best to be open to different cultures. For example, I've got neighbors who are Jewish. When I met Mr. Steiner I asked him if he was in banking, because my mother told me that so many of them used to do that. I was just making friendly conversation. Do you know what he said? He said, 'No, are you in the business of making crackers?' Now, I ask you, was that not peculiar? But did I act offended? No, I did not, I merely told him the truth. That I was a school teacher educating our future leaders."

"What did he say to that?" Kaitlin asked.

"He said he was going to go home and pray. They're different, those people, really different."

Suddenly, John felt a nudge around his feet. He thought his neighbor might be mistaking him for a table leg, then someone began rubbing his ankle. He kept his focus on the table but could feel Taffy's stare. She giggled, pining for his acknowledgement, but John adjusted his seat, ensuring that she would now only be able to reach that table leg after all.

"What is it you do on that ship, Mr. Chen?" Loretta asked, scooping a forkful of rice and shrimp.

"This and that. I no work now. Tired." He took a bite, which, he admitted to himself was quite good.

"Did it pay well?" she asked, her eyebrows raised.

"Mother! Please," Taffy chastised, "How tacky!"

"I'm just asking, because we all know this trip wasn't cheap." With her emphasizing the 'p' in 'cheap,' a speck of rice flew from her mouth and landed on the edge of Jim's plate. He grimaced. John Chen smiled cagily and continued with his dinner, ignoring Loretta's question.

Jim caught John's eye, and flicked the grain of rice back in Loretta's general direction, then said, "It's hard to believe it wasn't cheap 'cause we're all so close to one another." Loretta glared at him.

"I wouldn't say the Sea Frolic is cramped, Jim. It's a lovely cabin cruiser. I like it very much, Captain," Kaitlin, remarked, gazing at the head of the table. Jim looked at her seeming mildly shocked. In her late thirties, she was a woman in her last blush of youth, her eyes crinkling as she gave the Captain a smile he appeared not to notice.

Not to be outdone, Jim said with a grin, "Well, it's nothing like that ship we took the river cruise on. Remember that? Had a pool table in the salon. And how about that hot tub?" He nudged his wife.

"This ship has a hot tub, Jim," Kaitlin stated primly.

"Yeah, but nowhere big enough for what I had in mind," he winked. "Nobody likes to be crammed in there like you're taking a bath with somebody ya' don't know."

More discussion ensued as the Captain shifted the topic to things to do in Turks and Caicos. John listened and drank more wine, realizing too late that the alcohol had caused the headache to worsen, the throb becoming so intense he wondered if it could be seen as a bulge in his temples. He could endure the soreness from his wounds, but the pounding head was doing him in. There was nothing for it but to remove the glasses. Doing so, he hooked an earpiece at the opening in his collar. As the men were engrossed in a football discussion and the women arguing about a movie, no one commented on the change, except Taffy.

Turning towards him, she cooed in a low tone, "I like you without your glasses, John." Leaning over in her V-necked dress, John noticed she had one enormous breast hoisted unnaturally on the table while it's twin drooped below. She opened her mouth to gently bite her full bottom lip, her face in a little pout. Batting her eyes, his attention became distracted by a piece of lettuce stuck between her front teeth.

Her hand slipped down and rested on his thigh. "You know, I've got something in my room that would help those cuts of yours. You could come by and let me play nurse." She chuckled.

He withdrew her hand and placed it in her own lap, then stated firmly, "No. I fine." When he turned back he found Loretta watching.

After a simple dessert of chocolate mousse, the group dispersed to different activities. Ernie and Jim moved to the television and turned the sports channel on again. The women walked out on deck, the lone exception being Taffy, who remained close to John as he rose from his chair.

"It's a lovely night, John." She put a finger on her bottom lip that was newly crimsoned in a spackling of lip gloss. Her body assumed the posture of a little girl, one leg bent as she pivoted slowly to the left and right.

"Yes, I go sleep now." He almost gave his heels a little click and prepared to turn. Taffy wasn't to be discouraged so easily.

She extended her bony arm for him to hook his through, and asked, "Would you like to take a promenade around the deck? That's what a girl used to say to a gentleman in the old days."

He was tired of her uninvited attempts. With the others out of earshot, his smile disappeared and his eyes narrowed. When he spoke he dropped the fake Chinese accent and said levelly, "I said no."

She gave a little backwards jerk of her chin. "Oh!" He kept his eyes locked on hers and was about to take a step towards her. She became unnerved. Not by what he said, but by the coldness in his eyes and the threatening stance. He looked at her hard, in a way a predator eyes a potential victim. She turned, the hem of her dress making an orbit around her. Her eyes jumped to the stairs, but she didn't go that direction and instead made her way for the door leading to the deck, giving him a final glance with a concerned look. He smiled to himself and trotted up the steps to return to his room.

Happily, the headache seemed to be subsiding. He reached into his pocket for his key as he took the final step. When he glanced down the hall, he discovered Loretta at his door, her hand jiggling the knob. Finding it locked, she removed something from her pocket.

"Hey!" he called tersely.

Her look of shock confirmed his suspicion, and she backed away, swiftly returning whatever was in her hand to her pocket. When she spoke, her reaction was well-rehearsed. Her mouth formed an 'O' as she glanced at his room number and feigned shock.

"My heavens! Is this not my room? Oh, I'm so embarrassed. Please forgive me, Mr. Chen." She hurriedly moved her bulk past him, her stockings making a swishing noise. She stopped at the first door in the hallway and went inside.

He put his hand to the knob, confirming it was still locked, then put his key in and entered, seeing nothing untoward. This was an unexpected development, he thought to himself. Loretta and Taffy were two thieves working the cabin cruiser. He would have to act on this carefully, as he couldn't risk them finding the laptop or his stash of money.

Chapter 32

An Innocent Mistake?

Trevor and Nick were climbing the steps behind a young officer who was taking them to see Captain Patel and to collect Ray. They had pulled up to the High Cotton minutes ago after pushing the cruise ship out of Durango's path. The brothers were quiet, perhaps even pensive before they boarded and were greeted by Third Officer Pullen. She was about twenty-two, and spoke in an Irish accent with the predictable flaming red hair visible below her cap.

Her brown eyes twinkled as she said, "I can't believe what you men just did! It's so fantastic! I was scared, I mean, I didn't show it, naturally, but my heart---and then at the last minute---wait, no, the last second---you got your boat to move our huge ship! I'll never forget it. Never. Something to tell me grandchildren, you know, not that I have any now."

Nick gave her an awkward smile then replied. "Is the Captain waiting for us?"

"Oh, yes sir, she surely is," the girl answered, her long bangs fluttering as she batted her eyes. Her awestruck expression was glued on her face like a swooning groupie at a concert, and climbing the steps, she kept looking back at Nick with a girlish grin.

It perplexed Trevor that Nick didn't seem to be reveling in his moment of fame. Trevor had assumed Nick would have that annoying pleased-with-himself grin slapped across his face, the way he always did. Like the time Nick and Ray pulled an older couple out of the ocean after their small boat capsized. It was on TV news and written up in the Charleston paper the next day. Nick was thrilled with the attention the front page picture got him. He had milked it every time he met a girl. So why not now? He should be relishing this, at least the old Nick would have.

A tension swept over Trevor. Perhaps the brother he'd left years ago had disappeared… dissipated with age, and the thought filled him with a sad ache. He preferred the Nick who would have eaten up the adoration of this cute Irish crewman. That Nick seemed to be only a memory, and it made Trevor realize that all those years he had been away everyone else had moved on, changed without him. He didn't fit back into their world the same way. Following behind his brother, he accepted for the first time since his return that things would never be the same as when he had left.

*   *   *

They continued through the maze of the ship's interior, never seeing a passenger, though at one point Trevor could hear animated voices in a stairway's chamber. When Captain Patel saw them enter the navigation room, she excused Third Officer Pullen, who gave the brothers a lingering gaze before she left. The Captain faced them, her expression changing to an anxious smile.

"Gentlemen, I'm so grateful. Words could never express," she said, shaking Nick's hand, then Trevor's, who stood there with his wet tee-shirt and jeans clinging to his sculpted body. The Captain, noticing Trevor's state, couldn't help but give him a thorough inspection with her eyes, then recovered with, "You're soaked, Trevor. Let me call someone to bring you some dry things." It was a statement, not an offer. She got on the radio to Dawkins and told him, "Bring clothes for Trevor Starnes." Then giving Trevor another appraising glance, added, "His build is similar to Chambers'."

As she spoke, Trevor's eyes moved around the room, impressed by the spectacular 360 degree view. Far below, the ocean was as glossy as gunmetal. On a sunny day, the room was so bright it didn't need artificial lighting. And it was plush, decorated in high end Scandinavian furniture and computer workstations designed with ergonomics in mind. To his right were sleek ebony countertops, banking beneath an extensive array of navigational technology. It was impressive, looking as up to date as some small naval ships, but with all the luxuries.

"So, where's Ray?" Nick mentioned to his brother in a tone just loud enough for the Captain to overhear. Finishing the radio call, she gave them that tense smile again.

"About your friend, Ray…" Seeing a wave of panic cross Nick's face, she quickly interjected, "He will be fine, but he's down in the ship's medical center. It's just that he became faint and unwell after you left. He's being monitored."

"Faint?" Nick repeated, looking at Trevor skeptically.

Trevor said to Padma bluntly, "Give it to us straight. Did Ray have a heart attack?"

With only the three of them in the room, the silence was heavy before she spoke. "Well," she began carefully, "It appears that he did. The good news is that our medical personnel responded immediately. He's stable, conscious and alert, but the doctor said not to move him. We *are* equipped to care for him, and as I said, he needs to be monitored. When we reach Charleston he should be transported by ambulance to a hospital, and…" giving the slightest smile, added, "I would be happy to arrange that."

Trevor responded with, "Damn. Yeah, let's keep him here, but we want to see Ray before we leave."

Nick, an edge to his voice stated, "Yeah, I'm gonna need to see Ray *now*."

She formed her response as she gently placed her hand on Nick's arm. "And I'm more than happy to take you there, but first, could you wait a few minutes? I want you here for the debriefing. And I've gotten word the Coast Guard has arrived. Two officers are being brought up to speak with us. Your insight will be invaluable."

Before the brothers could respond, there was a knock on the door and the steward entered. "Excuse me, Captain. I have the clothes you requested."

"Excellent, Dawkins. Please put them in the lavatory." She looked at the slight puddle around Trevor and gestured to the bathroom door.

Trevor said to Nick, "Let me go change, and if the Coast Guard isn't here when I finish, we'll leave to check on Ray."

Nick had his cap screwed up in his hand, tapping it against his side. "All right," he replied, snapping the cap back on his head, "But make it quick. And no offense, Captain Patel, at this point I really don't care what the Coast Guard has to say. Ray is the priority here, not some rogue tanker that can't steer."

Trevor had already moved into the bathroom and closed the door. Ignoring Nick's outburst, Padma nodded acknowledgement to Nick and said, "I know I've already asked too much, but the Coast Guard will need to speak with you as part of its investigation. For them it will not be optional. Ray's in good hands, and we're equipped to address his needs. Perhaps it was best he was with us at the time. You see, he required a defibrillator…" she trailed off.

"Wow…" Nick sank back, bracing himself against the ebony counter.

In the bathroom Trevor had stripped off his sticky, damp things, piling them on the floor. He then rinsed the ocean water out of his black curls and used a towel Dawkins brought to somewhat dry his hair. Dressing in the clean garments, they felt warm, though a bit snug. He came out of the bathroom buttoning the bottom of the shirt, reluctantly leaving the chest open where the fabric wouldn't reach.

Then the navigation room door opened and two Coast Guard officers stepped inside with the First Mate behind them. "Captain Patel, this is Captain Perry and Ensign Sing," Chambers said. Both officers saluted, the Coast Guard Captain saying, "Captain Warren Perry of the medium endurance cutter, The Peregrine, Charleston Sector."

"And this is Captain Nick Starnes," she gestured to Nick. "And his brother, Trevor. You said you were ex-Navy SEAL, Trevor?"

"Yes," he replied, not elaborating. He stood tall in his newly pressed white pants and matching shirt. He knew he looked like a campy cruise ship showman, but at least he wasn't dripping and soggy. He took a good look at the Commander and instantly sized him up. He reminded him of an instructor he had at Annapolis--- thought he knew everything, without having to listen to anyone who didn't pull rank.

The officer in turn appeared to be making his own presumptions. Short, stocky and gray haired, the man was probably about fifty. He responded to Captain Patel's comment with two words, spoken in a deliberate tone to indicate his complete indifference. "Oh, really?" Then proceeded, "Captain, I'd like to get any additional information you have as quickly as possible. We've got a tight schedule and have to be on our way. You understand."

Trevor wondered if Nick would say that they were leaving for the infirmary, but he remained silent, waiting there with his jaw tensed as he looked from Captain Perry to Padma.

"Of course. I'm sure you're anxious to intercept Durango," Padma relayed. Then she moved her hand in the direction of five chairs that had been arranged for the meeting. "Let's sit down, then we'll get straight to the details of the incident. I've begun our own internal report. I'd be happy to forward a copy to you, Captain Perry, once it's completed."

The Captain eased onto the edge of the chair and said with a palm in the air, "Let me correct you right there, Captain Patel. We're not describing this as an incident."

Trevor could see her brow furrow. Padma replied, "Oh? Are you saying it was a direct act of aggression?"

"Absolutely not. Why don't you take a deep breath here and calm down. From what I--- or rather, the Coast Guard---can ascertain, this was a case of negligence at worst and probably more like an unfortunate error in judgement. We think it's a matter of Durango failing to keep watch on its relative position in the shipping lane. No need to take it personally," he chuckled.

Padma glanced at the brothers. Nick's expression was contempt. Trevor was unreadable, reflecting his military background. She redirected her attention to the Captain and stated, "Perhaps I need to get you up to date. These two men are responsible for the High Cotton not being *broadsided* by Durango. I radioed them for assistance and they agreed to help us at the risk of their boat and their lives. They moved High Cotton, changed her position in the water so that Durango passed parallel rather than T-boning her and causing considerable damage, perhaps *fatal* damage. They achieved this with seconds to spare. Trevor was nearly thrown from their vessel and crushed in the process. Had they not been able to move High Cotton, we would be having a very different conversation. *You*, or rather, the Coast Guard, would be conducting a body count, and most definitely reporting it as an *incident*."

The officer moved his eyes to Trevor's then back to Padma, opened his mouth to speak, then smiled and appeared to readjust what he was about to say. "Quite a story. But be reasonable. Durango could hardly be expected to anticipate a cruise ship parked out in the ocean with no ability to move. A ship like this is expected to be mobile." He gave a little wink to his Lieutenant. "Now, I'm sure everyone in this room will agree that this should be kept in the strictest confidence. We wouldn't want to make a mountain out of a molehill. We've discovered Durango has all the appropriate documents in order. It's flagged out of the Ukraine, but intelligence tells us the ship's registration and the license of its captain originated in China.

"Now, I did a little checking up on you, Captain Patel," he said in a chummy tone, "And I know that you commanded a cruiser in the Gulf. So you should know that things are touchy with China when it comes to situations in open water. What you don't appreciate here is that we are dealing with that age-old problem that affects so much of what we do, Captain, and I'm talking about politics." He reclined back in the chair, placing his hands behind his head and stretching his knees out. "The last thing we need to do here is overreact. No one wants to suggest it was an act of war. That's why we must keep this to the judgement of the boy's at the Coast Guard. I can assure you, that I'm going to have a word with Durango's crew to make sure they understand our laws inside U.S. territorial waters, and let them know what a scare it was for you."

Padma's face was flushed. She cut her eyes to Chambers, who was standing behind the two officers, hiding his shocked expression. Then there was a sound from the door, so he quickly trotted over to see who it was. Nick rose from his chair as well. A minute later Chambers walked back over to Padma and whispered something to her. Her face briefly registered surprise before she questioned, "And they are absolutely sure?" He nodded. Turning her attention back to Captain Perry she took a slight gulp then explained, "I've just learned that one of our esteemed passengers used his drone, which was streaming footage, to sweep over Durango and saw a body on its deck---covered in blood."

Ensign Sing let out a huff. The Captain moved his hand to instruct him to remain quiet. "Hold on here. A body? How could they be sure of what they saw?"

Padma replied. "In fact, it was two witnesses, and one was a crew member." The room was silent. The Captain raised an eyebrow but allowed her to continue. "This means that Durango is possibly traveling with no one at the helm, which would explain the lack of contact and the close encounter. That ship is headed straight for Charleston. It may not be an intended act of aggression, Captain Perry, but at this point you'll have to treat it as one. It must be stopped before Durango plows straight into the city's harbor."

"Yes, Captain Patel," he said, rising from his chair. "I can see how concerned you are. You have done the right thing by turning this information over to me. Don't you worry your little self any more about it. I won't be letting Durango 'plow into the harbor,' okay?"

Chambers intervened. "Captain, Durango never responded to our radio calls, not even our distress calls. There won't be time to stop that ship if you delay and no one is piloting."

"Not to fret, young man. Durango may have ignored your calls, but it won't ignore mine."

They began striding across the room towards the door with Chambers looking at Padma for direction. She said, a slight edge to her voice, "Escort them back to the hatch. Then return here."

He hurried to catch up and open the door for them as Nick moved out of the way. Padma and Trevor rose from their chairs, with Padma saying stiffly after the officers had exited, "I'm not sure what to make of that. What do you think?"

"I don't think you could have changed the Captain's mind even if you'd told him Durango had a nuclear weapon onboard." He saw her face go ashen. "I apologize, Padma. Just a manner of speech. But I would guarantee there's more going on than just misplacing their position in the shipping lane."

Her hand gave a slight tremble. "It just worries me. In these days it seems no tragedy is out of the question... my brother, he's there in Charleston, a doctor working at the hospital." Their eyes met and held tightly.

"At least we will be heading in behind them. We can keep an eye on things. Or are you still stalled?"

"Actually, I got word right before you and your brother walked in that we're fully operational now."

"Good. And you know, Padma, no one could be expected to anticipate you'd be immobile out here." Trevor gave her a playful wink.

"Yes," she said with a wry smile and the tension in her body lifting for the first time. "That is so true."

The moment of levity was broken by a loud metallic crash. Trevor hadn't flinched, unlike the others in the room who jumped to see that Nick had overturned a decorative silver captain's wheel from a high display. It rolled a few feet then stopped sideways on the floor.

Outwardly unphased, Trevor's throat was going dry, making it hard to swallow. It began to consume him, the pressure creeping into his lungs, leaving him with the feeling he got when breathing during a sandstorm. His attention narrowing and his frame of vision closing around him, he began having a flashback. The sound of gunfire rang in his ears and the peculiar odor of fish filled the confined space. A sense of hot lead rocketing past him had him wanting to drop and roll sideways, but he was too constricted. Then he felt the slice of muscle and the warm ooze of blood. His eyes adjusting to the dark, he knew exactly where he was. He was where it happened. He was on the only mission that failed him, his last.

Chapter 33

Did He Or Didn't He?

They were packing the equipment, their filming complete, at least for this stage of the exposé. Tenderly folding its propellers, Jason returned the drone to its case. Estevão was jerkily zipping up the computer bag, his hands still quivering as he mumbled about what he saw on Durango.

Jason was thinking to himself, *Yeah, I got it the first ten times you told me, and we're moving on...* He purposely re-focused his attention on how he could interview some of the participants of the tell-all.

After saving High Cotton from Durango, he had seen the fishermen enter the hatch, presumably to speak with the Captain and retrieve the third member of their crew. What a Kodak moment it could be when they are reunited with the old teddy bear they so gallantly left behind. Jason had achieved a brilliant shot of the hot one perilously dangling off the fishing boat at the moment he was about to be crushed by Durango. How great to contrast that with his soft side. That hunky hero could play well for follow-up interviews too, he considered.

This train of thought was interrupted by another outburst from Estevão, who clearly realized his ramblings were falling on deaf ears. Lord, Jason consoled himself, what more does Estevão need here? He had already explained to him that if Durango did have a dead body on its deck, it will be handled by the appropriate authorities, *i.e.* the Coast Guard. They had pulled up to the High Cotton minutes ago, parking next to the shrimp trawler---clearly prepared to do their job. Jason had gotten a shot of their boat, seeming a little small to be dealing with a big cargo ship like Durango, but that was the Coast Guard's call.

"Jason, please, you didn't see that grotesque display, that poor man, his head practically cut off, the blood, oh the blood..." Estevão shivered, then added, "You don't get it. The Coast Guard is here. I must tell them about it."

Ignoring him, Jason began clipping down the interior stairwell, his footfalls echoing. Estevão followed prattling on, his voice sounding whiny. That accent that had seemed so cute earlier was beginning to grate on Jason's nerves.

"You did not see it, so I have to report it. I won't sleep a *weenk* if I don't know that there is justice for that poor man. The Coast Guard will probably want to get more details from me." Raising his brows, he added perkily, "Perhaps you should *feelm* this." And with a moment of vanity in his voice, asked, "Is my hair okay from that wind?"

Estevão's idea of speaking with the Coast Guard gave Jason an idea in turn, that he would like footage of the conversation between the Captain, the fishermen and the Coast Guard---but not using the drone and laptop. The conference will probably take place in the navigation room, so the drone wouldn't help. It would need to be safely stowed away in his cabin. If the authorities learned that he had footage of the corpse, they could confiscate his equipment, and that just wouldn't do. No, he'd use his phone to record what happens on the bridge. It would have to suffice. He picked up his pace, saying over his shoulder, "Now Estevão, remember, this isn't about you."

"Jason, you are not *leesenning*," Estevão continued. "Why you are being so stubborn? I know it is not about me. It is about the dead man."

Jason had almost reached the door to the hallway. "It's like I said, the Coast Guard will deal with it. Besides, after I take my equipment to my room, I intend on recording the Captain's talk with these men. If the moment is right, I'll tell her about 'the body'," he said with air quotes. He cheered himself inwardly for getting that last bit out without an eye-roll.

"That is fine, but *I* am going to tell them now. They should know there is a *keeler* on Durango!"

Jason stopped and turned around to face Estevão as he considered the point. Exasperated, he acquiesced, "Alright, I guess we'll go now, but only because we don't want to miss any possible footage, all right?"

"Yes, *queeck*," he was tugging on Jason's sleeve. "They are probably talking to our crew this very minute!"

"Yes, yes, I've got it." Jason said, snapping his arm out of Estevão's grip. "But slow your roll here, Estevão. If we do this, I can't risk the Coast Guard seizing *my* drone and laptop---and that's exactly what they'll do if we tell them I've got the body on video."

Curling a dark lock through his fingers, he said, "Oh, of course, I see what you mean. So here's what I'll tell them. I'll say we didn't film it, we were doing live streaming, *jes*?" He again reached to pull Jason's arm towards the stairwell, but caught only air.

Reluctantly, Jason agreed with the caveat that even if threatened with jail or torture, they would not reveal the laptop footage. In fact, Jason was scheming to find the right place to hide the equipment, so that when they entered the navigation room it wouldn't be vulnerable in his hands.

Each anxious to be the first on deck, the two ran back up the three floors, bursting out shoulder to shoulder into the restricted area. Panting for breath, they found themselves needing to cross in front of a prominently perched seagull that had a chip out of its beak. The gull, staring intently, didn't budge, only let loose with a large, gooey deposit on the deck's floor. The two hesitated, allowing the other the option to go first, then following that with increasingly urgent nudges. Estevão took the first step.

Using him as a human shield, Jason jetted past the bird making a beeline to the large vent with a hooded cover he'd spotted during their brief delay. He stowed the laptop and drone behind it, then stood up ready to deal with Captain Patel and company. But before he could take a step, he felt the brush of Estevão passing him, excitedly charging through the gate to ascend the final steps to the navigation room. Jason ran after him. "Wait!"

Excitedly, Estevão's hand rose to knock, only to be stopped. "Calm down, will you? I've got this," Jason said in a reassuring tone.

Estevão nodded, but as soon as Jason tapped and Chambers answered with a crack at the door, Estevão blurted out, "I must speak to the Captain and the Coast Guard! It's urgent!"

Instead of admitting them, Chambers slithered out an opening he created and then closed the door behind him. "The Captain and the fishermen are debriefing the Coast Guard and can't be interrupted. What do you need, Estevão?" And with more than a tinge of irritation, he added, "And why is Cummings with you?"

Jason, sliding his arm over Estevão's chest, pushed himself between the two, and replied, "We were live streaming---not recording, mind you---when Durango passed the High Cotton. We saw..." getting a firm bump from Estevão, he corrected---"that is, Estevão saw, what he believes was a dead body on Durango's deck."

"I did see it! It was there, covered in blood! A man..." Estevão rattled off.

"A dead body, on Durango's deck?" Chambers asked ironically.

"Yes, yes!" Estevão shouted.

"He's adamant that is what he saw, trust me," Jason added.

Chambers hesitated, giving both a hard stare, then reluctantly said, "Wait here."

He slipped back through the door and closed it behind him. Through the glass, Jason watched him go over and whisper to Captain Patel, who was seated next to the fishermen. Across from them were two Coast Guard officers, both uniformed in monochromatic navy. He then noted that upon hearing Chambers' news, Padma's face showed a glimmer of surprise.

Waving Chambers away, she moved to speak to the older of the two officers, a stocky man with curly gray hair. Jason could see her effort to remain neutral in expression, and noticed from the man's profile, his reaction appeared calm to the point of flippant. He raised one hand slightly as he spoke, then as he turned his head, Jason could see he was smiling. Chambers cut in, saying something directly to him, his face serious. The man shook his head and made a placating gesture as he and his junior, a man about thirty and of Asian descent, rose from their chairs.

The fishermen remained seated, their faces expressionless. Captain Patel rose and stood behind them as the Coast Guard Captain gave them all a quick salute before turning to make his exit. Jason found it interesting that the salute was not reciprocated. The two made their way towards the door as Chambers rushed ahead to open it.

As they stepped through, Jason heard Chambers say, "These are the two men who were using the drone, Captain Perry, Jason Cummings, who is a popular reviewer, and our crew member, Estevão Gencio."

The Captain nodded curtly. "Excuse us please, we're in a hurry."

The two stepped aside, but Jason wasn't going to be put off like that. He was not a primary schooler tattletaling. "Captain, you've been informed about the murder victim on Durango?" he said in his most official tone.

Having already passed, Jason saw the Captain's shoulders stiffen. Without turning around, he replied, "We'll be in touch with Captain Patel. It will be at her discretion as to what, if any, of our findings you will be told."

Undeterred by the rebuff, Jason persisted as the two began descending the steps. "Will you be boarding Durango? My thousands of followers will want to know."

He stopped and faced Jason, the lines in his face forming an angry frown. His furry eyebrows, sprinkled with gray, were knitted together. "Do you have proof of what you saw?"

Jason quickly answered. "No! No, it was a live stream, not recorded."

He nodded, "I thought so. This is a way for you to have your 'fifteen minutes,' isn't it? Make up a story about somebody dying to scandalize the brush with Durango?"

"Certainly not! I don't 'make up' anything! I'm a reputable journalist!" He saw the other officer give a slight eyebrow raise, and look from him to Estevão mockingly.

"Journalist?" the Captain repeated, addressing Chambers. "I thought you said he was some kind of reviewer?"

"He is," Chambers answered, seeing Captain Patel and the two fishermen emerge from the navigation room.

"What's going on, Chambers?" she called out. "Why are you holding up these officers?"

"I'm not, exactly…"

Jason cut him off, moving closer to the two men, neither of whom was aware that his phone was discreetly recording the interaction.

"Captain, all I'm asking is this: are you going to investigate the murder of that poor man or not? I wouldn't want your fine officers to run into a dangerous murderer none-the-wiser." he suggested innocently.

"I am not about to tell you how the United States Coast Guard is going to respond to this call. Furthermore, you're not to inform the public of anything until Captain Patel gives you the go ahead, do I make myself clear? And until I speak with Durango on the radio, this entire episode will be kept quiet. Not a word."

Jason scoffed, "You can't stop the free press, Captain. Besides, you say you're going to speak to them on the radio? Is that all you're going to do?" Then turning to Chambers, "Surely you tried to raise them on the radio before, Chambers. Did you get a response? I'm assuming not."

Chambers started with, "Ah, we attempted to reach them repeatedly---"

"Well, Captain?" Jason stated, crossing his arms and looking pointedly at the junior officer.

"Mr. Cummings!" Captain Patel called out. "I cannot have you speak to a commanding officer in this fashion. Besides, if you persist in delaying the Captain's departure, we'll never know what's happening with Durango, will we?"

Jason saw that the fishermen were watching with interest.

The Captain looked at Padma and nodded agreement, then made the pronouncement, "Plenty of these big tankers are on a deadline and ignore radio contact from other ships, but I can assure you that will not be the case with us." He did an about face with his junior on his heels then disappeared into the stairwell. Chambers sheepishly glanced at the Captain, who gazed back stonily, then signaled with her chin in the direction the Coast Guard officers had taken. Turning, he followed them through the metal door.

Captain Patel then turned her attention to Jason. "I have an update for your followers, Mr. Cummings." Jason looked at her questioningly. "I just received word that we're back online. We'll be resuming our return to Charleston shortly."

Jason moved his eyes to the taller fisherman, who seemed not to notice nor care what the Captain had said. He was searching the sea in the direction of Durango.

Chapter 34

Yes, It Is Serious

He was leaning against the Sea Frolic's railing, cigarette in hand and deep in thought. The night was black as coal dust with a sliver of moon, the stars so distant they were barely pinpricks in a dense sky. The boat eased through the water, its wake foaming and the engine purring. John Chen was alone on deck and glad of it.

When he left his room earlier he had to walk through the salon to reach the deck. His shipmates were sitting around a table, each with a fistful of cards. It comically reminded him of the paintings of dogs playing poker. Jim Gaines evoked the high stakes player in his visor and smoking a cigar. Ernie clutched his cards against his chin, his eyes darting left to right. Loretta was puffing her cheeks in and out, glancing from her hand to the pile of dollar bills. Taffy, seemingly bored, announced, "I'll call," right before she let out a big yawn. Glenda responded with raised eyebrows and another look at her cards before she poured herself more wine.

Miraculously John Chen tiptoed through unnoticed, glasses on and with double vision. He wanted a cigarette to think. Taffy and her accomplice, Loretta, were the reason why. How would he deal with these two women, thieves operating as a team? It was one of those unexpected developments that occur sometimes. All the planning in the world cannot prevent unpredictable behavior. There were occasions a person's free will got in the way. How these situations were handled was at the discretion of the agent. The man in the field had the liberty to act in any manner necessary to preserve the mission. Of course, at The Great One's next meeting all would be dissected, everyone having an opinion on the actions taken, but 'John Chen' was relieved that The Great One so far had always backed him. Satisfied, he took the last drag off his Marlboro, flicked it into the sea, then left to put his plan into action. He was nothing if not decisive.

Captain Stewart wasn't at the helm when John knocked on the half-opened door, then peeked inside. The operational zone faced a broad window overlooking the front deck, currently giving view to the pitch-black night. The room's primary illumination was a folding lamp bolted to the control panel. Buttons and monitors added some degree of brightness. Among the dials and knobs, John noticed screens with live video feeds of the port and starboard sides of the boat. He wondered where else cameras were hiding. The walls were covered in nautical maps and a cork board arranged with pictures of Sea Frolic's more recognizable guests.

Stepping inside, he found a younger man in charge of Sea Frolic's journey to the Turks and Caicos. Turning to face him in a swivel chair, John gave him a half bow and began, "Please excuse. I speak with Captain. Very important."

In his mid-twenties and dressed in a polo shirt and chinos, the young navigator said, his dark brows furrowing, "He's in his quarters right now. How can I help?"

John noticed the French accent, so replied in French, "*Oui, s'il vous plaît,* tell him that I discovered one of the passengers attempting to rob my room."

"*Mon Dieu!*" he exclaimed, then pausing, he seemed perplexed as to how to proceed. He finally replied, "That is an accusation most serious. I am sure this is a matter of misunderstanding."

"I agree," he continued in French, "it is serious. You now understand the importance of my speaking with your Captain---immediately." He faced the young man, unwavering, until he stepped out of the doorway and gestured, "Shall I accompany you, or wait here?"

Clearly the young gentleman was inexperienced in such matters. He looked at the boat's controls then to the doorway. Eventually, he moved a lever and made an adjustment on the keyboard. Sweat was visibly pooling on his upper lip. Wiping it away, he rose from the captain's chair. "Wait here."

John sat down in the swivel chair, his fingers drumming the arms. Studying the photos from previous cruises, he could see that the Captain had chosen only shots of attractive people scantily clad in bathing suits that no woman or man would wear in North Korea. Neither Loretta nor Taffy would make the cut for this board. He inwardly smiled at his little joke then looked to his right to find a single picture in a gilt frame of the Captain and a pretty dark haired woman. Prominently beside it, was an exquisite box of Swiss chocolates, the kind Americans love to give to their paramours. Plucking one of the largest caramels, always the most desirable flavor in the box, he took a bite. His face scrunched up, realizing it was a liquid cherry. He spat it out and replaced the remaining bit.

A few minutes later the navigator returned. "You may speak with Captain Stewart in your quarters. He should be there shortly."

"*Oui, d'accord*," John replied with a slight nod to his head.

He left, seeing the form of the Captain turn the corner ahead of him. When he reached the entrance to his room, he was already there, appearing to examine the doorknob. He looked up upon hearing John's approach.

"Ah, Mr. Chen. Shall we step inside?" the Captain stated in his smooth baritone.

"Yes, please do." Removing his key, John unlocked the door and the two entered.

The Captain stood at ease, his posture diffusing as he said, "I've just examined the lock on your door and don't see any evidence that it's been tampered with, so what's all this about?"

John dropped his key on the dresser, then stated with cool composure, "I return to room after dinner.

Found lady---Loretta---at door, something in her hand to pick lock."

He smiled and cocked his head. "Hardly an open and shut case, Mr. Chen. It may have been her own key. She probably drank too much wine at dinner and got the rooms mixed up. Happens all the time."

"No. She want to steal. Other one, the daughter, she try to keep me with her, so mother could steal. She try kiss me. Now I no feel safe. I want off boat. Very scared. Very upset. I no want to have to tell police."

"Oh, Mr. Chen, you don't want to get off the boat, not with the Turks and Caicos waiting at the other end of our journey, and here I thought you were beginning to have such a good time. I'll tell you what, why don't you let me have a little talk with Loretta in the morning. She comes across a bit strong, I can see that, but I'm sure this is just a misunderstanding, like Gabriel in the navigation room told you. No need to be frightened, a strong chap like yourself." He reached out to playfully slap John on the bicep, but John was out of the way quick as a cat.

Now at the window, John narrowed his eyes as he pushed the curtain aside to look out, merely as a tactic to appear to be considering the Captain's offer. He then turned back to face him. "You talk to her. But you talk now. I no want to wait. I need know now."

Considering John's escalated emotion, he acquiesced. "Fair enough," the Captain reluctantly agreed. "I'll go have a chat with her *now*."

John nodded and followed the Captain to the door then closed it behind him, keeping the handle pressed down. Waiting a few seconds, he cracked it open again, so he could listen to what transpired in the hallway.

A minute later he heard Loretta's voice on the stairs. "Really, Captain. It's late and I'm tired. I cannot imagine what is so urgent." There was the sound of her door opening then closing. Muffled voices drifted down the hallway. Then he heard Loretta's indignant cries. "He what? Why, that little chink! Accusing *me* of being a thief, if that doesn't beat all. Me, a deacon of my church. If there's anybody we should be suspicious of it's him! He's the one coming here and can't even speak English! How do you even know that's what he really meant? I'm good at reading people, Captain, and he isn't who he says he is. I could tell the second I laid eyes on him. Man can't even look you square in the eye!" The outrage oozed from her shrill shreaks.

As he eavesdropped, her statement about questioning who he really was became concerning, although it was possible she may have made the comment for dramatic flair. Then again, he considered, takes a con to know a con, right, Loretta? And I don't like to share.

The Captain's voice was low, the words spoken so softly John couldn't make them out. Loretta answered back, her voice quieter. Then her door opened. "Well, I'll think about it. But I don't see how we can be civil to somebody like that, accusing me of such a thing, and poor Taffy! Bless her little heart, he scared her to death. And Captain, please let me reassure you, I'm a tolerant person, not like that Glenda who doesn't like Canadians, of all the crazy things."

John delicately closed his door. A few seconds later there was a tap. "Who there?" he called out meekly.

"Mr. Chen, it's the Captain again."

He opened the door to find the Captain with a pained expression. He attempted to give John a smile, his hat tucked under his arm where he had removed it for Loretta. John stepped aside for him to enter.

"I spoke with Loretta, as we discussed," he started, seeming to choose his words carefully. "She's upset, and I think understandably so. Perhaps it would be best to drop you off after all. We could make a stop in Savannah first thing in the morning. You could depart there as long as you have your passport."

"Yes, Captain, I have it. That be good, very good for me."

The Captain nodded appreciatively. "I've learned that on a boat this size, if the guests don't get along it can ruin the trip for everyone. We've still got a long haul, so since you're agreeable I believe it will make things easier for everyone. And of course I wouldn't want you to be onboard and feeling unsafe," he added with a slight rise in his voice.

"Yes, Captain."

"But regrettably, John, I won't be able to refund your money."

He gave a nod of understanding, the switch back to his first name noted. He replied, "I see."

When he left, John locked the door and leaned against it with a cruel smile on his face. Loretta and Taffy had better enjoy what's left of their trip, because they hadn't seen the last of the chink.

Chapter 35

Thank You, God

Ray Carter lay blissfully in a haze that was not quite awake and not quite asleep, the sounds of someone tapping on a computer keeping him relaxed. The memory of the doctor's voice sifted through his mind, telling him to take it easy, saying he needed a stress test. It kept echoing over and over, get those tests done, this was serious. Dreamily, Ray let one side of a crooked smile draw up. He and the doctor both knew what those tests he was supposed to have gotten a month ago would say, and here was the proof.

That numbing sensation in his fingers had been nagging him every time he really got working, like a few weeks ago when he was helping Jenny in her garden. Holding the shovel he couldn't quite keep his grip right, couldn't keep that compression out of his chest so he could take a full breath. He blamed the excess sweat and panting on his age, and Jenny never questioned it. When had he gotten so old that nobody was surprised by his body failing except him?

Softy rubbing his thumb across his fingertips he could almost feel the way he had been losing his hold on the outrigger lines. He recognized how much harder he had to work now for the same actions he'd always done. He thought of the times Nick would get to hustling him. He'd blame his woozy fingers on the beer. But it wasn't beer making his hands feel drunk.

Exhaling, his head heavy on the pillow, he knew this was his last working day on the ocean. His body had made the decision for him. Not Nick. Nick's 'ums' and 'errs' bounced through his mind as he thought of him working up the nerve to tell him they should sell. He had thought he was telling Ray something he didn't already know, thought he would need convincing. But Nick was the one who needed to reassure himself, the one who needed Ray's validation that it was the right choice.

Perhaps, Ray wondered, he should have told him then and there. That might have taken the question of continuing on with the Esmerelda off the table. But he couldn't bring the words to his lips to quit on that boy. Couldn't say it should be over. Ever since Cam passed, he'd been there, and God, how good it felt to be needed. As a result, he never missed anything, never let Nick or Trevor down. He supposed, selfishly, he wanted to keep his perfect record.

He and Jenny never had their prayers for a baby answered. In spite of that, he had two wonderful sons. When the boys came over, the house was filled with the raucous noises of youth. He and Jenny treasured every second of the chaos, though, of course, they didn't dare let on or the brothers would have gotten more rambunctious. Trevor loved to keep everyone entertained with his wild stories while they sat around the dinner table. And every now and then he'd let Nick get a word in. Their banter kept everyone in stitches, sometimes laughing so hard it hurt.

Those boys may not look like Jenny's, but they have her heart. Even Trevor, who would deny it up and down because he thought he had to act so damned tough, had a heart of gold that could be as soft as butter after one word from Jenny. Jenny made sure that wall he built around his feelings was at least one protecting a good soul. And Trevor learned from Jenny that every person has a story we'll never know, that they always deserve our patience.

Nick never needed that kind of coaching. Still, Ray could see Jenny's influence in the way Nick treated his own little girls, and how sweet it was to see both of those babies stretching their arms out for 'grandma Jenny.'

Yes, it didn't take long after Cam died for Nick and Trevor to learn to love Jenny and her tender ways, and for damned sure they loved her cooking---mighty fine soul food---the way any good Southern boy raised right would do. Trevor and Nick never had to put on a show of joy when she made them something; they oozed genuine love and gratitude. And in turn, so did Jenny, and Ray's heart would feel like it was about to burst watching them. Jenny knew those boys needed her, and in the end, that was enough for her. It was surely enough for him. Thank God for that. Amen.

Chapter 36

What's a Doomed Durango? We're about to find out! #CummingsAndGoings

Jason braced himself to steady his phone. He panned from the two Coast Guard officers returning to their cutter over to the shrimp boat. The contrast was stark. Rust cracked through old paint in a few places and ropes hung limp with age. He zoomed in on the boat's name, 'The Esmereld.' Flinching at the peculiar name, he then noticed that there used to be another letter. Apparently long, long ago there was an "a" on the end. Further scrutiny revealed that the "E" and "m" were slightly different shades of sun-bleached red than the other letters, indicating that at one point in time vanishing letters had been replaced, but clearly the whole boat was left to fade now.

Jason questioned aloud, "Why would two hot young guys want to make a living on such a dilapidated old boat? Doesn't make sense to me."

Chambers, who had somewhat reluctantly been holding open the hatch door to indulge the filming, cleared his throat to indicate that time was up. He gestured to Estevão, who, taking Jason by the arm, made room for the hatch door to swing shut.

Just as Jason was getting a dim, but enjoyable, shot of Chambers' bronzed forearms flexing as he locked the door, the radio buzzed. It was Captain Patel instructing Chambers to return to the bridge to escort the Starnes brothers to the infirmary. He responded obediently.

As Jason realized that Chambers would be leaving them, he remembered the nagging feeling in his stomach, the one that had been there since the meeting with the Coast Guard. It was what that condescending officer had said---that he would radio the Durango, and not to worry, that they would *answer him*. Jason couldn't help but give his head a shake as he thought of the man's arrogance. It's a ludicrous idea to radio a suspected murderer to ask, *Hey, so, is there a dead body on your ship*? As if a murderer would answer, *Well, as a matter of fact, sir, you caught me! There is a body! Would you like to hop on board to collect evidence and arrest me?* The scenario was not only laughable, he knew it would never happen. For whatever reason, the possibility of a murder having taken place on the Durango was of no concern to the Coast Guard. But was that where it should be left?

Jason was a journalist. His job was really one of important public service. Who else keeps the government and its agencies in check but the press? And this was not 'Fake News.' He knew it. He had proof. But like hell would he be the one to go chasing after that boat. He was no Miss Marple on steroids. He needed an ally. It was then he realized that the taut, shapely bum staring him right in the face was his best chance. Not that he was looking, it's just a natural occurrence on stairs.

As the trio reached the top level and Chambers briskly began to turn down the hall towards the bridge and the awaiting brothers, Jason stammered, "Uh, Chambers... hang on a second."

Chambers whipped around with his lips pursed in a line. He clearly had no interest in delaying his orders from the Captain. He cocked an eyebrow as if to indicate this.

Estevão, who had been trailing the two like a determined child, remained closely behind Jason. Jason knew this because he could feel his hot breath lapping at his neck. Estevão really needed to get back to work. Wasn't someone looking for him and wondering why he was getting nothing done? It didn't speak well for a ship to give employees the freedom to wander aimlessly and accomplish nothing; this would need to be in the review.

"Look Chambers, I've been thinking about, you know, the whole dead body on the Durango issue..." he hesitated. "I don't get the impression that the Coast Guard is taking it very seriously."

Estevão, leaning over Jason's shoulder like a trusty girl-gang sidekick added, "Oh no, they are most definitely not. They are going to let a murderer get away! How could they live with this? Ay, Santa Maria!" He crossed his chest as Jason stepped back in front of him forcefully.

Before Jason could go on, Chambers let out a deep sigh and explained, "No body means no murder. For them it's that simple. There's nothing more we could have done."

This time it was Estevão giving Jason the firm shove. Jason winced then said, "Well, suppose I could show you the body." He batted his eyelashes innocently.

Chambers replied haughtily, "What? I specifically remember your saying you had no film."

Jason gave a half smile, then replied, "Ah, since then I realized a miracle has occurred. The drone was recording after all!"

Chambers stood unamused. He was clearly mulling over this new information. Finally he replied evenly, "How quickly can you show me this footage? I am assuming the 'miracle' has occurred despite the fact that you were worried your film would be confiscated?" When Jason didn't answer Chambers frowned, cocking his head to one side. "So, I will be counting on you to make a quick copy while I take the Starnes brothers to the infirmary. Then I'll expect to meet you there."

As recognition of Chamber's command, Jason replied, "Deal."

While Chambers proceeded to the navigation room, Jason pivoted and began to make his way to the stashed drone and footage. The thought of where all of this would go from here began to cross his mind. Clearly Captain Patel would rather walk the plank than not follow protocol, so how could they ensure action? Even if Chambers had the best intentions, more would be needed.

Certainly the Coast Guard would attempt contact with Durango, but would they get an answer? It was hard to know for sure. Their radio-guy until now had done an excellent job of stone-cold silence, but was it because he was a stone-cold corpse? No response seemed likely. Would they have the capacity to stop the ship, and if so, would they board? Was the killer onboard?

Jason's mind spinning, he realized there were too many variables to predict an outcome. Someone needed to be ready with the facts. But not him. *Someone* needed to take action, if necessary. It had to be someone who could get there, to Durango and the Coast Guard. Most likely someone with access to a boat… and someone cool under pressure… someone who perhaps had Navy SEAL training… and someone who would be willing to be a hero should it become necessary. A grin crossed his face. Yes, the Starnes brothers would do nicely.

Chapter 37

Again?

Nick and Trevor walked out of Ray's room with the pungent smell of antiseptic lingering. The echoes of two monitors trailed behind them, one pinging in a two-beat rhythm and the other beeping faster in irritating discordance.

With his fingertips on Ray's door, Trevor drew in a long breath, unable to look back as a memory was surfacing. The clinical sounds and smells were stirring a familiar unrest, his heart quickening as his hand slipped off the knob to drop by his side.

He purposely put his thoughts back to Ray, how even woozy from sedation his smile couldn't be tempered, although it may have been a little more crooked than usual. He wouldn't let them see him down; he'd do anything to make sure they left laughing. And they did, at least until the door closed. Ray always used his humor and gusto to keep those around him at ease. He never let it be about him, and you'd never see it keep him away from what was important.

Nick's voice broke the silence. "How did I know he'd be acting a fool? I mean complaining about how they wouldn't let him have a beer." He chuckled. "I guess he's telling the truth that he isn't nearly as bad off as those 'fussy' doctors and nurses would have us believe."

Trevor's mouth drew up on one side as he replied, "Yeah, I wasn't sure what we'd be walking into after what the Captain had said. Then Ray's in there flirting with the nurses trying to get them to spoon feed him and slip him something 'real' to drink. I guess we don't have as much to worry about after all."

"Well, Ray, that devil, tellin' us his doctor's already been talking to him about his heart, and that this has happened before! I mean, damn! I wouldn't have had him out today had I known he's supposed to be taking it easy." He shook his head in a mixture of frustration and admiration.

Trevor quipped, "Well that's exactly why he didn't tell you. I mean, hell, does Jenny even know? We gotta lay into him for this when he gets back home. And God, him joking about that one poor nurse's leopard thong visible through her scrubs. He's shameless!" Running a hand through his salty locks Trevor added, "But that's Ray."

"Damn sure is. We'll call Jenny back on the mainland. You think she's got any more of that coconut cake?"

Exchanging shoves and relieved laughter, the brothers emerged from the infirmary, the door clicking shut. "I guess we better be heading back," Nick announced. Trevor nodded. Then footfalls were heard as someone came around the corner to face them: Chambers.

"Excuse me, Captain Starnes." He stated officially.

Trevor gave him an appraising glance, noticing that overzealous writer was just behind him with a laptop and a well-groomed Latin man. He knew how to make an impression, that was for sure. He recalled the Coast Guard officials didn't seem too impressed, however.

Chambers continued, "You see, I know you're both aware that there are some concerns regarding Durango."

Nick cut him off. "Yes, concerns that have been explained to the Coast Guard." He raised his chin as if to indicate, 'are we done here?'

Chambers exhaled deeply. "Well, it would seem that way. And yet, one of those concerns didn't seem to be of importance to them. Largely because..." He cut his eyes to the other man, "At the time we couldn't provide proof."

Trevor interjected, "Proof of what, exactly?"

"This is Jason Cummings, from earlier. You may remember, he's a travel reviewer onboard. He was flying his drone when Durango was passing so close to us. He saw, thanks to the stream from the drone, the body on Durango's deck. The... well, *dead* body, to be clear.

As Chambers was speaking, Estevão persistently kept clearing his throat as Jason waved him away.

A "Mmmm..." escaped Nick as Chambers continued. "The Coast Guard didn't take this revelation to heart because Jason," a tense smile passed over his face as he continued, "didn't realize he had recorded the footage. And without seeing said body they wouldn't consider it anything other than these two just thinking they saw something."

Jason stepped forward, chest puffed, "But you see I had the wonderful discovery since they left, that I *did* in fact record! Chambers here, has seen it and agrees, it is definitely a dead body."

"Why are you telling us?" Trevor could see a favor was coming on, but couldn't determine what.

Chambers nudged a shoulder in front of Jason, causing the brothers to take a half step back. "Well, the Coast Guard ignored the information. Totally. And we have no way to show them this before they reach the Durango."

Jason, determinedly inching forward, continued, "And we're worried that they won't be able to make contact, because murderers aren't likely to answer radio calls, therefore, they're likely to get away with it!"

Trevor cocked an eyebrow, unimpressed by the dramatics. "You need to get a copy of that footage to Captain Perry. That way he *will* take your claim seriously. And then he can proceed with the most accurate information."

Chambers was the first to respond, "It is very difficult to send a digital file this large at sea, you know. And it's not like I have the number to his satellite phone. He and I didn't exactly swap digits."

"I am sure you gentleman can find a way. Where there's a will…"

Jason huffed, "It's just that time is of the essence! They'll get to that ship very probably before we could send them that information. And they may ignore it even if it does get there in time."

Nick retorted, "You know those cutters are equipped with all the latest gadgets and intel. It's kinda their thing. They go to ships all the time without a prep meeting."

"And Chambers will give them a heads up," Trevor added officially. "Gadgets aren't the only thing that cutter is equipped with. There's a lot of sophisticated weaponry, too."

"Naturally," Jason replied, "But I don't want it to end up like a traffic cop unknowingly stepping up to a car and getting his head blown off."

"Very descriptive," Nick responded sarcastically. "But I still don't see why you're telling us. What is it you want us to do? Be The Hardy Boys and follow along in case we need to swoop in and…" Using air quotes, he added, "Save the day." Chuckling, he elbowed Trevor, who was standing a little too stiffly.

"All we're asking is that we'd like for you to be sure you take a route back to Charleston that goes by Durango and the cutter. It's where you'll be heading anyway. Just as a precaution. We aren't saying you need to go all Avengers or anything. Just perhaps be in the vicinity. And maybe check in to be sure they've received our footage," Chambers explained hopefully.

"Exactly," Jason added like a car salesman closing a deal. "We really just want you there for our own peace of mind. So we can keep in contact and be sure that these murderers are brought to justice."

Trevor noticed Jason had his phone out, held conspicuously like it was recording. Nick turned his head and the two exchanged a knowing glance. Truthfully, they weren't asking for anything too unreasonable. And the brothers weren't known for letting justice go unserved. They both groaned that grumble that meant they would begrudgingly accept.

"Great! So it's settled then!" Jason smiled, still recording. He handed them his card and said, "Be sure to check out my twitter and #CummingsAndGoings to follow your story. You'll be famous!"

Trevor rolled his eyes and thought to himself, every crackpot with a phone thought the world was watching his social media. Turning to Chambers, he said, "Get that footage over right away. The Coast Guard will be the real heroes here. But we'll humor you and pass by. Okay?"

The men all shook hands. Then the brothers, trailed by Jason and the Latin man who couldn't stop sharing how great this all was, walked down to the hatch door.

Returning to the Esmerelda, Nick started the engine as his brother untied the line. Jason remained in the hatch's doorway, phone in hand. They pulled away, ignoring him until they were far enough out that they saw the ship's door finally close. Nick pulled Esmerelda's throttle back and said, "Come on, old girl. It seems we have one more mission after all."

Chapter 38

The Cold Sea Awaits

"All right," Nick began, "So we follow the course of Durango back to Charleston, easy enough. We should also then be following the Coast Guard. I expect we'll catch up to them at this speed, but then what? I mean, I get those guys's concerns. That Coast Guard Captain definitely seemed full of himself, but then again, he's the expert. What are we gonna do when we roll up on everybody? Be like, *Hey guys, just checkin' in to be sure you're---ya' know---doing your job.*" He raised an eyebrow at Trevor as he shook his head.

Trevor had been staring at the sea ahead, and for the first time looked back at his brother. He half rolled his eyes then said, "Well, I don't exactly know. I don't see what we could really do, other than just a drive-by to see what we see. We may get a little intel over the radio to hear if Durango is answering them. But I can't imagine the Coast Guard flagging us down and asking us for help or some shit like that. And they certainly aren't going to say too much over radio channels about the situation. But maybe we'll get lucky and see them making an arrest as we go by. Then we'll have something to tell everyone on High Cotton when we get back."

"Yeah, it'd be cool if we could see a little of the action so we can tell Ray. Something exciting to distract him, and you know how he loves to rubberneck." They both laughed. The Starnes brothers had learned long ago to keep tension at bay through laughter, and it came to them easily.

The journey was quick despite the glassy calmness of the sea beginning to crack. They could feel the swells breaking over in increasing succession and size, but the Esmerelda cut onward. Trevor made his way towards the bow and was reenacting the cliched 'Titanic Scene' when Nick called him back.

"Oh come on, couldn't you just hear Celine singing me on?" Trevor joked throwing an arm around Nick.

"Oh yeah, but you were a little less Rose and more thorn!" Nick flicked his hand toward the radio, "But check it out. I've been listening and getting some of the Coast Guard calling to Durango."

"And let me guess, it's been a very one-sided conversation?"

"How did you know?" Nick responded sarcastically. Then mimicking the Coast Guard Captain, he added, "Now, they may not have answered *you,* but they will answer *me.* I'm important. They would never ignore someone *important.*" The brothers broke out into laughter.

After a few minutes of listening to the Coast Guard's unreturned communications, the cutter became visible on the horizon. Just beyond it was Durango. Nick quickly pointed out that neither ship was stopped. However, they weren't going at top speed, either, because Esmeralda was quickly gaining on them.

Trevor had not taken their current 'mission' seriously until this point. He knew how the chain of command worked and that the Coast Guard would be following a protocol. Someone high up the ranks would be calling the shots, and there would be no intentional deviation. The Coast Guard knew how to handle difficult situations; it was part of their job. Those officers were trained in dealing with hostile people who didn't like them riding up to their boats and asking questions. But how often did a cutter encounter a tanker-sized ship that they had to order an all-stop? Or a ship that refused communication? That couldn't happen often, not in this part of the sea.

There was nothing more difficult than being on a mission and waiting for orders when it had become clear the original plan wasn't working. Trevor had to assume that was exactly what the cutter crew was doing now. The whole *you stop because we are authorized officials* thing wasn't having an impact. A small cutter wouldn't be able to intimidate a large ship unless it had serious weaponry and Trevor doubted that was the case here. That tanker could run it over and keep going. So he wondered what they would do. He supposed the Navy could issue a fighter plane scramble, but unless they planned on firing on

Durango, it may not have an effect, and that Coast Guard Captain was so politically antsy he doubted that would happen. A sea interception of a vessel of that magnitude would take time to coordinate. There would be a lot of people who would have to approve the plan before additional support by air or sea would be sent in. But time was not on their side. Durango was making its way towards Charleston rapidly. Padma's warning of 'an act of aggression' was beginning to ring true. The cutter may very definitely need their help.

Trevor could feel himself there with them, the tension of a mission about to go awry thick in the air. He began to feel the delicious hint of adrenaline igniting his senses, every synapse coming to life and ready to fire. His forte was making a quick read of a bad situation and knowing what to do before he even thought about it. Most military men like to stick to the books, follow the plan and the orders. The hope is that those were what protected you. Someone else thought things out and decided the best possible scenario. When you went off-script you were taking a chance, relying on your team's intuition and your own ability to communicate and redesign a plan instantaneously. You would be accountable if it went wrong. But you could also clench the mission for your team. Embodying that thinking and those skills is what makes an excellent SEAL. Trevor thrived on that energy. And for the first time since his discharge, he admitted to himself that he missed it.

Suddenly his name was echoing around him and he realized that Nick was calling to him. Snapping around he yelled, "Yeah!"

"Dude, speak up over there, you gotta help me with this. What do we say? Do we do it? I can't believe this is a serious question…"

"Believe what is a serious question?"

"For fuck's sake. The question of helping the Coast Guard! You act like you weren't just right here listening to me talk to them. What do I say? You may be a SEAL but I'm Captain Average over here. What do they really think that I could do? That we could do with Esmeralda…"

Trevor's head ticked to the side and he could feel that vein in his neck give an excited little pulse. They needed him.

*   *   *

The cutter and the Esmerelda only converged briefly. The meeting had been quick. *Time is of the essence,* had been overemphasized. Nick could barely follow the quick synopsis and what the Coast Guard wanted to happen. They worked efficiently. It was lucky for them that they were able to confirm Trevor's service as a SEAL so easily. They had clearly recognized that despite being discharged for his injury, he had been one of the best. Trevor would have never described it that way, but Nick knew he was.

But what they wanted seemed ridiculous. It was obvious they were out of better options, and Nick could tell they would do anything, say anything, to get them to agree. But how could they not? The real question was---could it work?

What they wanted was insane. He attempted to communicate that to them as he let the whites of his eyes bulge and his eyebrows remain arched in skepticism. But they weren't paying attention to him. They were paying attention to Trevor. And Trevor gave nothing away. He had his game face on. Nick never understood how he could hold that neutral expression in any situation necessary. But did he hear what they were asking?

There was never a point where they requested their help. It seemed that just by taking the meeting it meant they agreed. Isn't that government for you? Almost as soon as they had boarded the cutter, they were shuffled right back off.

Stepping back aboard the Esmeralda, Trevor called out, "Ok Nickie boy, you know what to do." Except he had no idea what to do. How was it that everyone else was following these ideas so clearly? They were ludicrous! Was he the only one who needed more details? All he knew for sure was to gun-it. So he headed to the wheel. But that was the easy part. The rest of this plan was far from simple. In fact, as far as Nick was concerned, it was crazier than being asked to move that cruise ship.

*　　　　*　　　　*

That was it. The plan was in place and there was no time to sweat the details. No time to deliberate action. Trevor was back. For the first time since his discharge he felt that vibrant buzz of life, the body's chemicals that flowed when fight was the choice, not flight.

Nick wasn't enjoying the rush of anticipation the way he was. Nick liked life to be predictable. He was great when he was in his element and never had an interest in pushing himself beyond that. It had always frustrated Trevor, who saw more potential in his older brother than he did in himself. Nick had lived a safe life, which was fine, most people did and were happy enough. But today he would be forced to go to the limits. Trevor would take him under his wing. And for the first time Nick would get to see the skills that he was so proud of in action. And finally he would be able to talk about a mission with his own brother after its completion.

Grinning, he went over and removed the towel covering his M1A1-SOCOM rifle. Throwing its sling over his shoulder, Nick said, "You are a little too calm about this, you know that? What happened to just doing a drive-by? Are you psychic? You just happened to have that rifle on you today? What, were you planning on being called in to save the day?"

Trevor paused to look his brother in the eye. "You know as well as I do that I got kicked out of the hero business, okay? I brought this," he said, giving his shoulder a slight lift, "because I thought---look, I don't know for sure what I was thinking. Maybe I really am psychic," he joked, "or maybe I just wanted to have it with me for old times' sake. Let's leave it at that…" He paused and walked over to the bench and placed the rifle back down. Then he said, "I didn't come out here to save anybody. I never wanted to start down this road with the cruise ship in the first place, you and Ray did. Remember? But here we are." Patting the fixed blade knife he carried on his belt, he asked, "You still have your knife on you, right?"

Nick nodded. "We went over this earlier, remember?" then reached around, removing his own from the sheath on the flank of his belt.

"Good." Trevor replied, back to business. There was no time to hash out feelings. Time was ticking. Nick would have to deal with their reluctant-hero status later.

Trevor slipped his Glock 23 out of his waistband holster and put one in the chamber. He also took off that ridiculously tight shirt he'd been given on the cruise ship and slipped on the Grateful Dead tee shirt he had in his bag.

"Is this really the time for a wardrobe change?" Nick teased.

*　　　　*　　　　*

They were gaining on Durango now. The Esmeralda sprayed them with a fine salty mist, leaving their tanned skin tacky. The swells kept the Esmerelda bobbing in a steady thud, thud, thud pattern. It was just enough to rattle your stomach, but not enough to empty it.

Nick stood grasping the wheel with white knuckles, his grip both helping him balance against the turbulence and to channel his nerves. He didn't want his little brother to see him so shaken. Sure, he wasn't practiced at going on life-threatening missions, but his brother had nearly died on his last one, and *he* wasn't breaking a sweat. In fact, no one but Nick appeared to be worried. Naturally the Coast Guard could take a sigh of relief--- they weren't the ones doing this, he and Trevor were. They had decided it was of *critical importance to our national security* that the brothers take over and execute this absurd idea. And was this really of critical importance? In a post 9/11 world it seemed that national security had become an umbrella to get people to agree to anything. How do you really say 'no' to national security?

Nick didn't understand how a boat not stopping was really a national security issue. Although, the Coast Guard seemed convinced that it was highly likely the ship would proceed into the Charleston Harbor at full speed and cause mass destruction. Durango had now missed its appointment to rendezvous off Sullivan's Island to pick up a Pilot to direct it in. Durango had seemingly thrown out all rules and regulations so far, so maybe it was likely that the ship was indeed on a terror mission.

It seemed to be doomed to cause trouble. Trouble for the cruise ship, for the Coast Guard, and for Trevor and himself. Or was it that he and Trevor were just doomed to have to deal with Durango? It had been pulling them in all day, forcing them towards impossible tasks. And here they were, full throttle, nets unraveled, weapons ready, harpoon locked, and Trevor's shoes neatly placed under the bench behind him where a clean towel waited.

*   *   *

Trevor's hands worked quickly with the precision he knew he could count on. Untying from here, retying to there. Move this up, take that off. Fold this here, attach to there. Cut here, tie to this. Deliberate action was all there was time for.

When he was done, the nets had been neatly removed from the outriggers and detached from the floaters and wooden panels needed for shrimping. The nets for each side of the ship were cone shaped to accommodate catching shrimp. The shape made them heavy and thick on one end, and on the other came to a smaller five foot diameter where the shrimp would collect. Using sturdy small cordage he instructed Nick on how to help him weave together the narrow ends of the nets. They were in poor condition and broken in many places from the torque of the rope. Small frayed ends fanned out in every direction and gave the nets a shaggy appearance. They reinforced them as best they could with the limited supply they had. Then in the precise, deliberate tone of a commander, Trevor explained how to get the ropes into position.

334

Ticking his head to the side he could feel his blood pumping, humming through his veins. A foggy memory of walking through a tight corridor and stopping just before a doorway floated into his consciousness. He could see himself turning to look back, expecting to give a silent direction to someone who wasn't there but was supposed to be. He blinked and quickly inhaled the salty sea air and turned back to look at Nick before the memory could take hold. He wasn't ready to deal with all of that right now.

Quickly reviewing the plan with Nick, he noticed the bits of sand from the nets that stuck to his skin like glitter. "Okay then," he said, nearly distracted by the shimmer. "We're ready for you to punch it, Cap'n. I should have everything else ready soon."

*   *   *

Trevor braced himself holding steady against the increasing jerks of the Esmeralda, the waves unrelenting as they closed in. His breathing was slow and steady. Behind him the long trawling nets were meticulously placed, each gently coiled like two cobras into neat piles. From the center of each pile, bright orange cordage was attached. The placement of the netting was strategic; it needed a clear path and to be angled for a smooth exit. Once it reached the target, all he could do was pray that it would become instantly entangled in Durango's propeller.

Trevor's finger hovered over the trigger, waiting. He knew being a good marksman was all about patience. In that moment all he sensed was his shot. He didn't feel the beads of sweat tracing his black brows and threatening to fall into the creases of his eyes. He didn't hear the drumming of the ocean. He blocked out the feeling of hot coals smoldering in his shoulder.

Thwoop! He felt the gun release, the orange cordage soaring out over the water.

He pivoted sharply and grabbed the second harpoon. As the cord and net whooshed over the side of the boat, the gentle hum of the friction was exhilarating. Pressing the harpoon down into the pneumatic barrel, he grunted against the immense pressure, not wanting to waste a moment. And with a swift swing, the gun was poised and waiting again for the trigger's release. The first netting was still making its way over the side of the boat, the loud grinding of resistance competing with the ocean's spray. The salty air stung, but he refused his eyes the relief of tears. His vision must stay crisp. The turbulence of the net beside him was increasing, violent sounds of ripping, catching, straining. He swallowed hard, steadied his breath, took aim and his trigger finger released.

He felt the firm jolt of the harpoon. The crisp whoosh of the rope. Nick's cheers from behind him erupted. The barrel tapped against the rail as he let the gun fall to his side and raised his other arm in jubilation. He would never usually do something so celebratory, but Nick's enthusiasm overtook him. One fist pump wouldn't hurt his reputation. And how could he not? Both harpoons went straight into the void of the churning propeller, the line of the netting following quickly behind them.

Then he felt the loud smack of another wave against Esmeralda's bow. Frothy water blasted him. He reached to regain his hold and steady his balance, and just as he felt the reassurance of the gunwale, he detected something sliding over his foot. It was hot, burning. Quickly blinking the salt from his eyes, his flesh flamed in pain from pressure and friction. Then as quickly as he had registered the heat, his entire body felt a jerk and then the cool water submerging him.

Chapter 39

Hope You Enjoyed Your Stay!

The streets of downtown Savannah were dotted with historic buildings. Grand trees shaded small landscapes near elegant shops with elegant prices. Scattered along the way were bistros and cafes.

Outside one cafe, was John Chen sitting peacefully and admiring the Haitian Monument, the sun glinting off its bronze patina. Taking the last sip of his espresso, he considered that the barista knew how to make a good brew. Satisfied, he replaced the small cup in its saucer. With a glance down at his phone he could see his Uber Black driver was nearly there.

Pushing back from the wrought iron table, he rose and re-buttoned his suit jacket effortlessly with one hand, while the other flicked a tip onto the table. The tip was generous, but he wouldn't be bothering to weight it under the dish. He smirked with the thought that that little waitress better be prompt at bussing if she hoped to find the tip before the wind did.

The early evening was giving off that golden magic-hour glow. Everything seemed softened and more picturesque in the honeyed light. He noticed how it complemented the chestnut Gucci loafers he had discovered packed in his bag.

As the car pulled up in front of him, he waited stiffly for the driver to get out. When the young boy didn't understand, John impatiently cocked his finger at his luggage, indicating it would need to be loaded. He recognized the driver's unheard 'ah-ha' and he came around, opening the door for John then loading his bag.

The smell of chemically engineered flowers filled the cab, clearly emanating from the tacky flower clip on the air vent. A cup holder-sized container of gum rested in the arm rest. Clearly the driver was under the deluded impression that people were wooed by cloying odors and publicly shared gum. He was undoubtedly wearing drugstore cologne, discount shoes, and big box store clothes. Pity, John silently mused, if he wanted to be the one riding in the car instead of driving it, he had a lot to learn.

The first half of the ride to the airport was just as he liked it, silent. But it seemed to suddenly occur to his driver, Chet, that he had not gotten John's input on the music selection. Abruptly he asked, "How's this music for ya', er sir? I can change it to whatever you like." He paused then added enthusiastically, "Really, I've got satellite radio in here. Anything you want, I got it."

John was hardly impressed by radio variety, and he wasn't in the mood for his own music. He didn't like to share. "This is fine," he replied blankly.

Chet looked into the rearview mirror, attempting to make brief eye contact as he said, "Oh, okay. Great. Anyways, we're already close to the airport."

John, who had intentionally left his sunglasses on, didn't turn his head. Just gave a vague, "Ah..." in response.

Chet, seemingly emboldened by this brief discourse continued, "So you're heading out today?"

"Clearly."

"Yeah, I guess it's a good time to go. I suspect you're not the only one leaving, ya' know... on account of what happened."

Turning slightly toward Chet, John replied, "Oh? What was that?"

Chet's face lit up as he explained, "You didn't hear? It was crazy! These two ladies evidently had too much to drink last night out by the water, you know, along East River Street. There's some good bars along there. And well..." he threw his arm around the passenger seat turning to face John at the red light. "They think it must've been that one fell in the water, and the other tried to pull her out or something. But they both had to be either pretty gone or terrible swimmers, 'cause they ended up drowning!"

"You don't say."

"Oh, yeah. And I was there this morning when the police were pulling out the bodies! It was for sure exciting. But, ya' know, they haven't had too much on the news about it. They like to keep stuff like that

hushed up. Don't want tourists like you rushing off."
He chuckled to himself. "Don't get me wrong, I don't
mean to laugh, it was a real tragedy. Those ladies
didn't deserve to die."

"Oh, of course not," John replied with a faint smile
crossing his lips.

Chapter 40

Remember That Time...

Nick stood at the helm with his legs slightly spread to balance himself while Esmeralda bucked against the waves. One hand fiercely gripped the wheel, the other clenched the throttle to have precise control.

The old girl was impressing him. She had been at top speed for a long time now and showed no signs of giving up. That was the thing about having an older boat. Sure, it didn't have the bells and whistles of a new one, and perhaps she wasn't as reliable overall, but Esmeralda had soul. They had a history together and when the chips were down, she never failed them.

He and Ray had spent many a long night working on the old gal' to keep her up, but they didn't mind. The few times she'd given them engine problems, she made sure it was when the sea was calm and Jenny had packed them extra lunch. On the days when a gnarly storm rose up unexpectedly, Esmeralda gritted her teeth and got them home. She might moan and groan a little more than she used to, and her paint may have faded one too many times to get a decent luster anymore, but she had heart. She wasn't backing down on her mission. She would end her service in glory. Nick smiled in praise of the boat, then adjusted course.

It took every skill and trick he knew to get her in perfect position for Trevor, who was on deck looking intently ahead. Suddenly, Trevor gestured a thumbs-up to indicate that she was on target. Nick held her steady. He knew he didn't have an easy job, but he also knew that Trevor's part required greater skill. Luckily, Trevor thrived under pressure. He always loved to perform 'under the gun.' Nick watched as he braced himself and carefully raised the pneumatic harpoon to take precise aim. Never doubting, Nick knew his brother would make the shot.

The whoosh of the first harpoon was satisfying, but it wasn't time to celebrate yet. Both harpoons were needed to tangle Durango's propeller to the point of completely jamming it. Nick watched as the worn netting rushed over the bow and into the fizzy ocean. The nets were hardly in mint condition, but they were serving this purpose well.

Seeing the green nylon moving so fast brought a memory to Nick's mind, his first working trip on the boat. He had finally convinced his parents that at the hardy age of seven he was ready for a day on the water. He knew it was tiresome and sometimes brutal from all the stories and complaints his dad and Ray loved to tell over dinners upon their return.

Nevertheless, he wanted to show them how useful he was. His dream was for those two men---his heroes--- to forget that he was just a boy. Like his dad, he wanted to be a fisherman.

The day had gone well, at least in Nick's mind, until the end when they were dumping the catch. Absorbed in watching the wriggling shrimp as the men flushed them out of the webbing and into the coolers, young Nick hadn't paid attention to where he was stepping. Just like their catch he became impossibly entangled. Furiously, he tried to free himself before his dad or Ray noticed, but the more he struggled, the more the nets tightened. Without knowing it, his dad and Ray were dragging him closer and closer to fall into the coolers. Finally, Ray saw what was happening and stopped to cut him free. Nick went home rope-burned and bloody, and it would be two years before he was allowed to work on the Esmerelda again.

He returned his focus to Trevor just as the second harpoon reached its target, seeing the other pile of netting arc out after the first, rushing overboard like a falcon after its prey.

Without hesitation Nick let out guttural whoops and hollers. As he cheered, all the tension, doubt, and fear was squeezing out through his vocal cords. It was a sweet release. Trevor was so damned good. Nick always knew he was, but seeing him in action and under pressure today and not faltering for a moment, filled Nick with pride. That was his baby brother saving the day, *again*. He was back. Nick knew he was back the second Trevor turned around with that grin on his face---his grin, the one Nick hadn't seen since he'd left the SEALs.

Nick flipped his hat and was surprised to see his elation reciprocated when Trevor let out a victorious war cry and fist-pump. Nick stooped over to grab his hat, then stumbled as a sudden wave gave the Esmeralda a jolt. He lurched forward but caught himself before he banged his head. Snatching the cap he stood up boasting, "Damn near knocked myself out stumbling over that wave! Ha!" he laughed, replacing the cap. "Dad would've been pissed to think that with all the action we've been through today, a little choppy water was what got me." Smiling to himself he looked up in anticipation of Trevor's snarky response.

Were his eyes deceiving him? He thought he was looking where Trevor was standing, but all that was there was the trailing netting and a little sea foam.

"Trev?" He half shouted not wanting to seem panicky. He thought about Trevor playing games earlier, staying underwater as a prank. But this wasn't the time for joking, and Trevor knew that. Nick had to rub his ear, a piercing racket suddenly thrumming into his head. It was getting harder to hear. When no response came from Trevor, he began making his way over.

More metallic groans filled the air. Grinding and straining, the metal-on-metal scraping sent prickling waves through Nick's spine. It seemed to grow louder and louder each second. He couldn't help but clap his hands over his ears. The relentless screeching gave him the cliched nails on a chalkboard sensation. It was so consuming he could taste the all-encompassing

sound. Attempting to focus despite the demanding
noise reverberating in his skull, he began walking
again around the bow, every step the sound louder
and more excruciating. His heart beat faster in alarm.
Where was Trevor?

Now he was running. Back and forth, his eyes
scanned the deck. He knew before he reached the edge
he wouldn't be finding Trevor onboard. He grabbed
the small life preserver and ripped it from its hold as
he made his way to the bow, the Esmerelda still
charging forward through the choppy water.

Shouting down into the froth, his eyes searched for
Trevor, the grinding sounds clamoring painfully in his
ears and clouding his mind. Anxiety made his hands
uneasy as he listened for a yell from his brother, yet he
knew he wouldn't be able to hear even if Trevor was
calling to him.

In a split second, Nick determined that if his
brother had gone overboard he was an excellent
swimmer and could easily tread water long enough for
him or the Coast Guard to pick him up. It was the best
case scenario, but there was another possibility he
considered, his stomach tightening. If he got hung up
in that netting... Trevor would quickly become so
entangled he'd have to be cut free. Nick needed to
help and he needed to do it now.

Reaching around he felt for his knife sheathed on
his belt, then tapped the other knife he kept in his
pocket, which he knew was dull, but there was
nothing he could do about it at that moment. He took
a deep breath and grimaced momentarily at what he

must do. He grabbed hold of the remaining section of netting and let it hurtle him overboard.

His muscles tensed against the blast of icy feeling water, his skin shocked by what felt like the stabbing of a million pinpricks. Gripping tightly, his hands scraped against the rope's frayed edges. He could feel each fray sinking into his flesh like a cheese grater. Propelled through the water, he was coughing from the rush of salty sea. His vision temporarily lost, his ears still throbbed with the unyielding screeching. He was nearing the sound, but couldn't understand what was causing it. Then Nick felt his heart skip a beat. It was the same thing he was rocketing towards. The propeller.

Chapter 41

Lost At Sea

The tug of the netting was slowing but Nick's mind raced. He was following the same path his brother had undoubtedly followed, moving through the torrent water towards Durango's churning propeller. A wave submerged him, leaving him disoriented and unsure. Was the netting really slowing, or was his brain working so quickly that time had almost stopped?

No. The movement of the net was definitely more sluggish, which meant that their crazy plan was working---the nets were jamming the propeller. The screams were coming from the grinding of metal and gears fighting the hopeless entanglement. This meant that Durango would eventually float to a stop despite a throttle telling it otherwise.

Throttle... throttle... The word throttle scratched through his mind more urgently than any of the sounds he had heard that day. It echoed through his head like a broken record, thundering along with the propeller's screech and he could tell by the vibrations surrounding him, he was almost upon it.

"Trevor!" he called, his voice drowned by the racket. He pushed his face underwater in hopes of seeing him, but had to come up. The shock waves from the sound were like torture.

His gut wrenching, he knew he only had seconds, seconds that wouldn't allow him the time to save both himself and his brother. The most difficult decision of his life must now be made in an instant, then carry on and live with the consequences.

The giant propeller, now in front of him, had only a few feet between its final churns and his ability to flee to safety. He let his hand release its grip on the netting. Then he turned ninety degrees and swam with all the strength he had left. His legs and arms pumped with the veracity of an Olympic swimmer, despite the drag on the water coming from behind him.

His body pressed onward, carrying him away like a lifeguard rescuing a listless child. His mind was telling him to turn around, to go back. He could still save his brother if he just tried hard enough. Breaking to the water's surface he gasped for air and tried to look behind him. But his body wouldn't indulge it.

The piercing screeches intensified, the soundwaves flooding into his ears and masking his own screams.

Then they were both superseded by an unmistakable noise, something he was anticipating but had hoped so heartily that it wouldn't come.

It was the Esmerelda speeding forward obediently, her throttle still fully engaged, just as he'd left her.

Like the netting, she was crashing into the mouth of Durango.

She seemed to be yelling with him. Screaming her outrage at his oversight. At how he set her up for failure, groaning over the end of their partnership. Shrieking for what she had undoubtedly done to one of her most beloved people. For what he made her do. They wailed together for Trevor.

Nick rolled onto his back letting his agony echo into the air and his tears drip silently into the water. He floated, paralyzed from grief and anguish.

Chapter 42

Rebirth

His thoughts gelled as slowly as his mind was moving now, coming out of a drug induced unconsciousness. He remembers floating. The screeches. His brother. The cascading anguish, the tears and the loss of the Esmerelda. Did he want to awaken?

He had a vague recollection of the Coast Guard picking him up. His hand went to one ear. The ringing had stopped, so had the pain. If only the pain in his heart could go away by the prick of a needle.

When he opened his eyes he was unsure if he had been asleep for minutes or hours. Long enough to be in dry scrubs and to have left a sizeable drool spot on the pillow. Sitting up, the anger returned to him, instilling a renewed determination. He wanted to face those who were responsible. Turning over, he set his bare feet on the floor, wobbly at first, then set out for the cutter's navigation room.

Passing a few crew members who stared at him questioningly, no one stopped him. He did his best to maintain the facial expression of someone coherent. Though his legs were carrying him, with each step he was surprised he was walking. He felt a strange disconnect, his brain and limbs seemingly in two different places.

He found the navigation room with surprising ease, staggering in and flopping into a swivel chair. Swirling around in the fun spinney chair, he admired all the gadgetry and the organization, each person silently tending to his or her duties. He then gazed out the window to see Durango floating nearby like a red sore on the skin of the ocean that he desperately wanted to pick at so he could see if it would bleed.

"I thought you said he'd be out for hours," someone said.

"He should be," another answered. "He must have the constitution of an elephant."

"Captain," an Asian looking officer called out. He was addressing the man who had earlier been on the High Cotton, the officer who had blown-off the idea off that a murder had been committed on Durango. It was his dereliction of duty that had cost Trevor his life. And the man speaking had been with him. Nick stared at them with seething hatred. The officer continued, "We've got permission from the Charleston Sector Commander to board now."

"Good," the Captain replied. "Prepare to launch."

"Yes, sir. And sir?"

"Yes, Sing?"

"Allow me to say, sir, that plan of yours was brilliant. To act so quickly and improvise so effectively. It will surely be mentioned in future textbooks. I mean, so imaginative to use the shrimp nets to stop her. Incredible."

"It was a group effort, Sing. That SEAL may have been the one to come up with it, but it's hard to say we had to move so quickly."

Outraged, Nick began to speak but nothing came out but a gurgle. Then he cleared his throat and growled, "That SEAL you happened to be barely mentioning there---the man who gave up his life, and yes, definitely the man who had the brilliant idea of using MY nets to stop that fucking ship AND the man who made the two harpoon shots that carried it out, is my brother! And why are you mother fuckers not out there searching for him?"

"Captain!" a female officer called out, wearing large headphones and pulling one side down from her ear.

"I don't believe you are in a condition to be out of bed, Mr. Starnes..." the Captain began.

"Captain Starnes to you!" Nick bellowed, his words slurring. "My boat may have been destroyed because *you* didn't do your job, but it doesn't change the fact that I was her Captain!"

"Sir!" she called out again.

"I apologize. Captain Starnes, your brother---"

"My brother had more honor than all the men on this ship combined. What are you shitheads doing to find him? He deserves a burial..." Nick cried out, his s's coming out as shs's.

"Captain," the officer said more urgently.

"Just a minute, Seaman," Captain Perry replied impatiently.

"And another thing---" Nick continued, wanting to rise from his chair but his legs were too buttery.

"But Captain," the girl insisted.

"Seaman! Did you not hear what I said?"

"She knows you're an idiot," Nick said with a giggle.

Ignoring Nick, she persisted, "Captain, the SEAL, he's on the radio. You'll want to hear what he has to say. What he has discovered..."

"What do you mean? I told him to stay put! Don't tell me a military man isn't abiding orders!"

Their conversation washed over Nick like a gentle surf, slowly sinking in. "SHEAL!" he shouted, a wobbly hand raising into the air, "Is it my brother? Why the fuck didn't you tell me? He's alive?"

The Captain pursed his lips and cut his eyes to several officers in the room before saying, "We tried. Many times, in fact I was--"

Nick cut him off again, but this time to shout in triumph. "I should've known that devil would figure out a way. He always finds a way. Yep, he always does it! Saved you idiots, that's for sure," he kept rambling in relief. He had the idea to run and grab the radio to talk to his brother, but with each swivel of that comfy chair his eyelids grew heavier, until he was just listening.

"Sing! Are we prepared to launch?"

"Yes, Captain."

The Captain turned to Nick. "Well, *Captain* Starnes, we're leaving to board Durango. We'll bring your brother back with us."

Nick smiled but was too woozy to say anything, so instead he stuck out the tip of his tongue in reply.

The last thing he heard was the Captain saying, "Somebody get this man below. I don't want him passed out here and in my way."

Chapter 43

Anchovies Anyone?

Climbing inside the hold, Trevor found it dark and dank, with overpowering odors of decaying metal and mildew clinging to the air. His hand wandered along the wall, assuming the light switch would be there. His fingers discovered that it had been removed and the wires capped. Strange, he mused, that someone would intentionally move a light switch away from where it was needed.

He kept going through the darkness with the doorway's pale light behind him. He touched a heavy black curtain framing an area in the hold. The structure created a hallway in what would usually be a wide open space. Going around it, his bare feet stepped cautiously on the grated floor, his ears listening intently for any sounds that could be heard over the horrific screeching of the propeller. The noise made him want to grit his teeth. His head twitched slightly as he felt the vein in his neck pulsing again. Every nerve in his body was at attention as he kept his pistol raised and his finger poised over the trigger. This was why he carried a Glock. He knew even wet he could count on it to fire.

Almost in darkness, he found the light switch, fluorescents flickering into an underwhelming glow that gave just enough illumination to lead him to the stairs for the upper deck.

The wailing of the propeller could stop any time now, he thought to himself, feeling a migraine beginning to wrap its tentacles around his brain. He began climbing, hoping that the screeches echoing off the hold's metal walls would diminish as he rose higher. His gun was poised and steadied by both hands. It had always bothered him how in movies they acted like it was so easy to aim a gun, as if one arm in a general direction would do. It was ludicrous. Intense focus and a firm grip from both hands were needed to make a bullet's trajectory even close to where it's intended. On he went, steadying himself with his back skimming against the railing, crusty with crackling paint and rust.

Prepared for someone to appear around the corner, he also listened for movement behind him; he was even alert to his damp feet possibly slipping or faltering over something sharp. But what did happen he was not prepared for. He did not see that coming, not one bit. Those were the moments God sent to you when you were getting cocky, to take you down a peg and keep your head in the game.

By the force of the impact, he suspected that the propeller was ripping off the ship or something had just hit Durango. As a result, he fell down the stairs like a toddler learning to walk. Surprisingly, he had managed to flip around before slamming into the bottom two steps, his butt taking the brunt of the impact. It was a mark of his training that the fall didn't shake the pistol out of his grip and that his finger still rested inside the trigger guard. Adrenaline kept him from worrying about the bleeding and bruising he endured. With focused attention, his finished his way to the top.

As he prepared to exit the stairwell he had a feeling of *deja vu*, as if he had been there before. He had been on many missions, but none that made him think of this, yet he couldn't shake that feeling of familiarity. And he couldn't help but feel like someone was supposed to be there with him, covering his back. Nick remained on the Esmerelda, and that was where he wanted him, so why did it seem like someone should be there?

He swept across the deck quickly and methodically towards the navigation room. No doubt some asshole was in there planning his next move, some last ditch effort to get out of being caught. But getting closer, no one was visible.

He prepared to breach the door, expecting a possible killer on the floor or behind a tight corner. As he rushed in, he found it empty. Yet clearly someone had been there. The room had a smattering of blood across the floor and on the controls. It was dried. Hours old at the very least. So where was he, or worse still, they? Off for a nap? Bleeding out in the shower? Only one way to find out.

As he prepared to enter the captain's quarters, he hesitated. It was that feeling of *deja vu* again. Something felt so familiar.

He glanced down at a piece of trash in his path and he did a double take. He knew the packaging, had eaten that very snack before. His mouth went dry remembering the taste and the revolting smell. Why did Asian people love anchovies? And why did they think they were a vending machine food? His mouth drew up into a half smile recalling the bet he'd lost that led him to try dried anchovy in the first place.

The smile quickly vanished as he could see in his thoughts the soldier he'd made the bet with. The guy who was supposed to have his back. Instinctively he looked over his shoulder, knowing he wouldn't be there. "Just like you weren't there the last time I needed you," he scoffed, then headed down the hall.

He made quick work of checking the area. Whoever had been on Durango was no housekeeper. Trash and debris were everywhere, paired with the lingering stench of piss and body odor. The blood trail went to the bathroom and shower. The water pressure on the ship couldn't have been anything great, because congealed clumps of blood and shampoo lingered around the drain, as well as puddles of semi-clear water on the floor. So it hadn't been that long since the bather had left. Then he considered, how curious to bother shampooing when you were bleeding out.

Through all the foul odors of the disheveled ship, anchovy consistently fought to the forefront. It would be a long time before he would want a Caesar salad, he decided, reemerging on deck.

For nearly a month his head had been free of pain. Had not reminded him of his injury. Now it wouldn't subside. Maybe it was from the propeller's screech, or that damned anchovy smell, but he could feel the pain re-emerging from deep inside his skull. Could feel it taunting him. Feel it wanting him to remember, remember...

He sighed, trying to press it back down to where it had been hiding all this time. For months he had attempted to conjure up what had happened, yet got no response. Superior officers had 'needed' him to remember. They had him try all the tricks of the trade, and some he was pretty sure they had just made up in desperation. Nevertheless, the slippery memory remained in the shadows of his mind. So why the hell did it want to present itself now?

Walking back around the deck, a trail of blood caught his eye that wasn't visible from his approach earlier. The blood, like in the navigation room, was dried and browned from the sun. As he swept closer, moving along its path, a new scent entered his nostrils. An aroma as distinct as anchovy, but with a slightly sweet tinge. Almost like rotting peaches. If only that would be his luck. To find on the other end of the odor an old bushel of peaches turning to a putrid moldy liquid in the sun's rays. But the closer he got his stomach assured him, it wasn't peaches.

Crumpled in a heap of dried blood was a man's body. There was no need to rush and check if there was a pulse or if a tourniquet should be applied.

Blistered from baking in the heat, the bloodied skin looked like a barbecue chicken forgotten in the oven too long. His clothes were twisted and ripped. The blood on the floor had been smeared indicating there had been a struggle, and clearly the victor was the one who had walked off leaving the once crimson trail. It was also clear from the blood splattered on the surfaces all around, that someone had hit an artery. So perfectly named art-ery for the way it splattered everywhere, a-la Jackson Pollock.

Keeping one eye on his surroundings, he took a toe and nudged the body so that the man rolled onto his back. He really wished he had shoes on right about now, his high school gym teacher's lectures on bloodborne pathogens coming to mind.

The man's shirt had been ripped so violently that it was split all the way down to the hem, revealing a hairless, bloodied chest. The man's face was coated in congealed 'barbecue sauce,' swollen but distinctly Asian. Chinese? It was hard to tell in the state he was in.

As much as Trevor did not want to touch the corpse, he needed to check for identification. That would be the first thing the Coast Guard would want to know, and he knew they would be boarding Durango any minute now.

Mindful of the fact that the person who walked away from this exchange could still be on the ship, he kept his pistol raised in one hand while he checked the pockets with the other. Nothing. The next thing was to examine tags. He could at least get a possible idea of his country of origin by examining clothing labels. The tag had been cut from the shorts, so he checked his shirt. As he moved the collar back, he realized it too had no markings.

Disappointed, he was about to let it go, but paused. Something curious caught his eye. He pulled the collar further back. Miraculously the oozing blood hadn't covered an area slightly above the collarbone. And there it was. A tattoo.

Such an unusual place for a tattoo, even for a small one. His eyes locked on the marking. It seemed familiar. Was it the angular script? The elongation of the numbering? He could have sworn he'd seen it before. But he would remember. Yes, he would definitely remember someone having the number thirty-three inscribed so distinctly. Puzzled, he let the fabric slide through his fingertips as he rose.

Having barely stood up, he saw the hallway. Had that been there before? It didn't seem to fit. It looked clean, freshly painted. His intuition told him that was where he needed to go, and he trusted his gut. His pistol leading the way, he signaled for Banks to follow him. He didn't look back to be sure Banks saw his signal, he never needed to. He knew he could count on him.

Suddenly something clanged as he reached the end of the corridor. The sound came from his left, so he switched his position to track into the darkness on that side.

The fire alarm started wailing. It was so loud. One of those hateful corporate devices designed to force you outside even if you wanted to stay. He continued to move forward. It was so dark. So deafening. His eyes weren't adjusting quickly enough. He kept blinking to clear the bright spots from his vision. That white hall he had been in had been so bright, too bright to look back to be sure Banks was still in pursuit. It would cost time. He kept going.

The hall reeked of anchovy. Why did it have to smell of anchovy? Then he remembered, he was in a warehouse. A warehouse that housed dried anchovy snacks. The uranium deal was going down in the back room. He was almost there.

Was the hall growing? It seemed so long. His eyes had finally adjusted. He blinked the final bright spot away. Then he suddenly jumped back as a face filled the hole in his vision where the bright spot had been. He was in all black, pistol raised. Trevor shot him. He watched the body fall to the floor. He was dead, at least he slumped as though dead. He had a tattoo on his collarbone that Trevor noted before he turned to look over his shoulder to check on Banks for the first time.

He wasn't there. But Trevor had known he wouldn't be there. How had he known? Banks was supposed to be there, so how did he know he wasn't? Just as he looked back the body was gone. He wanted to search for the man. He never got the chance. A tremendous blast hit him in his chest, then his upper arm, then finally a crack to his head. As he slipped out of consciousness he could feel the warmth of his own blood pooling around his shoulder.

The bullet had not penetrated his Kevlar. A ricochet had sliced his shoulder. The blow had knocked him out.

For the first time since his last mission, Trevor remembered. He remembered it all. He remembered the man he had just found on the deck.

Chapter 44

A Star Is Born

The cardiac ward, a place usually filled with tension and the steady beeping of monitors, was now humming with a new energy. The kind of buzz that happens when a celebrity is in the midst. The halls were deserted, save for a baritone voice echoing nearby, chased by the gasps and gushing of nearly every attendee on the floor.

Room 261 had attracted a considerable crowd, with visitors spilling out into the hallway, standing on tiptoe trying to see. Staff and even a few patients, sat on seats, the chair arms, corners of the bed, countertops or leaned against every surface in the cramped, minimalist space. That is, everywhere not consumed by the numerous floral arrangements and gift baskets. But no one seemed to mind the close quarters. They were all too enthralled with the story, each and every one of them captivated by the charming grin and epic tales of Ray Carter.

The area filled with laughter and Ray shook the bed with his jolly chuckle. Then with a mischievous grin, he placed his hand on the night nurse's arm beside him and said, "I tell you what now ladies, all this storytellin' is making my throat dry." His hand moved to his neck.

"Oh, no, Mr. Carter!" said Shirley, a young attendant. "You can't leave us hanging like that. You've got to finish the story."

Under his brows he looked up expectantly, then said, "Well, it's just this ol' water don't quench my thirst the way a Coke does…" he trailed off.

Megan, a nurse in her thirties, nodded her head in understanding and said, "Will someone run down to the fridge and get this poor man a Coke!"

There was shuffling through the crowd as two young girls in scrubs rushed off. Then she continued, "It's not every day we get a real live hero in here. And this is the closest I'll ever get to top secret information." She indicated for him to lean forward so she could fluff his pillows. The room filled with murmurs of agreement.

Frantically the two girls pressed their way back through with the Coke. "Straw?" one cooed, as the other poured it into a cup of ice.

After swallowing, he gazed at her with a little smile. "Ah, perfect, just what I needed. I tell ya', you fine girls are spoilin' this ol' fool." There were actually a few men present, but Ray directed his attention exclusively to female staff members.

"After all you've done it's the least we could do!" Yasmin explained, her large brown eyes flickering long lashes.

"Ya'll quit distracting him so he can get back to the story, I want to know what happened next," attendant Lara said. She eased her hip onto the edge of his bed and flipped her blond ponytail over her shoulder.

Ray grinned. "Okay, okay, I don't want anybody fussin' cause of me, so let me see... Where was I?"

"You were making the suggestion to Captain Patel that maybe your boat could move the cruise ship," Megan said.

"No, that's not it," Shirley corrected. "You were telling us about Trevor getting on Durango. What happened then? CummingsAndGoings said on twitter that he found a bomb! What did he do then, disarm it?"

"I'll tell you everything, but remember..." Ray said, his finger going to his lips while he made a "Shhh..." sound. They all nodded gravely. He continued, his voice low, each of them leaning closer. "Well, he found the body first---the body covered in blood."

"Ohhh..." they said in unison. "Was the killer onboard?" Shirley inquired, her blue eyes showing the whites.

"No, nobody was onboard---at least nobody alive," he chuckled, "but Trevor didn't know that. Luckily, I had brought my gun and loaned it to him. He searched everywhere, but the only thing he found---aside from the body---was the bomb. And don't you know, that ship was headed straight for the harbor? They figured she would have slammed right into the Battery! The bomb was so powerful this very hospital would have been blown to bits! All of Charleston would have been wiped out."

"Oh, Mr. Carter," Yasmin said, lightly touching his hand. "What kind of bomb was it to do so much damage. It wasn't… a nuke was it?"

Ray looked down. "I don't want to scare you little ladies," he paused.

"Tell us!" they all cried in unison.

"It was."

Shirley's hand covered her mouth. Yasmin said in a whisper, "What did they do with it?"

Ray looked from left to right, checking to see who else was listening. "Trevor figured out the thing was on a timer. But the timer was turned off. Somebody'd cut the wire so the bomb wasn't gonna to explode! But here's the tricky part…" They leaned in again, so close Ray could feel their breathing on his skin. He had always known how to tell a story, and these fine girls sure were a good audience. He continued, "The scariest thing was that If Durango had gotten all the way to Charleston harbor and smashed into the Battery, that bomb might have gone off anyway. So tonight, you all go home and kiss your boyfriends and your family, because if it hadn't been for me, Nick and Trevor, none of ya'll would be alive!"

"Oh, Ray!" Lara said, moving closer to hug him. "Thank you. Our country thanks you."

"That's right," they all agreed, their fingers touching his arms and shoulders. Shirley held his hand.

Then Megan stood back and asked, "So where is it now?"

"Durango?" Ray asked.

"The bomb!" Megan clarified, a note of fear in her voice.

"Nobody knows. The Coast Guard and U.S. Navy used tug boats and took Durango off somewhere. And the bomb was still on it."

"Wow!" Shirley gasped. "Where did they take it?"

Ray shrugged. "Trevor said they got it somewhere where they can go over it with a fine-toothed comb. They want to find clues. You see, nobody knows who sent Durango."

Yasmin said solemnly. "Do you think it was terrorists?"

Ray put a hand to his chin. "I've sure thought about it. I reckon anybody who wanted to do that kind of damage would be a terrorist, but I don't think it was like them guys who did 9/11."

"It had to be. I bet it was Jihadists," Shirley speculated, proud to have used the word.

Ray shook his head. "Trevor told me the guy who was dead was Asian."

"Asian?" Megan replied, all the nurses looking puzzled.

A voice came over the intercom. "This is Doctor Patel. I need all fourth floor staff to check in at the nurses station as soon as possible."

"Uh oh," Shirley muttered. "We'd better scatter."

They all rose and slowly made their way out the door. Ray called out, "How about one of you pretty things bringing me an ice cream? Vanilla would be fine, and if it has to be one of them frozen yogurts, I suppose I'd go along with it. I wanna get better, you know." He winked at Shirley, who gave him a sly smile then left.

Chapter 45

Into The Night

Nick and Trevor left the Coast Guard administration building after several hours of waiting and questioning. It was their third trip there. Nick hoped it would be the last. The two had been interviewed by the Charleston Sector Commander, a Naval Intelligence officer and her entourage, and a few others in suits who never introduced themselves. It seemed absurd that all of these government types couldn't keep Nick's story straight, asking him the facts over and over. It felt like *he* was the terrorist and they were trying to trick him into confessing. It was downright insulting.

It had been seventy-two hours since Durango was intercepted and the Esmerelda lost. They were driving home through historic downtown Charleston.

Nick broke the silence, one hand gesturing, the other holding the steering wheel. "I can't get it out of

my head. All this, all the people, the history---
everything would have been blown to kingdom come.
A single change in events could have meant
unbelievable tragedy." He looked at Trevor. "And no
one's talking about it! They're walking around with no
idea how close they came to being obliterated, because
the authorities insist on keeping information from the
media---minor details, ya' know, such as a nuke ready
to blow barely fifty miles away!"

"Well, the timer was off. Somebody deliberately
disarmed it, so technically it wasn't about to explode."

"Are you fuckin' kidding me? If Durango had hit the
harbor wall or another ship, that thing would have
gone up like a firecracker---killing everybody within
miles in the process, not to mention years of radiation
poisoning. Yet the public is oblivious."

Trevor blew out a long sigh. He didn't want to rush
his response and come across as condescending, but he
also understood all too well what was happening
behind the scenes. "That's true. But it's for the best.
I'm sure you can see that. Everybody knows bad guys
exist in the world, but part of saving people isn't just
saving them from the bad things. It's saving them from
themselves, the nightmares of knowing what could
have been, but wasn't."

"Okay, I know the public might have panicked, and
God knows what could have happened then. What I'm
saying is, they don't appreciate what they were saved
from." Then calming, Nick added with a chummy
punch to Trevor's shoulder, "Of course, it's no worries
as long they've got you, me and Ray around, right?"
They laughed, Nick continuing to air his thoughts.

"Lord help us if Ray gets another tale to add to his repertoire." He shook his head. "I don't think the people at that hospital could take it. He was practically selling tickets to the staff. Felt like we were going to visit Denzel Washington the way they had to wait in line to get in his door."

"Yeah, poor Jenny has the bar set awfully high by those doting nurses, and he's practically extorting sodas and ice cream from them."

"And telling them all the stuff he's not supposed to." Nick rolled his eyes, "The things that were intended to be 'classified,'" he said with air quotes. He laughed again. "I can hear him now. 'Remember, this has to be just between us.'"

Trevor mused, "Actually, it's a miracle the media hasn't learned the facts with Ray's loose lips. I guess mainly that's due to Jason Cummings never getting past Jenny to have an interview with him. That dude is relentless."

"Definitely, almost as bad as the guys we just left. I'm telling you, I am sick and tired of answering the same questions asked fifteen different ways."

"You can't take it so personally. They have to be careful. You know that in today's world nothing can be taken for granted."

"I get what you're saying, but damn!"

"That's why there's beer, big brother," Trevor said with a wink. "And it looks like fate wants us to have one, because there's a parking spot front and center on King Street, plus it's big enough for your truck. You know that doesn't happen without divine intervention!"

"Why not? This place looks a little trendier than our usual beer joint, but I'm ready for a cold one. In fact, I'm so thirsty I'd take a Corona with a little umbrella dangling off the side."

"I'm in," Trevor said.

They climbed out to be met by a warm spring evening, on the verge of darkness and the air pungent with blooms. Tourists strolled along the sidewalks lining the narrow street, no one noticing that their saviors were in their presence. A couple exited from what looked like a large, sliding barn door. Before it closed, Trevor took hold and he and Nick walked in to be greeted by a sound system playing a top hits station. The decor was dark wooden floors and heavy ceiling beams, the walls adorned with antique horse brasses and equestrian equipment, bits, bridles, and old saddles. A shiny bar with tractor seats acting as stools had Nick bee-lining for the only two empty places next to each other.

Five minutes later, after each took a long pull from his beer, Trevor wiped his lips and smiled at an attractive waitress across the room.

"You know her?" Nick asked.

"No, just being friendly."

Nick chuckled, "Oh, right." He looked back to where the pretty girl had been, but she was gone. He returned his attention to Trevor. "Seeing your new friend over there reminds me, have you heard anything from Captain Patel?"

"Actually, I got a new phone this morning since we all lost ours on Esmerelda..." Trevor paused, seeing Nick's expression become pained then go neutral again. "Anyhow, I was able to call the cruise line and leave a message for her. She called right back, and we talked for a few minutes. She's doing well, still very appreciative of what we did, of course."

Nick nodded. "That's good. And yeah, you're right, we lost a lot of good stuff on Esmerelda. I had some expensive fishing gear and don't forget that Dad's old Colt went down with her."

"What about my SOCOM?" Trevor countered.

"What about my tuna?" Nick volleyed.

"Oh, shit! The tuna! It's on the bottom of the sea, preserved in your cooler." The two laughed, then became serious as a sadness followed.

Someone turned the television volume up on the flat screen over the bar. They could hear a news announcer say over the din, "The drownings were at first believed to be accidental, the authorities assuming that the mother had fallen in the water with the daughter jumping in to save her, resulting in both tragically drowning. However, once police obtained autopsy results, they learned that the deaths of these women were indeed no accident. Investigators wouldn't say what evidence led to this conclusion. City Police Chief Sandra Metzinger also wouldn't tell us what, if any, leads they have in the case. Furthermore, she didn't reveal if the crime was committed by a man or woman, but inside sources told WJCL News that investigators are operating on the assumption that the killer was a man. No witnesses have come forward as yet to confirm this, and as we've said, no suspect has been identified. Back to you, Marcia, and the rest of the WJCL News team." An anchor woman replied back, "Thanks, Stan. We'll be anxious to get more updates concerning these murders in beautiful downtown Savannah."

Trevor saw the man's head next to him shaking as he remarked, "Tsk, tsk… tourists can get themselves into all kinds of trouble." He was now facing Trevor. "Can't they?"

Without being obvious, Trevor looked the man over. Nice clothes, in fact, expensive suit. He was Asian and extremely fit. He also noticed that his knuckles had some old wounds on them. The man suddenly pulled his hands away and turned back to speak to the voluptuous redhead next to him.

"Who was that?" Nick asked.

Trevor's brow creased. "I don't know. He was running his mouth about what was on TV."

"Oh. I hope they don't turn the volume up if there's more reporting on Durango. They might show our pictures. Right now the last thing we need is for somebody to want us to tell them the whole story, which we can't, and I'm sick of it, anyway."

As if on command the brothers looked back to the television to see Jason Cummings standing at the Charleston harbor, holding a microphone. Nick put his hand over his brow to hide his face while his eyes remained deadlocked on the screen.

"It's just rehash," Trevor remarked. "Cummings has pretty well exhausted all of his leads."

"Yeah, but he's been plugging his yet to be released 'documentary.'"

"True," Trevor agreed, "But he may find that his documentary gets held up due to some national security issues. Then again, I'd say he's done pretty well off Durango without it."

While Trevor was speaking, his peripheral vision had continued watching the man next to him. He told himself to cool it. Still, he could feel his pulse quickening. He drained his beer and slapped the mug on the counter, saying to the bartender, "No, thanks," when asked if he wanted another. Turning to Nick he said, "You ready?"

"What's the hurry?" Nick said, chugging the last of his drink.

Trevor cocked his head. "I thought you wanted to remain---" then he said in a theatrical whisper, "incognito?" He stood up, putting some cash next to his empty beer glass. He then saw that the man next to him was also leaving, heading to the door with the redhead hanging all over him like a sloppy drunk.

The brothers made their way through the crowd, as the popular bar had filled since they'd arrived. Once outside, the relative quiet greeted them with darkness illuminated by what looked like an 1800's lamp post. Trevor looked sideways to see the man and the redhead leaning against the building their lips together in a long kiss. Her hands snaked all over his body, coming to rest on his collar. She pulled it back to kiss his neck. Instantly, something caught Trevor's eye before the woman's head blocked the image. He moved quickly, striding over. The man, seeing him, pushed her back. She stumbled, bracing herself on the wall.

Trevor's face held a smile as he extended his hand. "We didn't get a chance to meet. My name is Trevor."

Narrowing his eyes, the man slowly raised his palm and the two shook, a powerful grip held by each. "Jin," he stated, spoken almost as a challenge. His stare never wavered from Trevor's as their fingers dropped to their sides. The redhead was giving Trevor a toothy smile.

"Enjoy your stay in Charleston," Trevor remarked. He turned, then, pausing, he added over his shoulder, "Stay safe. Tourists can get themselves into all kinds of trouble." He quickly caught up to his brother.

"What the hell was that?" Nick asked before they reached his truck.

Trevor replied lightly, "Just being friendly again. Listen, do you mind leaving on your own?"

"You're not coming?"

A sly smile crept over his lips. "I'm thinking about that cute waitress, wondering what time she gets off."

Nick grinned. "You dog! I knew it."

Trevor shrugged. "She may not be interested, but I want to give it a shot."

"Not interested!" Nick replied skeptically. He knew all too well how women were always interested in Trevor. "Okay, little brother." He opened his door. "Don't do anything I wouldn't do!" He climbed in and cranked the engine.

By the time Trevor backtracked, Jin and the woman were no longer outside the bar. He trotted down the street in the opposite direction, stopping after he'd gone a full block. With them nowhere in sight, he rushed back and went inside.

It was noisier, the patrons having to raise their voices to be heard over the music, his heart and the song thumping in unison. His eyes scanned the crowd with the concentration of looking through a rifle scope. He made a circuit of the room, then stopped at the bar.

The bartender recognized him. "You're back! What will you have?"

Trevor gave him a friendly smile. "You remember that couple sitting next to me, the guy with the redhead?"

"Oh, yeah," the bartender replied.

"Did they come back in?"

He shook his head. "Haven't seen them. They left when you did."

"Thanks," he said, hurriedly making his way to the door.

Back outside, he was pondering the possibility that Jin and the woman had taken a car. If so, he had no chance of finding them. He walked back up the sidewalk in the direction of where he and Nick had parked.

The night felt warmer, humid with no breeze. Downtown was lively, people coming and going from a restaurant next door. The level street, brightened by street lamps, gave Trevor a view ahead: a hotel van pulled over. The last passenger got off and slammed the door. The vehicle pulled into traffic.

It was then he saw it. Nick's truck had been parked in front of the van, the lights on and the backdoor open. His brother was helping Jin get the woman into Nick's vehicle. Seeming passed out, Nick had her by one arm, Jin the other.

Panicked, Trevor began running. He called out, his voice drowned when Nick slammed the truck's door. Now, both Jin and the woman were in the backseat. Nick was getting in behind the wheel.

Trevor yelled again. "Nick, stop!"

It was too late. Even sprinting, he couldn't reach them in time, as Nick had moved into the traffic flow. Trevor, helpless, watched the tail lights slipping away, then go around the corner.

*   *   *

He kept running, as fast as he could, dodging pedestrians and flower boxes outside the shops. A few times he bounded into the street to go around people, then back onto the sidewalk to avoid oncoming cars. In the distance he could see the truck make another turn. Still going full speed, it took another minute to sprint to the corner. His breathing was coming in one-two beats. Searching for the truck and seeing no sign of it, he tried not to let his imagination go to the possibilities of a ruthless killer in Nick's backseat. Jin may need Nick's vehicle, or his clothes, or identification. Then hope returned; Trevor could see congested traffic ahead due to a red light. His now burning lungs were giving out. Then he spotted the truck.

Nick had pulled under the enormous canopy of downtown's most exclusive hotel. A uniformed doorman assisted patrons inside and directed cars through the valet area. Their vehicles maneuvered with difficulty around Nick's truck that had its blinkers on and no one inside.

Trevor didn't stop to speak to the doorman. He jumped into the revolving door that spit him out into a huge marble-floored lobby. He saw shops, a cafe and a bar surrounding a plush seating area with potted palms. A fountain trickled over a statue of Venus.

Unsure of what direction to take, Trevor spotted the elevator area off to one side. From there his eyes moved to the front desk, carved in mahogany with a black marble counter. Nick was standing there, holding a red purse, its sequins glittering. Sucking in several restorative breaths, Trevor headed that way.

"Here, you are!" he exclaimed as he reached his brother.

A front desk clerk that had been checking someone in was now asking Nick what he needed. Nick turned around to see his brother, and surprised, said, "What are you doing here?"

"That waitress had finished her shift and left by the time I got back."

"Oh."

"May I assist you, sir?" the woman repeated to Nick, looking over some spectacles and seeming impatient, as others were waiting.

"Oh, sorry!" Nick said, his attention returning to the woman. "I dropped off one of your guests a few minutes ago. She left this in my truck…"

Trevor cut him off. "There it is!" He reached out and grabbed the purse. The woman glanced at him, brows raised. Trevor explained, "I just saw her gentleman friend. He asked me to bring this up to their room."

"He did?" Nick asked, sounding skeptical.

"That's right. I passed him as I walked over here." Then looking at the clerk, who was walking away to assist someone else, he remarked, "Thanks! We'll take care of it."

With the purse in one hand, he used the other to direct Nick towards the hotel entrance. "I'll return the purse. You had better move your truck. It's causing problems out front."

"Okay, yeah. But I doubt I'll find a parking place. I'll probably have to circle the block before I can pick you up."

"That's cool. This shouldn't take long."

Nick hesitated, searching his brothers face. "Are you all right? You've got sweat on your forehead."

"Do I? I walked," he shrugged, "It's gotten hot out. By the way, I was surprised you gave those two a ride. How did that come about?"

"I had to pull over. Carly texted me. Next thing I know that dude is tapping on the passenger window, saying his girl was having difficulty walking and the wait was too long to catch an Uber."

"Was she drunk or drugged?"

"Drugged? No. She'd had too much, that's all. Anyhow, he told me they were staying here, so I saw no harm in helping. It was a short drive and she was in no condition to wait for the Uber. I suppose the purse got left behind, because he had difficulty getting her out without my help. The doorman insisted I stay behind the wheel so I could quickly move my truck."

"Always the good Samaritan," Trevor said, slapping his back. "Listen, I'll run this up to them, and look for you when I get out front."

"Great. Try to hurry it up. Carly said one of the girls has a fever."

"You got it."

Trevor headed for the elevators. When he turned around a few seconds later, Nick was gone. He opened the purse and found a key card to a room. He then heard the sound of elevator doors opening. Instead of climbing in, he stood there, his fingers flipping the card over and over in his palm.

Epilogue

Three Weeks Later

The sloop moved across the water as gracefully as a pelican skimming for fish. Trevor was at the helm, unable to keep the grin off his face. The mainsail was taught with wind, the sailboat nearly sideways as she slid through the water sleek as a seal. Nick was with him, tying off the jib.

"She's a beauty, Trev!" Nick called out. "I can see why you bought her."

Nick was glad to see Trevor excited about the boat. He rarely spent money on himself. Was this a new trend? Now if he could get him out of that sketchy apartment it would be even better. Actually, Nick didn't care about Trevor's shabby apartment. It was his mother and Carly who wanted to see him living in a nicer place. "One suitable to attract a decent woman," his mother had said.

"Did you see Esmerelda mounted in the cabin?"

Nick nodded. "It looks great, and it's the right place for it." They were talking about the piece of wood Nick had plucked from the ocean before he was rescued by the Coast Guard. He had given it to Trevor, though it wasn't an easy decision to part with it. Now he could see that it had been the right choice. Trevor had the wooden piece mounted and framed with a brass plaque that had the Esmerelda's name and her years of service.

"I want to get Ray out here as soon as I can."

"You could start a tourist gig," Nick suggested jokingly. Trevor gave him a questioning look, so he placed his hands in the air, and said, "I can see it now. Sail with the hero, Trevor Starnes, and get a tour of the Charleston harbor after traveling out to sea to where he stopped Doomed Durango."

"Wise ass," Trevor retorted. "But you know, that's not a bad idea. But not for me, for you. I think you and Ray should refurbish an old shrimp boat. Fix it up so it has plenty of seating rather than fishing gear. Have the side of the boat painted in bright colors. *Doomed Durango tours conducted by the heroes, Captain Nick Starnes and his trusted sidekick, Ray Carter.*"

Nick burst out laughing. "Dude, you're making Ray sound like he's Robin and I'm Batman."

Trevor replied, "Well, you both can't be Captain, uh, I mean Batman."

Then Nick considered, "It would be a good tourist draw. At least for a while, while it's still fresh on everybody's mind. Which reminds me, have you seen the documentary yet?"

Trevor shook his head. "Not interested."

"Oh, please. How can you not be interested in your big moment on screen?"

"I've already had three calls from guys on my team giving me a hard time about that film."

"They're jealous, that's all," Nick said mockingly.

They lowered the mainsail then brought the boom across, the yacht seeming impatient to get her canvas full of wind again. Once the switch was made she was gliding even faster across the water. Nick's gaze followed the sea to the shoreline. They raced along, enjoying the sound of the wind crackling the sails and the boat cutting a sliver of wake through the water. Then he began thinking about something he had seen yesterday in the *Charleston News and Courier*, something that had made him alarmed and uncomfortable. He looked back to the helm, Trevor's eyes indiscernible behind sunglasses.

He cleared his throat and said as he continued to study the water, "I happened to catch something in the newspaper. Did I tell you? Ever since the articles appeared about us and Durango, Carly took out a subscription. Anyhow, it was about a murder. They don't have any clues about the victim or the killer."

Trevor's expression didn't flicker. "Oh yeah?"

"Yeah. It said a body was found in the harbor. They're thinking it had been in the water for some time. No identification, but they were able to determine the man was Asian. His neck was broken." He paused, waiting for Trevor to comment, but he didn't. Nick continued a little awkwardly, "Uh... seems strange, doesn't it?"

"That they could tell what race he was after being in the water for so long?"

"No. The coincidence with Durango, ya know?"

"The dead guy on Durango?" Trevor clarified.

"Of course the dead guy on Durango! How many dead Asians have we run into lately?"

"You think there's a connection?"

"I don't know. I'm just saying it's odd."

"What, like the man in the harbor could have been one of Durango's crew members?"

"Maybe. There had to have been more than one person onboard. They needed two to pilot it, and of course, somebody had to cut that man's throat. So where did the other one go?"

"Good question."

"But here's the thing. From what little was said in the article, it sounded like police investigators are working on the premise that the guy was killed then dumped in the harbor. Naturally they said nothing about Durango." He stopped, waiting for Trevor's response. Again, nothing. "That makes me think three people were involved, not two."

"Three crew members and one kills the other two?" Trevor replied skeptically.

"Something along those lines."

"I'm sure Naval Intelligence has already looked into any possible connection. Though we probably won't learn any more facts other than what the local police reveal."

Nick knew that Trevor could probably pick up the phone and get classified intel about Durango and probably the murder, but he didn't bring up the point, because he knew Trevor wouldn't say. He had asked him to find out where Durango's port of origin was, but he wouldn't do it, or if he did, he wasn't telling.

His thoughts shifted to the real question he wanted answered. It came out as a statement. "You know, you never did tell me about that night, when we went to the bar, and I took that guy and the girl back to their hotel. I had to circle the block three times before you got back outside. What took so long?"

Trevor turned to look at Nick, then cocked his head and said, "Well, it took longer than I thought to break that man's neck, and then get back outside so you could pick me up."

"Not funny."

"It kinda is. You're wondering if I killed that guy, right?"

"I want to know if you had anything to do with it, that is, assuming he was connected to Durango."

"I had nothing to do with killing anybody that night. Do you believe me?"

"If you say so, then I believe you." And it was true. If his brother looked him in the eye and said he didn't do it, which is what he just did, then that was good enough for Nick.

"Great. End of discussion."

"End of discussion," Nick said, about to reach out his hand to shake Trevor's before realizing that the gesture might appear odd. And yet, it would let him know that he really meant it.

Trevor slapped a hand on Nick's shoulder instead. "Not to change the subject, Inspector Clouseau, but

I've got lunch and some beer below. Do you mind bringing me a sandwich and a cold one?"

"While I get one for me, I'll grab one for you."

They enjoyed the lunch then started back as storm clouds brewed behind them. Their cheeks ruddy from sun and wind, Nick's tension had disappeared. Passing other yachts, Trevor was immensely pleased that his was faster. He guided her with ease, slipping through the choppy waters, then reaching the dock at dusk. As they secured the boat and gathered their things, bloated raindrops began to fall.

Walking to the car, Trevor was whistling, tossing his keys. They drove with the stereo blaring to a Grateful Dead song, and even though he was ridiculously out of tune, he had Nick singing too.

They were home, safe. Ray was going to be fine. Charleston was still a beautiful city. It had been a day like any other day. They sang happily, like boys again. "What a long, strange trip it's been..."

The End

Meet the authors, C & C Beamer

C&C Beamer is the writing team of Christine Beamer Seropian and Caroline Beamer. Christine is a public school teacher and yoga instructor, who is married and lives with her husband and their Doberman, Zeus. Caroline is a former journalist and novelist: PIVOTAL POINT written as Caroline Kean and DRAGON WIND as C.S. Beamer. Both live in the North Carolina mountains. This is their first collaboration.

Doomed Durango

Made in the USA
Columbia, SC
27 July 2020